# Stealing Chevy

Rachel Lane

# Contents

# Chapter 1

The walls were flat black, and spotlights lit the stage, illuminating a shiny center pole. Recessed lights above the bar lent dim lighting to the thick, hazy atmosphere of cigarette and cigar smoke. Most of the patrons had a drink in their hand and watched the changing stream of naked girls on stage. Young girls, who changed with the song—blondes, brunettes, redheads, and everything in between. All of them had soft, youthful skin, G-strings, and bare breasts, and were covered in fine, alluringly scented glitter. They moved their bodies and crawled on the stage floor with sexy, arousing moves to music that had distinctive rhythms.

Chevy had long brown hair, hazel eyes, and full, luscious lips. She had a model-perfect face and a seductive, mischievous smile. Everyone noticed her, so her father had kept her close, pampered, protected, and shielded from the harsh world. Now Chevy was grown, and on this night, in this place, her world had changed. Here with her G-string, naked breasts, and newly acquired erotic moves, this was Chevy's time to sparkle in the spotlight.

A man sat at the corner table next to the stage, quietly observing her. A thin line of smoke streamed upward from the end of his cigar, adding to the already hazy atmosphere. Watching her attentively, he held up a hundred-dollar bill, gave her a nod, and set it on the table next to his amber-colored drink.

On her knees beside the pole, moving seductively and grinding to the music, she paid more attention to him than the other patrons.

The man held up another hundred-dollar bill.

She kept her gaze in his direction, dancing just for him, watching as he took another puff of his cigar. The red-orange end glowed brightly, revealing another bill, then it was dim once more. The hundred-dollar bill sat with the others next to his drink. As her song ended, she made her way off the stage, passing the next girl waiting for her cue.

The walls and rooms backstage were all painted the same unforgiving flat black. Chevy hurried into the dressing room. Inside was a wall of makeup tables and a couple racks of lingerie-style costumes that hung neatly next to the wall.

Jen sat looking at her reflection in the mirror. Slowly and meticulously she touched up her makeup. It seemed that there was something troubling her. Her wavy dark hair made her big blue eyes stand out, and her nipples sat prominently on a perfect breast job. She glanced at Chevy in the mirror as she hurried in.

"There's a guy holding up hundred-dollar bills and setting them next to his drink for me," she said with excitement.

"Remember," Jen coached, in a flat tone that lacked joy and enthusiasm, "give the man a sob story. Mom's a drug addict, dad's in prison, you're trying to better your life. They hear that, they shovel money your way."

Chevy nodded.

"No one likes to hand money to anyone who says their dad owns a chain of hunting stores. They don't like to hear how you ran up Daddy's credit card too many times and he cut you off. Trust me," Jen smirked. "It loses sympathy."

Chevy looked in a mirror, checking her makeup and fixing her hair.

"You look great." Jen handed her a tube of lip gloss.

She rolled the gloss across her lips, looking in the mirror as she handed it back.

"Beautiful," Jen assured her. "Go knock 'em dead."

Without a word, Chevy turned and was out the door.

###

The brown-haired man sat quietly in the corner, the end of his cigar glowing red-orange as he took small puffs.

"May I?" She stood at the side of his table.

He had a receding hairline, and what was left was thinning at the crown.

He tilted his head toward the chair while maintaining eye contact.

His face was round with a squared chin. His pleasant features made him seem relaxed, patient, and understanding, while the white dress shirt with the two top buttons undone washed out the color of his skin.

He smiled, pushing the bills her way. "This is yours," he said. His smile showed sincerity, while his eyes had more to say. Looking her over closely, he picked up his drink, circled the glass to twirl the ice cubes, and took a sip.

She glanced down, noting the placement of the bills and allowing them to sit.

"So, where are you from?"

"Kentucky," she answered with a cute little drawl.

"What brings you to Boston?"

"A lot of crap. Sometimes a new start is a good thing." She half smiled, with a story behind her eyes.

"Come on!" He repositioned himself in the chair. "You're a pretty girl. What do you need to get away from?" He picked up his cigar and leaned back, preparing for a long answer, and looked at her closely with an observing eye.

She shrugged. "Just stuff. Mostly my parents," she said, noting that the way he looked at her made her feel uncomfortable.

"Uh-oh. What's going on with your parents?" He paused. "Let me guess, divorced?"

Chevy looked at him, that uneasy feeling growing. He was more than probing; he was fishing—for what, she just wasn't sure yet. "My mom has an addiction problem. I've only seen my father a couple of times. He's been in and out of prison."

"You have family or friends around here?" the man probed as the end of his cigar waved in the air.

"No, I'm an only child. My grandma passed away a few years ago. She was the only grandparent I had." Her eyes shifted sadly toward the floor. "You could say she was more my mom with the wisdom of a grandparent." She smiled.

The man shrugged. "Well, no family is perfect. Some are just a little better than others," he offered.

"Thanks." She nodded in acknowledgment of his attempt at comforting words. "What about you?" She wanted to move the conversation along.

"I was born in New York, along with three or four million

6

other people," he answered with a humorous chuckle. "My father was a businessman and had to travel a lot. My mom stayed home with my brother and me. She took good care of us—actually, both of them took good care of us."

"What do you do?"

"Business—sales mostly." He pulled the corner of his mouth to the side, appearing bored. "It gets lonely."

"I understand." She nodded and looked at his drink. "Do you need another?"

The man held his hand up. "No, I'm good. I have to drive." He winked.

She laughed.

"This is yours." The man pushed the money toward her, then signaled for her to wait. He leaned to his side, pulled his wallet from his back pocket, thumbed through it, and tossed several hundred more on the table for her.

Her eyes grew in size and her eyebrows raised, making horizontal lines across her forehead. "What's this for?" She looked at him.

"For talking to me. Most women in places like this only want to give me a lap dance." He made quotation marks in the air. "Or go for a ride. You're a nice girl. Your grandma was clearly a good person. You don't belong here. Take the money—go to school. An education doesn't get you as far as it used to, but it will get you somewhere other than here. What's your name?" he asked, looking at her and holding out his hand for her to shake.

"Chevy."

He laughed. "Your mom named you Chevy?" His eyebrow raised in surprise.

"No." She smiled. "My mom named me after my grandmother, Charlotte. I love Chevy trucks. I used to have one, an older one." She paused and leaned toward him. "My grandmother would say she could hear Chevy coming, meaning my truck." She smiled and leaned a little closer. "It needed a new muffler, but I thought the loud rumble was kind of cool. The name stuck."

"Well, Chevy, it was nice to meet you," he said, seeming

sincere.

She smiled. "Likewise." She picked the money up from the table, paused, and looked at him. "Thank you."

He nodded politely. "You're welcome."

Jen walked up, put her arms around Chevy, and leaned toward the man. "Did you want a lap dance?" Jen asked seductively.

He looked at Jen. The corner of his mouth moved sideways and he hesitated. "No, I'm good," he said quickly, the crease between his eyes deepening.

Jen moved around the table and straddled him, pushing her breasts purposefully into his face as she moved in a slinky motion up and down his front.

Chevy shrugged and mouthed, "Want me to take her away?"

He looked at Chevy as best he could from around Jen, and with a discreet side-to-side motion of his head, he briefly closed his eyes and indicated no.

### 

Chevy stood in front of the clothing rack, changing into her clothes, while Jen sat at the dressing table, looking in the mirror and running her fingers through her hair. "Do I look okay?" Jen asked, fussing with the front.

Chevy glanced over while pulling her jeans on. "You look great. Where are you going?" she asked, knowing that Jen only fidgeted with her hair when she was going out.

"Remember the men on the yacht the other night?"

"Yeah, I remember you telling me about them." She buttoned her jeans.

Jen leaned to her and whispered, "They wanted me to come back tonight." She looked at Chevy and smiled.

Chevy's eyes widened, and she stepped closer, speaking softly. "You're going to that yacht without Austin or Tyler?"

"Are you kidding me? If I take Austin or Tyler, then I have to claim the profit." Jen turned back to the mirror and looked at Chevy in the reflection. "Do you have any idea how much money the men paid?"

Chevy pulled her orange sweatshirt over her head. "How much?"

8

Jen's tone became defensive. "Eight grand goes a long way for me."

Chevy's eyes widened. "Really?"

"My parents don't pay my bills. Why do you think I'm here?" A resentful tone came through.

Chevy stared at Jen dumbfounded—she knew the situation.

Jen looked away. "I'll be able to pay some of my father's attorney fees." She looked at her reflection.

Chevy laid her hand on Jen's arm to get her attention. "That's great to cover bills, but at what price? My parents don't pay my way, either. My father cut me off—you of all people know this. You know that's the only reason I'm here, stripping for perverted horny men and on several websites trying to collect sugar daddies." She stopped for a moment, searching Jen's face. This isn't fun for me." Chevy let go of Jen's arm. "What I take home shows this isn't fun, but those men will tuck money in a G-string like it grows on trees, and I have tuition to pay." She paused. "You're the person who told me never to do any jobs without Austin or Tyler," she reminded her.

"It was good advice," Jen said, pulling her eyes from her reflection in the mirror and looking at Chevy. "I have some bills to take care of."

"Bills?" Chevy questioned.

"Something like that."

Chevy gave her a deductive look as she started pulling her hair out of her sweatshirt. "You're not being completely honest."

"I have to pay my father's attorney."

"I thought you had that covered. Your father made good money."

"Yeah, but the government frowns on white collar crimes. Something about embezzling investors' money makes people cranky." Jen wanted to lessen the seriousness of her family's situation.

Chevy finished pulling the length of her hair from her sweatshirt. "I thought you said that happened almost two years ago. Hasn't it been swept under the rug yet?"

"The government suddenly decided to freeze all the accounts, seeing that my father was filling our saving and investment accounts with embezzled money." Jen twisting off the top of her lip gloss and smeared it across her lips to make them glisten.

"Oh!" Chevy sat down at the makeup table next to her. "This is a new development," she said, sympathetically.

Jen's eyes started to well.

"Aren't some of the accounts solely in your name? I thought you said your father covered his tracks. He made it look like he was depositing part of his salary into the accounts for you and your brother." Chevy looked puzzled.

Jen looked at her. "You know this whole thing is embarrassing. My father was money hungry and careless," she said with a burst of anger and resentment that she normally hid.

Chevy leaned to her supportively. "You don't want to go any place without Austin or Tyler. They are bouncers for a reason. They come with us on off-site jobs just in case."

"Nothing ever happens."

Chevy bent down to zip her backpack. "Are you trying to convince me or yourself?" she asked over the sound of the zipper. "What about the guy who couldn't keep his hands off me earlier? Austin had to toss him out. I would say that shows why we need them. But you are correct, aside from touching, nothing ever happens. For a drunk attorney or CEO every now and then who's having a bad day, getting a little out of hand makes them feel empowered again. They know we have bouncers who will be their safety net."

Just then knuckles rapped against the back of the dressing room door. "Ladies, you ready? We'd like to go," Austin asked.

"Be right out," Chevy yelled.

With her purse in hand, Jen stepped to Chevy and whispered, "This is an upscale establishment. We have upscale men."

"We're strippers." Chevy stared at her. "These men are here because their wives are off somewhere shopping or on another vacation. They're lonely rich men that have plenty of money and little else to make them happy. Austin and Tyler are here just in case."

"The attorney's expensive," Jen growled, looking away. "I would like to go back to school one of these days. I'm not dividing the money with Austin or Tyler." She headed for the door, then suddenly stopped and turned to Chevy. "If by chance something were to happen, I'm going to the Patriot Marina, slot 828."

"The Patriot Marina. 828," Chevy repeated.

"They're on a huge yacht. Becky thought they were Italian or Greek, and they were perfect gentlemen to her."

Jen pulled the door open and walked out, pulling it shut behind her. "Chevy will be out in a second."

Chevy stared at the door, contemplating, then picked up her backpacks and opened the door. "Ready," she announced.

### 

The breeze was chilly when Chevy stepped into the parking lot and walked toward her hybrid car. Every time she looked at it she remembered standing in the dealership on the showroom floor. The smell of new car mingled in the air with the scent of thick cologne from the salesmen who scurried around prospective customers.

"I don't like the black and white," she had told her father as they stood there looking at the shiny car. "I would prefer the solid black or yellow one."

"What the hell is wrong with this one?" her father barked.

She looked at him. His wording told her he wasn't going to budge.

Her mother nudged her father with her elbow. "John," her mom scolded.

"I don't like the black and white," she told them with her lips puckered unpleasantly. "I like the black—the black is mysterious, intriguing, and sexy," she told her parents as her eyes widened with excitement.

"Great!" her father said. "That's what I want…to send you back to college in something mysterious and sexy." He shook his head and half chuckled. "Sorry about your fuckin' luck!" he said abruptly. "Take it, or else you can walk!"

11

"John!" her mom hissed, irritated with him.

"I don't like the white stripes. It looks like a skunk." She frowned.

"Chevy, give us a moment," her mom asked sweetly.

She stepped away, purposefully close enough so she could hear them.

Her mother quickly leaned toward her father. "John, she's not a little girl. You have to stop this. First, you protected her and spoiled her into insanity, then you're angry when she wants the car she likes best. I told you not to spoil her rotten, but you wouldn't listen to me."

"Yeah, well, you don't know," he replied, belittling her.

Her mother paused. Chevy could just imagine the cold stare on her mom's face.

"Do not take that tone with me," she heard her mother warn sternly.

She listened as her father backed down. *Hardheaded man*, she stood there and thought, recalling the impatient look her father gave her. *Mom is the only person he will back down for.* It was either this black and white hybrid or her old beat-up truck—although she doubted her father would send her back to school in the truck. If it would make the distance was questionable.

"See you tomorrow!" she heard Jen yell from across the parking lot.

Chevy pulled her hands into the sleeves of her sweatshirt. "Be careful," she replied as she unlocked the door, tossing both of her backpacks in the passenger seat next to her. The black leather seats were cold, reminding her of the other two cars she preferred over this one.

A picture of her and Brandon hung from her rearview mirror. Brandon's face was pressed next to hers, and both of them were smiling. He was pleasant-looking, with short brown hair and light eyes. He was tall and had a nice smile and a dimple in the center of his chin. Hanging with the photos were several strands of Mardi Gras beads she and Brandon got when they were in New Orleans a year earlier. It was a fun, wild time her father knew nothing about. He didn't know about her boyfriend, either. When she was home, the beads and picture were placed neatly under her driver's seat, out of sight.

Tired, she started the unloved hybrid she referred to as Skunk.

###

Chevy pulled in front of a two-story 1920s-style house—she was home. The house had taupe siding trimmed in white and a white front porch with thick round pillars. The front door was white, and decorative glass panes flanked each side. The porch lights were recessed, giving just enough light for her to see.

In the second-floor window a light was on. Chevy smiled, knowing Brandon was waiting for her. She paused on the porch and pressed the remote for the car alarm. *Better safe than sorry*, she thought as the alarm chirped in the background.

Inside, she set her backpacks next to the long, narrow table against the wall and tossed her keys on the top. She noticed the mail that sat waiting. Grumbling to herself, she shuffled through the envelopes and paused at the one from Harvard.

Plucking it from the pile, she ran her fingers under the back, tearing it open. The top of the letter was marked STATEMENT. She took in a deep breath to release the stress she felt building and pulled the paper out. In big bold letters at the bottom was written, "Now due $13,853.16." She felt the muscles throughout her body tighten and her blood pressure surge with the sudden warm flushing of her cheeks. She took in another breath and closed her eyes, feeling the stress of the bills increasing. "This was supposed to be four easy payments," she mumbled in frustration. She let out her breath and opened her eyes.

Her mind raced. Rent was due in a week and a half, insurance was due in four days, then electric, gas, water, Internet, phone, and the credit cards her father had stopped paying. She set the statement on the table.

She turned for the steps and shut the closet door that Brandon always left open. As her feet moved up the hardwood steps she heard the sound of soft music. She pushed open the door to their room. The covers on the bed were pulled back, but there was no Brandon. Her excited smile and beaming eyes

13

momentarily shrunk. She looked to the bathroom to see a flickering light coming from the crack under the door. She pushed the old wood door open to see Brandon in the huge claw-foot bathtub with mounds of bubbles. Candles littered the bathroom around the base of the tub, the perimeter of the bathroom, and on the sink, windowsill, and shelf. Her excited smile and beaming eyes instantly lit again. "Wow!" she said, stepping into the bathroom.

"Are you getting in, or are you going to stand there?" He gave her a devilish smile and winked.

She started peeling off her clothes. "This is such a girl thing," she said with excitement. "I wanted a hot bath."

"That's where my sweatshirt went. I was looking for it," he said, watching as it hit the floor.

"Don't worry, it was comfortable."

"Was it?" he replied, running the back of his hand down the side of her soft, smooth skin, looking at how her body curved in all the right places. Her breasts were full and round, sitting impressively in place.

She stuck one foot in the hot water. "Oh—" She closed her eyes momentarily and sighed. "That feels good." She stepped in and slowly sat down, facing him, and leaned her head against the tall porcelain back. "This was just what I needed. I was thinking on the way home about a bath—a nice hot bubble bath," she moaned.

"Water?" Brandon offered. "I knew you would want some." He handed her a bottle.

"Yes," she replied, twisting the top off, and took a drink. "You would never believe the night I had. You know, I had two guys trying to put their hands on me. Austin had to threaten one and throw the other out."

"I bet Austin loved that." He laughed. He's like the Incredible Hulk with Swedish white blond hair and fair skin.

"I don't know." Chevy shrugged and stared up at the ceiling. "Austin didn't seem in the mood. He grabbed the guy and showed him to the door. That was the end of it."

"Did the guy have too much to drink?" Brandon asked as he pulled the bubbles to his side of the tub.

"I think so. They were both groomed businessmen—I wasn't paying much attention to them. I don't care, as long as they stick money in my G-string and keep their hands to themselves."

"Physically removed him, huh," Brandon repeated, taking a drink of his water.

"Yep!" She pulled her eyes from the ceiling and looked at him. "Then some man kept watching me tonight, more than most of them do. He kept putting hundreds on the table for me, even tossed in a few hundred more because I talked to him and didn't automatically want to give him a lap dance or go for a ride. The money is great, but there was something about him that made me uneasy." She leaned forward with a serious expression and took another sip of water, thinking.

"What was strange about him?" Brandon asked.

She thought for a moment. "I'm not sure exactly. He was nice. He was polite. He just wanted to talk. I felt like he was evaluating me somehow. Looking for something. I'm not sure. It was just weird. It wasn't anything he said or did. It was a strange feeling I've never gotten before."

"You know every guy that comes in the club is going to evaluate you."

"Of course." She splashed water toward him. "This guy was different. I can't quite put my finger on it. It was just weird."

"How much did he give you?" Brandon asked.

"Um…Thirteen hundred."

"Wow." His eyebrows raised.

"We need every bit of it for bills."

Brandon pulled her in front of him, to rub her shoulders.

"Mmm. That feels good," she groaned.

"Let me talk to my father. I know he'll cover all the bills and your tuition."

"I've never met your father, and I'm supposed to accept assistance from him? Besides, my father should be taking care of it."

"He should be, and he's not," Brandon replied.

"Give me a few more weeks. I have a few of those sugar daddy sites that will help." Chevy turned in the tub, straddling him, loving the feel of his wet body next to hers. "Maybe you should find a sugar mama." She smiled, her lips glistening. "You're sexy."

Brandon pulled her close, kissing her warm, wet skin.

She tilted her head back, closed her eyes, and moaned.

"You want some rich woman all over me?" he asked, giving her neck little kisses.

"If it's helping to get us through school and you aren't emotionally vested, then why not?" She delicately kissed his lips between words. "You're amazing in bed. You would be a great fantasy for some rich woman."

He snickered. "It's easy for you, you can lay there and fake pleasure. I have to perform. How could I fake arousal when my penis and testicles crawl into my abdomen and won't come out?" He grabbed her butt cheeks and pulled her closer to him.

She kissed his neck and looked into his eyes. Her hand reached from under the layers of fragrant fluffy white bubbles and touched the center of his lips with her index finger. "Shhhh...You think of me," she whispered. "You think of my soft skin." She pressed her lips to his neck, kissing slowly up to his ear.

He ran his hands along the tops of her thighs and squeezed her butt in the palm of his hands.

She pressed her hips against him, feeling him growing between their abdomens. She kissed up the side of his face, running her hands over his shoulders and across his chest. "You think of my breasts." She kissed his forehead.

"The way you put them in my face?"

"Yes." She raised herself slightly, moving side to side to run her nipples across his lips. "You think about sliding into me—making love to me," she whispered in his ear.

His tongue ran around her nipples as he moved her hips—positioning her over him—and pulled her down.

Her nipple slid from his mouth as he slid into her.

Her head tilted back, feeling his length stretching inside her. "Oh my God...yes...this is what you think of," she said as she slid up then back down on his length.

###

The man sat in his hotel room with the light mounted next to the bed on and his laptop open and running in front of him. Next to his laptop was his amber-colored drink. The top of the screen read SUGAR BABIES. He flipped through a series of photographs of women looking for sugar daddies. Then before him was a picture of that cute girl from The Club. Next to her cute picture was the unforgettable name—Chevy.

"Well, well, well…Who do we have here?" the man said, pausing to view her profile. "You're just a perfect little candidate, aren't you?" He picked up his glass and took a sip, contemplating.

# Chapter 2

Surrounded by white fluffy covers, Chevy's head rested comfortably on her pillow and her body curled next to Brandon's, their noses almost touching. The room was illuminated by the light of another pleasant fall morning. Beginning to wake up, she moved under the covers, then suddenly opened her eyes, blinking rapidly to focus. Hurriedly, she reached for her phone and looked at the time. "Shit," she mumbled, tossing the covers back.

The comfort of Brandon beside her forced a smile and a happy moan as she stretched then put her hand to the side of his face and kissed the delicate tip of his nose.

He opened his eyes and lifted his head. "Chevy?" he muttered.

"I'm going to be late for class," she said softly. Her feet hit the floor, making light thumps against the wood as she hurried. She opened a dresser drawer and pulled out a lacy yellow thong and bra, then hurried to the bathroom. Unlit candles lined the floor and shelves where they had left them. On the tile in a neat pile were her clothes. She picked up her jeans and quickly pulled them on. At the pedestal sink she splashed some water on her face, lathered, rinsed, ran a toothbrush over her teeth, then threw her hair up in a clip. She pulled a gray sweatshirt from the closet. "I have to go," she whispered, leaning over the bed kissing Brandon's forehead.

"I love you, too," he mumbled, mostly asleep. "I will see you after class at the café." He opened one eye, trying to focus.

Chevy smiled. *He's so sweet*, she thought. "I love you," she told him.

She watched him snuggle back into his pillow. "Lunch at three in the café," he mumbled to himself.

"Yeah. If I'm a little late, just wait. I'm going to go to the gym after class and take a shower," she told him quickly as she hurried out of the bedroom.

"All right."

She hurried down the stairs. As she grabbed both backpacks she saw the letter sitting there, ominously waiting for her. Her muscles begin to tense, and she shook her head. "I will deal with it later," she mumbled, grabbing her keys from the table and heading out the door into the crisp autumn air.

###

Chevy sat at the makeup table putting on glittery powder when Jen come through the door. "Nice to see you're still alive."

Jen gave her an unimpressed glance as she set her bag down and peeled off her jacket. "Of course I'm alive. Did you honestly think you would see me on the back of a milk carton?" she asked, hanging her jacket on the back of her chair.

"I was concerned. Did you make the money you expected?"

"Yes!" She smiled, relieved. "It's a huge help."

"That's good," Chevy looked back down at her leg, continuing to apply glitter.

Jen slowed. "What's wrong?"

Chevy shook her head. "I just have a lot to contend with, and it's wearing on me." She picked up a backpack from the floor and set it on a chair, seeming deep in thought, as she pulled a tub of lip gloss from the bag and put it on.

Jen looked at her. "What's weighing on you?"

"Just the similar shit that you're dealing with," Chevy answered. "Brandon wants to ask his father to cover my part of the bills and my tuition."

Jen searched Chevy's face. "That's *good* news," she replied with a confused look.

Chevy paused and looked at her. "Then why don't I feel comfortable with his father's help? If I passed his father in a store I wouldn't know it. I have never met him or seen a picture." Chevy tensed. "Plus, it makes me feel like I'm not handling this myself. Does it matter how I get the bill money, or just that I get it?"

"You've never met his father?" Jen repeated slowly. "That's odd. You guys have been dating for over a year."

"I didn't give it any thought until last night. Now I've been thinking about it all day. We've both been busy with classes. I

19

was just seeing where this was going, and this year has flown by. It never really crossed my mind until last night when he offered. In all fairness, he has never met or seen pictures of my family, either. My parents don't know I'm dating anyone. My father would flip." Chevy rolled her eyes, imaging her father's reaction.

Jen laughed. "Then just wait till your father hears what you are doing to cover the bills. He'll forget all about the boyfriend." She snickered, brushing her hand in the air.

Chevy gave her an unamused look.

"This really bothers you, doesn't it?" Jen stopped laughing.

"Yeah, it does."

"What does his father do?"

Chevy shrugged. "I don't really know. Some sort of a businessman. He travels a lot. That was the answer Brandon gave me, and that's the answer I was satisfied with."

"Ask him. I'm sure he will tell you. Brandon adores you," Jen said reassuringly.

Chevy leaned down, shoving her jeans and sweatshirt in a backpack. "I'll talk to you about it later." She got up and stepped toward the door. "I need to get out there and make some money. Sitting back here thinking about it isn't going to solve any problems." She opened the dressing room door to loud music that flooded in.

"Chevy," Jen said, catching her attention. "You and I, we aren't strippers. We're two women trying to contend with financial issues."

With a somber and burdened expression Chevy pulled the door shut the music fading to almost a silence again.

Jen sat for a moment, contemplating. Suddenly Becky came in.

"What's wrong with Chevy?" Becky asked as she moved to the wardrobe rack to change her thong and heels.

Jen shook her head. "Chevy's having a bad day."

Becky pulled on a different thong. "Oh," Becky squealed, as she looked in one of the mirrors at her butt, admiring her smooth-looking skin and the defining shape of her curves. "I like the rust-colored thong. It goes with my red hair and looks good against the color of my skin—don't you think?"

Jen sighed. Becky was always lacking. For Becky, every moment was about showing off her body to whoever would look. Flirting with men, sex with anyone who would shove money her way, getting drunk or screwed up on whatever drug she could get—that's what filled her mind. She always seemed to have some new biker boyfriend named Bruno or Fang who had poor social skills and lacked intelligence. That was Becky. She was super cute, but soon enough, she would look like the riffraff she hung out with. Sometimes Jen felt sorry for her, but she also thought Becky was lucky. She lived in her small mind with small expectations. She seemed to have little pressure or concern, just the pleasure of day-to-day life. Jen looked at Becky. "Yes, I agree that's a great color for you." Giving Becky a weak smile, she watched her pranced out the door without a care in the world.

The dressing room was quiet once again, with only the low rumble of bass from the stage. Jen looked at herself in the mirror. Her makeup was going on slow and she thought about the distorted perception she was giving people. She undressed for men, danced erotically, gave them lap dances, and rubbed her breasts in their face. To be thought of as one of the Beckys of the world disgusted her.

She felt angry at her father for embezzling. It had left her in an awkward situation. She could transfer to a community college, but it would put her at a disadvantage when getting into a decent law school. She wanted to be a corporate attorney for a large corporation—that took a good college, Ivy League. She didn't want to be a small-town attorney defending locals who couldn't make decent choices or pay their bills. Just another few months until the next semester, and she would be back in class. She hoped the attorney she wanted to become wouldn't be unraveled by what she had to do to get there.

She stared at herself in the mirror and, seeing her dull-looking lips, leaned over and shuffled through Chevy's backpack, looking for her lip gloss. She was pushing the clothes to the side when she saw Chevy's notebook. Chevy had written "Bills" on the front cover. Jen paused, then arranged the clothes neatly over the notebook and headed out the dressing room door.

She stood in the dark hall, watching Chevy on stage. Her movements lacked erotic quality and passion, and looked forced. She glanced down, wanting to help.

### 

Several hours later, Chevy walked into the dressing room and picked up the powder puff to apply more of her fragrant glitter.

"Hey, Chevy, I went in your backpack for some lip gloss," Jen said, hurriedly touching up her makeup so she could get back out there.

"That's fine," Chevy replied as she turned her focus back to the powder.

"I saw your notebook."

Chevy paused. "Writing the bills down helps me see what's owed and figure out how to organize and plan."

"I'm supposed to go back to the boat tonight. Becky's been there. I've been there several times. I felt safe. Each time they paid me eight grand. I know you need the money. You can go tonight instead of me."

Chevy looked at her. "I'll consider it," she said slowly, going back to her glitter.

"Let me know." Jen turned and glanced at the clock above the door. "You have a few hours before we close," she said as she disappeared out the door.

Chevy stood there playing with the powder puff and the powder—allowing the idea to roll around and the temptation to grow.

### 

Chevy pulled into the marina parking lot into slot 828 and sat there looking at the impressive yacht at the end of the dock. Hesitantly, she turned off her car, Skunk.

As she walked down the long pier, a pleasant-looking Italian man with dark hair, light eyes, and a fair complexion came around the side of the yacht, holding two glasses of wine. "You have arrived!" he said loudly with a heavy accent. He set the wine down and stepped off the yacht. "Welcome!" he said,

22

holding his arms open to greet her. "My name is Sandro."

"I'm Chevy." She smiled.

He held out his hand to help her as she stepped onto the yacht.

"Thank you."

"I knew you were coming, so I poured you a glass of wine. I hope you like wine, and I hope you like red," he said politely, picking up the glasses and handing one to her.

"Thank you." She rolled the wine around the glass, smelling it, then took a sip. "Red is my favorite."

### 

The end of a cigar sat smoldering in an expensive crystal ashtray. The man from the nightclub was sitting back in his black leather chair, his laptop open and running. The light on his desk was the only light on in his office. A small glass with several ice cubes and amber liquid was beside his ashtray. He sat there quietly waiting. The time in the corner of the computer screen read 3:31 a.m.

"Is this the girl you wanted us to get?" Sandro asked from the screen, looking into the camera as he pulled a passed-out long-haired girl into the camera's view.

The man paused. "That isn't the girl we talked about the other night." He puffed on the end of his cigar.

"Jen. You mean the girl named Jen, whose father embezzled money from his company?"

"Yeah, that's the one we talked about, Jen, but this girl is better," he said. "This one doesn't come with a high-profile father."

"Did you do your homework on this one?"

"Yeah, I met her. This one's safe. She'll bring a lot of money with that all-American face."

"Did you check her out?" the Italian man asked again.

"No, I didn't, but trust me—we have been doing this for how many years. The girl's name is Chevy. What kind of hick names their daughter Chevy?" The man took a puff of his cigar, making the end glow red-orange.

"Do you want to send this girl through the rooms and send her home?"

"No, no, take good care of this one. Keep her happy. We'll auction this one as a wife. She'll bring big bucks from one of the wealthy businessmen overseas. This one has an air about her, and she is genuinely sweet. She'll probably be thankful to get out of her crappy life." He sipped his drink.

"Overseas then?"

"Yeah, we'll keep her overseas."

"We're leaving now then—"

"Do the norm," he instructed.

Across the desk from the man, a woman in a robe and pajamas sat in a comfortable leather chair. "You didn't do your homework on this one?" she asked. "Do you really think this is a wise idea?"

He turned off his computer, looking at the woman with arrogance. "Like I said, who would name their daughter Chevy? A hillbilly? Hillbillies aren't well educated, and they don't have means. They can be a passionate bunch, but that hardly makes up for sophistication and the right contacts."

The woman shook her head and raised her eyebrows as she looked at him with an unconvinced stare. "If you say so…but you better be careful. I hope you are correct, because one wrong girl could be disaster."

He looked at her with loving eyes. "I have everything to lose. You're a great woman." He glanced at their family picture, which sat next to the light on his desk, a picture of the two of them with their son. He stared for a moment at the image of his wife with her chin-length graying blond hair. She was even more beautiful now than she was all those years ago when he first met her.

She walked around his desk to the side of his chair and leaned over.

He looked up at her.

She patted his shoulder and kissed his forehead. "I love you, sweetheart. After all these years I have grown rather dependent on you. Just be careful. I need you here with me, and Brandon needs us to get him through college. He can't take over the business until he finishes."

"Sure he can."

"Honey, first we have to tell him what you do," she reminded. "You still have to sit him down and explain."

"We will one of these days, when the time is right. I'm not sure how he'll take it. He has always been more of a crusader for justice, a little too much for my liking."

"I'm sure he will be fine," she said, patting his shoulder again.

He put his hand on her arm. "I love you, sweetie." He looked at her.

"I'm going back to bed." She smiled as she made her way around the desk.

"I'm right behind you."

She paused at the French doors. "All right," she said, then went through the open side.

# Chapter 3

The room was dark, but the curtains on the French doors
that led to the balcony were open, allowing a small amount of
light in from the star-studded sky. The room smelled like wood
and scented candles. John suddenly woke up. He picked up his
phone from the log night stand and pressed the side button. The
time lit up, 3:43 a.m. He set his phone back down beside the
antler light. Rolling onto his back, he rubbed his face with his
hands, then tossed the covers back and walked across the
hardwood floor to the bathroom. Moments later, he crawled
back into bed.

Ruthie lovingly rolled the covers over him as he got back
into bed, then snuggled against his side and wrapped her arm
around his chest as she kissed his cheek. "You okay, babe?"
she asked.

"Yeah," he replied. "I'm fine."

"Having trouble sleeping?"

"A little bit."

"What's wrong?" she asked, noting his unsettled spirit.

"Chevy popped into my head. I just woke up."

"If you're worried…" She looked at his profile and his lips
as the muscles in his jaw tensed. "You can call Chevy if you're
that worried. I can send her some money so you don't look as
though you're giving in," she offered.

"I want to go back to sleep." He rolled to his side.

"All right," she conceded, knowing she had at least planted
the idea. For such a stubborn man he was so easy, so moldable.
"I love you," she told him sweetly, snuggling her head against
his back.

"I love you, too," he mumbled, pulling her hand against his
chest.

### ###

Brandon woke up in their fluffy white covers with his head
snuggled comfortably in his pillow. He reached out his arm,
feeling Chevy's side of the bed, then suddenly realized: no

Chevy. He opened his eyes. trying to focus on her side of the bed, and lifted himself to his elbow. *No Chevy?* He paused, trying to process her absence. *This isn't right.* He looked at the floor for her pile of clothes. No pile. He pushed himself from his elbows to his hand, looking for her pile at the end of the bed. No pile. He looked toward the bathroom—the door was open, just as he left it the night before. A soft light from the bathroom window cast a shine on the ceramic tile—the bathroom was empty. No Chevy.

He reached to this night stand and picked up his phone. It was 9:33 a.m. He had no missed calls. He pressed the button for his phone log. In big letters was her name. He tapped Call and hit Send. It rang once, then jumped to her voice mail—her phone was off.

He looked around the room, trying to wake up. "She never shuts her phone off," he said to himself, thinking.

He pushed the covers back and sat on the side of the bed, as he wiped the sleep from his eyes. He made his way to the window, and pushed back the curtain—no Skunk. Her spot beside the curb was empty. "Did you go over to Jen's after work? Did you fall asleep?" he asked the air, letting go of the curtains.

Getting ready, he checked his phone repeatedly. No calls, no texts. Nothing.

###

Slowly, Chevy woke up. Glaze covered her eyes, her head pounded, and a drained, sluggish feeling permeated her body. Her head was lying on a pillow, and she could feel drool running from the corner of her mouth. Slowly, she lifted her head, which felt like a pounding brick. *Pillow?* she thought, then rubbed her face with her hand, wiping away the drool. She looked around, trying to focus.

*Where am I?* She didn't remember the pillow. She didn't remember the room, either. She looked around at the king-size bed she was on, the pillow under her, the white bed covers, and the two-layered headboard, which was covered in a mustard-colored fabric. She didn't remember any of it. The room was large, with a lot of cherry woodwork, flooring, and crown molding. The ceiling held recessed lights, and on either side of the bed were lights that were mounted to the wall. There was a small window with beautiful curtains. Under the window was a white sofa and a wood coffee table. In the corner was a desk, and across from the bed was a built-in chest of drawers, closet, and entertainment cabinet.

*What do I remember? Men, laughing dancing. drinking the wine...Ah...yes—the wine*, she thought.

Her pounding head made it hard to think about much of anything. Pushing herself onto her hand, she waited for the pounding to let up. *I got drunk and passed out? Hmm...that's odd.* She looked down at her clothing. It was all there. Nothing felt or looked like it had been removed. Her body didn't feel as though it had been violated.

She rubbed her eyes with the heel of her hand and stood from the bed. Her legs felt like rubber, and she struggled for energy. She grabbed the door handle and twisted. It came to an alarming stop. Stunned, she panicked.

She twisted it again; another sudden stop. Her heart skipped a beat and her mind went blank. *What? This can't be right!* Her heart began thumping in her chest. She mumbled little prayers under her breath. She tried the knob again. Another sudden stop. She pulled the door toward her. It only wiggled in place.

### 

Brandon waited outside of Chevy's morning class, looking at his watch every few minutes. The strap of his brown leather satchel was across his torso, hanging at his hip. In a dark sweatshirt and a fitted winter hat, he waited anxiously, listening for the professor to stop talking. Impatiently, he looked down at his watch again. The doors opened a few minutes late and a flood of students made their way out and dispersed down the halls. He watched everyone who came through the door until only a few stragglers were left in the classroom, packing up. Eagerly, he stepped through the doorway expecting to see her meticulously putting her notebook away. He looked around at the few people. None were Chevy. He walked to the professor. "Excuse me. Did Chevy make it to class today?"

28

The professor gave him a blank look. The deep creases between his white eyebrows grew deeper as he tilted his head to the side and he looked at Brandon, struggling to recall a person named Chevy.

"I'm sorry," Brandon quickly corrected himself. "Charlotte Westen," he said, glancing at the professor's open attendance book sitting on the podium in front of him.

"Ah…yes, Charlotte. Now that name rings a bell." The professor ran his finger down the left side of the book to the *W*s. "Today Charlotte missed class," he said matter-of-factly, with nothing more than a glance in Brandon's direction.

Brandon looked at the attendance book.

"Charlotte hasn't missed any classes before today, and her scores are quite good," the professor offered, then looked at Brandon. "These are private records, if you don't mind." He shut the attendance book.

Brandon looked at him, wondering what would keep Chevy from class. Suddenly, somewhere in his mind what the professor said finally connected. "Right! Of course, confidential information," he repeated, taking a few steps back. "Thank you for looking."

"You're quite welcome."

Brandon turned and made his way out of the classroom, checking his phone again, this time turning it off and then back on to see if any messages came through. None. Impatiently, he tried her again. It went straight to voice mail. "This is Chevy. I will call you back just as soon as can." Then the annoying tone. Frustrated, he went to their usual café, found a table, pulled out his laptop, and waited.

### 

Chevy sat on the bed and held her head in her hands. Her stomach was empty and rumbling with hunger.

Suddenly, she heard the door knob rattle, the sound of metal against metal: a key sliding into the lock. She froze, not knowing who was on the other side, why they had locked her in, or what they were going to do to her. Her throbbing head raced with wild ideas and overly vivid images. She scanned the room for a place to hide, but nothing popped out at her. She watched the knob and heard the lock click open, and the handle began to turn. Chevy's heart started to pound, unsure what was going to happen. The door started to open.

### 

Brandon tried to focus on a paper as he watched people come and go from the café, none of them Chevy. He restlessly peered down at the time on the corner of the screen, 5:21 p.m. He had to be at class at six. It was a lecture on the legality of foreign trade. He picked his phone from the table—it hadn't made a sound. Reluctantly, he stood and put his things back into his satchel.

Sitting in class, the lecture slid to the wayside. He moved in his chair uncomfortably and doodled in the margins of his notebook. He needed to stay to receive points, then he could concentrate on Chevy.

###

Through the crack at the door frame by the hinges, she could see a camel color. From around the door came a very pretty woman with long dark hair and big chestnut eyes.

"You are up," she said with a heavy accent, carrying a tray. A warm smile crossed her face as she pushed the door shut with her hip. "I wasn't sure what you enjoy eating, so I brought you several things," the woman said sweetly, setting the tray on the end of the bed and sat down beside her. "My name is Veronica." She held out her hand.

Chevy looked at the woman's hand apprehensively, then shook it.

"Where I come from, women hug." Veronica smiled.

Chevy's head pounded. "You hug," she repeated.

"Yes," the woman said.

Chevy leaned toward the woman and gave her a hug.

"I bet your head is booming. I brought you lots of water. If you drink the whole glass and wait about fifteen minutes, your headache will subside," she assured Chevy, picking up the glass of water and handing it to her.

Chevy sat there and looked at it.

Veronica smiled. "It is fine—drink. You'll feel better."

Chevy put the glass to her lips, unsure, then drank it

quickly. "Where am I?" She wiped her lips with her fingers.

Veronica leaned closer to Chevy. "We are on the boat going overseas. Whatever you do, you must be sweet and cooperative."

### 

Brandon walked toward the main doors of the nightclub, where Austin was collecting cover charges. "Hey, is Chevy here?"

"No, Chevy's not here yet. She was supposed to be here at nine—I think."

Brandon pulled Austin aside. "What time did Chevy leave last night?"

Austin put his hands in the air in front of him. "Man, I'm not sure what the problem might be between you two, but I don't want in the middle of it."

"No." Brandon shook his head. "It's nothing like that. Chevy didn't come home last night, she never went to her classes, she didn't show up at the café where we meet, and now she's not here at work." He looked at Austin.

"Man, I don't know what to say."

Brandon stepped closer. "What time did Chevy leave last night? Was it the normal time? Did she leave with anyone? Did she plan to go home with one of the girls after work?"

"Um," Austin started slowly, trying to recall. "When the rest of us left. Tyler and I walked everyone out. We made sure they got in their cars."

"Did they go out after work and get breakfast?"

"Let's ask the girls if they've talked to her." Austin opened the door and yelled for Tyler. "Hey, man, come out here and work the door for a minute? We're trying to find Chevy."

Tyler stepped outside, taking Austin's place.

Becky stood at the bar in a thong and pasties. Austin leaned on the bar to get her attention. "Hey, have you seen Chevy?"

Becky's long straight red hair almost covered her pasties. The tray in front of her had several drinks. "I saw her last night," Becky paused, flirting with Brandon as she smacked on her gum. "What's wrong?" She shifted her eyes back and forth.

"Chevy didn't stay the night at your house, did she?"

31

Brandon asked.

"No." Becky paused, observing him intently. "Chevy is always in a hurry to get home to you." She smiled, stepping closer with a twinkle in her eyes. "I can see why she's in a hurry."

Austin lightly swiped his chin with his index finger and nudged Brandon's arm, signaling for Brandon to follow him behind the stage.

"Jen," Austin called out, as he tapped the dressing room door with his knuckles.

"Yeah! Come in, I'm just powdering," Jen said loudly.

"I've got Brandon with me!"

"Brandon. Yeah, I'm good, Come in!"

Austin opened the door to find Jen standing in front of her makeup table, one leg on her chair and a big powder puff in her hand as she dabbed on glitter.

"Hey, Brandon," she said.

"Have you seen Chevy?" Austin asked.

Jen paused, glancing at the clock on the wall, and went back to her powder. "No. I'm sure she'll be here soon. Why?" she asked, shifting her eyes between them, waiting on the reason for the question.

Brandon stepped closer. "Chevy never came home last night. She never made it to class or the café we normally meet at. Now she isn't here at work. This isn't like her," he said with concern.

Jen put the powder puff back in the container, pulled her leg from the chair, and blinked—thinking.

"If you see Chevy, or hear from her, would you please let me know?" Brandon asked.

"She really didn't come home last night?" Jen said, slowly.

"No." Brandon pulled the flap of his satchel open and pulled out a notebook. He jotted down his number twice and ripped the paper in half. "I'm going to wait a few more hours. Then I'm calling the police to report her missing."

Jen nodded as he handed half the paper to her and the other half to Austin.

"All right, man," Austin said. "As soon as I see her I'll give you a call."

Brandon gave Austin and Jen a quick glance. "I appreciate it." He noticed Jen's slow movements as she stood there, seeming to be thinking hard about something.

"Okay, man," Austin replied as he and Brandon headed out of the dressing room.

### 

Jen watched Austin and Brandon walk out and pull the door shut behind them. She stood there, numb. Her mind raced somewhere between guilt, the yacht, and concern for Chevy. All kinds of possibilities played in her mind. She turned to the mirror and stood there, staring at the sparkly powder that covered her body. She looked pristine on the outside, but on the inside she felt tarnished, ugly, and foul. "Where's Chevy?" she whispered to her image in the mirror.

# Chapter 4

Brandon pulled up to the house to see that Chevy's spot beside the curb was still empty. He hoped to see her moving about, but the house was dark expect for the porch lights he had left on. He sat there for a moment, put the car in park, and stared at the top of the steering wheel. When he got out of his car he starred at her spot by the curb with a glum expression, then slowly started for the house.

Inside, the closet door was hanging open, the way he always left it. He put his coat away and shut the door, moving slowly, struggling to decide if he should report her missing or not. Sitting on the steps staring at his phone, he turned it on, then off, then on, then off. Then he set the phone beside him on the steps and looked at it, pondering. He decided to dial her number one last time.

"This is Chevy—"

He hit End, not wanting to hear her voice on the recording again. Taking in a deep breath for bravery, he looked up and dialed the non-emergency number for the police.

"Yeah…I need to report my girlfriend missing…" he began.

### 

He hung up the phone and sat, waiting. Disgruntled, he watched through the wavy, distorted glass that flanked the front door. After a while, headlights flashed in front of the house as a car pulled in behind his. He could hear one side of the car door shut, then the other. Through the glass he watched as one dark figure then another in lighter-colored clothes came to the door. The silence was heavy. He was about to make her officially missing.

From behind the wavy glass an arm reached for the doorbell. *Ding-dong* rang through the house.

He stood, taking in a deep breath and swallowing hard before he pulled the door open.

"Did you call about a missing person?" the older and huskier of the two men asked in a deep voice.

"Yes. My girlfriend." Brandon nodded. "Please come in."

"So, what's going on?" the younger, smaller officer asked as he stepped in.

Brandon shut the door behind them. "Let's have a seat in the kitchen." He led the way down the hall, which opened into a large living room, dining room, and kitchen area. He took a spot next to the island.

The older officer had on heavy cologne and looked to be in his late forties or early fifties. He had short reddish-brown, stick-straight hair that stuck out all over his head and a pitted complexion. "I'm Detective Hemming." He set his handheld radio on the counter. "This is Patrolman Becker." He motioned with his thumb to the muscular officer standing a few steps behind him.

"Brandon." He nodded politely, holding out his hand for Hemming.

Hemming seemed well seasoned—pleasantries weren't needed.

A photo that lay on the counter caught Hemming's eye.

"You can have that. It was taken about a week ago." Brandon pushed the photo toward him.

Hemming picked it up and briefly looked at it. "Her name?"

"Chevy."

Becker repeated her name with a cocky tone. "Chevy?" He chuckled. "Like the truck?" He smirked.

Brandon looked at him, unamused. "That's what everyone calls her. Chevy. Her name is Charlotte Westen," Brandon clarified.

"Westen...like the store? Westen's?" Becker laughed, poking fun.

Brandon stared at him. "Yes, her father owns the Westen's chain."

Becker's smile instantly melted and his laughter came to a silence.

"By all means," Brandon sarcastically encouraged, "continue laughing about how funny this is. I'm sure her father isn't going to find this humorous. Perhaps you can call him yourself and inform him his daughter is missing. Why don't

35

you go ahead and laugh while you're informing him. Let's see how he reacts?" Brandon challenged, giving Becker a cold stare.

Hemming stared at Becker until the younger officer finally noticed his disapproving grimace and looked down at the floor.

Hemming pulled out his notepad. "So, you said her name is Charlotte Westen and everyone calls her Chevy?" He looked at Brandon, making sure he had it correct.

Brandon nodded. "That's right."

"Birthday?" Hemming asked. "Where does she live?"

"March 28, 1995. Here." Brandon pressed the tip of his finger to the counter.

"Student, I gather?" Hemming asked, noting the stack of textbooks on the counter.

Brandon continued to nod. "Undergrad in business at Harvard," Brandon replied. "Since her father owns a large chain, he wants her to major in business. But Chevy's true interest is psychology."

"So there's conflict between her and her parents?" Hemming paused his pen, looking at Brandon.

"I wouldn't say that." Brandon shook his head. "I haven't heard anything unpleasant about her mom. Her father can be stubborn, rigid, and unmovable—so I'm told."

Hemming studied Brandon. "Do you and her father get along?" Hemming asked, with an intimidating glance.

"Can't say." Brandon shrugged. "I've never met him. Chevy hasn't told him we're dating. She said her father is very protective of her and can be unreasonable."

"This almost sounds like she's afraid of him," Hemming suggested, shifting his weight and watching Brandon's reaction.

"Afraid?" Brandon repeated and laughed. "No." He shook his head. "She just knows how he'll react."

"So when was the last time you saw her?"

"Yesterday. We meet at the café for lunch after her one o'clock class. We spent some time there, ate, talked, and did classwork like we normally do. Then she went to her Tuesday afternoon class. After class, she goes to work," Brandon told him.

"What does she do?" Hemming asked, with his pen against his paper, ready to write.

Brandon said with a touch of apprehension. "Chevy works at the Club."

Hemming paused and looked up from his notepad at Brandon.

"She's a stripper!" Becker blurted out.

Brandon tilted his head and looked at him in amazement. "Social skills?" Brandon asked, squinting. "You haven't been on the force long, huh?"

"Becker!" Hemming nudged Becker with his elbow and gave him a sour look.

Becker looked abashed.

"All right," Hemming said slowly, going back to his notepad. "Your girlfriend is a stripper. How long has she been a stripper? Has she ever done this before"—he moved his hand in the air—"not come home?" He suddenly seemed to take more interest.

"I know how this looks," Brandon admitted. "Chevy comes from a good home with lots of friends and family. She also comes from money. Her father opened his first store when she was little. Chevy has always been a daddy's girl. This is her third year at Harvard. She ran up the credit card too many times, so her father won't cover her expenses any longer. Now she has tuition, rent, and utilities, among other things. Obviously, waiting tables isn't going to cover it. She signed up on a couple sugar daddy sites and also started at the Club. She has a friend at the Club, Jen, who has similar financial concerns. She prompted Chevy to join her. They specifically selected the nicest club around, wanting to keep this as tactful as possible. She's been there about two months. Although she makes good money, she doesn't pull in as much as the other girls do. Let's just say she's not really stripper material. She just wants to get through school."

"Drugs? Alcohol?" Hemming asked.

Becker laughed. "She's going to show up as soon as she sobers up, comes down from her high, or gets done with her boyfriend."

Brandon glared at Becker, then looked back at Hemming. "Neither. She'll drink once in a while when we go out, or when she's around people she's familiar with. We went to New Orleans for Mardi Gras last year—we both had way too much to drink." Brandon smiled. "To answer your question, she's not a drinker. She prefers water. Drugs, she doesn't go near them." He cut his hand through the air, punctuating his words.

"We need to wait forty-eight hours before we make it official," Hemming informed him.

Brandon looked disgusted. "She's been missing since sometime last night. Aren't the first few days the most critical?"

"Ha!" Becker interjected. "As soon as she comes down from her fix and escapade with her other boyfriend, she'll surface." He laughed.

"Becker!" Hemming bellowed. "Go get my clipboard from the car."

Without a question Becker turned and headed down the hall. His hard-soled boots thumped against the wood floor.

Hemming watched the front door close, then looked at Brandon. "I'm sorry about him. He hasn't been on the force long. He thinks he knows it all and hasn't seen anything yet."

Brandon crinkled his face. "He leaves a lot to be desired."

"Have you called her friends and family?" Hemming softened.

"Yes and no," Brandon quickly responded. "I went to the Club, but none of her co-workers have seen or heard from her. The bouncer, Austin, said that after work, he walked the girls to their cars like he normally does. They didn't go out for breakfast, and know one knows where she is."

"Tell me, did you call her parents? Could she have gone home?"

Brandon shook his head. "No, I didn't call them. They don't know we are dating and living together. I have their numbers; Chevy gave them to me in case I ever needed them. But tell me, if you were in my position, would you call? How do you start that conversation?" Brandon waited on Hemming's response.

"I get the point." He shifted his position beside the counter.

"You can have a seat," Brandon offered. He watched Hemming try to get comfortable.

"So, is it possible that Chevy could've went home?"

Brandon paused, bobbing his head back and forth. "Sure, but not likely. That's not like Chevy to just leave. She's never done that. She has school and her job. When she commits herself to something, she doesn't walk away or not show up. If there was some sort of emergency at home, she would have called to let me know. She's from Kentucky, so it's a long drive."

"What part of Kentucky?"

"Rudle Mills—I'm told it's a small town."

"Hmm. And you didn't call her parents," he repeated, thinking out loud. "How is everything between the two of you?"

"Us?" Brandon looked at him. "It's fine. I got her a ring. I haven't decided when to give it to her yet, Christmas, New Year's, Valentine's Day, her birthday…" Brandon's voice trailed off, the momentary twinkle in his eyes fading.

Becker walked back though the front door, clipboard in hand. "You had it in the trunk," he said, irritated.

"Thanks," Hemming replied, taking the clipboard and setting it on the counter.

Becker looked at the clipboard then at Hemming and continued standing there.

"What kind of car does she drive?" Hemming questioned.

"Hybrid Cooper. It's black with a white stripe over the top. Someone ordered it, then decided not to take it. The dealership couldn't sell it, so her father got a deal. Chevy hates the stripe. Says it reminds her of a skunk."

Hemming smirked. "I can't say I disagree." He jotted down the description. "Do you have her plate number?"

"No," Brandon shook his head.

Hemming looked at the picture of Chevy again. "Has she said anything about strange men hanging around the Club, or maybe someone odd from one of the websites?"

Brandon thought for a moment. "Not that I can think of. She did say that the bouncer had to toss a few guys out of the club the other night, but nothing abnormal. The websites…She had a few dates recently to feel out chemistry, but she didn't mention anything weird."

"I wouldn't suppose you know which websites—her user names and passwords?" Hemming sounded particularly interested.

"I do." Brandon held up his finger for him to hold on and went to retrieve the information. A moment later he returned with a notebook and flipped a to a page that listed the websites.

Hemming pulled out his phone and took a picture. "You mind if I check out these sites?"

"Of course not. She's missing. I want her found."

"I'll put an APB out on her car." Hemming looked at Becker. "Go back to the car and put out an APB on Charlotte Westen's vehicle."

Becker glanced at the radio sitting on the counter.

"Do it from the car," Hemming said slowly, gave him a cold look.

Becker trailed down the hall again. As the door closed behind him, Hemming turned down the volume on his radio and leaned toward Brandon. With a crease between his brows, he asked in a quieter manner, "What about bank accounts? Do you share a bank account, or do you have separate accounts?"

"Both," Brandon answered. "We both have our own accounts, and we also have a joint checking." Brandon paused. "The checking has been a test to see how we behave with the finances, how we communicate, and to get a better handle on what each of us feels is important."

"Has any money been taken out?" Hemming asked.

"That's one thing I haven't looked at."

Becker came back in. "Did you catch that?" Becker asked, coming down the hall, his shoes thumping against the floor.

Hemming looked over to Becker and turned the volume up on the radio. "No. What'd I miss?"

"The APB." Becker had a twinkle in his eyes. "A call came in a while ago about Charlotte's car. It was reported at the

40

Patriot Marina. The spaces are numbered and rented, and she parked in someone's space. When her car didn't move, the people called the police wanting it towed. The car is still sitting there."

"The marina," Hemming repeated in a tone that indicated something had clicked in his mind as he raised his eyebrows. He looked at Brandon. "We're going to check out the car. I will keep you posted." He pulled a card from the clip board. "This is my number. If anything changes, you call." He held out his hand and looked at Brandon.

"Do me a favor. Keep him away," he said, gesturing at Becker. "I need Chevy found, not Becker screwing things up every step of the way."

"This is my call," Hemming said bluntly. "Becker won't be near this."

Becker looked put out.

"Thanks," Brandon's nodded appreciatively and shook Hemming's hand.

### 

Brandon sat down on the steps and looked through the railing at the picture of them on the long narrow table across from the stairs. The smell of Hemming's cologne was hanging in the air, a lingering reminder that Chevy was missing. Now, he felt even more lost then before. Not knowing where she was, if she was all right, or if she needed him put him on edge.

Later, in bed, Brandon looked across his pillow to her side. He wanted to rest his mind with some simple answer. He squeezed her pillow, causing the scent of her hair to come alive as though she were right there beside him. He pulled the length of her pillow close and wrapped his arm around it—pretending it was her.

# Chapter 5

The strip club was busy for a Wednesday night. The dark atmosphere was hazy from cigar and cigarette smoke. Hemming looked around and came to a stop at the bar, flipped open his wallet, and looked at the long-haired bartender. "I need to speak with the owner," he said, showing his badge.

The bartender looked at him as she leaned over, reaching for a glass under the counter. "What's this about?" she asked, making a drink.

"A missing persons report," Hemming replied, leaning his elbow against the bar as he put his badge away.

A moment later the bartender set the drink in front of a man sitting several seats down, then disappeared into the back through a swinging door.

The bartender came back through the door with a dark-haired, middle-aged man close behind. He was wearing a polo shirt and khakis.

"Hi," the man said, holding out his hand. "I'm Carl, the owner."

"Detective Hemming." They locked hands and shook.

"How can I help you?" Carl asked.

"I need to speak with you and your employees about a missing person report on Charlotte Westen. You may know her as Chevy."

A sudden expression of concern crossed Carl's face. "Come," Carl said, motioning for Hemming to follow. "It'll be easier to talk in the dressing room," Carl said loudly so Hemming could hear him over the music.

Carl went down the length of the bar and came through a swinging half door. "I'm going to have Austin"—Carl gestured to the bouncer who was leaning against the wall—"round up the girls in groups. I assume that's okay? I still have a business to run here."

"That would be fine." Hemming looked over at Austin, a pale-skinned bodybuilder type, as he approached.

Carl leaned toward Austin's ear. Hemming watched as Austin nodded, then headed for a couple of girls off to the side of the stage.

"Come this way," Carl motioned, walking along the side of the stage into a dark hall, then into the dressing room. A light dusting of fine glitter covered the chairs and floor, and a nice fragrance filled the air. Hemming noticed the drastic change in atmosphere from seductive in the rest of the club to one of hope and tranquility in the dressing room. Jen came through the doorway first, Becky behind her, then a few others trailing behind them.

Carl looked at the pretty faces waiting in front of him. "This is Detective Hemming," Carl said. "Chevy is missing. If any of you know anything, you need to tell him."

Jen tilted her head down, shifted on her heels, and leaned against the wall, fidgeting.

The room was silent. Only soft thumps of music could be heard through the wall.

Jen sighed, pulling her head up, and looked at Hemming. "Chevy did a private job last night," she stated.

Carl looked over at Jen at the same moment Hemming did. "What!" Carl said loudly. "You know the rules about private jobs. It's to avoid problems like missing people," Carl scolded.

Jen looked at him, nodding, and rolled her lips between her teeth, taking her reprimand. "Yes, I'm aware."

Hemming pulled his notepad from his pocket and started writing. "Who did Chevy do a private job for, and where was the location?" He paid close attention to everyone's reaction.

"I went to a yacht at the Patriot Marina twice," she admitted. "The guys were nice. They were foreign, and they paid well. They wanted me to come back. They spoke fairly good English. Chevy has financial issues, so instead of going back to the yacht for the third time I thought I would be helpful and let Chevy go in my place. I have financial concerns, too, but Chevy is new to financial problems, and she's new to this world. I thought I would help her out."

"Damn it, Jen!" Austin stepped forward, pointing at her. "You know better!"

Jen tilted her head down, took a deep breath, and nodded in agreement. "You're right. I know better," she said strongly.

"Sit down!" Hemming ordered in a deep bellowing tone.

Austin looked at him and leaned back against one of the makeup tables.

Jen put her hand in the air, motioning for Hemming to take it easy on him. "You can tell Austin to sit down, but he's right," she said, glancing at Austin. "I do know better. I trained Chevy, taught her to never going anywhere, meaning private jobs, without at least one of the bouncers." She gestured to Austin and Tyler.

"Did you get the names of these men, any of them?" Hemming questioned.

"They introduced themselves, but most of their names were foreign, so I don't remember them. There was one guy, Sandro, he was fortyish, sort of handsome, very gentlemanly and polite. Dark hair, light eyes, great smile—I would say Italian." She spoke slowly, trying to recall. "He had very porcelain skin with rosy cheeks and wavy hair."

"Were there other people aside from the men?" Hemming asked.

"There were some women, but they seemed shy. They didn't want to make eye contact. The few I saw were in a different section of the yacht."

"And you didn't think this was...at all odd?" Hemming asked in an accusing tone as he stepped closer to her.

"Did I think it was odd?" Jen repeated defensively. "I was there to make money, not evaluate the people. They were foreign."

"You didn't think any of this was out of the ordinary?" Hemming reworded the question.

"Really?" Jen questioned him with wide eyes. "Let me see here," she said slowly, looking up while thinking about her words. "I'm a stripper, so I see a lot of weird people and things. Did I think the foreign people seemed different than me? Odd, maybe." She looked at Hemming sarcastically. "Foreign people normally do have behaviors, mannerisms, and attire that are different from ours. Foreign to us?" Jen paused again, moving

44

her hands up and down in front of her as though weighing the idea. "Yes, it did seem odd to me," Jen nodded. "Yes, the foreign people did seem…foreign."

"All right then." Hemming wanted to move on. "Where did you go to meet these men?" he asked, glancing to Becky, who was leaning against the wall in a pair of tall platform heels and a G-string, her breasts bare.

"The Patriot Marina, slot 828."

Hemming jotted down the slot number, noting the way Becky shifted on her feet, fidgeted, and looked around at everyone in the room with more intensity at certain points of the conversation.

"How big would you say this watercraft was? Was it a boat or a yacht? Did you happen to notice the name of the watercraft?"

Jen paused, trying to recall. "It was a large yacht. I'm not sure how many feet, maybe around two hundred. There were several levels." She continued to think. "Maybe four levels."

"Anything else you can remember?"

Becky shifted again, looking around nervously.

"Well, the décor," Jen continued. "There was a painting, kind of an abstract painting in blacks and creams. It was beautiful, so it caught my eye—I could pick it out if I saw it. A few of the men had on rings that were gold. They looked like class rings. I didn't think much of them. I guess the oddest thing I noticed was the women. I only saw a few. One was very blond, with very pale skin—she caught my eye—I could point her out. The other woman looked Middle Eastern, maybe. She didn't seem to speak English. She had darker hair, light eyes, and was young, rather pretty, chesty—very chesty. She looked like Chevy."

Hemming abruptly shifted his attention to Becky, stepping in front of her and looking at her intensely. "Can *you* recall anything?" He held his hands behind his back, waiting.

Becky looked nervous and stammered, "I— I—" She shrugged and blinked.

He continued looking at her, waiting. "You know something. Did you notice anything noteworthy?"

45

Becky eyes went wide and she shook her head, her red hair swishing around her face.

"Are you going to tell me you weren't on the yacht?"

"I didn't say anything," Becky replied, her light-colored eyes looking nervously at everyone in the room. "How did the questions shift from Jen to me?"

"I know you didn't say anything. I am asking you if you noticed anything that would be helpful," he told her.

Becky gave him a blank look, not sure how to respond.

"You were there, too. The question isn't if you were there. You're not in any trouble. The question is what you may have seen that can help us find Chevy."

Becky stammered. "Um…"

### 

The area around Chevy's car was taped off. Investigators were taking pictures and going through the car.

Hemming walked toward her car, noticing the metal 828 sign that it was parked in front of. He looked around at the yachts, but none of them seemed as large as Jen described. All of the yachts and boats were dark, no one on them. He pulled his phone from his pocket and scrolled through his contacts. He saw the name he was looking for and dialed.

### 

Jason Ward was half-asleep as fumbled for his phone. "Agent Ward," he answered.

"Agent Ward, this is Detective Hemming from Boston PD—"

"Hemming," Ward repeated. "I take it you have something for us?" He rubbed his hand over his face, trying to wake up.

"Yeah," Hemming replied. "I got another missing girl from the Patriot Marina."

"What do we have this time—a runaway, prostitute, addict, what?"

"No," Hemming said. "This one is a college girl by the name—"

"College girl!" Ward flipped on the light beside his bed and sat up.

"This is a girl by the name of Charlotte Westen. She is a

third-year business student at Harvard. Her parents own the Westen's chain—you know, the hunting stores," Hemming clarified, looking around the marina for anything that would catch his eye.

"Oh, man," Ward sighed.

"Here is why they took this one. Apparently, this girl and her father had a falling out over the use of a credit card, so he cut her off. She's been working as a stripper the last couple months trying to keep up with the bills and tuition. According to the boyfriend, stripping is something new. She's also listed on a couple sugar daddy sites."

"Sugar daddy sites. I know which ones," Ward groaned. "So they think they have a stripper."

"Oh yeah—but you're going to love her nickname." Hemming chuckled.

"Huh?"

"Chevy—everyone calls her Chevy."

"We all knew this was bound to happen sooner or later," Ward remarked, moving to the side of his bed and putting a hand on his knee.

"I spoke with the co-workers at the Club. One of the women said she'd been doing private showings on a yacht for a group of foreign men."

"Shit. You would think some of these girls would have a little more—"

"Sense," Hemming said, loudly. "Well, I hope you're ready. These foreign men you guys have been watching just snatched the wrong girl. As soon as the media finds out the Westen girl is missing, it's going to be national news."

"All right," Ward grumbled. "I'll start making calls. I'll have our forensics team there ASAP. Get the report on my desk yesterday."

"I'm headed back to the office now."

### 

Thursday morning in Rudle Mills, Kentucky, Mike Roots was sitting at his desk, a new desk in a new addition to the police station specifically for the detective bureau. Mike's fellow detective Ken Trudell was leaning against the door

47

frame of Mike's office, a file in hand, when Mike's phone rang. Mike turned in his chair and answered his phone. The look on his face grew serious, and he pulled his chair closer to the desk, grabbed a pen from the pen holder, and began jotting down information on his notepad.

"Westen?" Mike repeated for Ken, while his pen paused on the paper. "The Westens live just outside of town," he said with a Southern drawl. The lines between his brows deepened as he frowned.

Ken pulled himself from the door frame, walked to Mike's desk, and leaned against the top with the palms of his hands, waiting to hear more.

"Yeah…" Mike said. "Chevy…" He looked at Ken. "I've known her since she was a toddler. I'm familiar with the Westens." He scribbled "missing!" on the notepad for Ken to see.

Ken's eyebrows rose.

He scribbled more information. "All right. I will go have a talk with the Westens…When are you sending the fax?" He paused for an answer. "All right. I will be in touch." He hung up the phone. He sat back in the chair, tossed his pen on the notepad, and stared at it. "You'll just never believe…" he said slowly, his words trailing off. "Chevy's missing." He looked at Ken.

"Our Chevy?" Ken repeated with disbelief, pointing to his chest. "We takin' a trip out there?"

Mike nodded. "We have to." He paused. "The Boston police department is faxing over the information."

Suddenly the fax machine started.

They watched as Chevy's photo emerged, with the report under it.

Mike pushed himself from his desk, shaking his head. "Man, I don't want to see that. You grab the report?" He picked his keys up from his desk and headed out the door.

"We'll read it on the way," Ken said as he collected the fax from the printer, hurrying out the door behind him.

### 

Ken sat in the passenger seat of the unmarked navy blue

48

squad car, reading the report. "It says here Chevy's boyfriend reported her missing late last night. They apparently live together and share bills, and she has been working at an exotic dance club trying to pay her way through college." He looked at Mike, stunned.

"Chevy stripping?" Mike asked, dumbfounded. "Come on, you know I don't want to hear that. Chevy's like one of my own daughters. Do you know what kind of image pops into my head?"

"Man, I bet she's a hot little number." Ken grinned.

"That shit isn't funny!" Mike told him, looking back and forth between Ken and the road. "What if we were talking about your girl? What's wrong with you?"

"We're not!" Ken replied, with a twinkle in his eyes. He smirked.

"I don't care how good-looking Chevy is, she's a kid compared to us. Man, what's wrong with you?" Mike asked. "You got some wires in that head of yours twisted? And what the heck was that part about Chevy paying for college?"

"I know. I found that part interesting." Ken looked at the report. "It says she has to pay her own way," he repeated, confused.

"Pay her own way!" Mike repeated, mulling over the idea. "The Westens have more than enough income to put Chevy through an expensive Ivy League college like Harvard," he said, thinking aloud. "They're loaded. Why does Chevy need to put herself through school?" Mike tried to wrap his mind around it. "The police have to have this wrong."

"John's too protective of her," Ken agreed, then continued reading.

"Get this..." Ken said a moment later, glancing over at Mike. "Chevy and her father had a falling out over purchases on a credit card. Apparently, her father will no longer cover her expenses." He looked at Mike.

"Who, John? John did that?" Mike replied, with an expression of complete disbelief. "Are you sure?"

Ken looked at him equally astonished and shrugged. "That's what the report says."

### ###

The Westen home sat off a back country road in a heavily agricultural area, with woods sprinkled between the cornfields. The home was nestled in a cluster of trees down a long paved drive. It could be partly seen from the road only at certain times of the year, when the foliage was sparse. They had a big lodge home with a huge wraparound porch supported by cedar logs in fieldstone bases.

John and his wife, Ruthie, had been friend of theirs since high school. They had been to countless hog roasts and other kinds of get-togethers at John and Ruthie's house over the years. It wasn't that long ago that Mike could recall being over at John's, helping with one of the truck engines, while a pint-sized Chevy ran around in the hot sun with pigtails and a Popsicle in her hand, wanting to give her daddy red Popsicle kisses.

As the home grew closer, Mike looked at the double front door that stood ten feet tall. Thirty feet on either side of the front door were double French doors that opened onto the porch. At night, when the outside lights were on, the house was particularly impressive.

He remembered when the Westens were building the house. Ruthie and John worked closely together, helping each other complete the house. John was a tall man, six foot five, thin, with long legs, big muscular arms, light blue eyes, and blondish hair that he always kept buzzed. He was a nice guy with a big heart, and he would help anyone, but he could also be a jerk. His egotistical, macho attitude would occasionally pop out, making people wonder how Ruthie could put up with him. Occasionally, Ruthie would look at John with a particular expression and tell him, "Knock your shit off!" A sparkle would come into John's eyes, and another macho comment would fly from his month so he could feel in control, but each time Ruthie tossed out that particular look and phrase, his macho attitude would temper.

Ruthie was a very attractive, radiant woman with a killer figure, enough love for a million people, and always a heart of gold. She had the mercy of a saint yet could be as fierce as the devil. She wore her age well; she looked far younger than she really was. Her medium-brown hair was highlighted with various shades of blond. She had class, style, and grace, but she was never afraid to get her hands dirty.

Mike wondered how they would take the information he was about to give them. He put the squad car in park, took in a deep breath, then let it out—preparing himself for what he needed to say and bracing himself for how the Westens were going to respond. To hear such news first thing in the morning wasn't going to make for a good start to the day. They rang the doorbell, then waited.

Ruthie pulled the door open and stood in the doorway in a pair of jeans and a loose-fitting sweatshirt, a cup of coffee in her hand. She smiled the instant she saw them. "Hey, guys! Come in." She backed up, gesturing.

As Mike stepped in, Ruthie gave him a big hug and kissed his cheek, then hugged Ken as he stepped through the doorway. "It's so good of you guys to come by!" she said, closing the door behind them. "John and I just finished breakfast. The boys got on the bus a little while ago. Are you guys hungry?"

Mike put his hands up. "No, thanks." He shook his head.

"You never turn down food," she commented with a questioning glint in her eyes. "You have the appetite of five men and never gain an ounce. The only time I have ever seen you turn down food was when something was bothering you. Wait a minute." She paused, seeing their trouble demeanor. "What's wrong?" she asked.

"Can we sit down? We need to talk to both of you," Mike said reluctantly.

"Okay." She braced herself for whatever was coming. "I'll get John. Go have a seat. Can I get you some coffee?"

"No, thank you," Mike said.

Ruthie stopped Mike before he started into the great room. "Should I add some Kahlua to my coffee?" she asked sweetly, looking up at him with her pretty green eyes.

"Since when do you drink?" he asked.

"Since you're here at seven in the morning, clearly upset about something, won't eat, and have to talk to us."

Mike nodded. "That Kahlua might not be a bad idea."

Her eyes shifted between them, analyzing. "All right, extra Kahlua," she said slowly, then turned and headed for the kitchen. Moments later, she emerged with her cup of coffee, a bottle of Kahlua, and John.

Mike and Ken greeted John, then sat in the chairs across from the sofa next to the fieldstone fireplace, which stretched to the ceiling. Above the mantel hung a big moose head that Ruthie got on a hunting trip and was extremely proud of. She put the bottle of Kahlua on the coffee table next her phone. She and John sat on the sofa. "All right." Ruthie looked at them. "I'm as ready as I'm ever going to be. What is it?"

Ken looked over at Mike, who let out a sigh and put his head down.

Ruthie looked back and forth between them, nervously waiting.

Finally Mike looked up. "There's been a problem with Chevy," he said, with difficultly.

Ruthie froze.

John stared blankly, waiting for more.

"Chevy was reported missing last night by her boyfriend."

In sequence John and Ruthie tilted their heads in the same direction.

"Boyfriend?" John said.

"Missing?" Ruthie said as she leaned forward and blinked.

The pause in the room was deafening. Ruthie and John looked at each other, then back at them. "Chevy's missing?" Ruthie asked.

"Chevy has a boyfriend?" John shook his head with surprise and repositioned himself on the sofa, as through irritated.

Ruthie put her hand on John's leg, patting it comfortingly. "You need to stop being so hardheaded and unreasonable."

The crease between John's brow deepened and his eyes narrowed. He took in a deep breath and let it out. "You knew Chevy had a boyfriend?"

"Yes." She rubbed his thigh and took a big drink of coffee. "Yes." She nodded. "The reason Chevy didn't want you to know is because you're ridiculously overprotective. Chevy's

52

not a little girl anymore. She's a woman, and until you accept that, you're just pushing her away."

John sat there with his jaw clenched tight.

Mike held out his hand to interrupt. "Have either of you heard from Chevy? Has she come home, by chance?"

Ken flipped to a blank page in his notepad.

Ruthie shifted her eyes between Mike and Ken. The notepad made this more real. "No." She shook her head, observing Ken. "Chevy isn't here. The last time was about two weeks after school started when we had the hog roast."

Mike began nodding, remembering. "That was an especially good hog," Mike commented to break some of the tension. "My family had a great time."

"That was a good hog. My kids loved it, too," Ken agreed, with an awkward smile.

Ruthie tried to recall. "Chevy came home that weekend and left that Sunday around noon, or one o'clock. She had to get back to school. The last time I spoke with her was…" She looked at John, trying to remember, then looked back to Mike. "About a week ago…no," she corrected herself. "It was Sunday. I talked to her Sunday night. Chevy said she had a big report for one of her classes."

"Did Chevy say anything else?" Mike asked.

"Not really. We talked about her classes. She said they were going well." She shrugged. "I know that's not helpful."

Ken jumped in. "Did Chevy tell you where she was working?"

Ruthie squinted her eyes, looking confused. "Chevy's going to school. She doesn't have a job. Isn't school a big enough job?" she asked, realizing Ken was looking for a particular response.

"She had better be looking for a fucking job. I'm not paying for her to fuck off anymore!" John barked.

An instant expression of anger covered Ruthie's face as one eyebrow rose and her nostrils flared. She took in a deep breath, closed her eyes, and let it out, trying to calm herself, then looked up at the ceiling. "Just how much do you think a normal job is going to cover at an Ivy League college?" Her words

53

dripped with irritation, and she turned to John with an intimidating stare.

Mike glanced to Ken, then watched their interactions. "So there is some tension about school. What's going on?" Mike asked.

"Chevy goes off to college and thinks she needs to run up the God damn credit card every semester." John's voice raised.

Ruthie tossed her hands in the air. They made a slapping sound as they hit against the top of her legs on the way back down. She reached for the bottle of Kahlua, poured more into her coffee, and took another large gulp.

"You gave her the card! I told you not to!" she hissed, then turned her eyes to Mike and Ken. "He gave her the card."

John looked at her, then to Mike. "Yeah! For things she needs, not to go on a twenty-three-thousand-dollar shopping spree. How many times has she done this?" John shook his head with a bitter laugh.

Ruthie grumbled. "You're still acting as though I approved the shopping sprees or told her shopping sprees were a dandy idea. I never told her to do that anymore than you did, so don't you give me that accusing tone. Don't you dare make this sound like my doing."

"Then do something about it!" he snapped at her, then looked at Mike, still shaking his head. "Un-fucking-believable!" He waited for Mike to agree with him.

Mike sat looking at them. He had never seen them argue.

"Then why don't you correct the problem? Makes sense, doesn't it?"

Ruthie's eyes widened with anger. "I talked to her. Did you? What do you want me to say to her that I haven't already said or done?" She gave John an angry glare that made Mike lean back. "Don't you dare sit there and ask me how I dealt with her. I tried to deal with her—unlike you, who leaves the discipline up to me, but by God you sure can criticize and pass the blame, huh? How dare you!" She glared at him, shook her head, and threw herself back into the cushions.

Mike sat silently, watching them, before he said, "Perhaps some realism dealing with shopping sprees from you"—Mike

54

looked at John—"would temper Ruthie's frustration. Ruthie is a touch fierce at the moment."

John said nothing and shook his head.

"You know what the problem is?" Ruthie said. "You and Chevy are just alike. You are both stubborn and determined to do things your way, coupled with being downright naïve."

"Noooo…" John disagreed, drawing out his response and shaking his head.

"Then give Chevy clear boundaries," Ruthie suggested. Suddenly, Ruthie looked at Mike. "So Chevy is missing!"

"She was reported missing last night." Mike nodded.

"How long has she been missing?" John jumped in and asked.

"Apparently since the previous night. She never came home from work, so her boyfriend reported her missing late last night."

John chuckled. "See, she did get a job." John smiled proudly, as though he had won something. "Maybe you're right. Chevy's like me. She went out and got a job," John taunted.

Mike and Ken glanced at each other. "Well," Mike said slowly. "I'm not sure this is going to sit so well." He paused. "She has been working as an exotic dancer." Mike watched as Ruthie's and John's faces fell.

Ruthie picked up the bottle of Kahlua and poured more into her coffee. "That's great! Our daughter is now a stripper because you have to be an ass!" she said loudly, fighting with emotion.

John sat there, stunned—like a deer caught in headlights.

Ken chimed in. "Makes you feel a little funny about strip clubs now doesn't it? I don't think I'll ever be able to go into another one. The visual of any of our girls naked and covered in glitter on a shiny gold stripper pole turns my stomach. That just isn't right."

Everyone starred blankly at him with stunned and twisted expressions.

"Hey! Enough! What's wrong with you? I should have left you in the car," Mike scolded.

"Thanks, Ken, for that wonderful visual of my daughter. Maybe my husband here will see what cutting her off has caused." Ruthie crinkled her lips and looked at John. "Great job, honey." She patted his leg. "I don't know why we didn't think of it sooner. We could make a mint. We could put strip clubs in all our stores!" She straightened and looked at everyone with a surprised grimace. "Chevy can be the main show. Hell, we can put stripper behind the counters. Men will buy anything with a perky pair of boobs in their face! Mike, Ken." She gestured with her hand for their input. "Keeping up with the personalities of Hollywood wouldn't hold a candle to stripping with the Westens. Too bad all three of our kids weren't girls." She forced a smile.

Mike gave a subtle nod, then looked at John. "Being a parent is hard. Sometimes we don't make the best choices for our kids, but we always have the best intentions. We always want to do right by our children, and we learn through trial and error. That's why grandparents seem to have all the answers: they've already made the mistakes. Unfortunately this gets a touch worse."

John looked blankly at him.

"She's also signed up on several sugar daddy websites."

"Good Lord!" Ruthie said, glaring at John. "What about co-workers? Could she be at school working on that report, or did she and Brandon get into an argument?"

John looked at her. "His name's Brandon?" he asked, realizing she knew a lot about the boyfriend.

"Yes," Ruthie replied. "If you were willing to accept that Chevy isn't going to stay your little girl forever, then she would talk to you, and you would know his name."

Mike held out his hand to calm the tension between them. "This is one of the things we know—her phone goes straight to voice mail."

Ruthie nodded. "She turns off the ringer when she's in class or in the library. Her screen comes on if someone calls or texts, so she sets the phone beside her where she can see it, but she never turns it off." She grabbed her phone from the coffee table, dialed, and put it to her ear looking hopeful.

They watched as her hopeful look turned to disappointment.

"It went right to voice mail," Ruthie said, distraught, and set the phone down.

Ken chimed in. "Apparently the Boston police felt there is more to this case then just a missing person. The FBI has been contacted. One of Chevy's co-workers told the detective they had been doing private shows for a group of foreign men on a yacht."

John asked, "Why were her co-workers able to leave the yacht and she wasn't? Didn't her co-workers wonder where she was?"

Ken looked down at the report, skimming the lines. "It says here, Chevy and her co-workers went to the yacht by themselves on different nights. All of them went alone, which is why it was dangerous and made it easy for something like this to happen."

Ruthie's sat quietly, put her hand over her mouth, and looked down at the floor. "Do the police believe Chevy's..." She paused. "No longer alive?" The color drained from her checks. "Is this why the FBI has been contacted?"

"No," Mike replied quickly. "Let's not get ahead of ourselves. We have no indication based on the report anyone feels she's not alive. I haven't gotten the report from the FBI yet. I should hear from them today."

Ruthie shook her head, trying to make sense of it. "Normally the FBI isn't called for several days...What am I not understanding? Why is the FBI already involved?"

Mike sighed, pushing his mouth to the side. "That's a very good question," he said, reluctant to answer. "I'm going to guess—and I'm only guessing"—he looked at her and held his index finger in the air—"the FBI already had an alert with the local police. Something about Chevy's case was similar to the FBI alert. That's my guess. We get alerts on cases the FBI are following, and if we come across something similar, we give them a call, and they're on it right away."

John chimed in. "Is the yacht still there? Can't you get a search warrant?"

Ken gave him a disappointed look. "It says in the report the yacht isn't docked there any longer."

Ruthie squinted her eyes, thinking. "She's not just missing. It looks like she has been kidnapped," she said, slowly turning her head to the side.

Ken continued. "You also have to keep in mind, you're the Westens. Chevy isn't just any girl. This is going to be all over the media by noon." He raised his eyebrows.

Mike shook his head. "I believe the concern is that she's been taken out of the country. I haven't gotten the report from the FBI yet, but they don't waste any time—especially on a case that's going to be high profile."

"Out of the country," Ruthie repeated. "But then it's international law—we are in a gray area, a bunch of legal red tape with other countries that may or may not cooperate." She shook her head, as she stared down at the floor, realizing the gravity of the situation.

John put his arm around her and pulled her to his side.

Mike looked at John, then at her. "We should hear from the FBI soon. As soon as we get back to the office I will give them a call, and I will relay any information they give me."

### 

Two hours later, Ruthie sat in the kitchen by the French doors that opened onto the back patio. On the table next to her was a cup of coffee. She stared out the window as if into a void of thoughts and feelings she was trying to decipher. No call yet.

She watched from the window as John drove around on the tractor. She could hear the rumble of the motor, which grew louder and more distinctive as the red tractor came into sight, the fainter as it rolled across one of the hills in back then disappeared. A while later, she saw the blue tractor pulling a pile of wood, then trailing out of sight. She watched this a half dozen times. *Busywork*, she thought to herself. When John had trouble coping, she could always gauge the severity by how much random busywork he did, and how many times he changed the type of busywork—she called it physical fidgeting. He was having more trouble than she could ever recall.

She reached for her coffee and noticed her hand trembling. *Too much coffee,* she thought. Then the doorbell rang. She slid back from the table, excitement plastered on her face as she hurried toward the door—then she paused. She stood there, fiddling with her coffee cup, looking reluctantly at the door and deciding she needed time for whatever was standing on the other side.

When she eventually pulled the door open, in front of her stood two FBI agents. Both men had navy blue jackets with the letters FBI embroidered on the breast, khaki pants, dress shoes, and short dirty-blond hair. She gripped the cup of coffee in her hand like a child clutching a blanket, surprised.

"Are you Ruthie Westen?" the agent who looked to be a bit older asked.

"Yes, I'm Ruthie."

"I'm Agent Jason Ward, and this is my partner, Agent Tim Cook."

"My daughter was reported missing last night…" she said, looking horrified to see them.

"That's correct," Ward replied.

"Isn't it normally a couple of weeks before you guys are called?"

"Could we come in?" Ward asked. A news van was sitting along the road in the distance.

She nodded her head. "Of course." She quickly ushered them in. "My apologies…I'm not thinking clearly." She eyed the news van in the distance as she shut the door.

"That's a fair question. Normally, we are called later, but there may be a tie-in with other cases we are working on. It made sense to get involved now. We would like to speak to you and your husband."

Ruthie pulled the coffee cup to her chest. "We can sit in the kitchen by the French doors. I'll call my husband." She pointed them to the table as she picked up her phone and dialed.

She glanced around as it rang.

"You have reached John Westen—"

She pulled the phone from her ear, hit End, and redialed.

"You have—"

59

She pulled the phone from her ear again and hung up. She forced a smile. "He must have equipment running—not able to hear the phone. He should be in soon. Would you like some coffee?"

###

A few hours later, she was still at the kitchen table, looking out the French doors and pushing and rolling the tips of her thumb and index finger together. Suddenly, John came through the garage door off the kitchen, with a case of beer tucked under his arm and an open one in his hand.

"Where have you been?" she asked. Relief danced in her eyes.

John looked at her. "Why the hell do I need to be questioned the moment I come in?"

She raised her eyebrows and an odd expression brushed across her face, She was stunned at his response. "You're my husband."

"You don't need to know where I am. If it's important, I will let you know!"

She sat there, blank, her mouth open. Slowly, her eyes narrowed and a glare formed. Her nostrils flared. "Ever stop to think that something important was going on and that's why I was calling you?" She tapped the end of her index finger against the top of the table.

"What would you have to tell me that would be important?"

"You left me to sit here by myself with two FBI agents. Not only did I sit here alone, I felt very abandoned at a time when I need you. I was also embarrassed that Chevy's father appeared to not give a shit. Why wouldn't you pick up the phone?" She looked at him. "I was worried about Chevy, and then you. I had no idea if you were off having trouble with your emotions or out there hurt."

"You don't need to worry about me," he barked and took a drink of his beer. "Ya know what? I don't have time for this crap. If you want to be a fucking bitch, then I'm leaving." He began to turn.

Complete disbelief washed over her face. "I'm not being a bitch," she said, stunned. "I'm asking you where you were.

60

There's a difference between a question and bitching. Should we go over them? I'm not being a bitch, but I can be." She stared at him.

"Well, I didn't want to be fucking bothered! But no! All you want to do is fucking bitch!"

"What?" she said, baffled by his reaction. "Do you hear what you are saying?" She tossed her hand in the air, trying to keep her patience. "I asked you a question. If you think my question was bitching, then you have been drinking too much and you're really confused. Shall I take a bitching tone? Shall we do a little comparison?"

"All I know is, you had better not be like this for the truck pulls."

"I don't even want to go to the truck pulls," she replied, looking out the French doors.

"Well, we can't cancel!" he yelled.

"Yeah, John, I know, I am well aware. I didn't say I wouldn't go. I said I didn't want to go. What's your problem?"

"I have stuff to do," he said in a hateful tone.

"Babe," she said, to get his attention.

John simmered down for a moment.

"I know this thing with Chevy isn't fun. It's stressful. I don't know what to do, what to think, how to feel, or how to react—my emotions and thoughts are a jumbled mess. Please don't take your frustration out on me. You know I'm not bitching at you. I can see you're having a hard time with this, too. Don't be mean to me. If you don't know how to handle this, either, then we'll figure it out together," Ruthie assured him, putting her arms out for him to walk over and hug her.

"I'm not doing this with you! All you want to do is fucking bitch about everything. I have things to do," he barked as he headed out the door.

As the door shut, she pulled her arms from the air, put her forehead against the palm of her hand, and sighed. After a few moments, teardrops began to fall from her chin. With tears in her eyes, she got up.

###

Several hours later, she sat in the office trying to go over

61

paperwork when her phone rang. She glanced down at the caller ID—Crysta.

Crysta was a lifelong friend. They grew up together and had gotten each other into and out of a variety of troubles over the years. Now Crysta and her family lived in the Westens' farmhouse and watched over most of the corporate business dealings and accounting for the chain.

"Hello!" Ruthie answered.

"So what's going on?" Crysta asked, concerned.

Ruthie drew a blank. "Huh?"

"I just saw on the news—Chevy's missing."

"That. Yeah. She was reported missing last night by her boyfriend."

"So John knows about the boyfriend now?"

"Yeah...he knows."

"Did he come unglued?"

"No, not too badly. He took the part about her boyfriend much better than the part about her being a stripper to cover her financial expenses," she told Crysta, as she glanced at another pile of papers on the corner of her desk that needed to be filed. "Oh, and the sugar daddy websites that she's also listed on."

"What?!..." Crysta exclaimed. "You're kidding!"

"Wish I were," Ruthie said as she rolled her chair to the other end of the desk, turned to the filing cabinet, then paused, suddenly filled with emotion. Tears welled in her eyes. She put her hand over her mouth, trying to collect herself so Crysta wouldn't hear the quiver in her voice.

"Robert saw John. He was over at Bill's house," Crysta told her. "Robert said John was drunk, taking about what a bitch you're being. This is out of character for him, but I figured you guys just had an argument of some kind; he is always sweet loving and kind. Every once and a while I hear him spout off about something, but that's not normal and nothing like what Robert described. Then I saw the news and put two and two together. John's having a hard time coping. Why didn't you call me?"

"I just didn't think of calling. I've been here all day, first dealing with Mike and Ken, who came first thing this morning.

Then two FBI agents came a little while later. I thought I was going to get a call from Mike about the FBI, but I had unannounced FBI agents at my door instead. Then John didn't want to answer his phone. I sat here with two agents by myself. When John finally came back, I asked him where he had been, and he went off about how I'm always bitching at him. I was floored."

"What a jerk!" Crysta replied. "Don't worry, babe, he just doesn't know how to cope. If he can't handle being at your side, then I will happily take his place. He can get lost at some brewery."

"It looks like you have the job. I think aliens snatched my husband, because right now he's not my loving husband. I don't know who he is."

"Just give him some time. In the meantime, you have me."

### 

Ruthie heard the garage door open at 4:20 that afternoon. The boys were home.

"Mom! Mom!" they called through the house.

Ruthie closed her eyes, preparing herself.

"Hey, Mom." Nicholas poked his head into the office. "Why are there television vans outside? And what's for dinner?" He pulled his head out of the door and yelled down the hall to Alex, "She's in here!"

Ruthie looked up from the papers. "I ordered pizza. It should be here any minute."

"Are you all right?" Nicholas stepped into the office. He was tall, like his father, with the same build.

She looked at him, appearing dazed, lost somewhere in her thoughts. "Yeah," she responded quickly.

Nicholas was closest to her. They understood one another. She couldn't hide anything from him, and he could see right through sugarcoating. She thought about the FBI agents sitting at the table with her. *My daughter is missing and my husband has checked out.* "No." She looked at him. "I'm not all right," she said, as tears began to well in her eyes.

Alex walked in the room and asked, "Why are there news vans outside?" Then he saw the emotion on his mom's face.

Nicholas walked over, squatted his long legs in front of her, and reached his hand to the side of her face, pushing her hair behind her ear. "Mom, what's wrong?" he asked, looking up at her with his father's dazzling blue eyes.

Alex stood behind him, also waiting to know what was going on. Alex was a touch shorter, stockier, with his mom's face and the same green eyes. He had light brown hair, not as dark as Chevy's and not as light as Nicholas's.

She searched his features—they were like hers. "Are you ready for the shock of your life?" she asked them.

They waited, nodding.

"Chevy's missing," she told them. "The police and FBI are trying to find her. The one thing they do know is she's not dead," Her voice cracked.

Without another word Nicholas stood up, pulled her from the chair, and hugged her. "It will be all right, mom." He wiped her tears.

"It's all right," Alex stepped behind her, hugging her from behind.

"How do I look? Do I look all right?" she asked them, trying to pull herself together.

"This is not your best moment, but you don't look bad. You look upset, but you should look upset," Nicholas said.

"I was hoping the pizza would get here before every news station on the planet." She kept wiping her tears that weren't slowing.

"It's all right mom," Alex said. "I'll be right back." He looked at Nicholas. "You got her?"

Nicholas nodded. "Yeah." He looked back at his mom as Alex left the room. "Don't worry. I'll take care of the pizza," he assured her.

She thought about it for a moment. "Thanks, but I rather you not be gobbled up by a swarm of reporters."

"Mom, I'm fine. Its pizza and reporters," he said, looking at her. "What did Dad do?"

"Nothing. Don't worry." She shook her head.

"He was a jerk, wasn't he?"

"Why would you ask that?" Her eyes shifted back and forth.

64

"Because he can't handle emotions, and the moment he has to deal with emotions, he becomes a jerk. He loves you."

She stood there and looked at him, wondering how it was that her fourteen-year-old son had such knowledge and wisdom, while her forty-three-year-old husband couldn't handle his own emotions.

"Okay," Ruthie said. "If you want to handle pizza and reporters, go ahead."

"You know, you're the best mom." He smiled.

She hugged him. "You're the best Nicholas I could have."

He looked at her and smiled more. "Am I the best son?" he asked, with a silly expression.

The look drew a smile to her face.

She raised onto her tiptoes. "Of course you are," she whispered in her ear. "But if you repeat that to Alex, I will deny it. I love your brother, too, and don't want him to feel hurt or unloved," Then paused. "Wait—You weren't surprised about Chevy," she realized.

He smiled. "As soon as I saw the news vans I looked at the news on my phone to see what was going on. We saw Chevy's missing."

Her eyes widened. "You knew." She shook her head. "I should have thought about your cell phones."

"I knew you would tell me and would be upset."

"I'm fine."

"You're working on paperwork like a squirrel on speed, and Chevy's missing—come on now."

From upstairs Alex yelled down, "Mom, Channel Eight just pulled into the drive!"

She looked at Nicholas blankly.

Nicholas smiled and kissed her forehead. "You always start cleaning or doing things at high speed when you're upset." He headed out of the office to collect the pizza and fend off reporters.

# Chapter 6

At the fairgrounds, trucks with thousands of dollar of customizations under their hoods rolled in one by one on big tires. They came in long lines, honking randomly with excitement over the continuous sound of diesel engines rumbling, black smoke trailing behind them. Some were Cummins, some were Duramax—everyone had their preference.

This passionate group of people were hardworking, honest, and respectful, and they played as hard as they worked. Most of them were the good ol' folk America was founded on, and all of them loved their family and friends. Their cowboy boots and hats were a symbol of a lifestyle. The women were pretty, tough, and not afraid of hard work or getting their hands dirty—much like Ruthie.

People came from all over the nation to the Westen truck pulls, which had started twelve years earlier, when John and some of his friends got together and pulled their trucks at the fairgrounds. That group of friends told their friends, who told their friends, until the good ol' boys now rolled in from all over. Most of them arrived with campers, trailers, or fifth wheels as they prepared for the weekend.

### 

As the trucks were finding their spots at the fairgrounds, hundreds of miles away on rolling seas Veronica sat on the corner of Sandro's desk. "I don't feel this Chevy girl is a threat," Veronica told her husband. "I can let her wear some of my clothes and let her out of the room. I feel she will do fine. She's sweet."

Sandro sat comfortably in his office chair and looked at her. "You feel this girl is ready?" He leaned his elbow against the arm of his chair and looked into her eyes.

"I do," she assured him, her eyes sparkling with certainty. "Besides, she needs to be happy and well adjusted if we're introducing her to potential husbands."

Sandro held two fingers over his lips, listening. "All right, if you feel she is ready." He looked at the papers in front of him.

"I do. This Chevy girl will do fine." She smiled and pushed herself from the corner of his desk with a spring. "I will get her ready." She started for the door.

"Don't take her around the children yet. Let her become acclimated to you and her new surroundings first," he suggested.

"Of course. There's only so much a person can take in at once. I was thinking." She paused. "As long as she does well today, I'd like to take her off the boat when we reach port and take her shopping for clothes. She's going to need something suitable to wear."

He looked at her. "As long as she does all right, I have no problem with that. The sooner she adjusts, the better. This Chevy girl is going to be a nice paycheck. I think Sweeden has an auction coming up." He smiled with a glint in his eyes.

She lifted her eyebrows and headed for their bedroom to get clothes for Chevy.

### 

Chevy was sitting in her room looking at herself in the mirror when she heard the key twist in the lock. Veronica come through the door with an excited smile. "I brought you clothes," she announced, walking to the sofa and patting the seat next to her for Chevy.

Chevy sat down beside her.

Veronica looked at her warmly. "I think you are about my size, so I brought you these. They are mine," Veronica said, holding the clothes up for Chevy to see. They are typical Middle Eastern clothing. I pulled out the blue, cream, and gold one. I thought they would go best with your coloring." She smiled.

"Are you Middle Eastern?" Chevy asked, looking at Veronica's jeans and shirt.

"That's where I am originally from. I have clothes from all over the world. There's a bathroom across the hall." She pointed. "We will be at port soon. I want to buy you clothes. You will be more comfortable with your own clothes," she said

67

warmly.

Chevy gave her a puzzled look. "Why did you kidnap me? To buy me clothes?"

"No, I did not. They did. But don't worry, they have good plans for you," Veronica assured her, leaning closer. "I like you. You're nice. Most of the women are mean, strung out, or some kind of unpleasant." She made a sour face. "I don't normally allow people to wear my clothes, let alone buy them new ones. Whatever you do—cooperate. Stick with me, and you will be all right. Make sure you do what I tell you. Even if you don't understand something, do it, and I will be happy to explain later."

Chevy began to nod slowly, looking unsure and doubtful. "Okay."

"So which one would you like to wear first?" Veronica asked, with an eager smile, like they were two kids at a slumber party playing dress-up. "I was thinking you would come to dinner tonight. I don't normally have other women I can talk to."

Chevy sat there, apprehensive.

"But I must tell you"—Veronica gave her a warning look—"you have to behave with all proper manners. There are a few other women that you will see. Limit your conversation with them. You want to maintain class."

Chevy nodded.

"But first," Veronica continued, "a shower. Come with me." She stood from the sofa and headed for the door.

Chevy picked up the cream outfit with ornate edging and followed. She stepped into the hallway and looked around, taking in everything she was seeing, hearing, and smelling. The hall had more woodwork and thick crown molding. Recessed lights illuminated the hall. Veronica twisted the black door handle and walked in ahead of her. On one side was a big Jacuzzi tub inlaid with creamy brown marble and a large marble shower with a glass surround, several shower heads, and jets. There was a huge mirror that went from the back of the sink to the ceiling. The sink was a glass bowl that looked as if it had thousands of cracks.

There was a variety of elaborate candlesticks by the Jacuzzi, and a large plant with big wide leaves fanned out above the tub.

Chevy said nothing and looked around, taking it all in.

Veronica pulled out the drawers near the sink. "Here are combs, a variety of brushes and hair ties. Feel free to help yourself." She pushed the drawers back in and opened the cabinet. "The hair dryer is under here, along with shampoos and conditioners." Then she pointed to a table. "That is your makeup table. In the drawers is everything you could possibly need." She smiled. "I will be back to check on you. When you are done, go back your room and wait." She leaned close. "As long as you go back to your room and wait the door will remain unlocked. If you want more freedoms and privileges, you must show me that I can trust you. Don't wander the yacht and look around. I will show you part of it when I come back to get you for dinner. Trust me, and do as I instruct," she encouraged with a loving smile. "I know being here is nerve-racking," she sympathized. "They have good plans for you. No need to worry."

### 

Meanwhile, back in Boston, Brandon turned on the stove when he heard the doorbell. He opened the door to see two FBI agents. "I'm Agent Ward and this is Agent Cook. We need to ask you some questions about the disappearance of Charlotte Westen."

Brandon looked at them, wide-eyed, and paused. "Sure. Come in."

"No," Ward corrected with a shake of his head. "We need you to come with us."

The look on Brandon's face grew more serious. "Sure," he said reluctantly. "I need to turn off the stove and make a few phone calls to my father and attorney. I'm not saying anything without my attorney. You mind if I bring some class work until they arrive?"

The agents looked at each other, then Ward nodded. "That'll be fine."

He left the door open for them to see themselves in while he gathered his things. He picked up his phone from the table inside the door and dialed. "Hey, Dad. I have two FBI agents here who are detaining me for questioning. I need you to send Rob…" He walked down the hall to the kitchen. "My girlfriend's missing. I reported her missing Tuesday night…" He flipped off the stove, which made a distinctive long beep.

"Yeah, I have a girlfriend. I told you, remember? Anyway, I haven't seen her since Tuesday night…" He shuffled papers and books into his brown leather satchel. "No, she's not a bartender…She's working on her undergrad…No, the whole thing is complicated. She dances…No, Dad….Come as quickly as you can, please…Huh? She does come from a nice family…" Brandon laughed. "She's never danced before…Chevy. Charlotte. Her father's John Westen. He owns the Westen's chain…Yeah, I know it's one of your favorite stores. I'll explain it all later…Okay…All right. Bye." As he hung up he put the strap of his bag over his shoulder and headed down the hall to the waiting FBI agents. He opened the closet door, pulled out his coat, and left the closet doors open like he always did.

Pulling away from the curb, behind the agents in his own car, he looked up at the house. It looked quiet and peaceful. The upstairs curtains were open, but unfortunately there was no Chevy waving him good-bye.

### 

Brandon's father hung up the phone and leaned back in his chair. The crystal ashtray on top of his desk held a half-smoked cigar.

He wore a particularly spooked expression as he sat there mumbling. "What hillbilly names their daughter Chevy? Westen's—the chain of hunting stores." He looked at the picture on his desk of his lovely wife, Judy; Brandon; and himself. "Charlotte Westen, Chevy. Of all the girls Brandon could date, it just happened to be the girl at the strip club." The world suddenly felt small and the walls of his office seemed to be closing in. His wife's words echoed through his mind. *If you say so, but you had better be careful*, he could hear her say, seeing that trusting look mixed with doubt. She had never

70

doubted him before. In all the years they had been married, he couldn't recall one time she had doubted him. *I hope you are correct. One wrong girl and it could be disaster for us.* He had naïvely dismissed her warning. His face turned an ashy white.

Just then, Judy walked through the open door. "Chris, sweetheart," she said, placing a glass of iced tea with a lemon wedge on his desk before looking at him. Her words and movements slowed to a stop, and her eyes grew larger. "Chris! Sweetie…What's wrong?" She hurried to his side.

Chris blinked a few times, trying to take in the depth of his error.

"I'm fine," he said slowly, as he stared into nothingness.

She leaned beside him. "No, you are not! You're not fine. I've been married to you for far too long. I know when something is wrong."

He continued to stare.

"What happened?" She felt his forehead.

Slowly, he looked at her.

"You don't feel warm. Are you having chest pain or dizziness?"

"Brandon's girlfriend…" Chris's voice trailed off. "Brandon's girlfriend is Charlotte Westen," he said, slowly.

"Charlotte Westen?" she repeated. She shook her head slightly. "Okay. I don't understand."

"Charlotte Westen—the Westen's chain," he explained.

"Yeah," she said blankly. "And…"

"Her nickname. They call her Chevy."

Suddenly, her eyes widened. One hand flew to her mouth, while her other hand clutched her stomach. "You didn't check her out," she said slowly, quietly.

"I thought—"

"I know." Judy closed her eyes and took in a deep breath, letting it out slowly. "You thought she was safe. Chevy Westen. You didn't know, sweetie, and with a name like Chevy,…Well…The damage is done. Now we need to figure out damage control." She picked up the glass of iced tea and took a big drink. "Have them drug her, keep her drugged, and get her back here. Drop her off somewhere. It doesn't matter

71

where." She looked at him. "Do it! Call now! Get her back here." She pointed to his phone.

"How can I? Chevy can identify too many people."

"Yeah. Well, we can have police poking around about kidnapping, or we can have them poking around about murder." She looked at him.

He ruefully chuckled to himself. "What kind of hillbillies name their child Chevy?" he mumbled, remembering his words from a few days ago and shaking his head in disbelief at himself. "The educated ones with money and connections," he grumbled.

"Sweetie, these aren't hillbillies, and Chevy is just a nickname." She leaned against the end of his desk, tapped her index finger to her lips, thinking. "So, we need a deflection, something to give people no reason at all to look any further in this direction if your name should happen to come up. First thing Monday you need to donate money to the local school. Philanthropists aren't kidnappers."

He looked up at her, still pale and coming to terms with the magnitude of his mistake.

"I know we have at least a hundred thousand we can donate. You can call the school first thing Monday, then the newspaper, and the news stations, so you have press coverage. People need a specific image of you."

"I need to let this sit for a while," he said flabbergasted.

"Not to worry, sweetheart." She stepped beside his chair, put her hands on his shoulders, and kissed his forehead. "For every problem there is a solution."

He patted her hand. "You go do whatever it is you need to do. I need a couple hours to take this in and think about how to address it. I do like your suggestion," he acknowledged, looking at her. "I have to think about our associates, too."

She patted his shoulder. "You need some time?" she asked, making sure he wanted her to leave.

"I'm good, sweetheart." He put his hand on hers.

### 

At the truck pulls later that evening, the rows of stadium seating had filled and the competitors were making last-minute tweaks to their engines. Ruthie was on the platform with the announcer. Everyone was ready to get started when she stepped to the front, microphone in hand. "I would like to personally thank everyone for taking your time and hard-earned money to be here this weekend. I have watched this event grow in the last twelve years from a handful of guys who wanted to spend a weekend having fun with their toys to the thousands of people this event has drawn today.

"Many of you, my husband and I know firsthand. Others we have not had the pleasure of meeting. One thing I will say—for all of us here—is that this is the nicest group of people I have ever had the privilege to be around. Each year I am amazed how everyone rolls in from all over the nation—perfect strangers who help one another with their trucks, or sit down and talk like they have known each other for years.

"Unfortunately, I need to ask all of you for your help and support. Our daughter, Charlotte Westen, who many of you know as Chevy, has been missing since Tuesday night. Some of you may have already seen it on the news. If anyone sees Chevy, or hears anything—I ask that you call the FBI. There are flyers by all the steps with the number so you can reach the agents working on the case directly. Please take a flyer, keep it with you just in case that odd moment comes up where you hear or see something that will help my husband and I bring our Chevy home."

As Ruthie looked out onto the crowds of people she suddenly realized that everyone was silent. The people who were standing had frozen. The guys getting ready to pull their trucks stood silent with solemn looks. Suddenly, the large outdoor viewing screen came on with a picture of Chevy's smiling face, and the silence became even thicker.

Ruthie fought to hold her emotion, but her eyes began to well with tears, and she was no longer able to speak.

The announcer took the microphone.

"Ruthie's right," the announcer started. "Everyone who comes year after year have been great people. Obviously, since we're missing Chevy it puts a gloom on the weekend, but instead of gloom let's continue with the truck pulls." His voice picked up pace and enthusiasm. "Let's have a great time. Everyone take a flyer—Chevy might be missing, but she's out there somewhere. If we all pull together and keep our eyes and ears open we can bring Chevy home. Come on everyone, let's make this truck pull matter!" He paused. "So what do ya all say, will it be a Chevy Duramax or the Dodge Cummins? Let's get started!" He pressed his fist into the air with enthusiasm.

With reluctance, the people began moving. Little by little voices began to fill the air once again.

"Come on, everyone, let's hear it for the great time were going to have this weekend!" the announcer said, with more enthusiasm, then clapped his hands together above his head, prompting the crowd of people to cheer. Slowly, the crowd began to follow his lead. Single claps started to resonate from the audience, then more, until everyone was clapping and cheering.

###

Meanwhile, back in Boston, Brandon sat in a small room painted a medium gray. The fluorescent lights inset in the ceiling above him flickered. He worked on a paper for a class, then read through a few chapters in a textbook, the whole while ignoring the giant two-way mirror across from him while he waited for his father and their attorney to arrive.

###

Behind the mirror in a dimly lit room stood Ward and Cook, with several other people from different government agencies.

"So, what do you think? Does the son know anything?" a dark-haired man in a black suit asked.

Ward looked over at him. "No, I don't think so. The surveillance team hasn't recorded any conversation that includes his son or makes any reference to him. Even if Brandon does know what his father does, it's not likely he helped with this one. They have been dating for a while. The son has too much time invested in the Westen girl to turn her over to the sex trade. Besides, Charlotte is too high profile."

The man in the black suit said nothing, just looked through the mirror at Brandon, observing him closely.

Ward stood there with his arms folded in front of him,

thinking out loud. "Cook and I have been working on this sex trade group for three years. My bet is, Dad isn't going to show up. He'll send the attorney and stay as far away from this as possible."

Cook looked at the man in the black suit as he took a step closer to the mirror. "The question is, will Dad have the Westen girl drugged and brought back when he figures out who he has, or will she conveniently never be seen again?"

A man in highly decorated military dress blues spoke from the back of the room. "We've been following and watching this for a long time. This is a smart group of men who have international businesses that are so intertwined it would take us the next two decades to unravel it in the legal system. I have SEALs who can get on the yacht, quietly take out the current occupants, grab Charlotte, sink the yacht, and it's done. No red tape, no legal jargon. The yacht won't be seen again. It will simply fade from radar during the night. It will go down in history like one of the Bermuda Triangle stories."

The man in the black suit stood there, continuing to look at Brandon through the two-way mirror. "It's that simple, huh?" he commented.

"Yes," the man in the dress blues replied.

Ward looked back at the man in the dress blues. "Now that's just a little unnerving."

"Which part?" the man in the dress blues asked. "The part about killing the people on the yacht, sinking it, or the simplicity of the solution I purposed?"

"All of it," Ward said with a frown and crossed his arms. "All of it!"

The man in the black suit added, "I see what you mean about taking everyone out and sinking the yacht being unnerving. However, he does have a point. We're dealing with not one or two people behind this. We're dealing with a group of men so intertwined, it would be a circus in the legal system. Most of these men aren't from the US, so we need to rely on other countries. I can tell you right now that some of those countries will cooperate, while others won't. The sex trade is their main source of income, so they will protect these guys at all cost before they assist us." He turned and glanced at the other men in the room before looking at the man in the dress blues. "It may be unnerving, but he has a point. It would be the easiest, quietest, and quickest way to rectify the Westen situation. No fights, no debates, no international tensions, or wars." He paused. "Before I decide anything, I want to see what Chris Roper is going to do. I also want this to play out a little." The dark-haired man looked back to Brandon. "Although taking everyone out is certainly the easiest and most peaceful for everyone, sometimes examples need to be made. Maybe Chris Roper needs to be that example," he suggested, watching as Brandon sat quietly, reading his textbook and making notes in the margins.

### 

At the truck pulls, Ruthie sat beside the platform in a row of bleachers. She watched as the trucks roared down the dirt strip. Their diesel engines screamed, and black clouds trailed behind them. Instead of enjoying the truck pulls and the crisp evening air, Ruthie sat there wondering where Chevy was. She looked over at John, who stood over by a line of trucks, talking with a group of guys. So far the one person who was the closest to her for the last twenty-some years and should be steadfast at her side was now the most distant and argumentative of all—at a time when she needed him most.

### 

Chevy stood in the bedroom, looking at the cream-colored outfit with the ornate edging she had on. It made her feel a little like a princess in a far-off land.

There was a small knock on the door, then Veronica came in and instantly smiled. "You look beautiful," she complimented Chevy.

Chevy turned from the mirror and looked down at the outfit. "I wasn't sure what to do with this." She held a long piece fabric in her hand.

"Like this…" Veronica giggled, taking the fabric and draping it over her shoulder. "Ready?"

"As ready as I am going to be." Chevy seemed a touch nervous.

Chevy followed Veronica down the hall, around a corner, and down a beautiful staircase that emptied into the entertainment area where she had been dancing and drinking the wine. *Oh, that wine*, Chevy thought, remembering the pounding headache.

Through another room the aroma of wonderful rich food filled the air. They walked through a beautiful bar, then into the dining room. There was a long formal table and chairs sitting on a gorgeous area rug. The table was set with cloth napkins, silverware, place settings, and lit candles in the center of the table, giving the room a soft, warm glow.

Veronica put her hand on the back of a chair and pulled it out. "Have a seat here. I have to get the other women, then I will be back and sit beside you. There will be five men who will come in and have a seat. Be your sweet and friendly self. The man who sits next to me"—Veronica patted the back of his chair—"is my husband, Sandro. I will introduce you when I get back." She patted Chevy's shoulder, turned, and walked away.

A few moments later, five men came in with drinks, speaking a different language and laughing. All of them were clean-cut, wearing dress pants and shirts, chunky watches, and strong cologne. She remembered the one man—he had greeted her when she arrived. He sat down in the spot Veronica's husband was to sit in.

He looked at Chevy and nodded.

Veronica returned with four other women.

Veronica's husband stood to pull out the chair for her, then pushed it back in as she sat down.

Veronica looked at her husband. "Darling," she said, catching his attention. "This is Chevy." Veronica glanced at her. "This is my husband, Sandro."

He held his hand out for Chevy, took hold of her fingers, and kissed the back of her hand. "It's very good to meet your acquaintance," he said in his heavy accent, then said something to the other men, who looked at Chevy, smiled acceptingly, and nodded politely.

Chevy smiled uncomfortably, not knowing what he said. She picked up her glass of water and took a sip.

"Gentlemen," Veronica got their attention.

The men looked at her, waiting.

She leaned forward in her seat and gestured to a woman who looked to be about twenty-five. She had long blond hair and might have been cute except for the hard lines etched into her face. "Let me introduce Jordan." She paused as the men made eye contact and nodded their heads toward Jordan.

"Next is Samantha," Veronica said, gesturing to a woman with long, wavy light brown hair, who seemed to be about Jordan's age. *She seems mean,* Chevy decided and the men nodded.

"Taylor," Veronica continued with a girl who looked to be all of sixteen. She had a great figure, porcelain skin, brown hair, and dark eyes, but she seemed lost. The track marks on her arms hinted at an unfortunate life.

"And finally we have Jada," Veronica finished, gesturing at a small-framed woman with large breasts, brown hair, and light eyes. *She looks a lot like me,* Chevy thought. As the men acknowledged the last introduction, waiters in white suits came through swinging doors with small bowls of salad.

As one course of the meal blended into another, Chevy watched the men talk with the women. She noticed each man slowly appeared to select one of the women. Interestingly, only Veronica or Sandro spoke with her.

Suddenly, Jada pushed the baby carrots that were on her plate onto the table. Then she spit one against the wall on the other side of the room. She stood and looked at Sandro as though fed up and angry, talking loudly in a language Chevy didn't know. Finally, she sat back down sideways on her chair and crossed her arms angrily in front of her.

Sandro looked at Veronica. "She wants to go home."

Veronica gave him a long look without saying anything. An expression came across her face that Chevy wasn't sure how to interpret.

Sandro raised his drink in the air. "Jada," he said, getting her attention.

Jada looked at him. "You would like to go home?" Sandro asked, in English.

"Yes!" Jada barked in a thick accent.

He nodded his head with his glass in the air. "Then so it shall be." He smiled. "It will be arranged," he told her kindly, taking a small sip from his glass.

Jada twisted back into her chair and faced forward, beaming with delight. "Well, it is about time," she said authoritatively in broken English. "I will show you. You do not mess with me." Jada glared in his direction.

Sandro said nothing and smiled at her.

Chevy sat there wondering, observing.

### 

Back in Boston, the doorknob turned in Brandon's small interrogation room. He glanced up from his book to see Rob Steinberg, their attorney, standing in the doorway. Rob was in his early fifties and had white hair, blue eyes, and a medium build. He had deep dimples when he smiled, but he was not smiling now. His air of experience and confidence was intimidating.

"Hello, Brandon," Rob said as he walked in and shut the door behind him. He took off his coat and draped it neatly over the back of his chair and sat down.

Brandon smiled and closed his book, pushing it to the side. "I'm glad you and my father made it so fast."

"It's just me," Rob corrected him. "Your father had some business to attend to."

Brandon said nothing, appearing distraught. He watched as Rob got comfortable, putting his black leather brief case on the table and opening it, before pulling his black-framed glasses from his shirt pocket. "Son, these glasses make me look distinctive and powerful, but frankly they're just reading glasses. I'm getting old, and my eyes aren't what they used to be," he said with an honesty that lightened the moment. "Well, son, let me tell you what the FBI has so far." Rob leaned forward, looking at him over the top of the frames. "Nothing. They have absolutely nothing. This is good from the standpoint that they have nothing incriminating on you. But they also don't have anything to pull their focus off you. Statistically, most crimes are committed by someone close to the victim. So

79

questioning the boyfriend normally helps give investigators direction. Now bring me up to speed," he requested, leaning back, ready to listen. "You're dating this missing stripper." He looked at his notes. "Chevy." He looked at Brandon and sighed, raising his eyebrows disapprovingly.

Brandon looked at him. "I'm not just dating her—she's my girlfriend. Chevy's a nickname. Her name is Charlotte Westen. She used to drive an old Chevy pickup truck that needed a new muffler. When she would drive to her grandmother's, her grandma would hear it before she saw it and say Chevy was coming. The name stuck."

"Interesting how she picked up such a name. Does she still have the truck?" Rob smiled and winked.

"She still has the truck at home. She drives a hybrid at school."

"Let's move past her name. How did you get involved with a stripper?"

"She's not exactly a stripper. She goes to Harvard. She wanted to major in psychology, but her father wanted her to major in business so she could take over his business one day. Her father had been covering all her expenses, but then they had a falling out. She ran up the credit card a few times, so her father will no longer cover her expenses. She started stripping to try to cover her tuition and the bills. This is new for her. Chevy needs to cover her own tuition, rent, groceries, and so on. She's completely on her own."

Rob looked at him over the top of his frames. "Now, when you say her father will no longer cover her financial expenses, be more specific. Her father used to pay for all that stuff, but now isn't able to?"

"No. Her father has a chain of stores. He *won't* cover her expenses."

"So you're telling me that she comes from means?" Rob gave him a doubtful look. "That isn't the picture your father painted."

"Are you listening to me or to my father, who hasn't met her?" Brandon's irritation grew.

Rob squeezed his eyebrows together, trying to understand.

"These stores, are they like Dollar General or something?"

"No. Her father owns the Westen's chain of hunting stores." He looked at Rob, waiting for it to click.

Rob smiled. "I've heard the name, but I don't know anything about them. What are they?"

"Westen's is a big store where you can buy all kinds of gear for hunting, camping, fishing, hiking, and such. They have more than a hundred locations all over the country and are very popular. I'm shocked you haven't heard of them."

"Oh..." Rob replied, slowly realizing the caliber of the problem he was dealing with. "I'm not much of an outdoorsman." He paused, then shook his head and changed direction. "The FBI agents are going to come in here and ask you questions."

Brandon nodded. "I expected that."

"If there's anything they ask that I don't like, then I will tell you not to answer."

"Okay."

"Before they come in here, I have to ask you." Rob paused. "How is your relationship with this girl?"

Brandon leaned back in his chair, his eyebrows raised at the question. "Chevy. Her name is Chevy. I got her a ring, if that tells you anything."

"So, presumably things are good between the two of you?"

"Very good."

"What about arguments? Do the two of you argue?"

"Never!" He shook his head adamantly.

"Is there any drug or alcohol use for either of you?"

"No drugs, ever!" Brandon gave him a sour look. "Sometimes we drink socially, but that's about it. We did go to New Orleans for Mardi Gras last year. We were blasted drunk, but that was it. We took a lot of photos. We had a hangover for two days." He smiled.

Rob forced a smile. "Right...okay."

### 

Brandon pulled in front of his house and found reporters camped out on the porch. *Great*, he thought. *Just what I need— reporters.* He glanced at the house. Something aside from the mob of reporters seemed wrong. He looked more closely. The bedroom curtains closed, but he could swear he had left them open. He put the car in park and watched the reporters hurry to grab their microphones while the cameramen scrambled to turn on their cameras and hoist them to their shoulders. The reporters were like a swarm of bees. *My God*, he thought. *I'm not out of the car yet.*

He got out and made his way through the reporters, who were shouting endless questions over each other. With his bag over his shoulder he shut the front door, leaving the pushy reporters on the porch. He set his bag down by the closet, then paused, noticing the door was closed. *That isn't right*, he thought. *I always leave it open, and close it when I return and put my coat away.* He chalked it up to the FBI agents. *One of them must have closed the door, and I didn't realize it.* He was too tired to care. He opened the closet door, put his coat away, and promptly dismissed it.

# Chapter 7

Sunday night, Chevy was in a tropical paradise with crystal-clear water, breathtaking waterfalls, beautiful beaches, palm trees, great shops, and amazing-smelling restaurants. She stood waiting outside a single-toilet bathroom—the need to go grew while she waited. Veronica stood at her side, both of them holding multiple bulging shopping bags. Finally, the bathroom door opened, and an older woman came out.

Veronica glanced in. Seeing no windows, she allowed Chevy to go in alone.

Eagerly Chevy hurried in and locked the door. Then she spotted a purse on the floor between the toilet and the sink. She paused for a moment, staring at it, then grabbed it. Quickly, she sat down on the toilet and began digging through it. There before her was the woman's phone. Chevy pulled it out and turned it on. No lock code! She dialed her mom's phone, listening as it began to ring.

### ###

Back at the Westen home, Ruthie and John were in bed asleep when Ruthie's phone rang. She opened her eyes, sat up, and reached for her phone. "Hello!"

"Mommy?" Chevy said from the other end of the line, starting to cry.

Instantly, Ruthie was wide awake and hit the Speaker button.

"Chevy, sweetie! Where are you? Are you all right?"

John rolled over and leaned up on one elbow, looking at her.

"I'm sorry," she cried. "I was just trying to get through school. I wanted dad to be proud of me. Nothing I do ever makes him happy." She sniffed.

Ruthie glanced over, seeing John's egotistic pride shrink. She put her finger to his lips.

"Where are you? Are you all right?"

"I'm on an island. Somewhere in Nassau. I was brought here on a yacht. There are a lot of different people on the yacht.

They drugged me. Mommy, please help me!" she pleaded quietly. "Someone is watching me. I don't know what kind of trouble I'll be in if they find me on the phone."

The desperate sound of Chevy's voice made Ruthie's eyes well. She tilted her head back and closed her eyes as she put her hand on her forehead, fighting tears. "Of course I'll help you. I've been trying to find you. All of us have, even Brandon."

"I want to come home." Chevy's voice cracked. "Please don't tell Dad. He'll just be mad at me. Please. I got on a yacht called the *Apoise*. My car is at the marina. Jen and Becky were on the yacht before me. They were paid a lot of money. Tuition—I have tuition to pay, so I thought since it went all right for them I would be safe." Her voice shook. "Please, Mommy, help me."

Veronica knocked on the bathroom door. "Chevy, are you all right?"

Startled, Chevy looked at the door. Her heart pounded in her chest. She hit End on the phone, quickly stuck it back in the purse, and tossed the purse on the floor.

### 

Ruthie heard a click. "Chevy! Chevy!" She began to cry. She put her hand over her face.

John said nothing and pulled her against his chest. He rubbed her back with one hand and pushed the hair out of her face with the other. "We're going to find her."

She sobbed, wiping the tears from her face.

He looked at her outline in the dark. "You okay now?" he asked, as he kissed her forehead.

"We need to call the FBI agents," she mumbled as she leaned to her side of the bed for her purse.

He flipped on the antler light.

She sat there shuffling through her purse until she found the small card Ward had given her. She dialed.

"Agent Cook."

"Cook?" Ruthie repeated. "This is Ruthie Westen, Chevy's mother."

"Yes, yes," he said sounding tired.

84

"I just got a call from Chevy," Her eyes started to well, recalling the sound of her voice. "She was crying. She said she was sorry, they drugged her, and she is somewhere in Nassau. She was on a boat called *Apoise*." She paused. "She said, 'Please, Mommy, help me.' Then the phone went dead." Ruthie's voice cracked.

"Who is your cell provider?"

"Verizon."

"I'm going to start working on this. Is there anything else you can remember about that call, like any background noise?"

"Hmm…" Ruthie thought. "No, nothing that sticks out. The background was quiet."

"All right. You sit tight. Try to get some sleep. As soon as I have any information, I'll call with an update. Now, if anything else happens, you call me."

"All right."

Cook hung up.

Ruthie pulled the phone from her ear and looked at it.

"Come on, let's try and get some sleep," John encouraged.

She tossed her purse on the floor as he flipped off the light. She snuggled next to him, trying to find comfort and peace.

### 

Chevy looked at the door. "I'll be out in a minute," she said loudly, so Veronica could hear her. Standing in front of the mirror with the water running, she evened out the makeup lines from her tears, shut the water off, took another look in the mirror, then headed for the door.

"Are you ready go back to the yacht?" Veronica asked, upbeat, as Chevy came out of the bathroom.

"Here," Chevy reached for a few of the bags. "Let me carry some of those. I'm ready, unless there's something else you need to buy while we're here."

"Not that I can think of," Veronica shook her head.

As they started to make their way back through the warm evening air, a woman walked quickly toward them—the same woman who had left her purse in the bathroom. Chevy felt nervous butterflies as she caught the woman's eyes for a moment when they passed.

###

Brandon closed every blind and curtain in the house. The reporters were still on the porch and crawling around outside like cockroaches. He never saw himself as a private person, but knowing reporters were lurking, trying to look through any crack they could, was unnerving.

He was finding little things out of place in the house, starting with the upstairs bedroom curtains. He would swear he had left them open. And the coat closet at the base of the steps—he had left that open, too. Then there was the towel on the bathroom floor. He always left his towels on the end of the bathtub by the door, not at the other end, where he found it. He always closed the closet doors in his bedroom, yet one was cracked open. The pillows on his bed seemed straighter than when he left. And the decorative ball that sat in a bowl next to his bed was on the floor. He didn't remember it being on the floor. They were just little things. It crossed his mind that someone had been in the house while he was gone, but both the back and front doors were locked when he got home. Was he being paranoid? He thought about one of the pesky reporters picking the lock and rummaging through the house while he was gone, but dismissed the idea as being farfetched. Nothing of value was missing.

He sat sprawled out on the sofa, flipping through the channels. In front of him was a half-eaten bag of popcorn. The idea of reporters in the house was weighing on his mind.

# Chapter 8

Monday morning Ruthie sat on a stool at the kitchen counter. She stared into her cup of coffee, slowly moving her spoon around.

Crysta walked in through the garage door and stopped. "Are the boys up?" Crysta asked, looking at her with concern, then glancing down at her watch. "I had to come in through the garage. Have you seen the reporters out there? Trying to get down the drive was like trying to push through a mob of zombies. It's was crazy!" She shook her head.

Ruthie sat there, staring into her coffee.

"You look like you just crawled out of bed with a hangover," Crysta told her, paying close attention.

"The boys…" Ruthie repeated, coming back from wherever her mind was. "Hmm….." She took in a deep breath and wiped her hand over her face.

"Riiiight," Crysta said, then walked to the base of the steps and yelled up. "Alex! Nicholas!" Getting no response, she disappeared up the steps.

A few minutes later Crysta came back into the kitchen. "All right, I got Nicholas up. Alex was already in the shower. I'll drive them to school."

Ruthie just looked at Crysta as her eyes began to well.

"What happened?" Crysta questioned.

She tried to talk. Instead tears streamed down her cheeks.

Crysta wrapped her arms around her. "It's all right. What happened?"

"Chevy called last night. She said she was sorry. She had been drugged and taken to Nassau. Then she asked me to help her." Ruthie stumbled over her words. "She was pleading for me to help her. Then there was a click and she was gone again. My baby was gone again, and I can't get to her to help her."

Crysta leaned across the counter and grabbed the box of tissues. She pulled one out and wiped the tears streaming down Ruthie's cheeks. "Did you call the FBI?"

Ruthie nodded. "Yes..."

"Okay. I am going to take the boys to my house for the rest of the week," she said. She pulled her phone from her jacket, scrolled through her contacts, and dialed. "Hi, Cheryl. It's Crysta Gotlie I'm calling on behalf of Ruthie Westen...Yeah...Ruthie's daughter, Charlotte, is missing, and Ruthie is having a particularly hard time coping. If Dr. Carter could call in a prescription for some Valium, Xanax, anything along those lines would really help..." Crysta's voice trailed off, waiting. "Great...Yeah, that number to reach me is fine...Okay...thanks," she said, pulling the phone from her ear and hitting End. She pushed Ruthie's coffee out of the way, then suddenly pressed her eyebrows together. She put her hand on the side of the cup, then dipped her finger in. "Sweetie." Crysta looked alarmed. "How long have you been sitting here?"

Ruthie shrugged.

"Your coffee's cold. Where's John? Does he know Chevy called last night?"

Ruthie nodded, staring at the counter top. "He's still sleeping."

Alex walked into the kitchen. "No breakfast?" he asked, then saw his mom sitting there with a lost stare. "Mom, are you all right?"

Crysta looked at him. "Yeah, she's all right. Your sister called last night."

"Is Chevy okay?" Worry filled his voice.

Crysta grabbed his hand and made purposeful eye contact. "Yes. She called. She's stuck somewhere she doesn't want to be, but she's alive. So I don't want you to worry. Your mom has too much to contend with right now, but she'll be fine, too. Do me a favor and get Nicholas. I'm going to take you guys out for breakfast, then to school."

Looking unsure, Alex slowly nodded, glanced at his mom, and headed upstairs to find Nicholas.

Nicholas came down the steps in a hurry with Alex on his heels. "Mom! Chevy called last night?" He walked into the kitchen to see her sitting there distraught. Worry instantly covered his face. "Mom." He put his arms around her. "Are you okay?"

"See…I told you," Alex said behind him.

"Yes, she will be fine," Crysta put her hand on his arm. "Come on, let's go. I'm taking you guys out to eat. I'll tell you all about this in the truck."

Alex was out the door like a shot. Nicholas took small steps toward the garage, looking back at his mom. "I love you, Mom. You sure you're all right?"

Ruthie nodded, pulling her eyes from the cold cup of coffee, and looked at him. Seeing him put a hint of a spark in her eyes. "Yeah, I'm fine." She forced a smile. "Come here." She held out her arms to give him a hug.

Nicholas hurried back across the kitchen to her hug her. "What happened?"

"Crysta will tell you in the truck. I can't talk about it," she said, as tears started to swell in her eyes again. "Just go to school, pay attention, and do your best. I love you, sweetie. I don't want you to worry."

"I don't know how I'm not supposed to worry, but I will try." He kissed her cheek.

Crysta walked to the door. "I'll come back and make sure she's okay," she assured him as they headed through the door. "I'll explain in the truck. Come on. It's nothing bad, it's actually good news," Crysta's voice trailed off as the door closed behind them.

### 

Ruthie sat slumped in a chair in the great room, wearing her pajamas, slippers, and robe. She stared at the wall. "Shower? No shower?" she mumbled. Her hair was pulled back and little strands stuck out like rays of the sun. Her phone rang. She reached in the pocket of her robe and pulled it out. "Hello." She sounded like she just woke up.

"This is Agent Cook. I have an update for you."

She sat up in the chair. "Yeah—"

"We traced the number that your daughter called from. The number belongs to a lady who is on vacation in Nassau. Agents met up with her this morning. She was completely unaware her

phone had been used. She did say that last night she left her
purse in a bathroom. There were two women waiting to use the
bathroom when she came out. One was in a particular hurry to
use the facility. The woman said she realized a few minutes
later that she had forgotten her purse and went back for it, and
she passed the two women again. She was glad her purse was
where she left it, and as far as she could tell her purse looked
untouched." He paused. "We did show the woman a picture of
Chevy, but she wasn't sure if one of the women she saw was
Chevy or not. The woman didn't pay attention to their faces,
but she did say that both women were dressed in Middle
Eastern clothing. She found it odd because the one woman
didn't appear to be Middle Eastern. Again, when we showed
her Chevy's picture, she wasn't sure. She said the person she
saw could have been Chevy. The brown hair was the same, but
the woman she saw had her hair pulled back." Cook sounded
disappointed. "Another interesting part was the yacht, *Apoise*.
It was in the Nassau port when you got the phone call last
night. The *Apoise* was also at the marina the night Chevy
disappeared. This part you will like. We were able to view
security footage of the port. Four men and two women got off
the yacht and never returned. A while later, two women got off
the yacht, one appearing to be Chevy with her hair pulled back.
Several hours later, the same two women returned with
shopping bags. Both women were in Middle Eastern clothing,
just as the lady from the bathroom stated. Unfortunately, the
yacht left port before we got there."

A glow came to Ruthie's face, and a hopeful spark lit her
eyes again. "I'm sure you can find it on radar, right?"

"Yes, Mrs. Westen, we can. I know you want your daughter
back. Trust me when I say we are working on this," he assured
her.

"All we need to do is intercept the yacht—right?"

"It's a bit more complex than that."

"I don't understand. My daughter is on that yacht. These
people were willing to drug her. What else are they going to
do? Aren't you going to go get her from that yacht?"

"Mrs. Westen—"

"Ruthie."

"Ruthie, I know you want her safe. There is a lot to this situation. Right now we are working on it."

"Wha— I…All we have to do is go get her!" She rubbed the heel of her hand harshly against her forehead, then over the bridge of her nose. She squeezed her eyes shut. "So what happens from here?" She rubbed her hand against her forehead in a circular motion and opened her eyes, listening.

"For now we're going to keep an eye on the yacht. We're tracking the owner, associates, business partners, and friends." Cook paused. "Don't worry. Know that we are working on it."

"Why are we making this harder than it has to be? Hell! I can go rent a goddamn yacht, hire some Navy SEALs, and go get her myself. We have hunting stores. I'm no stranger to firearms and ammo. If I can shot a moose, then I can certainly knock off a few kidnappers!"

"Ruthie, promise me you won't do any such thing."

Ruthie remained silent.

"Ruthie Westen…"

"I'm in my robe."

"Good! Now promise me you're going to stay that way."

"All right," Ruthie said begrudgingly. "Keep me posted. I want to know everything."

"Absolutely."

As she hit End on her phone, she took a deep unsettled breath. Then she sat there and cried.

### 

A few hours later Crysta came back into the house though the garage with two bags in hand. "Ruthie!" Crysta yelled, as she scanned the rooms, looking for her. "Ruthie!"

"I'm right here."

Crysta turned toward the great room but saw no one, just a dark room with the curtains closed and a huge ladder near the tall windows with one of Ruthie's cats sleeping on the very top. "Ruthie?" Crysta called again.

"Here."

Crysta looked around, taking small steps into the great room, still not seeing Ruthie. Then her hand rose from the

91

chair.

Crysta blinked. "There you are." She walked to the chair from behind and peered down at Ruthie.

Ruthie looked up.

"No wonder I couldn't see you. You scooted down in the chair." Crysta stood there. noting the absent look on her face. "Get up." She nudged her. "I'm going to get you a glass of water. Why are you sitting in the dark? You never pull the curtains closed."

"Reporters were standing on the porch, looking in."

"What? That's craziness." She shook her head. "There were some in the yard when I pulled in."

"I had to drag in the big ladder to close the curtains. Frank seems to like sleeping at the top."

They both looked up at the snow-white cat, who was sound asleep.

Crysta walked back into the kitchen.

"Agent Cook called," Ruthie told her.

"Hang on," Crysta yelled out. "I can't hear you. Wait until I get back out there."

Ruthie listened to the water run in the kitchen, then turn off.

"Here," Crysta said, handing her a glass of water.

Slowly, Ruthie reached for the glass.

Crysta picked up one of the bags. "I went to bookstore and picked up a novel for you. It's by Rachel Lane. *Half Past Midnight*. It sounded like a good book." Crysta handed it to her.

Ruthie looked at the cover, less than amused. "Yeah, I've heard of this author." She looked at Crysta. "Remember, I was telling you about her? She wrote the book I wanted you to read—*Messerfly*. It was a really good. She has a few other novels that looked good, also."

Crysta brushed over what she was saying. "Yeah, yeah. I'll watch the movie. I also got your prescription." She opened the bottle of Xanax. "Take a whole one." She handed her a small white pill.

Ruthie popped it in her mouth and drank down the glass of water. "Agent Cook called."

Crysta sat down, eager to hear more. She twisted the cap back on the bottle.

"He said the call last night was made from a cell phone. The woman is on vacation. She didn't know any calls had been made from her phone. But she did accidently leave her purse in a bathroom. There were two women waiting to use the restroom. The woman noted they were dressed in Middle Eastern clothing. The woman said she didn't pay much attention to their faces, but did note the one woman didn't look Middle Eastern. Cook showed the women a picture of Chevy, but she wasn't sure if it was her. The yacht Chevy said she was on was in the Nassau port, but by the time the agents got there, the yacht had left," she recited.

Crysta was riveted. "Oh my God," she said, wide-eyed, as though the seriousness of the situation hadn't really sunk in until that moment. "Where's John? Does he know?" She looked around, readying to get up and get him.

Ruthie rolled her head from side to side against the back of the chair, causing her hair to bunch up. "No," she said. "I thought about calling, but he left the house this morning with a full case of beer and got on the tractor, then headed for the back of the property." She looked disappointed.

"Oh." Crysta made a face. "Is drinking on the tractor a good idea?"

Ruthie tossed her hands up. "Probably not, but what do I say? Don't drink and drive the tractor? What's he really going to hit, a tree?" She looked stressed. "There are only so many fights I can fight. John's a big boy." She shook her head. "Let him hit a tree. Maybe it will knock some sense into him."

Crysta raised her eyebrows and blinked. "I can imagine John trying to cope by driving around the property drunk on a red tractor. It's amusing, ridiculous, and sad all at the same time. Sweetie—I'm sorry. I don't know what to say." Crysta shook off the visual. "So, now what?"

"We wait." Ruthie held a depressed stare.

"Wait!"

"Yep, we wait." She sighed.

Crysta looked at some of the animal heads on the walls, then back at Ruthie. "Are they going to track the yacht? Go get her, or something?"

Ruthie raised her eyebrows and blinked. "Well, that was the first thing I asked. But apparently I sounded like some uneducated desperate housewife who has watched too many movies. Then I just felt dumb. They are tracking the yacht. There's more to this than one missing girl. Unfortunately, one of those girls is mine."

Crysta searched her face. "I'm surprised you're being this cool and collected." Crysta knew Ruthie's temperament.

"Trust me. Don't think for one moment that I didn't think about renting my own yacht, finding a captain that can navigate it, stocking the yacht with firearms, even hiring a few Navy SEALs, and going to get her." She looked at Crysta. "I even told Agent Cook that."

Crysta winced.

"He made me promise I would stay in my robe." Ruthie frowned.

"But then I thought about Alex and Nicholas. What if something happened to me? How can I sacrifice the future of my other two children for Chevy? Does this mean I'm selecting my other two kids over Chevy? We have plenty of money. We can track down the yacht ourselves and get her..." She quieted and sat there silent for a moment before she began to cry again.

Crysta leaned over and hugged her. "I know, sweetie. It is going to be all right. You're not choosing any child over the other. They'll find Chevy, but it's just as you said. There's a lot more to this than one girl. You have to be patient."

### 

Chris Roper smiled in front of the camera as he stood beside the pretty news reporter. "Kids are the future. I feel this is incredibly important. All kids should have the best start they can." It was a charismatic performance, topped by him handing the superintendent of schools a personal check for a hundred thousand dollars.

The reporter looked at Chris and asked in an upbeat tone, "Why are you giving the school system a personal check instead of a company check?"

Chris continued to smile. "It's not just up to businesses and large corporations to assist in maintaining our future."

The reporter turned to the camera. "There we have it." She smiled. "Thanks, Chris. I am sure the opportunities your donation will create will serve this community for many years to come."

"That's what I'm hopping for." Chris smiled and gave a confident nod and grin to the camera.

### 

Neal Collins sat at his desk inside the small gray cubicle. There was a black phone at his side and a computer in front of him. Eight-by-ten photos of places he had been hung on the cubicle walls. They were dramatic photos filled with heartfelt emotion that captured horrific situations. He kept them in view, a reminder of the places, people, and stories he had encountered. He exposed what some people wanted to keep hidden and what others prayed would be revealed. His writing and investigative reporting won awards. When Neal Collins wrote, people paid attention.

His days of high-profile reporting had slowed to a standstill. He found an interest in a local news reporter named Megan Mitchells. Megan was by all rights very attractive. She caught his eye at a point in his life when he was restless. He gave in to the idea of a long-term relationship, quit his high-profile job, and decided to settle down in a small town in North Carolina. It was a place where money was plentiful and people took life at a slower pace. But the news in this small town was anything but exciting.

"Here's an address." His boss handed Neal a Post-it across the top of his cubicle wall. "Get it taken care of."

"An address," Neal repeated, looking up from the small yellow Post-it.

"Chris Roper. Donated funds to the school. Go collect all the information and write about it," his boss said in a demeaning tone, then started to walk away.

Neal stood up, rounding his cubicle wall after him. "Wait, wait, wait."

His boss stopped and looked at him impatiently.

"Do you have something with a little more meat?"

"Like what?" he asked, irritated.

"I have been an international reporter. I can dig up dirt. You seem to hand me stories on things like fall festivals. You know there is only so much you can say about the changing color of the leaves, carving pumpkins, and caramel apples. How about giving me the Dewey Spencer story? Embezzling—now that's more my style."

His boss rolled his eyes. "Dewey Spencer embezzled from nursing homes." He shook his head.

"Yes!" Neal said with excitement. "That's just the point. How much did he embezzle. What did Dewey do with the money? Has any one noticed red flags before this? How about his past? Has Dewey done anything questionable before this? Maybe something was missed with Dewey's previous employers."

His boss gave him an annoyed look. "Chris Roper donated to the school. Go cover it."

"See, that's just it." Neal began following his boss, prompting him to stop again and listen. "Men like Chris Roper are either nice, good-hearted guys, or they're underhanded jerks who only want to make themselves look good. It's sort of a way to redeem oneself. If he gets caught doing something sinister, a donation puts doubt in people's minds. They ask how a nice guy like Chris could do such a thing. No one really wants to hear about Chris Roper and his donation to the school." Neal paused and looked at his boss to emphasize his point. "Meanwhile, you got the guy just out of college covering Dewey Spencer's embezzlement. I'm a big-name reporter with big stories under my belt, and you hand me a donation to cover. Come on, throw me a bone with some meat."

"Do me a favor," his boss started. "Make yourself useful. Cover the donation. Take some pictures. Make it look good." He shook his head, turned, and walked away.

Neal stood there in front of the big picture window and looked out onto an overcast fall day full of vivid colors. He suddenly felt that familiar itch to chase a story. He walked back to his cubicle with the black-and-white eight-by-tens staring him in the face—a nagging reminder that he didn't fit in this small town.

He picked up his phone and dialed.

"This is Megan."

"Hey, babe."

"Oh, hi."

He was taken aback at her cold tone. His eyes immediately shifted to the pictures. "I was thinking about dinner tonight," he said sweetly, leaning back in his office chair, still gazing at the photos. "I was thinking about that nice Italian restaurant you like just outside of town."

"Hmm, no," Megan replied, sounding short and uninterested. "I'm covering the charity event tonight."

He leaned forward. "Babe, we talked about this. We decided you weren't going to volunteer for any extra assignments. You and I were going to have some us time."

"If I want a shot at being an anchor instead of just a reporter, I have to volunteer for more assignments and be more visible in the community. Do you have any idea the salary I would have as an anchor?" Megan asked, half scolding.

He sat with his elbows on top of his desk, staring at one of the photos.

"Right," he replied, understanding what was important to Megan—and it wasn't him or their relationship. He smirked. "You're right, babe. We'll have dinner another night," he said, wanting to hear her response.

"Great!" Megan replied, with enthusiasm. "Yeah, I will be right there," she said to someone in the background. "Give me a minute."

"All right, babe. You have fun covering the charity event. I'll see you at home later tonight."

"Okay," Megan said distractedly, obviously wanting to get off the phone. "See you later. Bye." She hung up.

He slowly slid the receiver back onto the base. It sounded notably louder to him than it ever had before. He looked at the yellow Post-it that he had stuck to the top of his desk. He stared at it as if he were waiting for it to go somewhere. That small piece of paper wasn't just any old yellow Post-it. It was a crossroads. That one assignment, the address scratched onto that Post-it, was a question. *Can I be happy doing this, an unfulfilling job in small town? Or is this a sign I need to move on?* He mulled over the answer. He glanced at the time that was displayed on his phone, 6:07 p.m. He got up, put on his jacket, and put the strap of his bag over his head. He pulled the Post-it from the top of his desk, folded it in half, and shoved it into his jacket pocket.

### 

Later that evening, Neal sat down in a tall wood booth in a dimly lit sports bar. There were several televisions. The one closest to him was showing the local news, which he glanced at from time to time. The waitress walked up, blocking the screen.

She smiled. "How are you tonight?" she asked sweetly. She was young, cute, and bubbly. "What can I get you?"

"You know what? I'll have coffee and potato skins. Have them toss on a little extra bacon and cheese for me."

"Sure. Do you want your coffee now, or with your skins?"

"I'll take the coffee now. It's a little brisk outside, and I would like to warm up."

"Not a problem." She turned and walked away.

The TV came back into view. It was a reminder of all the reporting he had done around the world and his current job. *Is it time to move on? If so, where?*

The waitress set his coffee on the table in front of him. "Here you go," she said, setting a handful of creamers beside his cup. "Anything else I can get you?"

He looked at her, glad she was blocking the view of the news for another moment. "No. I'm good. Thank you." He sipped the coffee, deciding to work on the story for the school donation. He could write the body of the story now and plug in a few pertinent details after the interview. He wrote for a while, until the waitress brought his meal. A report about a missing girl from Rudle Mills, Kentucky, on the TV caught his attention.

*This story has teeth*, he thought. He picked up a potato skin and took a bite, listening to the details of the story, paying close attention to the inconsistencies. The missing girl intrigued him. He flipped to a different page in his notebook and took notes. He sucked down his coffee and ate another potato skin.

"How is everything?" the waitress asked, this time with the coffee pot in her hand. "More?"

"No, no." He held his hand in the air. "Everything's great. If you could get me the check, that would be perfect." He smiled.

"Okay. I'll be right back."

In moments she was back, attempting to lay the check on the table as she walked by.

"Wait, wait, wait," he said, catching her attention before she could get away. "Here." He reached in his pocket, pulling out some bills, some change, and that folded Post-it. He handed her enough cash to cover the bill and a sizable tip. The Post-it that lay in front of him clawed at his soul. He shoved it back into his pocket. "Hey, thanks. You've been great," he told her as he picked up his bag, stuck his notebook into it, and headed out the door.

### 

Back on the yacht somewhere on the ocean, Chevy sat beside Veronica on a sofa in what Veronica called the salon.

To Chevy, it had the look and feel of an entertainment room.

Veronica had the television on with the volume turned down low so they could talk.

"Tell me," Veronica asked. "What is life like where you are from?"

Chevy smiled as she thought of home. "I have two younger brothers. The older one always loves to pick on me."

"Pick on you?" she repeated, trying to understand.

"We used to live in this big white farmhouse that my parents fixed up. There was a big red barn behind the house. Alex— that's the older of my two brothers—put a rake on the ground, and then covered it with straw so I couldn't see it. He sat in the barn all day, waiting. Finally, my father asked me to go to the barn and look for him. I took only a few steps into the barn when *bam!* Right in the face." Chevy smacked the palm of her hand on her forehead.

Veronica's eyes widened as she listened, imagining.

"I stepped on the teeth of the rake. The wood handle flipped up and smacked me right in the forehead." Chevy laughed. It's funny now, but at the time I wanted to kill him.

Veronica giggled.

Suddenly, there were three loud gunshots in fast succession.

Chevy leaned over Veronica, tucking her underneath her, and froze, looking around cautiously, listening, and waiting.

"It's all right," Veronica reassured her.

Chevy's heart pounded as adrenalin coursed through her veins. "Those were gunshots," Chevy said in a whisper, pulling herself off Veronica.

Veronica gently put her hand on Chevy's arm. "It's all right—Jada wanted to go home," she whispered.

Instantly, Chevy remembered the dining room. Jada had made a scene, spitting her carrots across the room because she wanted to go home. Chevy remembered the expression on Veronica's face. Now she understood the look.

Chevy sat up.

"Were you going to protect me?" Veronica asked.

"Yes."

"Have you been around guns before?"

"You could say that."

# Chapter 9

Crysta stood in the checkout line at the grocery store on Tuesday afternoon, her cart piled high. Feeding her own two kids was a challenge; now feeding Ruthie's teenage boys, too, was a losing battle. She peered around her heaping cart at the line in front of her with a dismayed expression, sighed, and turned to one of the magazine racks that lined every checkout. There before her on the front of a magazine was a picture of Chevy and Brandon. Crysta's mouth hung open.

It was a bad picture—Chevy had a drink in her hand while Brandon looked angry. The photo suggested major problems between them.

"Oh my God!" she said aloud, staring at the cover.

Crysta picked up the magazine, taking a few steps away from the cart to the next end cap. Most of the magazines had a Thanksgiving theme on the front, but then Crysta spotted another one with Chevy. She groaned, plucking it from the rack. "You have got to be joking!" she said out loud and shook her head with disgust, causing the people around her to pause and look at her before continuing with what they were doing.

Crysta glanced at the people around her then looked back at the magazine. The second one at least had a better photo. Chevy and Brandon were partying, but at least it was a good picture and they were both smiling. She mumbled to herself, "Ruthie's going to flip."

Crysta took a long look at the cover. She glanced over the rack again, then spotted another. "Oh, good grief!" she said out loud, seeing another headline: WESTEN'S PARTY GIRL MISSING! It was an awful photo of Chevy. She looked drunk, and this time there was no Brandon. Crysta piled two of the magazines in the cart and began reading the third while she waited in line.

### 

Back at the Westen home, Crysta came through the garage door to the wonderful aroma of food. "I see the reporters are on the road instead of crawling around the house. What did you do, go outside with your shotgun?" Crysta teased.

Ruthie smiled. "No, but that doesn't sound like a bad idea, not to mention rather humorous," she said, cutting vegetables for dinner. "I called Mike and Ken and asked them to either arrest the mob of reporters for trespassing or make it clear that trespassers will be shot unless they stay on the road."

Crysta sat in one of the tall chairs at the counter, looking at Ruthie. "I'm impressed. This is an improvement from yesterday. You showered, you smell good, and you did something with your hair."

"Well, I have to tell you, the Xanax is working." She glanced up from the veggies.

"I have something to show you—and tell you," Crysta said reluctantly.

Ruthie paused and looked at Crysta as she picked up her mason jar of iced tea. "Yesterday was just a bad day, an emotional day. Sometimes we have those," she said, seeing Crysta's reluctance.

Crysta put the three magazines on the counter and spread them out for her to see.

She glanced at them, set the tea back on the counter, and began cutting the vegetables again. "I like the one of Brandon and Chevy smiling the best." Then she read the one headline out loud. "Westen's party girl missing! Well. We all have our moments, and that particular moment was captured on camera. We all learn from our mistakes, and Chevy's going to learn from hers." She looked at Crysta. "Thank God, all the trouble you and I got into wasn't captured on camera or caught on tape. The trouble we would have been in." She laughed, remembering. "You had better stick those in one of the drawers over there before John comes home. Some moments he's my John, sweet and loving; the next he's mean and hateful. I never know which to expect. He comes home at random times. But I know one place he's not." She smiled, pausing and looking at Crysta with a twinkle in her eye.

"Where?"

"The strip club!"

Crysta laughed. "No, definitely not at a strip club." She

picked up the magazines and headed for the drawers across the kitchen by the pantry. "Is this drawer good?" she asked, pulling one open.

Ruthie glanced up. "Yeah, that works." She tossed the cut vegetables into a pan with something that had been simmering and smelled wonderful.

Crysta stuck the magazines in the drawer and pushed it shut. "I'm going to go. I wanted you to see those. I didn't want you to be caught off guard."

"Caught off guard?" Ruthie waved her hand in the air. "Not anymore. I'm loving this Xanax. It's sanity in a little white pill." She beamed.

"The doctor prescribed some for me when Robert was being a jerk a few years back."

"I remember that. I was ready to kill him. Well, figuratively speaking, that is." "It worked wonders for me."

"Yep," she said. "Now I know how you handled Robert so well—the composure of Xanax." She smiled tranquilly.

"All right, babe. I have to go. I have groceries in the truck," Crysta said as she started for the garage door. "Call me if you need me, or if you get any more updates on Chevy."

"Absolutely," Ruthie said, pulling meat out of the refrigerator.

"All right, love you." Crysta pulled the garage door open.

"Love you, too. Thank you."

###

John came in through the garage.

Ruthie looked over to see him happy, and happy to see her. "Hey, babe," she said. His eyes had a sparkle she hadn't seen in a while. "How was your day?"

John's hands were warm on the tops of her arms as he pulled her close, wrapping his arms around her and holding her close to his body. Reactively, she closed her eyes as his lips met hers.

"Mmm…" she groaned. "Can I have more of those kisses?"

"Another one?" he teased, kissing her again. "Like this?" he asked, hugging her. "Or like this?" he asked, kissing her and rubbing his hands over her breasts.

"Like that…" she said, with her lips pressed against his. "I like that." She looked at him. "I." she kissed him. "Love those." She kissed him more, a little deeper. "Lips."

"Yeah?" He held a sparkle in his eyes.

This was the John she fell in love with, the man she blended with so well. The man who made her feel alive, passionate, and whole like no other man in the world could.

"These lips?" he asked, as he leaned down, grabbed her butt, and lifted her onto the counter.

She loved him close to her. She loved the feel of his hands on her body. She wrapped her legs around his hips, drawing him closer to her.

The phone rang.

His arms were wrapped around her. Her head was tilted back, and his lips were against her neck. He reached for her phone next to them, looking at the display.

"It's the FBI." A serious expression came back to his face.

"Hello," she answered, hitting the Speaker button.

"Ruthie, Agent Cook. We sent photos to Detectives Roots and Trudell  that you and your husband need to look at. I need the two of you to verify if it's Chevy in the photos. The detectives are supposed to be on their way to your house as we speak. I just got off the phone with them. We will talk more once you view the photos."

Ruthie looked at John, a serious expression on her face. "All right," she said. "Thank you." She hit End and sat there for a moment, tapping the corner of her phone to her lips.

"So, I wonder if they found Chevy?" John thought aloud.

"I don't know." She shrugged, wondering. "We need to verify if it's Chevy in some photos, then we go from there," she repeated, trying to take it in.

John looked at the pan of food. "This smells great."

"Get two forks." She pulled her legs from around his hips.

"No plates?" He reached into the drawer and pulled out two forks.

"Why? It's just you and me."

"Crysta still has the boys, I take it."

"Yep. She's going to keep them for a while."

"Ha." He laughed. "Good luck feeding those two." He pulled a bottle of wine from the wine rack and poured himself a glass.

"Crap. She was just at the store, too. I didn't even think of it. I should have given her money."

He took a bite from the pan. "You'll see her tomorrow."

She took a bite. "Mmm…This turned out really good."

He moved in front of her again. "That's because you're the best cook," he told her, then kissed the end of her nose.

The sound of the doorbell rang through the house.

She slid from the counter and scurried to the door, eager to see the photos and even more eager for Chevy to come home. As she pulled the door open, she immediately saw the somber expressions on Mike's and Ken's faces. "Come in," Ruthie said, holding the door open.

John came around the corner from the kitchen.

Mike stepped in. "I have some—"

Ruthie interrupted. "Agent Cook called and said you guys were on your way with photos. Come. Let's sit down." She ushered them into the great room.

John sat on the sofa beside her and set his glass in front of him on the table.

Mike held a file folder in his hand. "I want to prepare you for what you are about to see. It's graphic, and it's going to hit to close to home." He opened the folder and laid out a photo of a girl that looked very similar to Chevy. She was lying on a simple stainless steel table. Her skin was pale, her lips were bluish, and her eyes were closed.

Mike put another photo on the coffee table. This one was close-up of the girl's face, from a different angle. He then put a few more photos out, all taken at different angles.

She looked intently at the photos sprawled out in front of her. John sat with his mouth clenched tight. "This girl is dead, isn't she?" Her voice started to crack and she looked up, her face suddenly a pale white, as her hands began to tremble.

John drank several large swallows of the wine.

"Is this Chevy?" Mike asked gently.

She looked back at the photos, and her eyes started to well.

She put her trembling fingers over her mouth. "That's not Chevy," she said, getting the words out with as much composure as she could muster.

John sat there with his head down, his jaw still clenched tight.

"Where did they find this girl, and why did they think it could be Chevy?" She asked, with force wanting to know.

Mike turned to John. "John, do you agree with Ruthie that none of these photos are of Chevy?"

"That's not Chevy," John agreed with his elbows on his legs.

Mike started collecting the photos. He pushed them together and straightened them against the top of the coffee table. "I didn't think they were her, either," Mike commented as he put them back in the file folder. "As for where they found this girl, and why they thought she might be Chevy, that's a question for the FBI agents. I wasn't given the details. Do you want me to ask?" Mike pulled his cell phone from his pocket.

"No!" Ruthie said hastily. "I will call them back." She reached for her phone.

Mike looked at John as he put his phone back in his pocket. "Is there anything I can do for you?" Mike asked him.

John was pale. He tried to smile. "You know, just another day. I'm good." He sat and took a few more drinks of the wine.

Ruthie had her phone to her ear, looking rattled. "This is Ruthie. I have Mike, Ken, and my husband here with me. I am putting you on speaker," she announced, glancing to everyone.

"Am I correct to assume the photos are not of your daughter?" Cook asked.

"That's correct. It was not Chevy," she said perturbed. "Why did you think it could be Chevy? And why didn't you forewarn me that we were viewing photos of a dead girl?" She was pissed. The lines between her eyebrows were becoming more prominent.

"You won't find this comforting. The yacht Chevy's on is being tracked and followed. This girl was pulled from the water by the following boat. She hadn't been dead long. I was pretty sure it wasn't Chevy; however, it's not up to me to make that call. It's up to the closest family members. In this case, that's you and your husband. I'm sorry to put you through viewing these photos."

"You said the yacht she's on is being tracked?" She repeated, relaxing a little, then suddenly getting angry. "Wait! You mean to tell me that you guys are close enough to pull this girl from the water before she sank but can't get my daughter?"

"There's a lot to this case. Your daughter's disappearance is being addressed by the FBI and by other government agencies that have been watching the situation for a while. It involves international human trafficking from a whole list of countries. Some of the countries are cooperative, but some aren't. It's a delicate situation. The FBI along with the other agencies are working to bring all of this to an end."

John didn't say a word as he got up and headed for the kitchen with the empty glass of wine in his hand.

Ruthie watched him walk away, open the refrigerator door, and pull out a beer. She shifted her eyes in front of her and looked disheartened.

"So Chevy's in a very dangerous situation," Ruthie stated.

"That's a hard question, and one I can't truly answer. I can tell you what I know, which is some women are used as sex slaves for a period of time, anywhere from a few months to over a year. Some are then sent home, while others never go home. As I understand it, it depends on how cooperative the girl is."

"So there's hope," she asked, unsure she wanted to hear any more.

"I believe so."

John came out of the kitchen and stood along the wall, keeping his distance, and drank his beer in huge gulps as he listened.

"Ruthie, we have to talk about this later. I'm in Boston. We are leaving to do some interviews about Chevy. Should I call you back later tonight when I'm done?"

"No, not unless you have more information."

### 

Hemming walked into the nightclub with Ward and Cook.

Austin funneled them into the dressing room, then rounded up Jen and Becky.

"Jen Calder. Becky MacNamara." Hemming gestured to each girl in turn, stating their names clearly for the agents. "Ladies, these are Agents Ward and Cook from the FBI. There's been a development, and they have a few questions to ask you. Please have a seat." Hemming motioned toward the chairs in front of the dressing tables.

Becky sat down reluctantly, smacking her gum nervously. Agent Cook looked at Becky, then took off his jacket and handed it to her. "Put this on, please. It's uncomfortable talking to you with your breasts exposed."

Becky looked embarrassed, then sheepishly put on the jacket.

Jen shook her head. "She likes to show off her breasts." She smirked. "She's never been asked to cover them before—at least not that I know of."

Ward pulled out some photos. "Have you seen this woman before?" he asked, handing Becky an 8×10.

Becky looked at the photo and blinked. "You're going to show me a picture of a person with their eyes closed?" She sat there with her head cocked to the side.

"Yes or no?" Ward asked, flat and monotone.

"I don't know. Her eyes are closed," Becky complained.

Ward pulled the picture from Becky's fingers and handed it to Jen.

Jen's eyes widened. "She's dead!" Her face turned pale.

"Have you seen this person before?" Ward repeated.

Jen took a longer look. "Yeah. That was the woman on the yacht that looked like Chevy—very chesty. She's dead!" she said with disbelief, staring at the photo.

"Really," Becky said loudly. "Is that a real dead person?" She pulled the photo from Jen's hand, looking at it and smacking her gum. "Cool."

Jen shook her head. "What's wrong with you? This person's dead, and you were on that same yacht." She waited for the seriousness of the situation to sink in. When Becky didn't seem to care, she rolled her eyes.

"What do you know about this person?" Ward asked.

"Nothing," Jen shrugged. "I saw her on the yacht. She spoke another language. I thought she resembled Chevy. I saw her for a few moments, then she went to another part of the yacht and I never saw her again."

Ward handed Jen another photo of a pretty Middle Eastern woman. "Have you seen this woman?"

Jen looked at the photo. "Yeah," she said slowly. "I'm pretty sure I saw her—only her hair was down." Jen continued to study the photo for a moment, then handed it back to Ward.

Suddenly, there was a puff of perfume in the air. Everyone paused and looked at Becky, who was playing with a perfume bottle. Becky paused as everyone stared at her. "What? It was an accident," she said, clueless. She put the bottle back on the makeup table.

Jen looked at her. "Be serious for a few moments," she scolded, looking back at Ward.

Becky made a face at her.

"What about you? Does this woman look like anyone you have seen?" Ward asked, handing the photo to Becky.

Becky stopped making a face and looked at the photo. "Umm…no. Never seen her," she said loudly, sounding sure of herself.

"All right," Ward said. He looked back at Jen. "What about this person?" He handed her a picture of a dark-haired man with porcelain skin.

Jen's eyes lit up. "Yes! That was the man, Sandro…" She looked at Hemming with excitement. "Remember, I told you there was a dark-haired man named Sandro."

Hemming acknowledged her statement with a nod.

"That's him," Jen said with certainty.

"You remember this man," Ward asked.

"Yes, his name was Sandro, or at least that's the name he gave me. We got along very well. He was really nice." Jen looked over to Hemming. "I told Detective Hemming there was a man named Sandro. I wasn't sure what nationality he was— Italian, or something like that. That's definitely him." Jen smiled and raised her eyebrows as she handed the photo back

109

to Ward. "So who is this man? Where's he from?"

Ward turned to Becky and handed her the photo. "What about you? Have you ever seen this man?"

Becky glanced at the photo and rolled her eyes. "Oh yeah, him. I asked him if he wanted a blow job, but he said no. I kept asking. He said he was married and that it was against the vows he and his wife took. He was boring," Becky crinkled her lip and rolled her eyes, smacking her gum.

### 

John was sitting on the back porch off the kitchen with a case of beer beside him, looking up at the night sky and all the twinkling stars. Some stars seemed so close in the dark country sky, while others seemed so far away. He finished another beer and tossed the empty can toward one of the big flower pots that sat on either side of the steps to the yard that he was using as a trash can. He missed. "Where are you, Chevy?" He looked up at the sky.

# Chapter 10

Chevy and Veronica were sitting in Chevy's room on the *Apoise*, a bowl of popcorn in front of them as a movie played in the background. Chevy was having a nice time with her new friend. Despite being drugged and taken, she was being treated like a princess, at least for now. "So how did you meet Sandro?" Chevy asked. "I imagine it's a wonderful fairy tale." She smiled and beamed, wanting to hear a hopeless romantic story.

The smile fell from Veronica's face, and her head tilted downward. The question took her back to another time and place. "It's a graphic and sad story," Veronica said. "But it does have a happy ending." She smiled through the hurt in her eyes. "Are you sure you want to hear it?"

Chevy looked puzzled. "I want to hear all about it. Tell me. I told you all about my difficult father."

"Well," Veronica started, seeming a little reluctant. "My father sent me to the store for spice. I was walking home with my parka covering my face and the bag of spice in my hand. I was ten at the time. I saw three men. They looked at me and stopped what they were doing. Instantly, I felt uncomfortable. I had never seen them before. One of them asked where I was going. I looked at him, then I looked back down at the ground and kept walking. I said nothing as I passed them. We were in an area with partially destroyed buildings where no one lived. When I started by the buildings, one of the men grabbed me, pulled me off my feet, and took me inside. I started to scream, but he put his hand over my mouth, so I couldn't. He tossed me down on the floor, then he came toward me. I scooted away from them as quickly as I could until I was against the wall with nowhere left to go. The man who grabbed me walked up and stood above me. He seemed so tall. Then he tried to reach for me. I kicked at him. The other two men came around from behind him on either side. Each of them took one of my arms. I remember trying to fight, twisting and pulling, trying to get away, but I couldn't. The man who had been standing in front of me reached out and pulled my parka from my face and hair. I kept kicking my legs. I was terrified. The man that stood in front of me started undoing his pants. The look in his eyes was evil, like a serpent. It was like no one was there. There was no emotion, no feeling, or thought for another human being. He was blank.

"He pushed down his pants. I remember seeing his penis. It was the first time I had ever seen a man before. It was this wrinkly hunk of skin surrounded by hair. He got down on his knees. I was still trying to kick him, so the other two men grabbed my legs. My body hadn't started to mature, so I hadn't experienced any type of physical or hormonal changes. I had no idea when the man started to undo his pants what he was going to do.

"The man had a lustful look as he held his hand on my knee. He put his finger to his lips. "Shh, I'm not going to hurt you," he said, and he just sat there and looked at me, waiting.

I calmed down. I was still scared because of the way they had a hold of me. But none of them were hurting me. They just held me there. After a few minutes, the man started for my pants. I was worried, but I wasn't scared like I had been. He began pulling my pants from my body. I kept telling him to stop. One of the men let go of my leg so the man could get my pants off. I had one leg free so I started kicking again. I was twisting, kicking, pulling, trying everything to get away. They grabbed my leg and pulled it back, holding me there.

"'She's a fighter.' The man smiled. Then he leaned against me, trying to kiss me with his slimy, dirty lips. He pushed my shirt up. I had no breasts, so he strummed my nipples with his fingers. He reached down. I could feel his fingers feeling me. Feeling, then rubbing me until the tip of his finger started to sink into my vaginal canal. Then he slid his whole finger into me. It took my breath away. It felt really tight, super tight, but not awful. I keep telling them to stop. He held his hand over my mouth He leaned on to me,

112

guided his penis to my canal, and pushed his penis into me. At first it wasn't hard. As he started to get hard, it went from not hurting to being excruciating. I started to scream, but he had his hand over my mouth still. Every time I started to take in a breath he moved his hand, but when I started to let out air to scream he covered my mouth again. I remember how my body felt as he thrust himself into me. The first few times he got harder and harder, bigger and bigger. Each time he entered my body, he ripped and tore my canal more. It was pain beyond pain. He could have cut some of my fingers off and I wouldn't have noticed. My body tore until it wasn't going to tear any more. I was just numb.

Everything became a blur. All three of them took turns, one after another. When they were done with me, they left. They left me there with my shirt up, my pant on one leg, at my knee. I don't know how long I laid there. Then I heard my parents yelling for me. I tried to stand up, but it hurt too much. I tried to crawl, but that hurt, too. It hurt to move, but crawling hurt less than trying to stand. I knew if I could get to where they could see me, I would be safe with them. Their voices rang out intermittently, coming closer.

'Mommy!' I tried to yell. 'Dad…' It was a quiet, soft, airy yell, so I reached my hand past the doorway. They must have heard me, because my mom's voice started to sound worried. 'Mommy!' I yelled, with as much force as I could muster.

"'Veronica!' My mom said my name with panic, then suddenly she was there beside me, pulling me into her arms.

"My father walked up behind her and looked at me. He was this ominous figure. He was a cold, mean man. I dumbly thought this would be the time he would be loving to me. I thought he would go looking for those men.

"My mom saw my pants down. 'My God! What happened?' There was more panic in her voice. She knew.

"My father pulled me from the shadow of the building.

"My mom covered her mouth and started yelling and crying. 'She's bleeding! She's bleeding!'

"My father looked at me. It was a horrified look. He

pulled my legs apart and looked at me. A repulsed look covered his face, like he had just seen something so disgusting. He pushed my knees back together and stood up.

"My mom was on her knees at my shoulders crying.

"My father pulled on her arm, prompting her to get up. 'Come,' he yelled. 'Leave her! She's been contaminated.'

"My mom shook her head, not wanting to leave me.

"'No,' she cried, not willing to get up, and pulled me into her lap.

"'Now! Come!' he demanded.

"'No! My baby!' She rocked me in her lap.

"'She is no longer holy,' my father told her."
Chevy's eyes grew larger.

"'Come!' He pulled hard on my mom's arm.

"'No, get her!' my mom shouted. I never heard my mom shout at my father. He stood there for a moment. Disbelief, coupled with anger. He kept pulling on my mom's arm and shoulder, trying to make her stand up. Finally, he punched the side of her head. 'Now, to your knees!' my father yelled at her.

"My mom turned and looked at him—no emotion, no tears, not one word—just looked at him. In the distance was a young man coming over to us. He asked my father if he needed help getting me back home.

"'No.' My father shook his head. My mom was starting to pull me into her arms. 'Leave her,' my father ordered.

"'This is your daughter?'

"My mom looked up at him, pleading.

"'She's been contaminated by men. I can get nothing for her now,' my father insisted.

"My mom was still pulling me against her.

"'Woman, now! You come,' my father continued to order.

"'No!' she cried.

Then my father started punching her, wherever on her head and face he could make contact with.

"'What are you doing?' the man asked, stepping

114

between them. 'I will help you get your daughter home,' the man offered.

"'She is a contaminated whore!' my father screamed.

"At the time I didn't know what *whore* meant, but I will never forget that word," Veronica whispered sadly and paused.

"The man got the strangest look on his face. 'Your daughter has been raped. That doesn't make her a whore.'

"'It does in the eyes of God,' my father insisted with a piercing look in his eyes, staring at the man and stressing his belief.

"This time he didn't ask Mom to get up. He grabbed her by her hair and tried to drag her away.

"'Let go or I will kill her!'

"I was on my knees, trying to crawl behind my mom. My father kicked me in the stomach. I hit the side of the building. I was stunned.

"The man said nothing and punched my father in the face. 'She's a child who has been raped, not a whore.' The man was angry and pointing his fingers at my father as he spoke. 'May God make you suffer as your daughter has!

"I remember my father's twisted nose. There was no blood, but his nose was laid to the side of his face, distorted and drastic.

"The man leaned down to my mom and whispered something in her ear. My mom hugged him, then looked at him through tear-filled eyes and nodded her head. That was the last time I saw my parents. The man leaned down to me as my parents started away. My mom was sobbing. His eyes were full of compassion. 'My name is Sandro. Don't worry, I won't hurt you. You will come with me, I will take care of you.' He gently pushed the hair out of my face. 'Come, let's put your pants on,' he said. He pulled my shirt down, then helped me back into the leg of my pants. He picked me up and carried me away. We met with a friend of his and got into a car. Sandro laid me in the backseat, then he climbed in on the other side and rested my head in his lap. His friend drove us to a hospital, where doctors took one look at me and started an IV. Then they gave me something for the pain. Sandro never left my side. He tried to explain everything the doctors and nurses did. They took me to an operating room. When I woke up, I remember the first thing I saw was Sandro's smiling face.

"He took me to his house. It seemed like a palace. There was a room ready and waiting for me. He came from a family with means. He had many siblings. Everyone was warm, kind, and loving. They lived in another country, a place with endless fields of grapes. Each night I didn't want him to leave, and he never did. The first night he crawled into bed beside me. I curled up next to him. I was scared, hurt, and alone in this new place. For the first week I didn't get out of bed except when I had to use the bathroom. It hurt too much to get up and walk, so Sandro carried me back and forth. When he had to leave, then one of this siblings or parents cared for me. When Sandro was next to me, I never felt alone. I felt safe. That is how it started. Not what you expected to hear."

Chevy sat there starring at Veronica with horror and held her hand over her mouth. "I'm so sorry. I had no idea." She shook her head, speechless.

"Well." Veronica shrugged. "People would bring me food. There were people that would clean. There were endless rooms that were beautiful, with gorgeous furniture, paintings, pillows, and drapes. There were vases and flowers," Veronica recalled with an excited gleam in her eyes, as though she was seeing and experiencing the wonderfulness all over again.

"For the first time in my life, I felt safe. Sandro and his family showed me nothing but kindness, unconditional love, and acceptance," Veronica said softly. "What happened was truly awful." Veronica looked at her. "Sandro's mom would tell me. "Sometimes blessings come in a disguise." She would give me big warm hugs and kiss my cheeks. His family was so wonderful, all of them. I ended up in a loving place. A strong contrast to the family I had been born into."

Chevy looked at her. "You married him…right? When did all that take place? To think about it, a person would assume he groomed you," she said, looking disgusted.

"Groomed me? I don't understand," Veronica asked.

"You were a child and you were raped. The fact that you are married to him would make a person think he was sexually messing with you," she said with big eyes.

"I was young with a man sleeping with me at night." Veronica shook her head. "He was never anything but good to me. Now that I think about it, he never pushed me. There was years that nothing happened. When I got better and felt like walking, he took me shopping. I got clothes—lots of clothes." Veronica smiled. "It was wonderful. He always allowed me next to him. I was his personal shadow. We grew very close. I loved being around him. He was fun and charming. There were times he would kiss my cheeks and give me hugs, but the whole family was warm and loving in that manner. He would even tell me that he loved me. It never went beyond that. Never," Veronica said, thinking back. "I was older when we became sexual. I began noticing him in a way I had never noticed him before. He had that clean-cut hair, his face always had stubble, and he always kept himself in shape. We had separate rooms by that time.

We married not long after that. But no, Sandro never pushed me in any way that was bad. I can't remember a time when he wasn't at my side or good to me.

# Chapter 11

Brandon walked in the door of his parents' house, bag in hand. The moment he came in out of the chilly autumn air he pulled the sleeves of his jacket from his arms and tossed it across his bag, glad he had on his cardigan. Hungry, he started down the hall for the kitchen.

One of the double doors to his father's office was cracked open a few inches. "I had no idea she was John Westen's daughter," Brandon heard him say, grabbing his attention. "I pick the pretty ones who have good resale. You've never, in all these years, had a complaint. The situation with this Chevy girl is getting out of hand. Make her go away. You know—send her home!"

Brandon swallowed hard, moving closer to the door.

"Look!" he started, in a heated tone. "I don't care what you do with her. I think we can both agree that if she's brought back she's going to talk. If she talks, there are a lot of powerful people around her who can cause us problems!"

Brandon stood listening, stunned.

"Get your own money out of her, then make her go away, never seen again."

Brandon's heart pumped hard in his chest, causing his face to turn red.

"I don't feel it will be a problem," Chris continued. "Rob is a good attorney, and if anything comes of it, I'm sure Rob can get him off. After all, there won't be a body. He had no motive, and her co-workers said Chevy was going to a yacht. None of it points to him." He paused. "What do you mean she's in transit?" He asked angrily.

Brandon pushed the door open and stood in the doorway. "What the hell have you done?!" he yelled.

His father looked up, surprised to see him. "Let me call you back," he said into the phone and hung up.

"You fuckin' bastard!" Brandon hissed, taking slow, purposeful steps into his father's office. "You sat there and let

118

the FBI interrogate me for how long? You even called Rob."
He stared at his father with rage. "How dare you play Russian
roulette with my life!"

His father looked at him with apprehension.

"You knew where Chevy was this whole time!" Brandon
continued to move toward his desk.

"Perhaps, son, it's time you knew," he said calmly.

"You're going to bring Chevy back here!" Brandon pointed
to the ground. "I know that she won't have so much as a hair
harmed on her!"

"Son, some things aren't that easy," he started delicately,
tapping the sides of his hands against the top of his desk.

"Yes, they are," Brandon shot back. "Where the fuck did
you take her?" He slammed his fist against the top of the desk.

His father gave him a stern look.

"Now!" Brandon slammed his fist down again, leaned over
the top of the desk closer to his father's face, and pushed the
phone to him. "Make the call, now! Get her back," he
demanded.

"Girls come up missing all the time. Especially girls like
Charlotte."

"Chevy. Everyone calls her Chevy," Brandon corrected him.

"What the hell kind of name is Chevy? It makes her sound
like a goddamn truck!"

Brandon grabbed the front of his father's sweater, pulling
him closer. "She's not a goddamn truck. She's my girlfriend!"
Brandon raised his eyebrows.

"She's a stripper! She's what every man wants," he barked.

"What the hell?" Brandon pulled him closer. "She's my
girlfriend." He shook him.

"She's a fuckin' stripper!"

Brandon pulled his father across the top of the desk. Papers
flew everywhere, his amber-colored drink splashed to the side,
the container of pens hit the wood floor and scattered, their
picture fell to the floor and shattered, and the phone dangled
from the side of the desk.

He let his father fall to the floor as he balled up his fist and
punched him in the side of the face.

His mother hurried in, her strand of pearls bouncing from side to side around her neck. "What is going on?!" Judy yelled, pausing just inside the doors when she saw Brandon crouched above his father, poised for another blow to his face. "He's behind all of this," Brandon yelled. The palms of his father's hands were in front of his face.

"Stop it!" Judy yelled, moving quickly to Brandon, her pearls swinging. "That's enough." She crouched down pulled on Brandon's shoulder.

"He did this!" Brandon yelled, looking at her with rage and hurt in his eyes. He waited to see her shocked reaction. "Dad did this! He took Chevy." There was no reaction. Her eyes met his with only guilt and regret.

The air whooshed from his lungs. "You knew!" he said, blinking, and stood up. His soul was crushed. "You?" He asked in a whisper.

"Brandon, why don't you sit down?" She gestured to one of the chairs.

"No, I'm not sitting down! How could you? Chevy's my girlfriend!" His voice was airy and disconnected.

His father stood up, straightening himself. "I rescue women from unpleasant circumstances," he said.

"'Get as much money out of her as you can'?" Brandon repeated. "Is this rescuing women from unpleasant circumstances? You sold her! Where the hell is she?" His anger was increasing.

"I didn't sell her."

"Brandon, sit down!" his mom ordered.

"What did you do? Where is she? She's still alive, so you get her, now!" Brandon demanded.

"Brandon," she began, hoping to calm him. "You know that your father has several business ventures. He travels a lot, and sometimes in the course of his travels, he encounters certain situations where he can offer a certain kind of assistance to people who don't have many options. Your father takes women and teenagers who have run away or otherwise have no place to go, and he sends them overseas, where they have jobs waiting for them."

"Jobs?" Brandon said with disbelief. "I can't wait to hear this! Something tells me these women aren't making tennis shoes, are they, Mother?"

"No, they aren't," she said reluctantly.

"One of the girls Chevy works with said they were on a yacht with a half dozen foreign men. This has sex trade written all over it!" Brandon kicked a chair across the room. "So while you two are trying to explain and justify sending young women and teenagers to be prostitutes in other countries, my girlfriend is somewhere being fucked by a string of men!"

"Brandon." She held out her hand, wanting to calm him.

"No," Brandon stepped back. "And the worst part is, I always knew there was something shady about him." He pointed to his father. "But you…" He put his fingers on his forehead, rubbing hard, pulling on his skin. "I thought better of you." He looked at her with disappointment.

"Look around," Chris said. "Look around at all of this. Your clothes. Your school. Who do you think pays your college tuition?" he asked, his voice getting loud.

"Apparently, prostitutes!" Brandon yelled, throwing his hands in the air.

"I worked for a lot of years to make sure all of us had a decent life."

"Off the backs of women? How many never came home? How many did you make"—he made quotation marks in the air—"go away? So how many times when I ate cereal in the morning and stared at the missing faces on the back of the milk carton were you personally responsible for it? You know what?" He pointed to his father. "I don't know where the hell you took her, but you had better bring her back here." He started for the door, then stopped short. "You have two days. Two days!" he yelled, then disappeared.

"Brandon, wait!" his father yelled.

"Brandon!" she called, almost simultaneously. "Brandon." She started out the door after him, turning the corner in time to see his back disappear out the front door, bag in hand. The door slammed behind him.

"Oh my God, Chris," she said with panic in her voice. She

put her hands over her mouth and began to tremble. He wrapped his arms around her. "Now what?"

### 

Sitting in an unmarked white moving truck a quarter mile away, two surveillance specialists were listening to Chris Roper.

They took shifts, listened, and watched six or more screens in view with the shift of an eye. "Time to make a call," the senior specialist said.

### 

"Hello," Ward answered, in a groggy voice with his head on his pillow.

"This is your friendly surveillance team."

"Yeah." Agent Ward rubbed his eyes and willed himself awake.

"I need to tell you a couple of things. First, Chris Roper was on the phone with one of the associates, the one who owns the *Apoise*—Sandro Nath. Chris wants your girl to 'go home,' as they call it." The surveillance specialist paused.

Ward sighed and turned on the light beside his bed.

"Nath, however, seems to have a different idea and told Roper that your girl Chevy is in transit."

Ward sighed again.

"However, Brandon Roper came home and overheard part of his father's conversation. I'm not sure what Brandon heard exactly, but they got into one hell of a argument. Sounded like it became physical. Judy Roper got involved, and Brandon stormed out."

"Crap!" Ward groaned.

### 

Sandro sat at his desk, staring at a fixed spot while tapping his finger against the top of his desk in fast repetition, contemplating.

He moved forward in his chair to the computer and clicked on the search engine. He typed in *missing woman United States*. Instantly, he saw result after result in big letters: MISSING: CHARLOTTE WESTEN. Some sites just had a name; other sites offered pictures. He clicked on the first site with a picture of Charlotte Westen. There before him was the Chevy he knew, her smiling face, long wavy brown hair, and sparkling eyes. His heart felt as if it would stop in his chest. He forced himself to read several of the websites, which clearly spelled out she was not the normal girl they thought they had snatched. The sooner he passed Chevy on to the next person or got her back to the States, the better.

He clicked on another website. The name Brandon Roper seemed to leap off the page. Sandro's eyes shifted to the name and began reading, disturbed to find that Chevy's boyfriend, Brandon Roper, was held for questioning by the FBI.

### 

A few miles from his parents' house, Brandon stopped at a gas station, pulled out all the money the ATM would allow, filled up on gas, and grabbed a coffee and a hot dog. Walking up to the register, he glanced down at the magazines that filled the front wall under the counter and did a double-take. "You have got to be shitting me!" he said out loud, stunned and staring.

There on the magazine racks were Chevy and him drunk in New Orleans. All of a sudden the odd things around the house that were out of place when he came back from his fun-filled thirteen hours of interrogation made sense. Someone had been in the house—one of those pesky reporters.

"Will that be it for you?" the man behind the counter asked.

Brandon gave him a blank look as he set the hot dog and coffee down on the counter. He picked up two magazines that had horrid pictures of him and Chevy on the front. "Here. These too," he said as he tossed the magazines on the counter beside the coffee and hot dog.

He got back into his car and typed RUDLE MILLS, KENTUCKY, in his GPS. He pulled out of the gas station and took a drink of his coffee with the sound of the GPS talking in the background.

### 

John lay in bed with the moonlight shining in through the window. He was wide wake, staring out the window, his mind racing. He thought for a moment about taking some of Ruthie's Xanax. Maybe then he could sleep. He looked over. She was sound asleep.

For some reason the moonlight seemed overly bright and intense. He pushed the covers back and sat on the side of the bed with his feet against the soft fibers of the area rug. He leaned over and rested his elbows on top of his knees and his forehead against the heels of his hands. Ruthie's words ate at him. He wondered exactly how much of this was his fault. *Have I been too hard on Chevy?*

With creaky-sounding knees he stood up and shuffled to the windows. He stood there in his boxer briefs, looking into the night sky. The moon seemed like a bright halogen headlight in an otherwise black sky. As he looked at the grayish spots on the moon, he remembered all the times he told his pint-sized Chevy that the moon was made of cheese. She would giggle and snuggle into her pillow with her fluffy covers under her arms. Her wavy hair flowed over her pillow in all directions. She would reach her hand to her father's nose, gently squeezing the end, wiggling it back and firth, and say, "Silly daddy, the moon is not made of cheese." Her cute little smile and sparkling eyes were unforgettable.

His blue eyes would get big. "What do you mean? How do you know?" he would ask.

"Because it would be fuzzy like the cheese Grandma gets out of her refrigerator. Yuck!" She would stick her tongue out, making a face.

"So how do you know the moon isn't the kind of cheese that doesn't get green fuzzies?"

"Cause mommy said so." She would giggle.

"Mommy said so," he would repeat slowly, tickling her sides.

The memory was vivid in his mind. He let it dissolve into times past and slide back into the filing cabinet of his memory. His eyes wanted to well. He reached up and touched the end of his nose as he stared up at the night sky and into the brightness of the moon. "Where are you, Chevy?" he muttered.

### ###

Sandro was sitting at his desk, pondering what he wanted to do.

124

Veronica walked into his study, her hair up and her long dress flowing behind her. She sat down in a fluffy chair across from him and sipped a cup of hot tea. "I think we should let Chevy go to Granada with me to drop off the children," she said casually, taking another sip.

Sandro paused, and leaned back in his chair, thinking. "You're very fond of her," he commented, watching her reaction.

A pleasant smile came across her face. "I am. She is very sweet. As much as I love you, I like having another female around I can talk to. You and I have a wonderful relationship, but there are some things that..." She paused and looked down, like she was thinking about the wording she wanted to use, seeming somehow sad.

He pushed his chair away from the desk. "My love, come," he said, motioning for her to sit on his lap.

She walked around the desk and he opened his arms. She sat on his lap, put her arm around his neck, and looked at him lovingly. The cup of tea sat in her hand and rested against the top of her leg.

"You look sad. Are you not happy?" he asked.

She set her tea on the desk. "Of course I'm happy." She touched her hand to his cheek and looked into his eyes. "You have been nothing but good to me. What's wrong? You're bothered."

"No, no, you first. Please. Why do you have a lost look when we talk about Chevy?" He wanted to understand.

She paused for a moment. "Hmm...Well, the idea of Chevy leaving does make me feel lonely. I don't want her to go," she admitted.

"You need the companionship of another female?"

"Do I need the companionship? I'm not sure that I need it, but I will miss her when she goes."

He smiled at her. "Then you need another female. I'm surprised you haven't taken a liking to some of the other women before now."

Her face twisted into a sour expression. "The other women." She shivered. "All these years, the other women have left much

125

to be desired."

He bobbed his head from side to side and chuckled. "That's very true. I'm sorry, my love." He looked at her apologetically and wrapped his arms around her.

"Why in the world are you apologizing?" she asked sweetly.

"Because all this time you've been longing for another woman to be friends with, and I never noticed. The whole point of a relationship is to work together, function as one, and do our best every day to love and cherish each other and make each other's life better. We are supposed to do everything in our power to ensure each other's wants, desires, and dreams come true. If you need a female friend, I have failed you," he said remorsefully.

She looked into his sparkling light eyes, smiled, and kissed his lips. "I love you, sweetie. You've been nothing but good to me. I didn't realize I was missing anything, or I would have told you. Most of the women leave much to be desired. Chevy is different."

"Yes, she is different. Then, you trust her?" he asked, needing to be sure.

"I do." She paused, making an uncertain face. "I hope I'm not incorrect about her. What am I missing?"

"There's something I need to tell you," he said reluctantly.

She pulled her arm from around his neck and put both of her hands on his cheeks.

"I got a call. It seems there is a problem with Chevy," he said with heaviness.

"A problem?" She waited, shifting her eyes back and forth.

"It seems her real name is Charlotte Westen. She comes from a wealthy American family that owns a chain of stores. The fact that she is missing is making national news."

She let out a breath of disappointment, pulled her hands from his cheeks, and squeezed her eyes shut. "And now what?"

"Chris wanted us to send her home but—"

"Send her home…" she repeated with a horrified look.

"Something in the center of my soul tells me not to." He stared in front of him. "How many women have come through here? Sending them home seemed both humane to them and

126

the world. One less strung-out mess the world had to deal with. Chevy, on the other hand…I can't send her home, or I would have done it already. There is just something about that girl that I can't quite put my finger on. I told Chris she's in transit, to the Ukraine."

Veronica nodded her head. "All right. That can be several weeks to a month, depending on the ships available and where the person is going." It was commonly arranged for women to be conveniently lost in transport. If anyone from any country or port ever questioned where they were, it was easy to explain that the person disappeared somewhere in route. "So what do you want to do with her?"

"You truly feel you can trust her?"

"As sure as I can be. Chevy seems trustworthy and loyal to her friends and family. It's how she talks and speaks about people. When Jada went home, she heard the shots and covered me. Her first reaction was to protect me."

"All right. But what about the children? That's a different situation entirely."

"I'm as sure as I can be, based on what I've seen. Could she turn? Maybe. But I think she's more solid than that."

Sandro nodded. "Then take her with you to Granada, drop off the children, and put her on a cruse ship back to the States."

She paused, unsure. "We have never done anything like this before. You are getting her a passport?"

"I'll make one appear. This is about to blow up, and I don't want to be part of it." He looked at her. "I was on a website reading about a missing girl from the States. It was Chevy. Not only does she come from a very wealthy family, but her boyfriend was detained by the FBI for questioning."

"The FBI's involved?" She took in a deep breath and let it out slowly.

"That's not all of it. Chevy's boyfriend—you're never going to believe this." Sandro shook his head.

"Chevy's boyfriend is Chris Roper's son, Brandon." He waited for her reaction.

Surprise crossed her face. "My, my…that is no good." She paused, taking it in. "So his son had no idea what Chris does,

127

or does he know and helped?

"His son had no idea. Brandon was the one who reported her missing, then was questioned by the FBI. Chris was telling me to send her home, then there was yelling in the background. Chris suddenly hung up." Sandro looked worried.

"Sweetheart." He took hold of her hand and rubbed the back of it with his thumb. "I've reached a point in my life where I'm questioning what we're doing and why. I honestly feel that I could lose everything with this one girl. You are what I want." He held her hand tighter. "I never want to be without you, or lose you. Knowing that this girl is making national news makes me realize what is truly important. We have more than enough money for the rest of our lives. I don't want to spend the rest of my life on yachts, ships, or in ports. Let's find a place to live, buy a house, and live out rest of our life. I always wanted a child or two. Would you like children?"

She looked deeply into his eyes. "Yes, I would. I always thought one day we would have kids."

"Let's get the children to Granada, send Chevy back to the States, and buy a house somewhere."

She nodded. "That would be great. I love you." She put her hands on his cheeks, looked into his eyes, and kissed him. "I'll follow you to the ends of the earth. I don't want to live without you."

# Chapter 12

The sun was coming up as Brandon drove slowly past a line of new vans with reporters sitting in lawn chairs on top of them. Some reporters were wrapped in fluffy sleeping bags to stay warm. Their cameras were on tripods, waiting to snap pictures. As he approached the Westens' long drive, reporters began moving from their chairs, snapping pictures, shouting a barrage of questions, quickly surrounding his car. He turned into the long drive, leaving the reporters at the road. In the distance was a huge home that looked every bit like the Westen's hunting stores, with pillars cut from big logs, antler lights, and more antlers at the top of each pillar that held up the roof. He took a sip of his fresh coffee and looked at the Mardi Gras beads that hung from his rearview mirror. The time he and Chevy spent in New Orleans was flashing through his mind.

When he reached the front of the house he took a moment to sit in the car with his elbow against the top of the door. He covered his mouth with his hand and pondered if this was the right thing to do. He got out of the car and stood looking at the house. From the end of the long drive the wraparound porch hadn't seemed so large. As he stepped onto it he realized its size. The porch had tables, sofas, large potted shrubs, and two French doors.

He stood at the front door, debating. He could hear Chevy's endless words about how protective and unreasonably stubborn her father was rattling through his mind.

###

Ruthie was laying on the sofa in the great room reading. "You're a fucking bitch!" Ripley's father-in-law told her as he laughed and snarled, the devil dancing in his eyes. "Give me time. I will get rid of you." He chuckled. "My son will believe me, not you." She could see the evil on his face.

She had read this part of the novel a dozen times. Each time she read it she wasn't able to focus or comprehend the words

129

any better than the time before. She stretched against the leather and looked past the novel at the wood beams of the ceiling, then shifted her eyes to the huge moose head above the fireplace. She was tired of waiting and doing nothing.

The doorbell rang.

Happy for the break, she set down the novel, got up, and headed for the door.

###

The door opened, and before him stood a woman in a black shirt and blue jeans who was obviously Chevy's mom, a well-kept woman who looked much younger than her forty-some years with light eyes, full lips, and a sexy smile. Her long blondish hair was darker underneath and full and wavy like Chevy's.

"You're Mrs. Westen, right?" Brandon asked.

"Yes. And you're Brandon." She smiled. "I recognize you from pictures Chevy sent me."

"Yes, I'm Brandon Roper," he said politely, with an edge of apprehension. "I need to talk with you and your husband about Chevy." He sounded troubled. He was wearing the same cream cardigan sweater from the night before.

"Please come in." She ushered him in, seeming happy to see him.

He stepped in and noticed a giant caribou head hanging on the wall.

"We can sit in here," she said, leading him into the great room. "Please sit down." She picked up her phone. "I'm letting my husband know you're here," she told him as she dialed. "Hey, babe…I need you to stop what you're doing. I'm sitting in the living room with Brandon…Okay, love you, too." She looked at Brandon. "John's on the back part of the property. He'll be here in a few minutes." She set her phone down on the coffee table.

"You have an impressive home." He looking around.

"Thank you. My husband and I built most of it ourselves. Well…We had most of the structure built, but everything else we did. We hung the doors, did all the bathrooms and plumbing. We did some of the windows, but not the high

130

ones." She pointed. "We did the kitchen ourselves, too. I like woodworking, so I made some of the furniture you see." She smiled proudly, watching him look at the moose head. "Like it?"

He looked at her, then back up at the moose. "I've never seen a moose up close. Is this a normal size? It's huge."

"I shot that one." She smiled. "It's a decent size—average. You look tired."

He looked down at the floor. "It's been a long week, and I had an incredibly upsetting night."

"Did you come from campus?" she asked, curiously.

"No, I went home. I thought I would go home for a few days, rest, study, and try to focus on classwork, it didn't go as I expected. I ended up driving all night to get here."

"Where do your parents live?"

"Wake Forest, North Carolina."

"That's a drive. You look like you could use some food. Are you hungry?"

"No, thank you. I'm not sure I can eat."

"When's the last time you ate? I was getting ready to make some breakfast. How about I make some for you? I'm a good cook. Come on into the kitchen with me."

Brandon followed Ruthie to the kitchen and took a seat at the counter.

She pulled one side of a double refrigerator open. "What would you like to drink? We have several kinds of soda, milk, chocolate milk, orange juice, tea—both iced tea and hot tea— coffee, beer, and grape Kool-Aid," she said. "The beer and Kool-Aid would be my husband's personal favorites. He's a child trapped in a grown man's body." She winked. "So what'll it be?"

"How about water."

"Bottle or tap?"

"Whichever is the closest."

She grabbed a large mason jar from one of the cabinets and filled it with water from the refrigerator. "Stop me if this doesn't sound good," she said with a smile, setting the jar on the counter in front of him. She opened the refrigerator and pulled out a package of bacon.

He began to hear a rumble growing louder. He turned in the chair and looked out the French doors. Slowly, an older red tractor rolled across the backyard just beyond the patio and into his view. Instantly, he remembered a photo he and Chevy had put in a frame and placed on the dresser in their bedroom. It was a photo of Chevy in cowboy boots, jeans, a red bikini top that looked like a bandana, and a cowboy hat, sitting on that red tractor. Her legs were crossed, with her feet by the steering wheel, and her head back. He loved that photo of her.

Now, there before him was that red tractor and Chevy's father. John Westen was a tall man with huge arms, broad shoulders, and light blond hair. Deep lines in his face made his serious expression seem that much more serious. He reminded Brandon of the Marlboro Man, but without the cigarette hanging from his mouth. When he stood from the tractor he appeared taller and broader than Brandon originally thought. He wore jeans and well-worn work boots that looked a little like cowboy boots. He reached to turn off the engine, then stepped from the tractor and onto the patio, pulling the light gray work gloves from his hands.

Ruthie pulled out a big pan from one of the cabinets.

John stepped into the kitchen and looked at Brandon with a sparkle in his eyes and a half smile. "So, you're Brandon!" he said, taking a few steps toward him.

Brandon stood up and shook his hand. "Yes, I'm Brandon. It's nice to meet you."

"You've got blood on your sleeve."

"My father and I had a disagreement."

"My wife says you might be able to help us find our daughter."

Brandon sat down, seeming lost. "This isn't easy for me. I want you both to understand that I love your daughter. I want her found, more than anything." He tapped his index finger on the counter. "I'm not sure what kind of trouble I might be in."

John leaned against the counter, crossed one leg over the other, and crossed his arms in front of him, getting comfortable and listening.

132

"My father is behind this. Somehow. Incredibly. I don't really understand it, but he knows where Chevy is." He looked at Ruthie, then John, waiting for their reaction.

Ruthie looked stunned and hopeful at the same time.

John's expression grew more serious. The deep vertical lines between his eyes grew deeper as he spoke. "What do you mean, your father's behind this? And if he is, why are you here telling us? Isn't this information for the FBI?" he asked coldly.

"Look," Brandon said. "I want her back here, and I want her safe." He took a deep breath. "I went home to my parents' last night. I thought I would take a few days away from school. I needed to write a few papers, and in order to do that, I need to be able to focus. I'm climbing the walls not knowing where she is. When I got home, I overheard my father talking to someone on the phone about how she's John Westen's daughter. My father didn't know she was someone important. He thought she was just a stripper. He was talking about getting his money out of her, then making her go away—"

"That's what the disagreement was about?" John asked.

"I never really knew exactly what my father did. He travels and talks with a lot of different people. He has a couple of different businesses. Or at least that's what he said. It ends up, he's trafficking women. I don't know how much involvement he has, but I'll speculate based on the way he was talking that it's substantial." He looked at them.

John looked at the floor, shaking his head. "Un-fucking-believable!" He moaned, then half chuckled and stared off into the distance. "Your dad never met Chevy?"

Brandon shook his head and let out a frustrated laugh. "No. I never took many of my friends home, especially the girls." He paused, thinking about it. "I can't tell you why, other than I knew from a fairly young age that something wasn't right. Something about my father seemed…off. I had nothing to base that feeling on. My father puts up an excellent front. But something nagged at me. Then, earlier this year, I went looking for my birth certificate in my father's files when he was out of town. I know, I should keep it myself, but I've just never needed it before, so I never took it from my parents' house. As

I was digging around, I found some files that looked out of place. There were company names I didn't recognize, and all kinds of account numbers. I jotted down anything I found to be odd or intriguing. And I copied some letters that didn't look right."

"So, let me get this straight." John shifted against the edge of the counter as he uncrossed his feet and recrossed them with the opposite leg on top. "You're telling me that your father had no idea who Chevy was and just happened to select the one girl who's your girlfriend. You're telling me your father's trafficking women, which you supposedly knew nothing about. Yet you suspected your father was up to something shady, so you started writing down account numbers, copying certain letters? You see how this sounds doubtful? Is it possible that you're being just as shady as your dear old daddy? The apple doesn't fall far from the tree, does it?" John shook his head and started to chuckle. "So why the hell did you come to my house?"

"John!" Ruthie half shouted at him.

John quickly looked at her. "I'm just pointing out a few facts."

Ruthie glared at him. "No, you're not. You're being a jerk!"

Brandon looked back and forth between them uncomfortably. "I'm here because I want Chevy back. The only people I could think of who want her back as much as I do is you guys." He looked at them. "Not the FBI. You guys. I also need to tell someone what's going on. I don't know what kind of danger I might be in." He paused, looking back and forth between them. "Would my father try to kill me to keep me quiet? I'm not sure." He looked worried. "Now that I know my father's responsible for a percentage of the faces on the back of milk cartons—still missing—never found—would he do something to me to keep me quiet?" He shrugged, unsure. "I don't want Chevy's to be the next face I see on my milk carton. I have a serious problem with that."

John stood there against the counter looking a him, his jaw clenched tight.

Ruthie broke the silence. "You look like you could use a

shower, get cleaned up, change clothes, and relax. Food will be waiting for you when you are done. John will bring your stuff in from your car. You'll stay with us. We have an extra bedroom with a full bath, so you will feel right at home. You're not allergic to animals, are you?"

Brandon smiled. "If I were allergic, I'd be in trouble with all the animals you have on the walls. Thank you, that's very kind, but I can find another place to stay."

"No. This is where you belong," Ruthie replied quickly.

"Honey," John said abruptly. "Don't you think it's a little odd that Chevy has been dating him for over a year and we've heard nothing about him?"

"No, as a matter of fact I don't. She's told *me* all about him," she said sharply.

"How do we know this is actually Chevy's boyfriend and that anything he says is true?"

"John, I've seen Brandon's picture before. Chevy loves and trusts him. And so should we." She forced a smile and turned to Brandon. "Come on. I'll show you which room is yours."

"Honey!" John rudely cut her off.

She took a deep breath and stared at him. "Not now."

"*I* haven't seen so much as a picture of him! *I* don't know that he's who he says he is."

"Trust me," Ruthie snapped.

"You don't know!"

She walked past him and harshly opened the drawer. She pulled out the magazines Crysta had left and slapped them on the counter beside him.

John peered down at the top magazine, the one in which Chevy had a drink in her hand and Brandon looked angry . The skin of his forehead pulled back slightly as his eyes enlarged.

"I really don't need a shower," Bandon said uncomfortably.

Ruthie looked at John, wanting to convince him.

"Listen to him!" John's voice started to rise as he repositioned himself against the counter, seeming to brace for an argument.

"John, stop!"

"No, I'm not going to stop. You tell me how it is they've

been dating for a year and I haven't seen or heard anything about him."

"Honey, please stop." A pleading look replaced her piercing stare.

"Let Brandon here tell us!"

"Honey!" Her voice got louder.

"Let him answer the goddamn question!"

Suddenly her voice got deeper. "John, that's enough!"

"Have him answer us," he demanded. He turned to Brandon. "What's your major?"

"You mean my graduate work? Law. International law. I have a year left." Brandon stared into the air for a moment and laughed to himself. "Oddly, it was my father who said that international law has very few attorneys and it would be lucrative. One of these days I would like to have a wife and kids. I need to be able to support them, so international law didn't sound so bad. Now, I realize my father was grooming me to deal with his legal issues."

John stood quietly for a moment.

Ruthie broke the silence. "I knew about Brandon. You know this. Remember, we had this conversation when Mike and Ken came to the house and told us Chevy was missing. She told me about Brandon six months ago. She didn't want you to know because she felt you would fly off the handle and be unreasonable. I just can't imagine why she would have such a strong opinion about your reaction," she barked sarcastically.

"When have I ever been unreasonable?" John asked with a laugh and shook his head.

"You aren't hearing me. You're being unreasonable right now."

"I hear everything. The problem is, you haven't said anything, and when you try you don't make any goddamn sense. Maybe if you had half a brain in your head."

Her mouth hung open. "That's great, babe! Show Brandon what an unreasonable ass you can be, and give him a perfect example of why Chevy wouldn't bring him home to meet you. That's great, honey! Perfect! Do you feel like a man now? Because you should feel like the jackass of the year." She stared at him.

"You still haven't answered my question," John said with a belittling laugh.

"Knock your fuckin' shit off!" she told him.

"You know what, Mrs. Westen," Brandon said. "Thank you for the hospitality. You're a sweetheart. John…" Brandon walked over and held out his hand. "It's been an experience meeting you. I need to go. I can see why Chevy didn't want me to meet you. I'll show myself out." He headed for the door.

Ruthie started after him. "You really are welcome to stay. He's just upset about Chevy. Not only is his little girl missing, but he has to accept that she was stripping to pay her bills, which he has responsible for. Now he was just told she was taken by your father. I'm so sorry you had to see that side of him. My husband really is a nice guy under those layers."

"I don't know what I was thinking. Chevy told me how difficult he was. I just had no idea he was so far beyond difficult. My father and I got into a pretty bad fight last night. I won't be going home or back to school. It's my understanding that my father isn't the one who took her, but he had her taken. I assume by one of his business partners." He stuck his hand in his pocket and pulled out a folded piece of paper. "I stopped at a rest stop last night and wrote down some of the phone numbers, addresses, and a few accounts from what I found. I don't know what my father is going to do now that I know he's involved." He pulled out a pen out and jotted something on the paper. "If you need me, here's my number." He handed the paper to her.

She nodded. "All right." She noticed his parents' address on the paper before she stuck it into her pocket.

### 

She stood in the doorway and watched him drive away, then let out a sigh of frustration as she shut the door and went back to the kitchen. She grabbed his glass and put it in the sink, saying nothing.

"Say it!" John said, leaning against the counter.

"Say what?" she snipped, as she wiped down the counter top.

"What's on your mind?"

"Nothing I wish to discuss," she replied with her lips squeezed together.

"Spill it!"

"There is nothing to spill." She finally looked at him.

"There's something." He stood with his hand on his hip, waiting.

"Nope." She rinsed the glass and hastily stuck it in the dishwasher.

"Damn it, woman!" he barked.

"You're a bastard!" she hissed as she turned to him, pointing her finger.

"Me?! How the hell did I become the bastard? I'm not the one who kidnapped our daughter, nor am I the genius who thought being a stripper would be a brilliant idea."

"Is this where we're going?" She stopped and looked at him. "Now you're going into arrogant mode." Her hands waved in the air on either side of her body.

"How the hell am I arrogant?" He chuckled in amazement, with his head twisting from side to side.

"I'm not doing this with you." She smacked the washcloths on the counter beside her.

"You're the one standing there with a problem, not me. Let's get this out in the open! How am I arrogant? That's what I'd like to know."

"You did this."

"How the hell do you figure that?" He laughed.

"You cut her off, and then expected her to pick herself up financially on her own. How could she possibly do that? How?"

"You're goddamn right I cut her off. She went on a twenty-some-thousand-dollar shopping spree, because she needed new clothes. We have clothes that we've had for ten years. That damn girl doesn't need a new wardrobe every fuckin' year."

"You're right. She doesn't need a new wardrobe every year. We got everything in the world for that girl. Did you take the time to go over that with her? Did you talk to her about it? Did you share your viewpoint? Did you even stop for a moment to understand her viewpoint? Do you know that some of the money she spent was on utilities, gas, food, and tuition, not just shopping. You're looking at the end number and not breaking down where the money went."

He stood for a moment, listening, knowing she wasn't finished.

Ruthie continued, "There isn't any other viewpoint other than yours—ever!" She sliced her hand through the air.

"How does any of this make me responsible for her decision to run around in front of people naked?"

"You send her off to a prestigious college, like Harvard, where all the other students have life handed to them. Now the problem is amplified because she needs to fit in with all the other girls, whose fathers hand them life on a credit card."

"You can't tell me that all the other girls come from money. There are kids there scraping by because they want better for themselves. Harvard has scholarships, so don't stand there and try to tell me that bullshit!"

"The majority of kids come from money," Ruthie tried to explain. "You sent her to Harvard so she'll have more opportunity. That also means she needs to fit in! You won't get your money's worth from an Ivy League education if you can't network with the best. You can't be in those circles unless you have the right tools. Clothes are one of those tools. You gave her no parameters and just quietly expected she would read your mind and understand your expectations. Unbelievable! Absolutely unbelievable!" She turned away, too angry to look at him any longer.

"Chevy's not stupid," he said loudly.

She turned back to him. "No, she's not, but you also need to tell her what you want and expect."

"Chevy should know I expect her not to run off to a strip club."

"Why not? It's what the other girls do who have to scrape by." Ruthie looked at him. "How do you think they scrape by?"

"Look, stupid, you need to get a clue!"

Her eyes widened. "What did you just say to me?" she said calmly. "I will not ever be talked to like that." She turned and walked away.

He walked after her, his boots thumping against the hard wood floor. "You're going to stand there and try to tell me that all the other girls who don't have their parents handing them money are stripping?"

"Yes, they are. But there's a difference between them. They have instinct, and neither you nor I have ever shown Chevy anything different than 'Here's your card.'" Ruthie walked into their bedroom to the closet where the large gun safe was. She twisted the combination and opened it.

"Just because I wanted her to have a little better opportunity than I did, I'm a bad father?"

"No." She tensed, frustrated. "I've never said you were a bad father." She looked around the gun safe for the right box of ammo. "You're good to all of our kids. You have a tendency to be a little hard on them, while I have a tendency to be a little soft. So, between the two of us, I think we're pretty good parents. But you have to explain your thoughts, ideas, and viewpoints—that you need to improve on." She pulled out a small box of .22 shells and closed the safe.

John pointed to his chest. "I'm not the one who did any of this, and I'm sure as hell not the one who encouraged her to go strip." His face reddened.

Ruthie turned to him. "Yes, you did!" She pointed at him. "Not directly—indirectly, but you did." She walked back into the kitchen with John on her heels.

"How the hell do you figure that?"

She stopped and turned to him. "Do you toss a toddler into a pool without swimming lessons? Do you take a swimmer ten miles out to sea then drop them off and say swim back? No, you don't! You don't do either of those without proper training. If you're a good swimmer and you always have your children at the pool with you, do you assume they will just be able to jump in and swim like you? Some kids could do it. Most can't. They need to be taught. That's what you did to Chevy, and now you're upset with her because she hasn't met all the expectations you didn't share with her." She gave him a disappointed look. "Shame on you." She grabbed her purse and stuffed the box of shells in.

"Where the hell are you going?"

She started for the garage door. "While you and your ego are here busy being right, I'm going to get our daughter."

"Where the hell is that?" He grabbed her upper arm to slow her down.

"If you would've shut your mouth and not been an ass to Brandon, then perhaps you would know." She tugged her arm out of his hand, turned, and headed out the garage door.

John stood there.

"North Carolina, a town called Wake Forest," she said testily.

### 

John's jaw was clenched tight, the anger clear on his face as he shut the door, knowing she would stop and come back in. He waited. He heard her truck start with the distinctive rumble of the engine. He continued to wait. Then he heard the truck back out of the garage. Stunned, he pulled the door open in time to see her put her pewter-colored extended cab truck in drive and speed away. Her wide, knobby tires were a streak of color shrinking down their long drive. His stomach twisted with anxiety.

He grabbed his keys, hopped into his own truck, and took off after her.

### 

Ruthie roared onto the interstate with the sun in front of her. She picked up her phone and dialed Crysta. The phone rang as she shot past the other vehicles like they were standing still.

### 

"Hello?" Crysta answered, standing by her desk at home with business files in hand.

"Hey, sweetie," Ruthie began, sounding rushed. "I want to let you know that Brandon, Chevy's boyfriend, came by the house this morning. I'm on my way to his parents' home in Wake Forest, North Carolina. If you get a call to come bail me out of jail, please do so."

"Ruthie," Crysta said slowly, setting the files down and removing what she was doing from her mind. "Are you all right? What happened?" She picked up her coffee cup and took a sip.

Ruthie hesitated for a moment. "Brandon showed up at our door and told us his father was behind Chevy's disappearance. John was a jerk to him, so, of course, he left. I'm so mad at John I want to hurt him. I left him standing in the kitchen. He always wants to be right, so he can stand there by himself and be right. I, however, need to go get my daughter."

Crysta could hear the distress in her voice—Ruthie was sweet, loving, kind, and giving, and she had the patience of a saint, but she could also be fierce. "Where is she?" Crysta asked. "Why don't you let he FBI agents get her? Come over. We can have some coffee. Have you had your coffee this morning? Or we can just go straight for the Kahlua and relax for a while," Crysta said, attempting to lighten the situation.

Instead of a giggle or small laugh, Ruthie's voice was still flat. "No," she said quickly. "I have to go. Know I love you. Keep my boys safe. If it comes to it—bail me out."

Alarmed, Crysta kept talking. "Ruthie, what else did Brandon say?"

"Wake Forest, North Carolina. Brandon's father's name is Chris Roper," Ruthie recited, as she glanced down at the piece of paper Brandon had handed her.

Crysta grabbed a pen and jotted down the information as fast as she could as Ruthie rattled off an address. "Ruthie, you need to stop. I will come get you. We can go together."

"I have to go." Ruthie hung up.

Crysta stood at her desk with her hand over her mouth. "Oh my God," she said aloud, looking around, not sure what to do next. Ruthie wasn't thinking clearly any longer. As she was standing there, her phone rang again. She felt a momentary spring of relief. "Hello?" she answered, not looking at the caller ID.

"Crysta?" John asked.

Crysta's heart sank. "John, what the hell did you say to Ruthie?"

"I didn't say a goddamn thing."

"Bullshit!" Crysta shot back. "You were a jerk, weren't

you?"

"No, I wasn't a fuckin' jerk. Maybe you're the jerk for jumping to conclusions because you don't know. That fucking Brandon showed up and said his father was behind Chevy's disappearance, so Ruthie left."

"John." Crysta paused. "I know Ruthie. How she's put up with you all these years, I have never understood. But I will tell you what: if I have to bail her out of jail, I will have your ass! You need to quit being an egotistical jerk and be the husband that she deserves, one who will cooperate with her."

"She's the one who left."

"Yeah, because you were being a jerk. She didn't want to fight with you, so she was quiet, right?"

"She wasn't hearing me."

"No. Ruthie was stroking your ego like she always does. She was quiet, right?"

"She wasn't hearing me," he repeated.

"No!" Crysta said. "Ruthie was stroking your ego, like she always does, and let you think whatever you wanted." She paused. "You need to come back to reality! Do you have any idea how many people think some of the things you say and do are dumb? But instead of saying something to the man who can never be wrong, they're quiet, allowing you to think whatever you want. They stroke that ego."

"No they don't." He chuckled. "You weren't there. You don't know."

"Really, is that the best you can say to me? I've known you way too long to buy in to that bullshit. Maybe other people who want to be your friends will pat your back and tell you what you want to hear, but I'm not those people. Save your bullshit for them. Ruthie's on her way to Wake Forest, North Carolina."

"Why the hell is she on her way to North Carolina?"

"Well, Mr. I-Know-Everything, that's where Brandon's parents live. She gave me their address. Do you want me to text it to you so you can pull it up on GPS?"

### 

Roaring down the interstate, Ruthie picked up the phone and

143

dialed information.

"I need Wake Forest, North Carolina, the non-emergency number for the police department," she said, then paused while she waited on the operator to find the number. She glanced down at her speedometer. "Just go ahead and connect me," she told the operator, then waited while the phone ring. "Yes, I have a question. Who is the chief of police?" She picked up the paper that Brandon have given her and put it against the center of the steering wheel to write.

Her head pinched her phone to her shoulder. "And can you tell me who the town manager is?" She jotted it down. "Okay, thank you so much. I appreciate it…You have a great day." She hit End, set the on the center console, turned up the music, and kept roaring down the interstate for North Carolina.

# Chapter 13

Somewhere in the Atlantic, Chevy and Veronica were walking down a hall on the lower level of the yacht. For a moment, Chevy thought she heard the chatter of children. As quickly as she thought it, she dismissed it.

Veronica stopped in front of a door, reached for the knob, then paused and turned to Chevy. "Before I open the door, I need to prepare you," she said with reluctance.

"For what?" She squinted, waiting.

"There is an aspect that's not the most pleasant. I don't like it, I didn't create it, and I can't stop it. Unfortunately, I have to go along with it. You know what…" She looked down and turned back to the door. "I'll show you and explain later." She opened the door.

There was a magnificent yellow room that contained five canopy beds with lacy white comforters and pictures of carousels. In the corner was a small kids' table with stools in primary colors. Sitting at the table were three little girls. Two of the girls appeared to be American; the other Middle Eastern.

Veronica walked in and turned, waiting on Chevy's response.

The completely stunned expression on Chevy's face said everything.

The girls looked up from their coloring books, ran to Veronica, and hugged her. "Chi! Chi!" they said with excitement.

*Chi,* Chevy thought. *So Veronica doesn't want the girls to know her name.* She wondered if Veronica was her real name or if that, too, was just a name for Chevy to call her.

"Ladies." Veronica looked at the girls, making eye contact with each of them, ensuring she had their attention. "This is Chevy."

"Hello, Chevy!" the girls recited with wide smiles, sparkling eyes, and little voices.

Chevy squatted next to them. "It's nice to meet all of you."

"Would you like to color?" one of the girls offered politely.

Veronica glowed warmly. "I brought Chevy to meet you. We don't have time for coloring. I believe that Miss Ginger is bringing you breakfast in a few minutes," she told them.

The girls cheered. One pulled on Veronica's pant leg to get her attention. "Chi, will you read us the story about the rabbit?" she asked, looking up with hopeful eyes.

"Of course I will, when I come back," Veronica told her sweetly. "I will be back later. Miss Ginger is going to bring you food, then we'll play dress-up. We get to go to another ship later tonight," she told them, sounding excited.

The girls smiled with delight as they gazed up at her adoringly.

"All right. I will be back. Maybe Miss Chevy will be able to come and play dress-up also." She pulled the door shut behind her and Chevy as they left.

"These are children!" Chevy said with horror, keeping her volume low, waiting for some justifiable reason why they were on the yacht.

"Yes." She looked into Chevy's eyes.

"Tell me they aren't going to—"

"Yes," Veronica said and paused. "You have it right. They are part of the trade." She crinkled her lips together and looked down at the floor.

"They are babies! The one looks no more than five," she whispered.

Veronica pulled Chevy beside the wall. "They're children, children who are meant to be loved by mothers and fathers, but these children either have no parents or were sold by their parents." Her eyes searched Chevy's face.

"What parent would sell their child, especially into this?"

"Most of them are orphans," Veronica explained. "I don't like it, but this is the way it works. Different men like different things, and some like them young. Keep your mouth shut and cooperate. It's in your best interest. Cooperate."

"They're children," Chevy protested.

"Yes, they are children, and they stopped being children the moment their parents died or sold them. I don't like it any more

146

than you do. That was my reaction when I found out. Regardless, whether I like it or not, it exists and will continue. There will always be some man somewhere who wants children. I can make all the arguments I want, I can even die trying to stop it, but there will be someone happy to take my place and keep their mouth shut. I know that as long as I am here, I can be good to every child I see. Other people I have met never show these children a shred of compassion. So I can either fight the system and lose, or make it as pleasant for them as possible. They aren't children—not anymore."

Chevy looked at her, speechless, then closed her eyes.

Veronica put her hand on Chevy's arm and rubbed it. "Are you all right?"

Chevy nodded, looking at the floor. "Yeah, I'm all right."

"I know it's a lot to take in." Veronica started to lead them down the hall.

"Where are we going?"

"I need to get the kids ready."

"Ready? I thought Miss Ginger was going to bring them food?"

Veronica gave her a long look and didn't say anything.

Chevy searched her face. "What do you mean, ready?" she asked slowly, not sure she wanted to know the answer.

"Ginger is going to bring them food. Then I'm going to tell them about sex, show them what sex is, and prep them so it doesn't hurt so much the first time."

"They're children," Chevy said, dismayed.

"Since you have so much concern, why don't you help me prep them?"

Chevy's eyes widened. "How do you prep them?"

"I tell them about sex—explain it to them, show them what it will be like. Men like the schoolgirl outfits, so I have them dress in school clothes and no underwear. I show them pictures and do some other things so their first time doesn't hurt so much. I help get them ready."

"You what?!" Chevy said with disgust, holding her hand to her stomach. "They're just little."

"Trust me, it's more humane."

147

"Than what?"

"Than being six years old, sold, and taken into a room with no idea whatsoever what is about to happen, and having a grown man force his penis into you!" Veronica moved closer. "Do you know what that feels like? I remember—vividly. I remember not being able to walk because I ripped so badly. I remember crying, and screaming. All it did was arouse them more. I would have been thankful if someone would've prepped me. Whether I prep them or not someone will buy them, and someone will take their virginity. I'm just making it easier for them. Wait until you hear one screaming and crying. Your view will change."

"My God," Chevy whispered, squeezing her eyes shut.

Veronica leaned closer. "I know they're children. But this can go one of two ways. I remember what happened to me, so I try to make it easier on them. Some of them don't let me. I don't force any of them. The ones who won't let me, I often hear screaming later. We have to transfer to a ship later tonight, always at night. It will be you, me, and the girls."

Concern came into Chevy's eyes. "A ship?" Chevy replied with apprehension.

Veronica held her hand out. "Everything will be all right, but we will need to stay low key. I'm very glad you are here to help me. The girls are sweet, but each time I have to do this it gets harder."

### 

No longer on the interstate, Ruthie looked down at the piece of paper Brandon gave her. She drove slowly past homes, the GPS talking in the background. She turned at the end of the street, then a house no one could miss came into view. Its architecture was unusual, with its white Roman-style pillars and rustic brick. It sat facing the evening sun, making it appear more distinctive.

The rumble of her truck was loud as it rolled slowly into the long circular drive. She turned down the music, pulled behind an older black car, and turned off the engine. The loud rumble yielded to sudden silence. She looked at the piece of paper to double-check the house number, then grabbed her purse and headed for the door. A small light caught her eye, guiding her to the doorbell. She pressed the small button, then heard the chime ring through the inside of the house.

The knob clicked, and the right side of the double doors opened. Ruthie smiled at a short, round-faced Hispanic woman with kind eyes.

"May I help you?" The woman asked in broken English.

Ruthie noticed the heavy scent of fall candles wafting in the air from inside.

"I'm here to see Chris. He's expecting me." She smiled sweetly.

The woman looked confused. "I'm sorry. Mr. Roper is currently in a meeting."

"Oh, that's all right. I don't mind waiting. I'm a touch early anyhow," she said, glancing at her watch.

"Hmm," the woman mumbled with uncertainty, pulling the door open further for Ruthie to enter. She gestured to a small sitting room at the front of the house. "You can wait here."

Ruthie smiled and walked toward the waiting room. She caught a glimpse of a man who must be Chris through a cracked door down the hall. He was sitting behind a desk, talking with someone.

Suddenly she turned and headed down the hall.

"Ma'am! You can't go down there!" the woman called after her.

Ruthie pushed the door the rest of the way open.

Chris looked over, pausing his conversation. The smile fell from his face.

"Ma'am!" the woman repeated anxiously. She turned to Chris. "I'm sorry, sir. This woman pushed past me."

Chris held up his hand. "Its fine, Rosa. I will handle it. Apparently, it couldn't wait," he said lightheartedly, while his smile looked forced. Across from him sat a younger man with blondish wavy hair and light eyes that held curiosity and intrigue.

"Chris, hi!" Ruthie said in an upbeat voice. "I'm Ruthie Westen, Chevy's mother." She walked boldly to his desk and held out her hand for him to shake.

He stood reluctantly to shake her hand. A smile emerged once more. "Ah, yes," he said, as he glanced uncomfortably to the other man.

"What happened to your eye?" she asked knowingly.

"Oh, that." Chris shrugged. "It was a fight with a ladder and the wall." He paused. "I lost." He laughed.

"I hate it when that happens," she said with a disbelieving stare.

His laugh faded when he saw her sour look. "I'm in the middle of a meeting."

"Yes, I can see that. My apologies for the intrusion," she said condescendingly. She turned to the man sitting across from him and held out her hand.

The man stood.

"I'm Ruthie Westen," she began sweetly. "My sincerest apologies for the intrusion. We have a topic of urgency to discuss. Would you please excuse us?"

Chris sat down and shifted in his chair, irritated. "We're in the middle of a meeting. Whatever the topic, I'm sure it can be discussed later," he told her, his voice now stronger.

Ruthie turned to Chris. "It can't wait," she replied sharply. "It's sensitive in nature, so speaking in private would be best." She turned to the other man. "Thank you so much for coming. Chris will reschedule at his earliest convenience."

The man reached for his brown leather bag, but seemed to be paying close attention.

"Look," Chris stammered. "Whatever it is, can you wait just twenty minutes? I donated to the local school, and I'm in the middle of an interview that I need to get back to."

Ruthie sat down in the chair beside the other man and smiled at him. "Oh, are you a reporter?"

"Yes, I am." He nodded with a twinkle in his eyes. "Nice to meet you. I'm Neal Collins."

Ruthie's eyes widened as a smile pulled across her face. "I've heard of you. You do a lot of reporting overseas on sensitive issues. You did a story on the diamond trade, right?"

Neal smiled. "Correct. You wouldn't believe what goes on," he said as he sat back in his chair, engaged.

She looked at Chris. "It's a scary world out there." She paused. "I certainly know," she said, and looked back at Neal.

Neal glanced at the diamond ring on her finger.

Ruthie followed his eyes, then looked at him. "Cubic zirconia. It's the least of the evils. I know all about the diamond trade. Horrifying!" She paused. "Why are you in this neck of the woods? I thought you were one of the big boys

"Haven't been inspired." Neal got comfortable. "It has to have meaning, or I can't do it."

She saw the restless look in his eyes. "Met a girl, huh?" She nodded.

A smile covered his face. "You could say that."

"I understand. Sometimes relationships are more important." She paused. "Clearly this girl isn't working out."

Neal hesitated, the sparkle suddenly gone from his eyes. "We barely talk," he told her with an openness she was surprised to see.

"I see. Time to move on?"

"Haven't decided. But it's looking that way."

She searched his face. "Let me guess, local reporter?"

"H-h-how—" Neal stammered.

"It's all right. It's the type you would attract. You don't do the flashy dazzle, so she's lost interest. She's looking for the big name, the big money, the big life, and the big shot. You need adventure, yet you're too down to earth and practical. If it doesn't work, move on." She winked at him.

Chris cleared his throat to get her attention. "This is all very nice, but we have an interview to finish. Please come back another time."

She looked at him. "No, it must be now. Privacy would be best."

"Look, I don't have time for—"

Ruthie looked at Neal. "What do you know about the sex trade or human trafficking?" she asked, getting comfortable in her chair.

Chris's eyes got wide and shifted between Ruthie and Neal. Then he stood, walked around the desk, and held out his hand to Neal, who reactively stood.

"Tell me, Chris," Ruthie continued. "Tell me about your business partners from overseas. Tell me about the missing girls. Why is it that when your business partners show up, girls go missing?"

Neal looked at Chris. "Are you sure you don't want me to stay? I would love to hear the answers."

Chris laughed. "We'll reschedule."

Neal looked at Ruthie. "It was nice to meet you," he said, with sincerity. "I'm feeling inspired." He pulled out a card from his jacket pocket and handed it to her. "If you run into any walls, call me. I get around walls." He smiled and winked, then gave Chris a long look, turned, and left the room, shutting the door quietly behind himself.

Chris sat down in his leather chair. "Well, Mrs. Westen—"

"Please, call me Ruthie. We're going to get to know each other very well."

"People go missing all the time. You better be careful. You don't want to cause waves." He gave her a warning look.

"I'm here in regard to my daughter. Are you feeling concerned?" She raised her eyebrows. "Although she's missing, I never said you were behind it or had anything to do with it. It's interesting you assume I'm here to make waves. Your son and my daughter were dating, and I figured you might know something that could help us find her." She gave him a knowing look.

Chris sat there and stared at her. "What do you want?"

"What if I *am* here to make waves? What then?"

"People do go missing." Chris gave her a warning look again.

Ruthie raised an eyebrow. "Please. Do I look scared of you? All you're accomplishing is angering me. Making me angry is not a good idea, but if you would like to test me and find out the hard way, have at it." She leaned forward. "Where's my daughter?"

"Why would I know where your daughter is?" Chris shot back.

"Come on. You just got done threatening me." She looked at her watch. "I need to be home in time to get my sons to football practice, and I don't have time for bullshit." She crinkled her nose. "Where is she?"

"Look, lady. I'm a big dog. You don't want to mess with a big dog. You, on the other hand, Mrs. Westen, you're a little dog. I'll squish you!" His eyes held an evil glint.

She repositioned herself in the chair. "You don't listen very well, do you? I told you, call me Ruthie." She picked up her purse and started shuffling through it. She pulled out the case of bullets and set them on the chair next to her.

Chris started laughing. "Honey, you're a little dog. Don't you need a manicure or something?"

She pulled the gun from her purse and sat there, relaxed, with her back against the chair. The gun in her hand was pointed at the floor. "The thing about big dogs"—she rolled her eyes—"is that you can always see them coming. They're well trained and usually don't bite. And if they do bite, they're put down. We little dogs are cute and cuddly. When we bite, no one cares, because we're small. We're thought to be controllable and harmless. You won't see us coming, and we have a nasty bite. Now, where's my daughter?"

Chris stared at her, the amusement completely gone from his face.

"I want names, addresses, times, places, everything." She gestured with her hand in the air.

"I don't know where your daughter is," he repeated, looking uncomfortable.

Suddenly, she pulled the trigger. A bullet shot through the front of his wood desk and hit his foot.

He yelled, pushed his chair back, and grabbed his foot. "What the hell is wrong with you?!" He reached for the phone.

"Go ahead. Call the police." Ruthie pulled out her phone. "I'll call Neal. That way it's fully covered. I'm sure the police will be intrigued to know about some of your business dealings." Ruthie raised an eyebrow at him, then nodded her head toward the phone. "Let's tell them all about it, shall we? I'll get in some trouble for accidentally shooting you. I'll sit in jail for a day until I'm bailed out, but it will also alert the police, and the FBI, who in turn will investigate you. Tell me,

153

what do you think they'll uncover?" She tilted her head. "There are a lot of opinions out there, but there's one people all over the world agree on. They want to put men behind bars for a very long time for taking women and children and selling them as sex slaves." She looked at him coldly.

"You're a fuckin' crazy bitch!" Chris yelled.

Ruthie laughed. "I've been called worse. And I'm not crazy. I'm a mother. I'll fight to the death to protect my children." She glared at him. "So what will it be? Will you hand over the information, or shall we call the police? You know"—she looked to the ceiling and put a bit of condescending speculation into her voice—"I have a good friend over there, the chief of police. I wonder if Jim's working this evening? It's been a few months since we last saw him. His mother is having health problems, you know. He and my husband like to go hunting. Jim gets a discount at the store, and we get to speed without tickets. It all works out. Jim's good people." She crinkled her nose at him.

The last of his cocky arrogance fell from his face. He sat there and looked at her.

"Time's up! What's it going to be, the police or the information? I figured you would be a little faster, seeing that you are a gamblin' man."

"I don't gamble," he replied matter-of-factly, pulling a pen from the holder.

"Bullshit!" she hissed. "I know as well as you do anyone who has any business sense gambles. We gamble every day. How is the stock market going to behave, how is the economy go to act for the next four quarters? Don't sit there and tell me you don't gamble. Chevy isn't the first girl you have sold, and she won't be the last. A man like you has to know who you're plucking from the country. Get the wrong girl, and people are going to make noise. People like me."

"You come in here and think I'm going to just hand you information?"

"Yes, you're going to give me what I came for. You won't gamble with this; you know what you're doing. Give me the information I want and send me on my merry way, or watch

154

me draw a whole lot of attention. You don't want my kind of attention. We both know this."

Chris grabbed a piece of paper from the printer behind him and started writing, then slid the paper across the top of his desk.

She grabbed the paper and stood up. "If I find out any of this information is incorrect, or you tipped anyone off..." She glanced at the paper then back to him.

Chris held his hands in the air and leaned back in his chair. "You don't need to make threats." He gave her a resentful scowl.

Suddenly the doors flew open.

Ruthie and Chris looked over. John's broad shoulders filled the doorway. The crease between his eyebrows was deep.

Ruthie's eyes danced. "Hi, sweetheart." She beamed. This is Chris." She gestured. "Brandon's father. We were just talking about how much Chevy means to us, and how we'd all like her back home. He decided to give us some information."

"Your crazy-ass wife shot my foot! For some reason she thinks I had something to do with your daughter's disappearance."

She turned to Chris. "Knock it off. We already weighed your options," she reminded him. "You decided giving the information was best."

"This is why you need to keep out of this," John said as he shut the door behind him and headed straight for Chris.

Chris picked up the phone and pressed a button. John reached down, ripped the phone from his hand, and smacked the side of Chris's face with the receiver. He turned to Ruthie. "Honey, call the police, then the FBI." He grabbed Chris by the front of his shirt.

Calmly, she pulled her phone from her purse and started dialing.

"All right, all right," Chris said, with a fearful look in his eyes. "Chevy's on her way to the Ukraine." He held his hands in front of his face so John wouldn't hit him again.

"Call. Get Chevy back now!" he demanded as he handed Chris the receiver.

155

Reluctantly, Chris took the phone. Slowly, he dialed and waited for someone to answer. John hit the speaker button and let go of Chris, allowing him to stand behind the desk.

"Hello," Sandro answered in his heavy accent.

"There's been a change of plans. Chevy needs to come back right away," Chris told him, looking at John.

"She was put on transport, last night—"

"Cancel the transport. Just get her back here."

"We spoke last night. She has already been put on transport. You know once we do this—"

"Yes, I know."

"Is everything all right?"

"Look, I don't care what you have to do, just get her back here ASAP."

"I understand. I will work on it and give you a call back."

"Great!" Chris heard noise in the hall. Seconds later, uniformed officers burst through the door with guns pointed. "Freeze!" one of the officers shouted as Chris put down the phone. "Put your hands up!"

They froze.

Half a dozen police officers filed into the study.

"Drop your weapon!" one of the officers shouted, his gun pointed at Ruthie.

Rosa rushed in behind the officers, speaking loud and quickly in Spanish.

"Ma'am!" One of the officers tried to get Rosa's attention. "Ma'am!" The officer put his gun away, then wrapped his arms around her chest, lifting her from her feet. Rosa's feet kicked at the officer's shins as he whisked her out of the room, while she continued to rattle on.

Ruthie held her gun in the air, pointing it at the ceiling. "Put it down or hand it to you?" she asked the officer.

"Set it down slowly!"

Slowly, she bent down, keeping eye contact with the officer.

"Bend at the knees!"

Slowly, she bent at the knees, carefully placing the gun on the floor in front of her.

"Kick it to me!"

Ruthie stood slowly, kicking the gun toward the officer.

When the gun was at his feet, two officers rushed her to the ground and put her in handcuffs. They picked her up and set her in the chair like a weightless doll.

From the hallway Rosa continued to chatter on.

"Will someone please take that woman outside?" one of the officers said, apparently annoyed with the persistent prattling coming from the hallway.

"What's going on?" Chris asked loudly.

"We had a report of shots fired."

"Let her go," Chris told the officers. "For God's sake!" Chris said as he put his hands down. "You guys are going to give me a heart attack." Chris gestured to John, who was standing by the corner of his desk. "This is John and Ruthie Westen. They own the Westen's chain. Their daughter, Charlotte, and my son have been dating. As I am sure everyone knows, their daughter is missing."

"I have a carry permit," Ruthie interjected.

Chris glanced at Ruthie. "My wife and I invited them here. I know they're having a hard time coping with their daughter's disappearance. I know Judy and I are having a hard time as well. Chevy's a sweet girl—"

"What in the world?" Judy came through the doors and looked around at the barrage of officers.

"Judy, sweetheart," Chris said. "John and Ruthie are here. This is such an upsetting time for all of us, with their daughter missing."

Judy looked around, her eyes wide. "Why in the world are all these officers here?"

He shook his head in frustration. "Ruthie has a carry permit, and she got her gun out to show it to me, only it went off accidently and hit my foot, but I am all right. Rosa must have heard the shot, and not knowing what was happening, called the police. John here was trying to make sure I was all right, and then the police rushed in, and now you're home. By the way, dear—our guests have arrived."

"Oh, good grief!" She looked around then at Ruthie. "Are you in handcuffs?" she asked, stepping closer. "Take those handcuffs off of her. Right now!"

The officers lowered their guns and put them away. "Is that what happened?" one of the officers asked.

Chris nodded. "Yep, that's what happened. Do you really think my son's future in-laws are going to come here to shoot me? In God's name, why? And if they were going to shoot me, why would they aim for my foot?"

The officer noticed the hole in the bottom of the desk, then looked up at Chris suspiciously. "What happened to your face?"

"That?" Chris felt his face. "When the gun went off I instinctively leaned forward for my foot and hit my face on the desk."

"Take the cuffs off of her," the officer instructed.

### 

Sandro picked up the phone and dialed.

"This is Jack," Jack Sweeden answered. Jack was a professional-looking man, well kept, older, with snow-white hair.

"Jack, it's Sandro!" His smile came through in his tone.

"Sandro!" Jack greeted him as he leaned back on the sofa and smiled. "How are you?"

"I'm well…I'm calling with a question. Do you have two rooms available?"

"For you! I always have rooms for you! When are you arriving, and how long will I have the pleasure of your company?"

"It'll be my wife, Veronica, and a woman from the States who's in transit. I think they will be there a few days to a week." He thought about the time frame as he spoke. "I may meet up with them at your place. I'm not sure yet. I haven't worked out all the details. My arrival is tentative."

"Transit," Jack repeated. "I'm having an auction this next week. It's a standard wife auction, not the special auction with the teens. Are we putting your transit woman in the auction?"

"No," Sandro said abruptly. "This one stays in transit."

"All right," Jack replied slowly, taken back by the abruptness of Sandro's reply. He changed the subject. "I was at an auction in Egypt a few months ago and brought back the most interesting vase. When you get here, I have got to show it to you—providing you can make it."

"Great!" Sandro replied. "I can't wait to see it. Was it plucked from the sea, or unburied?"

"I'm thinking it was hidden for hundreds of years. Well, then, I will see you if you get here, and I'll definitely see Veronica."

"Sounds perfect."

###

Sandro hung up the phone and sat at his desk staring at his desktop, thinking. The words "Freeze! Put your hands—" before the phone was disconnected were too drastic. He pushed his chair back, turned to his filing cabinet, pulled out some files, and laid them in a pile on his desk. He got up and headed out of his study to find Veronica.

She was sitting in the lounge on the sofa in front of her laptop.

"There you are!" he said. The urgency in his voice caught her attention.

She looked up from the computer. "Yeah, here I am," she replied. "Are we playing hide and seek?"

Sandro sat beside her, rattled.

"What's wrong?"

He leaned close to her, talking quietly. "I just got another call from Chris. There seems to be law enforcement of some kind at his home. Are you working on transport arrangements?"

"Of course I am."

"Let me do some of that. I need to get you, the kids, and Chevy off this yacht as fast as possible. Right now, I need you and Chevy to shred the files I laid out." He pulled the laptop in front of him.

"Do you feel we are in danger of getting caught?" She searched his face for his reaction.

"I don't know. But I want all of you off the yacht and somewhere else just in case."

She got up. "Okay." She paused. "If you are getting us off

159

the yacht as quickly as possible, what port should I plan on? I need to know where we are going so I can make the arrangements once we are in port," she said. "I'll have Chevy shred while I make the arrangements for the port."

"I'll get you to the port in Málaga. If anyone asks where you are going, you tell them you're on your way to the Ukraine. Drop the kids off in Granada at Falcone—I'll meet you in Barcelona at Sweeden's." He looked at her and took hold of her hand. "Did you get all that?"

"Of course I did." She touched her hand to the side of his face, leaned over, and kissed him.

###

Chevy was on one of the beds reading the children a story when Veronica came to the door and smiled. "Guess what I brought!" she said with excitement as she held up a bag of cookies.

The girls roared with delight seeing Veronica and the cookies.

"I brought milk, too," she said, stepping into the room. "Come on." She set out plastic cups on the table for them. "Each of you get five cookies, so no fighting or taking someone else's cookies. Does everyone understand?"

"Yes," they said together, nodding with delight.

Chevy put down the book and walked to the table. She picked up the carton of milk and poured it into the cups as Veronica passed out cookies.

Veronica watched as the girls began snarfing them down. "Eat them slow. Enjoy them," she said kindly. The brown-haired girl barely slowed.

She leaned down, causing the girl to pause. "Enjoy them, sweetie. Once they are gone, they're gone."

Without a word, she began eating slower.

"I'm going to put in a movie. Chevy and I will be back in a while." She turned to Chevy and nodded toward the door. "Come on." She pulled the door shut behind them. "My husband and I are going to trust you. We have never extended our trust to anyone else before, so please don't break it."

Chevy smiled. "You can trust me."

"Come with me." She motioned, proceeding down the hall to Sandro's study.

She sat down at the chair behind his desk. "Pull that chair over." She placed her hand on top of the stack of files then looked at Chevy. "We need to shred this stack. The shredder's right here." She twisted to the bottom of the bookcase and pulled the doors open, revealing the shredder.

"All right." Chevy looked at the stack.

Veronica sat in front of the computer on a website that said TRANSPORTS at the top.

Chevy picked up some files and started shredding. "Do you want me to shred the file folders that list what was in them, also, or do you want to hang on to them?"

"Shred them too," Veronica replied, focused on the monitor.

As she was shredding, Chevy came to a file labeled HOME LIST. The first sheet had a name, some information, and a picture of Jada. She paused, staring at the photo and remembering the gunshots.

Veronica turned and looked at her. Most of the stack was shredded. Chevy sat staring at open file.

"Are you all right?" she asked, seeing the open file and the picture of Jada.

Chevy abruptly looked up. "Yeah." She shook it off. "I wasn't expecting to see a picture of Jada. She was a handful."

Veronica put her hand on her shoulder. "Don't worry. You are not on the home list."

Chevy continued to look at Jada's picture.

"Are you all right?" Veronica asked again.

Chevy slowly began to nod, then looked up. "Yeah, I'm all right. I just had no idea how many people have…gone home." She paused. "I didn't give it any thought."

Veronica twisted her chair to face her. "May I level with you?"

"Of course," she said, pulling her attention from the photo. "You can always talk to me. I prefer that."

"The one who decided that you would be a good person to take made a very bad selection. The fact that you are missing has made national news. Because of this, my husband and I are

161

getting completely out of this business. That's why you are shredding these files." Veronica paused. "The one who had us take you wants us to send you home."

Chevy's sucked in a breath, looking alarmed.

"Don't worry." Veronica grabbed Chevy's hand and squeezed it. "You aren't going home like these women." She touched the file folder. "My husband and I are going to get you back to the States, where you'll be safe. We are taking a very big risk that you won't implicate us once you are home. I hope, as good as we have been to you, that you would not turn on us."

"Don't worry. I won't admit I know or have seen either of you."

"We need to drop the children off, then I will get you home. It's low key. No one knows, no one sees."

### 

Sitting in an unmarked white moving truck about a quarter mile away from the Roper home was a surveillance team. The two men sat listening with black keyboards in front of them and half dozen screens for them to view with the shift of an eye. "Hey, did you hear that?" one specialist said to the other, turning the volume up. "I'm sending this to Ward," he said as he began dialing Ward's number.

### 

Ward leaned forward in his chair and picked up his phone. "Agent Ward."

"You've got to hear this! I'm sending you the voice feed now," the agent spoke into his wireless headset while he typed on the keyboard and flipped through computer screens. "The Ropers' home is exciting today! A reporter, the Westens, and the police—it's starting to look like a party!"

"No one's dead, are they?" Ward asked, imagining the worst.

"Nope, not yet. Mrs. Westen isn't playing around, though."

Ward released his tense expression, took a breath, then began flipping through computer screens, looking for the voice recording the specialist was sending him. "I got it here."

"So the quick run-down..." the specialist started. "Chris was

162

with a reporter, Neal Collins—that's a name that will get your attention. So, take note that Ruthie and Neal have met. Ruthie shot Chris in the foot, then John Westen barged in. He roughed up Chris a little. Regardless, Chris blurted out that Chevy is on her way to the Ukraine, then the cops showed up for shots fired. Chris is giving the cops a big line of bullshit about what happened." The specialist laughed.

Ward leaned back in his chair and tilted his head back, looking up at the ceiling. "Great," he said sarcastically. "This is just what we needed. How the hell did the Westens end up at the Ropers?" He looked around in frustration, thinking.

"You want my opinion? I think it was Brandon." The agent paused. "He overheard his father last night on the phone, and they got into a big blowup. My guess is that he went to the Westens and—"

"Crap, that's right. I wasn't thinking about that. All right, thank you. Keep me posted, and keep the feed coming."

"No problem."

Ward hung up the phone. "Crap!" He stared at his monitor, contemplating.

### 

Ward walked into a conference room and joined a group of men sitting around the table and talking. "There has been a disturbance at the Roper home," he said. He looked at each one in turn.

"Disturbance?" The man in the black suit asked calmly, raising one eyebrow. He leaned onto his elbow, waiting to hear more.

Ward looked around at the men. "Apparently police were called to the Roper home for shots fired. Chris Roper was shot in the foot. He told police it was an accident. Give you one guess who that shooter was." He smirked.

The man in the black suit waited.

"John Westen," Cook chimed in.

Ward tossed a file folder onto the table and watched as it slid to a stop. "You're close. Ruthie!" He paused. "Both Ruthie and John are at the Ropers' home. Chris told police that Ruthie's handgun accidently went off when she was showing it to him. Apparently Chevy's on her way to the Ukraine." Ward paused again, waiting for everyone's reaction. "At least that's what Chris told the Westens right before police barged in. But let's keep in mind that we already know Chris wants this girl dead, based on the conversation from last night. Now this associate has Chevy in transit."

Cook chimed in. "If the associate has her en route to the Ukraine, then he's not going to kill her."

Ward tossed a hand in the air. "Providing this associate is telling the truth."

"Sure he is. This associate doesn't want any part of this. He doesn't want blood on his hands. He wants to pass her on."

"But we really don't know," Ward pointed out.

The man in the black suit rubbed his hand over his face. "This just keeps getting worse."

The man in the dress blues looked at the man in the black suit. "I can put special ops in multiple locations and take out this group—all at the same time. Sink the *Apoise* and we'll be done with it."

The man in the black suit tapped his finger on the arm of his chair, debating with himself.

Ward smiled as he looked around the table. "Yeah, I thought everyone would like this little pile of situational vomit, but wait—it gets better. The men we have watching Chris Roper noted a high-profile reporter, Neal Collins, at Chris's house. Chris donated a hundred thousand dollars to one of the local schools, so Neal was at the Ropers' doing an interview when Ruthie arrived. Although Chris explained the shooting as an accident, I got a hundred dollars that says Ruthie will drag Neal into this anyway, and Neal will happily dive in headfirst. Ruthie isn't going to leave this alone."

The man in the black suit sighed. "All right. We need to stop this, before the Westens turn this into an international incident. They have money and connections, while Neal has even more connections."

Cook looked over at the man in the black suit. "Do you really feel Neal is willing to take on a story of this magnitude? Remember, he almost got himself killed when he was investigating the diamond trade."

The man in the black suit looked at another man at the table. "If Neal starts digging, intercept him. Give him passports for both of them, bank accounts, credit cards, and have a plane waiting for him. Hell, just hand him the goddamn file. Send him to the Ukraine to buy the Westen girl back."

One of the men in the room looked at the man in the black suit uncomfortably. "Neal Collins is a reporter, not an undercover agent. We could be setting him up for failure, and we could get them both killed. This whole thing could blow up in our face."

The man in the black suit shifted in his chair. "You have a valid concern. However, if Neal starts after this…"

"Have agents keeping an eye on them so Neal can get in and out without any hiccups?"

The men looked around at one another.

The man in the black suit groaned. "If Ruthie's willing to drive ten hours to shoot Roper, then she'll involve Neal. I'm sure he'll be more than willing to chase a hot story. Especially one with sex trade written all over it. I want your men watching Neal, now!" He looked around the table at everyone. "The moment Neal looks like he is going after the Westen girl, I want to know. If he goes after her, we'll have undercover agents over there to keep an eye on them. We know his name and have read his reporting, but how many people know his face?" He looked around the table of men.

### 

Neal sat in his gray cubicle and put the finishing touches on the article about Chris Roper. He read through it one last time, proud of himself. For what the article was, he had managed to make it exciting. However, meeting Ruthie sparked an interest he couldn't shake. He googled Chevy Westen, then looked for as much information about Chris Roper as he could find. Big shipping companies, cruise ships, charter yachts, and fishing companies were just the surface of what Chris seemed to be into. The more he searched, the more partners and connections he found in every possible direction. This looked big, complicated, and tricky. Neal sat with stars dancing in his eyes

165

and a glow he hadn't had for a while.

He stood from his chair and grabbed his jacket.

His phone rang.

He paused and looked at the caller ID—UNKNOWN CALLER. He picked up the phone. "Neal Collins."

"Neal, Ruthie Westen." She sounded determined.

He could hear the rumbling of her truck and the radio playing in the background. "Yes, Ruthie. We met at the Ropers. How did the meeting go?"

"Before or after I shot Chris in the foot?"

Neal sat back down on the edge of his chair. "I would love to hear the whole story, but how about you tell me the parts you feel are most relevant?"

"My husband and I could really use your help finding our daughter. We're happy to pay all your expenses."

"Ruthie—May I call you Ruthie?"

"Yes, please. I prefer it."

"I'll tell you that this has come at a rather interesting time for me. Where can I meet you and your husband so I can get as many details as possible?"

Ruthie looked at the traffic in front of her. "I'm heading home." She glanced at the GPS on her dashboard.

"You shot Chris Roper and now you're on your way home?"

"The police let me go. When they showed up, Chris gave them one hell of a story. It was completely believable, off the cuff. I'm still impressed."

"Is the FBI involved?"

Ruthie looked in her side mirror at the trail of traffic behind her. "Absolutely. And there are several other agencies involved. Apparently, this has sex trade all over it, but I haven't been told, nor have I asked which agencies."

"Ruthie, where do you live? I will come to you." He started to pull down his 8×10s.

"We live just outside Lexington, Kentucky. Its rural. How are you with directions? I'm still in North Carolina. I'm on I-40, headed home, but I'm coming up on an exit. I can turn around if it would be easier."

"No, no. What's the exit?"

Ruthie glanced out her mirrors and veered onto the off-ramp. "I'm taking exit A22. I see a Cracker Barrel sign. Meet me there?"

"That works just fine," he said as he started collecting the things from his desk and putting them in a box.

Ruthie pulled off the exit ramp. "I'm looking for a street name."

"No, that's all right," Neal said, as he pulled the thumb tacks out of the 8×10s. "I can get around, and for those moments of uncertainly, I have GPS. We men no longer have to circle for hours or stop and ask for directions," he joked, putting the photos into a file folder. "As you get off the exit ramp, is the Cracker Barrel on your left or right?"

"My right," she replied quickly then laughed. "GPS, huh. Okay." She giggled and spotted the sign as she went through the intersection. "The Cracker Barrel is off of Spring Street."

He grabbed a Post-it and jotted down the street name. "Spring Street," he repeated. He walked around his cubicle to the copier and pulled reams of paper out of a box, setting them on the floor beside the copier. "I have your address. What is your number? It didn't come up on my caller ID."

"Its 859-555-1121," she rattled off.

He jotted down the number on the Post-it. "Got it. I should be there in about thirty-five minutes, give or take, depending on the traffic. It's six o'clock now, so it should be thinning."

"Sounds great," she said. "I really appreciate your help."

"Don't thank me yet. I haven't done anything."

"True, but you will. International issues are beyond my backyard. I can't move fast enough. I don't have a passport," she admitted.

"Right, right. Well, not to worry. I'm a man with passports and contacts." He smiled and hoped he conveyed confidence.

"Fabulous. I'll see you when you get here." Ruthie pulled into the parking lot.

Neal put the last of his things neatly in the box.

With his computer in his brown leather bag and the box tucked under his arm, he headed out of his cubicle toward the huge picture window. His boss came around the corner. "And where are you going?" he asked with disdain.

Neal saw a deep crease between his boss's brows and smiled. "I was just straightening up a few things that have been out of order. I do need to thank you for not giving me the Chris Roper story—that was a great call." He smiled and winked, continuing to walk away.

"Neal! I'm talking to you!"

Neal turned and took backward steps. "You have a good one." He put his hand up in a thankful gesture and turned back around, never pausing or slowing to hear what his boss wanted to yell about.

Neal walked out of the building into the parking lot. He got in his car and put his box of things on the seat next to him. As the motor started, the radio came on loud. Neal smiled. He didn't notice the surveillance team sitting across the street, their small earpieces allowing them to hear any conversation he had.

###

Agents Ward and Cook were talking with the other men around the conference table when the phone rang. Everyone paused as the man in charge of the surveillance team answered, then finally said, "Stay on Neal, and keep me informed." He hung up and looked at the man in the black suit. "Neal is on his way to meet Ruthie Westen at a Cracker Barrel as we speak. She's recruiting his assistance. Neal gave her every indication he would retrieve Chevy. It appears that he quit. He left with a box of personal items tucked under his arm."

The man in the black suit rubbed his finger over his lips as he listened. He took in a deep breath and let it out slowly. "I'm afraid it's time to give Neal assistance. I want him personally escorted to a plane and flown to the Ukraine. Hand him money, passports, and credit cards to make this as easy and expedient as possible." He looked over at the surveillance man, then at the man in the dress blues. "Have your special ops team on Neal. I want it to appear that Neal went over there and simply brought the Westen girl back by himself. It has to appear that none of our agencies had a hand in this. Have our informants

168

on the lookout for Chevy and Neal, and I want your special ops to take out anyone who tries to hurt either of them. The last thing I want is an international incident," he said, irritated with the compounding situation.

### 

As the men in the conference room hammered out the details, Ruthie sat at Cracker Barrel at a table for four by the window. She had a glass of iced tea in front of her and a small wooden game in her hand that was occupying her mind for the moment.

"Ruthie," Neal said, standing at the end of her table.

She looked up from her game. "Please, have a seat." She pushed the game over toward the condiments and glanced out the window just in time to see John's truck roll into the parking lot. "Oh, great." She sighed.

"What?" Neal asked, glancing out the window, not sure what he was looking for.

Ruthie rolled her lips under her teeth, bracing herself. "My husband, John, just pulled in. I should have thought to turn the locator off on my phone. He's been quite the jerk since we got the news about Chevy. Normally, he's a giant teddy bear, especially around me. However, he can be a bit egotistical and obnoxious at moments. With the news about Chevy, he's become a jerk of unrealistic proportions." She watched as John walked in and looked around, not yet seeing her by the window.

Ruthie looked over at him, smiled, and raised her hand to catch his attention.

He started toward them with long strides and thumps of his work boots against the hardwood floor.

"Well, here he comes. Brace yourself. I'm not sure what he'll be like," she told Neal. "Hi, sweetie," she said to John, looking at him lovingly.

There was a lot about John that reminded Neal of his own father. While John wore work boots and jeans, and had a hearty, rugged look, his own father most often wore a suit and tie, khakis if he dressed down. What was similar about them was not their dress, but the air they wore. They had the same

169

glint in their eyes that conveyed they would never be pleased and were never wrong. Kind words were few, and love was on their terms. Their negative comments about your shortcomings were used in abundance to highlight your flaws in an attempt to mask their own. They saw the world and everyone in it through a narrow lens that revealed only other people's idiocy and inadequacy, which was the only way his father and men like him could feel good about themselves.

Neal realized that he was now sitting with an unreasonable man. Just as he did with his own father, he wanted to get up and leave. Reporting had been an excellent way to do just that. Run to another country and uncover and report the dirt of the world, so no one would see his own dirt, his father, the man he couldn't please.

### 

The streetlights in the cul-de-sac were on as Neal pulled into the driveway in front of the garage. He sat there for a moment thinking about what he needed to grab from Megan's condo. The most important things to him were his photos, which were on his computer or already packed up in the box he took from work, then his clothes and toiletries. The most sizable thing he had was his bank account. He had been paid richly for the stories he chased and had built an account for that someday he would share with a wife and then kids. Now, that someday was on hold again. He got out of his car and unlocked the front door.

In the master closet he pulled out his suitcases and began filling them with his clothes.

*Ding...dong...* the doorbell rang.

Two men in plain clothes who were government of some type were standing there. "Neal Collins?" the man in the khaki-colored jacket asked.

"Yeah, that's me," he replied reluctantly.

"May we please come in? We have some important business of a highly sensitive nature to discuss with you."

Neal glanced at the black briefcase the man was holding. "Sure, come in. Have a seat."

The man in the khaki jacket laid the briefcase on the coffee

170

table.

"What is this about?" Neal asked, sitting in a chair across from them.

The man clicked one side of the briefcase open, then the other. "We're with the government. Which agency, you don't need to know. We're aware that you have started to investigate the disappearance of Charlotte Westen."

"Yeah, so?" He gave them a questioning look.

"We've been instructed to brief you on Miss Westen's situation and ask for your help in retrieving her. For a number of reasons, which are classified, we cannot get directly involved."

"What did you say your names were?"

"I didn't. Who we are and what part of the government we're from is irrelevant." He pointed to himself. "Smith." He pointed to his partner. "Heater."

"Those aren't your names, are they?"

"No, but it makes you feel better, and that's all that's important."

Neal closely observed them. "But I'm a reporter, and this is a big story. Why me?"

"We know about the work you did leading up to that piece on the diamond trade and the situations you had to deal with, and we know you're capable of bringing her home safely, with our behind-the-scenes support. You will eventually be able to write about it, but for now, it is a delicate situation. We are after a large international organization here, an operation that has been in the works for a long time. We don't want to jeopardize the progress we've made. We're getting close. You can spin it that you got a lead on where the girl is, then went in and rescued her yourself. But you'll need to wait to write about it until we've brought the whole organization down. You will have the eternal gratitude of the U.S. government, as well as Charlotte's family. Can we count on your help?"

Neal sat for a moment, trying to absorb what he'd been told. He thought about the dead-end job he'd just left, and the woman he was preparing to leave. Then he thought about Ruthie and her determination to get her daughter back. "Okay.

What's the plan?"

The agents filled him in on the situation and shared the plan. "We need to give you a few things before you leave the country. These are your credit cards," the man in the khaki jacket said, setting a small stack of cards on the coffee table in front of Neal. The other agent quipped, "Visa. It's everywhere you want to be." He smiled.

The man in the khaki jacket sighed. "My apologies. My partner is trying to be funny."

Neal grinned. "Well, that wasn't bad. It lacked the proper intonation, but you had the words right. Come on. You have to give him credit for that."

"No," the man in the khaki jacket said flatly. "I have to work with him. He's not as funny as he thinks he is. Let's stay focused. The cards have unlimited credit."

Neal raised his eyebrows and leaned his head and shoulders back, straightening his spine.

The man in the khaki jacket reached into the briefcase and pulled out a navy blue passport book. "This is your passport." He wiggled it in the air then set it beside the credit cards, then pulled out another passport. "This one's for the girl. She didn't have a passport, but she does now. It's so you can get her back into the country without problems."

"I already have a passport," Neal said, watching them.

"We know you have a passport. Now you have this one instead. It gives you more clearance. The PINs for the credit cards are all the same: your birth month and day, zero-five-two-one. You can use them in ATMs to get cash as you need it." He pulled out cash in several different currencies. "This is for the places you may go where an ATM may be hard to find. If you have any problems you can call us."

His partner pulled out his phone and dialed as he looked at Neal. The pocket of Neal's jacket began to ring. Neal looked over at his jacket, which was laying on the counter. He ended the call. "Now, you have our number," he said flatly.

Neal looked at him, then at his jacket, then back at him. "Umm, great."

The man in the khaki jacket continued, "You're dealing

172

with a high-profile case. Several government agencies have been watching and following this particular trafficking group for a while. This situation involves a dozen different men who have intertwined business dealings. These men have not only been careful; they have also been smart. They came from a number of different countries, which is the part that makes this so hard. There are too many different countries with too many different laws."

Neal nodded.

"You may be looking for a story to report, but know you're placing yourself on very dangerous ground. You need to go in and retrieve the girl, then come immediately back to the States. Don't sightsee, don't ask questions. Get the girl and get out of there. There are people who want this girl to disappear, while others appear to be protecting her."

Neal gave them an apprehensive look. "Just how dangerous is this situation I'm stepping into?" Visions of the diamond trade and guns pointed at his head replayed vividly in his mind.

"If you're thinking about your last situation, no. It's not that dangerous. We have agents and special ops teams that are watching this girl, and they are in place to ensure her safety."

Neal looked at them, disturbed. "Who exactly are you people?"

"We represent a team from several different agencies that are working together to shut down this human trafficking group and bring this girl home. Our bosses don't want this situation to get out of hand."

"So why are you here handing me passports and a variety of currency if you're watching her so closely? Why do you need me?"

The man in the khaki jacket sighed. "That's a good question. Allow me to be perfectly candid with you."

"That would be appreciated." Neal nodded and crinkled his lips together.

"The government doesn't want to appear like they had a hand in this. In the simplest terms, they don't want to harm their ongoing efforts to end trafficking. They would prefer that the reporter saves the girl." The man gave him a stiff smile.

173

"So the government doesn't blow their cover?"

"That's definitely part of it. This particular situation is pretty sticky. The government is taking great pains to keep this girl safe and get the two of you back home. It's easier if the reporter gets the credit and the government is able to maintain a low profile. The government is more interested in removing this group than being the hero."

"So, how many people are watching? Just how safe will I be?"

"There are people inside and outside. Our bosses desperately want to avoid any problems. They're very concerned the situation with this girl will get out of hand and cause international tensions, or worse. You're to get the girl and get out."

"What's missing in all this?" Neal questioned.

The man in the khaki jacket tilted his head and narrowed his eyes. "I guess I don't understand your question."

"The government doesn't allow someone to be a hero without something in return."

"You're putting yourself and Miss Westen in a potentially dangerous situation, and you're bringing back the girl so our government can lay low and appear like they didn't have a hand in it," he repeated.

"That's it?"

"That's it! If there is more, I don't know about it."

"Do you have a flight arranged for me?"

"Yes. We have a private plane waiting as we speak, to take you to the Ukraine."

"Whose plane?" Neal asked. "Even something as simple as the plane can be looked into and questioned. You can never have all your bases covered. I learned that when I was covering the diamond trade."

There was a knock at the door.

A crinkle formed between Neal's eyebrows as he stood.

"It's probably the movers," his partner said.

"Movers?"

"Since you left your job, we assumed you're leaving your girlfriend as well. It appeared you had a choice between your girlfriend and the story," the man in the khaki jacket said.

Neal pulled the door open. Before him stood six men in military fatigues. A very buff-looking man with chiseled features stood at the front. "Are you Neal Collins?"

"Well, as a matter of fact, I am."

"We are here to move your things."

Neal looked past the men to a plain moving truck in the driveway.

"Mr. Collins, would you please open the garage door so we can back up the moving truck?"

"I doubt I have that much," Neal replied as he walked to the garage door and hit the button.

The man in the khaki jacket put a package of Post-its on the table. "Place a Post-it on everything that is yours so they know what to take. Small items—toss them in a pile and they will box it up for you. Pack a suitcase with only what you need for a couple of days. If you forget anything, remember you have credit cards. You can buy what you forget when you get there." He paused, looked past Neal to one of the men standing behind him, then back at Neal. "They need your car keys."

From behind Neal a young man with a deep voice asked, "Is there anything you need out of your car?"

"No," Neal replied, turning toward the voice. "I brought it all in." Neal looked at the group of men who were waiting to start collecting his things. "How do I know you're going to return any of my belongings?"

"I can see why this could be unsettling," his partner said. "We have quite a few hours on the plane for us to explain more. The plane is waiting, and we need to get going." He looked at his watch, then past Neal to the man standing behind him.

"Your keys," the man repeated.

Neal looked at the driveway, possibly taking the last glance at his car. "I wanted a new car anyway." He reached in his pants pocket, pulled out the keys, tossed them over, and picked up the Post-its. "Give me twenty minutes."

A while later Neal emerged from the bedroom with a carry-on. Post-its were scattered on objects throughout the condo.

"All right," he said. "I have everything I need."

"Okay," the man in the khaki jacket replied. His partner nodded. The movers came up behind Neal. "Mr. Collins, sir, the piles that you made for us and the items you stickered, is that all of your belongings? Will there be any furniture, sir?"

"No, I don't have furniture. Aside from what's in the piles and the suitcases in the bedroom, the rest belongs to Megan."

"Sir, yes, sir," the man said with a respectful nod, and walked away.

Neal walked out the front door with the two agents. His car was parked alongside the curb by the mailbox. The moving truck was backed up to the garage and black drop cloths were draped on both sides of the truck. No one could see what was happening. The moment seemed surreal, like something from a spy novel. "This is a first," Neal mumbled.

### 

Veronica, Chevy, and the children were waiting to arrive in port when Sandro came into the lounge.

"Honey." Sandro motioned for Veronica to follow him into the hall. She gave him a curious look as he closed the door behind them. "I need you to take these documents."

She looked down at the large manila envelope in his hand. When she saw the name and address on the front, she looked up at him with surprise. "You want me to go there?" Her eyes widened. "You told me to never go there unless I was accompanied by you. You know Chevy is going to see this place," she said softly.

"I remember. However, Lou knows you are coming. I'm sure you'll be safe enough."

She looked at him, trying to decipher his intentions. Suddenly the loud, deep horn of the yacht sounded.

Sandro glanced around. "Trust me, the sooner I get rid of some of our entanglements, the better," he told her. "There is FBI and God knows who else looking for this girl. I don't want us to go down with Chris." He handed her the envelope.

Reluctantly she took it. The paper crinkled in her hand.

"You'll meet me in Barcelona," he told her.

She nodded. "Yes, at Sweeden's?"

176

Sandro lifted her chin with the tips of his fingers. "I love you," he told her, then leaned toward her and kissed her passionately.

She looked at him. "I love you, too." Her eyes sparkled.

Sandro let out a sigh. "It's time to go."

She turned and headed back to the lounge, uneasy. As she entered the room, she put on a light airy smile. "Did you hear that?" Veronica asked, with excitement. "We are here! It is time to go on an adventure!"

The children bounced from their places on the sofa with delight at the idea of something fun awaiting them.

Veronica picked up her backpack and stuck the large envelope into it. She didn't see Chevy watching her closely, narrowing her eyes at the envelope.

"All right!" Veronica called out. "Let's go!"

# Chapter 14

Several days later, when they arrived in Granada, Spain, Veronica and Chevy were in jeans with their hair pulled back. They walked through narrow, uneven streets of brick and cobblestone. The buildings were built close together—rustic, old, and quaint. Some of the streets were filled with vendors selling meats, vegetables, and breads.

Veronica paused at a corner and looked up at a street sign. "We need to go this way." She started down a long street, a girl holding each hand.

The girl holding Chevy's hand whined, "I'm tired."

Veronica stopped and bent down, sliding her backpack off. "I'm tired, too. It's just up the street. We're almost there, sweetie." She pulled a bottle of water from her backpack. "Do you want a drink?"

The little girl nodded. Veronica twisted off the cap. The girl took a long drink, then handed the bottle back.

"Better?" Veronica asked. The little girl nodded. "Girls?" Veronica offered the bottle to the others. They each took a drink, then continued down the street.

They stopped in front of an old gray stone building with intricate stonework around the windows. The building had two big double doors with old door knockers in the shape of lion heads. Above the door was a sign in a different language. Chevy leaned to Veronica. "What does that sign say?"

"The Falcone School for Girls," she said, then walked up the steps to the door. She grabbed hold of one of the knockers and pounded.

The door was opened by an older lady with brown eyes and dark graying hair that was pulled back in a bun. Chevy glanced down at the girls, whose hopeful bright faces turned dull. They looked around, unsure, and huddled close to her and Veronica.

Veronica led the way inside. The lady smiled and gave Veronica a big hug. She spoke to Veronica in another language, turned, and pointed to the stairs behind her.

The inside of the building had a rustic beauty. The walls were a combination of stone and plaster. In the middle of the room was a table with a flower centerpiece. She heard people speaking English with American accents, which drew her attention to a room with old pocket doors and beautiful woodwork. Several men in priest's collars were talking leisurely, sipping on drinks.

Veronica leaned to Chevy and whispered, "Those are the saints."

Chevy slowed, taking a long look at the four American men as they passed by. She felt a pull, wanting to go into the room and talk to them. Instead she stayed at Veronica's side with a tired girl gripping her hand.

As they started up the stairs, Chevy glanced back at the room of English-speaking men.

Veronica tilted her head to her. "She said the girls get the back room."

As they made their way down the hall, Chevy watched a woman lead a young girl dressed in a school uniform into a room. As they walked past the room, Chevy glanced over and caught sight of a professionally dressed man sitting on a bed. Chevy held her free hand to her stomach and looked down at the girl at her side.

At the end of the hall, Veronica turned into a bedroom that had two sets of simple-looking bunk beds.

"All right," Veronica said, putting a bit of excitement into her voice. "This is where you get to live. This is the school I told you about, so make sure you learn as much as you can."

The American girls looked sad. The Middle Eastern girl began to cry. "Please don't leave me here," she sobbed. Tears dripped from her dark lashes and ran down her cheeks.

Veronica hugged her. "Remember everything I taught you and showed you?"

The girl nodded, sniffing, trying to stifle the tears.

"It will be fine." Veronica pushed the hair out of her face. "Remember, we got you ready, so it won't hurt too much." She paused. "The men want love. They need love, just like you do. Love them, and for a little while they will love you back, with

179

their body." She looked at the little girl. "Remember that, all right?" She smiled sweetly and looked at the other two girls.

The crying girl kept nodding and wiping her tears.

"Now that goes for all of you," Veronica told them.

Chevy stood there, watching.

Veronica leaned down and kissed them all. "I love you girls. Be good, and learn all you can."

Chevy felt her eyes wanting to well. She choked back the tears, not wanting to scare the girls.

"Good-bye, Chevy," the girl who had held her hand said, wrapping her arms around her legs.

Chevy looked down at the sweet little face and innocent eyes that looked up at her. She leaned down and hugged her. "Now be a good girl, and just like Veronica said, learn all you can." She struggled to keep her voice from cracking.

### 

Walking back down the hall, from behind the closed door Chevy could hear the girl's stifled screaming. She froze.

Veronica leaned close to her and whispered, "That's why I prep them."

Chevy stared at the door. "We can't leave them here," she said quietly, but forceful and determined.

"We have to. Trust me when I tell you there are worse places we could leave them." She looked into Chevy's eyes.

Chevy had an empty look, as though rational thinking was no longer with her.

Veronica grabbed her hand, escorting her down the hall to the steps. "I need to get you outside," she mumbled.

Rounding the corner at the base of the steps was the older woman speaking that unfamiliar language again. Chevy looked over at the saints as they passed. Veronica's voice sounded rushed, fading to the back of her mind as she looked at the room of English-speaking men.

One man looked at her and gave her a simple nod, put his glass into the air, and smiled in greeting.

Veronica pulled her out the door, making the men a blur.

### 

The phone rang on Ward's desk. "Agent Ward," he

180

answered and listened.

Suddenly, he leaned back in his chair and waved his arm in the air to get everyone's attention. The quiet chatter came to a stop as everyone paused and waited. Ward leaned forward, reached for pen and paper, and started writing.

"All right. Thank you. I will pass the information on," he told the person on the phone and hung up. "One of the informants spotted Chevy in Granada, Spain. She was seen with a woman by the name of Veronica Nath, who is married to Sandro Nath, who owns dozens of ports and businesses, and has his hand in several shipping companies. He and a couple of his partners own the *Apoise*."

"One of the partners?" the man in the black suit asked.

"Yep," Ward quickly replied. "They dropped three little girls off at an underground brothel—Falcone School for Girls. The place poses as a boarding school. They have a very specific clientele, and all of them are extremely wealthy. I guess in the grand scheme of things, this brothel is the least of the evils. The kids are cared for, have good living conditions and good food to eat, and are well educated. If not for the fact that the children are forced to have sex with men, it would be a model boarding school."

The man in the black suit glanced around, thinking.

The man in the dress blues chimed in. "Would you like me to bring her back now? We can remove this group of associates," he offered once again.

"Not right now." The man in the suit waved in dismissal. "If I decide our only option is to take this group out, then we will handle them all at once, after Chevy is home and this has settled down." He looked at the surveillance man. "Reroute Neal to Granada."

"Wait!" Ward halted everyone. "Where do we think they're going to go from there?" He looked at the man in the black suit. "Do you think they'll go to Barcelona?"

The surveillance man leaned forward. "Are you thinking that they'll show up at Jack Sweeden's? If so, I have an informant there already. I can have him be on the lookout for Chevy—and this Veronica."

The man in the black suit looked over at him. "None of us really know where they are headed next. Let's go with your thought and assume they'll go to Jack Sweeden's. That's their only associate in that area. Get that plane headed for Granada." He looked at the man in the dress blues. "I want special ops around Sweeden's." He paused. "I don't know if that's where they're going, but just in case. Anyone who tries to hurt Chevy, Neal, or this Veronica, I want taken out of the equation."

The man in the dress blues gave him a simple nod, pulled a phone from his pocket, and began making calls.

### 

Chris Roper was in his office, his foot aching in its walking boot. He reached for his bottle of painkillers, took two more, and washed them down with the amber liquid. He was angry about having to donate a hundred thousand dollars to some stupid school to make himself look good and even more upset that his associate had Chevy in transit. He knew what transit meant. Sandro was wiping his hands of the problem. Never had Sandro done this. Then again, they had never had a problem with any of the girls before.

He dialed Sandro's number and waited as it rang.

The pain in Chris's foot was excruciating—another ring.

He pushed his chair back—the phone rang again.

He placed the hard walking boot on the edge of his desk, elevating his foot—still the phone rang.

The throbbing seemed to slow, which felt a little better—the phone continued to ring.

Sandro wasn't picking up.

Chris slammed the receiver onto the base and sat there with his drink in his hand and held an angry scowl. He thought back to the day when his father introduced him to the business. It was years ago and easy to pluck pretty, young, troubled girls from the streets and take them out of the country. It was a time when passports were barely looked at and were easy to forge. Security at airports was a mere formality, carried out with a wink and a nod. There were hardly any surveillance cameras, and getting a girl out of the country undetected was almost effortless. No one knew anything about human trafficking, sex

182

slaves, or child prostitution. Those who knew were either the dealers or the takers, and both sides looked the other way and kept quiet about the heinous things they did.

The throbbing in his foot began to subside as the painkillers started to take effect.

His phone rang.

He looked at the caller ID, hoping it was Sandro. Instead, it came up as INTERNATIONAL SWEEDEN.

Jack Sweeden was from Germany. During his travels in Barcelona for an auction, he came across a particularly old building that looked more like a castle and bought it. It was the old gothic architecture that drew him. He promptly moved himself and his German-speaking wife to Barcelona. The building proved to come in handy due to its size, configuration, and location. It was a great location from which to auction off the cream of the crop of women to the wealthy bachelors of the world. It was close to the water, so transports to and from his home were easy.

Wife auctioning was the most lucrative part of what he, Chris, and their other associates did. It was a win for everyone. Beautiful women could be sold from anywhere for hundreds of thousands of dollars, up to several million. This was a nice paycheck for doing nothing more than picking the right woman and plucking her from the country. These women were in their mid-teens or early twenties, typically runaways. In many cases, they were delighted to become the wife of some wealthy man who would appreciate them and give them a pleasant life. In turn, the men were happy to have a naïve young trophy wife who was compliant and moldable.

Chris picked up the phone. "Hey, Jack."

"Chris, I just got an interesting call," Jack said. His deep voice was tinged with an accent that was hard to place.

"I'm listening."

"First off, I've been following the Westen girl that went missing," Jack said. "Was she one of yours?"

"Why do you ask?"

"Curious."

"Yeah, she is. But I didn't know—"

183

"I saw they pulled her boyfriend in for questioning. I was shocked when I saw it was your son. Picking girls a little too close to your own backyard, aren't we?" Jack probed.

"That's a long story. I knew Brandon had a girlfriend, but I hadn't met her. I was at a strip club in Boston, where he's doing his graduate work, and this girl catches my eye. I go back to the hotel room and get on one of my websites, and guess who pops up?"

"This same girl from the strip club."

"Yep! She told me her name was Chevy, and I think, how could a girl with a name like that be any kind of trouble? So I give the go-ahead on this girl. Then my son calls a few days later and tells me to send the attorney. He reported his girlfriend missing a few nights earlier and he was being detained for questioning. The whole thing has spiraled from there." Chris looked at his glass.

"Well, Sandro called me. His wife and Chevy will be here tomorrow. They'll be staying for a few days to a week, then leaving. I let Sandro know it was rather good timing that I'm having an auction next week. I'll have four or five women, and I asked if I should include Chevy." Jack paused. "The interesting part is that I was told she is in transit. Sandro didn't elaborate. He told me he would be meeting his wife and this girl, staying for a few days to make some arrangements, and leaving again."

"This girl has been a pain." Chris glanced at his elevated foot and grimaced as he repositioned it. "Since the moment Brandon reported her missing, I told Sandro to send her home. Clearly he hasn't."

"Are you sure you want to do that? This is high profile and could get out of hand."

"This one girl has caused me so many problems. I say sell her and then send her home. Quietly. I want my money out of her."

Jack spoke slowly. "You want me to sell her, against what Sandro has asked me to do, then follow that by sending her home?" He sounded a bit taken aback. "How do you propose I do that? I'll have a lot of explaining to do to Sandro, and to the buyer who will leave empty-handed." He paused. "You know we have a reputation to uphold."

Chris waved his drink back and forth in the air. "Be creative. Things happen. Make it look like an accident, overdose, natural causes, or something believable."

"I see," Jack said flatly. "I'll tell you that after I got off the phone with Sandro, I thought maybe she was in transit at your request. I wasn't sure you knew about my upcoming auction. I called to make sure everyone was on the same page. I'll see what I can do. I'll tell you right now, I won't make any promises."

"Let me know when you have it resolved," Chris said coldly.

"I'll be in touch," Jack said, and hung up.

### 

Agent Ward's phone rang. "Agent Ward," he answered.

The call was coming from the surveillance truck a half mile away from the Roper home. "Chris just got off the phone with Jack Sweeden."

"Ah, yes. Little Sweeden," Ward said, so the other men could hear him. The words *Little Sweeden* rang in the ears of everyone and grabbed their attention. "I'm putting you on speaker."

"Veronica and Chevy are supposed to show up at Little Sweeden," the surveillance specialist told him.

"Did they say when?" Ward asked.

"Jack told Chris that they were expected tomorrow. I sent the feed to your computer so you guys can listen to it yourself. But here is the disturbing part: Chris Roper wants Jack to auction Chevy then 'send her home.' Chris wants Jack to be creative about getting rid of her. He wants it to look like an accident. Jack Sweeden didn't seem happy about the idea."

"Anything else?" Ward asked.

"Yeah, the auction is next week. He wasn't any more specific than that."

"Next week," Ward repeated. "Standard auction?"

"From what I could discern. Jack said he had four or five women."

185

"Okay," Ward said. "Keep us posted." He looked around the room making eye contact with the others.

"Of course," the surveillance specialist said, then disconnected the call.

The man in the black suit sat there. "Get our agents over there and get Neal into Little Sweeden."

The surveillance man spoke up. "Remember, I told you I already have an informant at Little Sweeden. The informant has already been brought up to speed—if any of them show up."

The man in the black suit looked at him. "Great. Make sure Chevy's protected. We need that girl brought home safe and sound." He paused. "Who is the informant?"

"He is a middle-aged man named Bruce. He was from Chicago, a banker. His daughter was trafficked several years back. He was able to follow her all the way to the Middle East, but she was killed before he could get to her."

The man in the black suit looked down and shifted in his chair, as though he didn't like the man's qualifications.

"Once this guy got back to the States, we needed to place him into a witness protection program. He was recruited from there, now is one of the butlers at Little Sweeden."

The man in the black suit leaned forward and folded his hands together on the table in front of him. "Make sure this informant knows what the situation is. There's a lot that could go wrong—and I don't want it to."

The surveillance man nodded.

### 

Neal was sleeping in a leather recliner on the jet when he was awakened by a loud buzzing. He blinked his eyes and rubbed his fingers against his eyelids, trying to focus. He looked over at the two men across from him.

The phone was just under the window. The man in the khaki jacket answered.

"Sure, all right," he finally said, after listening for several long minutes. "I'll let him know. You'll make arrangements for the driver? All right, I'll give him the update." He hung up and looked at Neal.

"There's been a change of plans."

Neal noticed the plane making a sharp turn in the air. "Instead of going to the Ukraine, we need to turn around for Barcelona."

"Spain?"

"Yes. Apparently there's information that Chevy's in Granada and headed for Barcelona. They're planning to arrive at a place called Little Sweeden tomorrow."

"Little Sweeden?" Neal repeated.

"Little Sweeden is a bed and breakfast, but every now and then they have what are known as wife auctions. Wealthy businessmen who want a wife or companionship will go to Little Sweeden and buy what they desire."

"So now I need to go and buy her?" Neal rubbed his face, still groggy. "You know what?" He got up from his chair. "Let me get up, get my blood flowing again. Adequate blood supply to the brain helps the comprehension process. Let me run to the bathroom." He yawned. "Then we'll talk."

The men waited.

A few minutes later, Neal was sitting down again, this time with color in his face and clear eyes. "Let's talk." He smiled.

"Little Sweeden," the man in the khaki jacket said.

"No, wait. Back up. Who spotted Chevy? Was she alone, or is she still with that woman you told me about and showed me a picture of last night? Veronica Nath."

"Chevy's still with Veronica. It was an informant that spotted them in Granada. Then we got information from another source they're scheduled to arrive at Little Sweeden some time tomorrow."

"You said that was a bed and breakfast?" Neal wanted to clarify.

"Yes, that's correct. We've added you to the guest list, so you're in for the auction. You'll check in at Sweeden's on Saturday. The auction is Thursday. You'll be in a specific place, so keeping the two of you safe will be easier. We'll send you in with a car and a driver. The driver is undercover and there to protect the two of you from inside Little Sweeden."

Neal looked at him. "So, now, instead of going to find them

and bringing her back, now I need to buy her?"

"Yes. You need to appear to be a wealthy businessman. We're going to need to get you some new clothes."

"I would hope so. I need to look the part."

# Chapter 15

Back in Granada, Veronica and Chevy squeezed themselves into the backseat of a tiny cab. They sat shoulder to shoulder with their knees to their chest. Veronica's backpack was squashed on her lap.

"This is one of the tiniest cars I've ever seen." Chevy looked at the small door handle.

Veronica pulled the manila envelope from her bag. "We need to go here." She held the envelope so the driver could see the address.

The man gave her an odd look through the rearview mirror. "You don't want to go there!" He said firmly, shaking his head.

"This is where we need to go," she told him.

"Señora, you don't want to go there."

"Yes, I do. Take us there."

"Look, señora, do you know what that place is?"

Veronica glanced at Chevy. "Yes, I know. Just take us there."

"Two beautiful women like yourselves." He turned in his seat and looked directly at them. "Do you have a death wish? Even I don't like to go there, and I'm an ugly man."

Chevy's sat there, looking uneasy.

Veronica shook her head as though she was frustrated, then reached over and put her hand on Chevy's, squeezing it to comfort her. "Yes," she told the man. "I know about this place. I have some papers I need to drop off. In fact, how about you not only take us there but you wait on us. We will be fifteen minutes, maybe a half hour, and then you can drive us to Barcelona."

The man arched his eyebrow at her. "Do you realize that Barcelona is an eight-hour drive from here?" He stared at Veronica as though she couldn't possibly be serious.

Her demeanor suddenly changing into capable, sure, and powerful. "I know exactly how long it takes. Not only will I pay the fare there and back, I will cover the meals, including yours coming back, and a hotel for you, along with a sizable tip," she offered.

"Sizable tip? How sizable?"

"One month's housing."

"Señora, are you kidding me?"

"No," Veronica said firmly.

"How do I know you are good for it?"

Veronica reached into her bag and pulled out a bundle of money.

The driver looked at the bundle, then at her.

"Now you know I am good for it," she told him as she pulled several of the bills from the bundle and handed them to him. "Here! We will start with this."

"Are you sure you want to do this? You know you can rent a car and drive there yourself for a lot less."

"I don't drive," she replied sharply.

The man put his hands in the air. "All right, all right, as you wish," he said, turning back around and putting the car in drive.

"Lost Row it is," he said softly, as Veronica sat back in her seat beside Chevy.

Chevy repeated, "Lost Row?" and looked at Veronica.

"Yeah, that's what we call it," the driver told her, looking at her in the rearview mirror.

"Why do you call it Lost Row?" Chevy asked.

The driver shook his head. "I take it you don't know about Lost Row?"

"I do," Veronica said, quickly.

"Lost Row is what we call this place where we're going. It's where lives are lost, souls are lost, virginity is lost, and people lose their wives, sisters, girlfriends, children, and neighbors. Even men are lost there—mostly, trying to retrieve their loved ones. Some people make it out of there. Most don't. I'll tell you, what you see in there will take your innocence."

"My innocence?" Chevy sounded doubtful. "How?"

"You go in there and you'll see things you never thought possible. It'll take your innocence," he said, sure of himself.

Chevy looked at Veronica apprehensively.

Veronica nodded. "It's true. When you were upset about the

190

girls, and I told you there are far worse places. This is far worse."

Chevy sat there trying to imagine a place so bad, so horrible that part of her innocence would be lost—permanently.

They rode down streets and around corners for twenty minutes or more, then the buildings around them began to hold a more ominous feeling of something dark, secretive, dirty, and evil. They pulled in front of a building that looked like all the others on the block. Its substantial wood double doors were protected with ornate but heavy wrought iron gates. Chevy noticed that the other buildings around them had similar doors and gates.

"I'm waiting here. If anyone tells me to move, I will pull up right there." The driver pointed along the front of the building to a place farther up the street.

"Perfect."

"Go on…" Veronica encouraged Chevy, nudging her leg to get out.

Chevy reached for the tiny door handle. The small door opened, and she climbed out of the backseat. She started for the trunk to get her backpack.

"No. Leave it. We won't be in here long," Veronica told her.

"What if he leaves?"

"He won't, and if by chance he does, we can replace it." She shook her head. "When we go in, stay close to me. No matter how surprised you are, do not let it show. Look, but don't show expression. Act like you have seen it all before," Veronica prepped her.

"Maybe I shouldn't go in. I can stay in the car." She looked at the place with reluctance.

"No," Veronica said. "I need to keep you safe and get you back to the States. You're coming in with me." She rang the doorbell, then rang it again. One of the wood doors cracked open just enough so the person who answered it could peer out through the iron gates.

"I'm here to see Lou," Veronica said.

The door opened further to reveal a clean-cut man. He was good-looking and had a thin build, but his shifty eyes and the

191

dark vibes he was giving off gave Chevy the creeps.

He opened the wood door, pulled a key from his pocket, and unlocked the iron gates. The gates were pretty, but now she realized they weren't decorative. They were security.

They stepped inside and stood there waiting as the man locked the gates, then closed the wood door and locked it with a single slide lock about midway up. Chevy didn't say anything, but noticed that the wood doors had two more slide locks, one going into the floor and one going into the top of each door frame. She found it unnerving. Instinctively, she nudged closer to Veronica, touching her side.

"I'm not sure where Lou is. We'll have to find him. Follow me," the man said, heading down the hall.

The plaster walls and old tile floors looked all right. Nothing was in great shape, but nothing was ugly. The man paused and stuck his head into a room that looked like an old study, with a shallow marble fireplace that looked like it wasn't functional anymore. Several men were relaxing around a table, doing various things. All of them had guns in holsters at their ribs.

"Have you seen Lou?" the man asked them.

The men looked over. "No," one said. The others shook their heads and went back to what they were doing.

"Someone watch the door," the man said. He turned to Veronica. "We get to go search for him."

Veronica shook her head. "You go find him. We'll wait."

The man looked at her suspiciously. "No, I can't do that. I don't know who you are."

"I'm Veronica Nath."

"How do I know that you're really Sandro's wife?" He sounded doubtful.

"You go find Lou, and we'll wait here."

"If you're going to be in here, then you are going to stay with me."

"Suit yourself." She shrugged.

The man started down the hall toward a stairwell with a small stained glass window. In this dark, dreary place, the light that came in through the glass felt like a small ray of hope shining in from outside.

Coming down the steps were two men, one of them grossly overweight.

"How was it?" the man asked.

"I think you drugged her too much," the large man said. "I think she's dead."

The man groaned.

"I like them more responsive."

"I'll check on her, see what's going on."

The large man leered at Chevy and Veronica. "Are they new?"

"They're not for sale. They're here to do business."

"They're very pretty," the smaller man commented.

"Like I said." He looked at the men as he stepped in front of Chevy and Veronica, shielding them.

Chevy's eyes shifted to Veronica, who stared blankly into the distance. As the men walked past, the large man reached out for Veronica. She looked at him and said flatly, "I have AIDS."

His face turned sour and he snatched his hand back. He and his friend scurried away, toward the front door.

The man snickered. He looked back at Veronica. "I see you have been around this before."

"I told you who I am. I've been around this for a long time," she said, unmoved.

"Come on." He continued up the steps.

At the top of the steps were a series of heavy, ominous-looking doors. The man opened the first door and walked in. On the bed was a completely naked woman on her back, her arms tied above her head, her legs laying open. She stared lifelessly at the ceiling. Her skin was pale and her lips dark, almost as dark as the circles around her eyes. The man walked over and felt her neck. "She's alive," he said, unconcerned. "I'll come back and deal with her after we find Lou." He turned and walked out of the room, motioning for them to follow.

He opened the next door on a man having sex with a girl on her knees. The man behind her held her hips, thrusting his

193

length in and out of her. She glanced over at the door. Her pupils were dilated and her hair was matted. Purple, blue, and yellow bruises covered her wrists, butt, and upper thighs.

"Looking for someone," the man said apologetically as he pulled the door shut.

From somewhere at the end of the hall was a woman screaming. Chevy took note and said nothing.

The man opened another door. Crumpled in the center of the room was a naked woman, chained to the floor, a locked cuff around her bloody ankle and an iron mask locked behind her head. As the man looked in, the woman looked up. "Please let me go," she pleaded, sobbing. "Please, please," she begged slowly reaching out her hand to him. He pulled the door shut, irritated.

Chevy's face began to flush, reflecting the rise of her pulse. Her breathing speeded up and deepened. She thought about how they were locked in this heinous place. She stole a look at Veronica, who appeared completely unmoved.

They continued down the hall toward the room from which Chevy could hear a woman screaming violently. "No...!"

"He's probably down here," the man said as they approached the last door. "We have one we just brought in. She's a real problem." He opened the door to three men trying to hold the screaming girl down so one could inject her. She struggled to get free, fighting with all her might, screaming at the top of her lungs for someone, anyone to help her.

One man stood at the side of her bed, holding down one arm and a leg. The second man straddled her, holding down her body and the other arm with both hands so the third man could inject her. The woman was kicking her free leg, bucking. She got an arm free and punched the first man in the mouth. Instinctively, he let go of her, stepping back as he lifted his hand to his mouth and looked at his fingers, seeing his blood.

The woman's eyes locked on Chevy. "Help me!" she screamed, struggling to fight them off. "Help!!" She screamed at Chevy with terror in her eyes.

Chevy looked down.

The man straddling her grabbed her free arm, holding it

194

down again. The man with the syringe quickly injected her and stepped back.

"No!" she cried. "Let me go!" Her struggling began to lessen, and her words started to become mumbles. Soon, the desperate look in her eyes became a glazed blank stare through dilated pupils.

The man straddling her looked over at the man she had punched. "Lou, you all right?"

He had short dark hair and light eyes. Something about him made Chevy want to shiver. He touched his hand to his lip again, then looked at the dab of blood on his fingers. "Enough of her!" he said, looking at the second man, who was climbing off of the girl.

"Are you sure?" the second man asked.

"Yeah, go ahead. We can't get money for her when she fights like this." He looked at the blood on his fingers again.

The woman lay there, limp. The second man pulled her shirt from her body. He pulled her forward enough to unclasp her bra. The bra slid from her body as her body slumped back to the bed. Her head flopped back at an uncomfortable-looking angle.

The man smiled. "This one has nice boobs." He ran his hand across her nipple, strumming it with his thumb as he pulled her skirt and underwear from her body, tossing them to the side of the bed. Eagerly, he pushed his pants down and lifted her legs by the knees. He bent down and licked her, then licked his finger before sliding it into her canal. "Oh crap!" he said excitedly. He eagerly lined up his penis with her canal and pressed himself into her. He tilted his head back and closed his eyes. "Oh man," he groaned.

Veronica turned her head.

"Oh! God damn! This feels good," he said in a throaty whisper, then he paused and looked at Lou. "Want to feel?"

Lou squeezed his lips together, shook his head slightly, and motioned his hand in the air. "No, you go ahead. I'm going to take the backside when you are done."

"All right." He continued thrusting himself in and out of her.

195

They stood watching as the man's penis slid in and out of her. Veronica took in a deep breath, letting it out and shifted her weight from one foot to the other as though she were bored. The man sped up, moving faster until he gave several long deep thrusts and groaned in pleasure, appearing to orgasm deep inside her.

The woman groaned painfully, laying listless on the bed with her eyes blank.

Lou looked at the woman as the man pulled his penis out of her, stood up, and pulled up his pants. "Flip her over," Lou instructed, moving around the bed. "Put her head off the bed," He glanced over, laying his gun on the bed and undoing his pants, then crawled onto the bed and lifted her ass into the air at the hips. He spit on his hand and rubbed his saliva on his penis before entering her ass. He thrust himself in and out of her as hard as he could.

"Christ, this feels good!"

Chevy looked down at her nails, trying to mimic Veronica's boredom. She looked back up to see him taking deep, long thrusts. The woman groaned in pain. All of a sudden, he picked up the gun, put it to the back of her head, and pulled the trigger. Instantly, her body went limp. Blood, brain, bone, and fleshy chunks sprayed across the floor as blood poured from her head.

"Are you done now?" Veronica asked, sounding irritated that she had to wait.

Lou turned and gave her an irritated look. "Are you in a hurry?" he asked as he pulled his pants up.

Veronica took offense at his question. "I am, actually. I have a driver waiting outside."

Lou looked at Chevy. "So, who is this you have with you?" The corner of his mouth pulled back, and the glint in his eyes made Chevy want to panic.

Veronica snarled at him. "She's a friend of ours. Eyes off."

He took slow steps toward them with a lustful smile on his face as he eyed the length of Chevy's body. "You sure about that?"

196

"More than sure. Eyes off. Do you have documents for me?" Veronica asked.

The lustful smile fell from his face. "If you didn't bring her for me, then why is she here?"

"This isn't a good area to leave your attractive friend waiting in a car."

"So why did both of you come find me?"

"I told your man here"—Veronica gestured with a nod—"to leave us downstairs while he located you." She looked over to him. "Your man told me he didn't want us out of his sight."

Lou shifted his gaze to the man. "Don't bring people up here!"

Veronica chimed in. "Look you two can figure this out later. Right now, documents." She paused, giving him an intolerant expression. "Sound good?"

Lou paused, upset with his man. "Fine. Come with me." He adjusted his shirt coldly and started for the door, then turned around to the other men. "You two clean this up." He moved his hand in a mopping motion.

### 

Lou unlocked a door on the main level. Thick, dark draperies let in no light, not even a hint. The inside of this room was much nicer than the rest of what they had seen. It had new-looking flooring, a fireplace, built-in bookshelves, and a desk by the wall with plush chairs arranged in front of it.

"I have the paperwork here," he said. He walked to the desk and tapped a file folder, then crossed his arms and waited impatiently as Veronica unzipped her backpack. She pulled out the large manila envelope and handed it to him.

He handed over the file folder and watched as Veronica slid it into her back pack. "Are you going to make sure it is all there?" he asked.

She looked up at him. "No. This is between you and my husband, not you and me. If you didn't hand me the right documentation, then my husband knows where to find you," she said confidently.

Lou looked at her for a moment, seeming alarmed by her words. He walked around his desk, pulled open a drawer, and thumbed through some files. He pulled some papers from a file. "Here. Sandro might need these, too." He leaned over his desk and handed her the papers.

Veronica pulled the file folder out, put the papers in it, and returned it to her backpack. "Is there anything else I need?"

Lou shook his head. "Not that I can think of."

"Then you may see us out."

"Sure." He walked them to the room with the table of men and poked his head in. "One of you let these ladies out," he ordered.

"You're going to let them leave?" one of the men asked.

"This is Sandro's wife and his friend. Try to show a little respect."

One man stood. "I'll let them out," he said, unenthused, and walked to the door.

He pulled the slide locks from the floor, then from the top of the door, then the center. He opened the door and unlocked the gate.

"Thank you," Veronica said, stepping through the doorway with Chevy close behind.

The gate clanged shut behind Chevy. The sound rang ominously in her ears. The place was once again under lock and key, the lost souls shut away, trapped in hell.

Veronica walked to the cab. She pulled Chevy in behind her, then shut and locked the car door.

"Ready?" the driver asked.

"Yes. Go, get us out of here," Veronica said urgently.

He sped away.

### 

They were several streets away when Chevy leaned forward, put her head in her hands, and started to cry.

Veronica rubbed her back. "It's all right. We're out of there."

The driver peered at them in the rearview mirror. "It's all right, sweet girl. You lost your innocence in there, didn't you?" he asked. "Everyone who goes in comes out upset. What's in

198

there isn't meant for human eyes." He put his arm over the seat and rubbed the top part of her back. "I'll get the two of you to Barcelona. Are you hungry?"

"Stop the car!" Chevy blurted out, pulling the door lock. "I'm going to be sick."

Instantly, the driver pulled over. Chevy opened the car door, leaned out, and threw up. She heaved until there was nothing left in her stomach, then sat up and pulled the car door shut, wiping her wet lips with her fingers.

The driver handed her a napkin from his glove compartment.

Her eyes were smeary with tears.

Veronica put her arm around her, curling Chevy to her side. "It bothered me, too." She shook her head. "I remember when that was me," she whispered, looking out the window at the sky.

Chevy looked up and saw the distress in Veronica's eyes. She laid her head back on her shoulder.

# Chapter 16

Nine hours later, Chevy and Veronica were leaning on each other in the tiny backseat of the cab, while the cab driver sped down narrow brick and cobblestone streets.

"All these twists are turns...I feel like I'm in a maze," Chevy said.

He slowed in front of an old gothic gray stone building that looked like a castle.

Chevy gazed out the window of the cab in the last of the evening light. The building was illuminated with lights from the ground. It had five levels and tall arches. Gargoyles were perched at the corners, watching. On one side was a square medieval tower.

Veronica leaned forward and talking to the cab driver. Their conversation fell to the back of Chevy's mind. She was more interested in the thick wood doors that sat inside the archway and the long, heavy wrought iron hinges that held them in place. The building was beautiful in a rustic, old world kind of way.

"Go, Chevy," Veronica said, nudging Chevy from behind. "I paid."

Chevy stopped looking at the architecture and pulled the small door handle. She climbed out of the tiny backseat, happy to stretch her legs. She stretched and looked up to the top of the building. The gargoyles looked more menacing when she was directly in front of them. The cab driver popped the trunk, and Chevy pulled out her bag. "We're good," she said, closing the trunk. She took several steps toward the building, and stared at it. She heard the small car door close, then Veronica stepped beside her.

The cab rattled away, the noise of its engine trailing off in the distance.

"What is this place again?" Chevy asked, looking again at the creepy gargoyle faces.

"It's Little Sweeden. We're going to spend several days

here while I arrange your route back to the States."

"Veronica," Chevy said, still looking at the building.

"Yes."

"This place is creepy."

"You think so? I think the old architecture is beautiful." She looked at Chevy. "Wait until you see the inside. It's gorgeous. There are lots of antiques. Jack Sweeden enjoys traveling all over the world to collect things from estate sales, antiques stores, auctions. Some of the furnishings are not only priceless, they are breathtaking."

"Oh..." Chevy's voice trailed off, unimpressed.

"Come." Veronica took hold of her hand.

Reluctantly, Chevy followed her to the door. Alongside the stone archway was a small rope that disappeared into a tiny opening in the stone overhead. "Pull it!" Veronica told her, excited.

"I suppose they didn't have doorbells hundreds of years ago when this place was built, huh," Chevy mumbled sarcastically, then pulled on the rope. Waiting, she turned to look at the cobblestone streets that disappeared around corners and old buildings.

The deep squeak of the door opening grabbed her attention, prompting her to turn around. A middle-aged man in a butler's suit said something in a different language. Chevy squinted, frustrated by the language barrier, then walked into a huge entry with a claw-foot table in the center of the room. The table looked old and had a big bouquet of flowers in the center. The floor was wide wood planks that creaked as you stepped. A massive area rug lay in the center of the entry under the table, helping to absorb the squeaks of the floor. All the walls were rough stone hung with paintings that had thick, dark, ornate frames and looked as old as the building itself.

She took in her surroundings while Veronica and the butler spoke. She suddenly heard the butler say, "American?" The word grabbed her attention.

The butler looked at Chevy and smiled. "I expected your arrival tomorrow," he said politely.

"Is it going to be a problem?" Veronica asked.

"Of course not." He shook his head and turned back to her. "We always have rooms for you." He looked back at Chevy and paused. "You're very pretty." He took her hand and kissed it. "And your name would be?"

"Chevy." She smiled.

He gave her a slight nod of his head. "You have a very distinctive name, for very distinctive beauty."

"Thank you," she said sweetly.

"I am Bruce, the butler. I have known the lovely Veronica for several years. It is a pleasure to have the two of you here. Tell me, would you like to enjoy some of the night scenery, or shall I show you to your accommodations?"

"No scenery," Veronica said. "We can see it a different night. Just the rooms, please."

"Are either of you hungry or thirsty? I assume that you haven't eaten yet."

"We did eat along the way. We had a long day. We'd just like to go to sleep."

"To your rooms it shall be," the butler said. "Follow me." He led them up the stairs to the second level.

The steps creaked even more than the floor. Chevy walked near the wall, trying to avoid the creaks. Upstairs there were halls that connected to more halls. It felt confusing and maze-like.

"Veronica, this will be your room," he said, twisting a door handle and pushing the door open. The room was sizable, with an old canopy bed covered in a rich cream fabric, expensive-looking chairs, a fireplace, and a bathroom.

"Please make yourself at home. If you need anything, pick up the phone and dial one. Is there anything I can get you before I show Chevy to her room?"

"No, I'm fine. But I do need to see what room Chevy will be in."

The butler smiled at her. "Then I will show you right where Miss Chevy will be." He turned back into the hall.

Around the corner on the opposite side of the hall was another door. "This is the room Miss Chevy will be in." He opened the door and turned on the light. It had another big

202

canopy bed, fireplace, chairs, and a bathroom. Above the fireplace was an old pendulum clock that ticked louder than she had ever heard a clock tick.

"Well, señoras, I will leave you. If you decide you need anything, remember, pick up the phone and dial one." He held his index finger in the air.

### 

The pendulum swung, and the tick of the clock consumed the room. Chevy tossed and turned. It was one thirty in the morning. The images of the horrible place the cab driver had called Lost Row were playing in her mind. The cab driver was correct: what she had witnessed took her innocence, innocence she wasn't going to get back.

The tick of the clock seemed to grow louder with each swing of the pendulum. Each time she closed her eyes, she saw the girl chained to the floor, her hand outstretched for help. She heard the scream of the last girl. The stale smell of the place still lingered in her nose.

She decided she was hungry. she pushed the covers back, walked to the fireplace, reached up, and stopped the pendulum. For the first time since she got there she heard the most wonderful sound: silence. As for food, she could dial one, but it was late, and finding the kitchen couldn't be that hard. Her need for something to eat propelled her to the door. She paused and slowly pulled the door open, trying to be quiet. The hinges squeaked. "My God," she said to herself. "Everything needs oil." She left the door open.

The boards creaked beneath her feet as she tiptoed through the hall. She moved closer to the wall, looking for a less-worn path that would make less noise. She found an area that didn't squeak too much along the baseboard.

She found a stairwell and descended. At the bottom of the stair she came out into a dark hallway. Like the upstairs, it was a maze of rooms and twisting halls. She spotted a partly open door down the hall, a light on in the room behind it. She heard two men talking in another language. The door suddenly swung open, flooding the hall with light. The men were carrying a naked woman, limp and lifeless. Her eyes widened. She froze, then stepped quietly to the wall and headed back down the hall in the opposite direction. Her heart was pounding in her chest. She came to another hall, then turned around and moved as quickly as she could, staying close to the wall. She made several turns until she came to double pocket doors at the end of the hall. She slid one back and slipped into the dark room, then pushed the sliding door back into place.

She stood there for a moment, facing the inside of the doors. Her heart pounding in her chest.

"I trust you are finding everything all right?" a deep voice asked from the dark.

Chevy jumped and screamed.

Suddenly a light flipped on. In a chair sat the butler. The top of his shirt was unbuttoned, and a drink rested in his hand on the arm of the chair. "Not to worry. You can scream all you want. Sound doesn't travel in this place," he told her in clear English. "Is there anything I can get you?"

Chevy's chest heaved.

He stood from the chair and walked to her.

She watched his every movement, his every step, scanning the area around them.

He took another step toward her and stopped. "It's okay." He held out his hand. "Come," he encouraged her.

Chevy stood there, untrusting.

"It's okay." He motioned again, giving her a kind smile, asking politely, "How about we dance?"

Something about the look in his eyes made her want to trust him. She took a cautious step toward him.

"May I have this dance?" he asked, taking several more steps to her.

She was ready to run when his hands met hers.

"Does my Chevy like to dance?" he asked charmingly.

Chevy searched his face. "I suppose so," she said, softly, reluctantly.

He stepped to one side and then to the other in a swaying motion, her hand in his, close to him. They were dancing in the huge, beautiful room without music. He began to whisper into her ear. "The main areas are wired for sound, so be careful

204

what you say. If it's something you don't want to be heard, then whisper into the person's ear."

"Is my room wired for sound?" Chevy whispered.

"No." He shook his head, and leaned to her ear. "There is supposed to be a man from the States who will be here to take you home."

Chevy jerked her head away and looked at him.

He leaned back to her ear. "He's going to take you back to the States. I will point him out to you. Whatever you do, it must be perceived that you have taken a liking to him. That way the other men will leave you alone. These men are looking for permanent companions—wives. There is an upcoming wife auction."

"Wife auction," Chevy repeated, wanting to feel panicked. She saw home, school, Brandon slipping through her fingers and felt herself sliding into a unknown abyss of horrific things that could happen.

"Don't worry. Cling to the man from the States. He is coming to take you home. I'll point him out to you." He spun her around and pulled her close to him once again. He whispered, "Be very careful talking to me. No one must think we share any knowledge of this sort." He held her body close to his as they danced in the silence of the room. "Don't drink the wine unless I give it to you. Think of me as your guardian angel." He dipped her.

Chevy gave him an unsure look. "It was nice dancing with you, Chevy," he said quietly, pulling her up from the dip.

"I was looking for the kitchen," she told him. "I wanted something to eat."

"Absolutely!" he said, and winked. "Well, then, Miss Chevy, allow me to escort you to the kitchen and then back to your room." He pushed one of the doors open and stepped into the hallway, holding Chevy's hand to guide her.

# Chapter 17

Brandon sat on the hood of his car and looked out across the beautiful Ozark Mountains. He had always wanted to watch the clouds roll in, to see that rolling fog. He didn't know where to go. He had no plan. He knew he would be easy to find if he stayed with family or friends, and he didn't want to involve them.

He sat there struggling to comprehend what his father did for a living and that his father had taken the one person who was most important to him. School was now less important than figuring out life and his new place in it.

His phone rang from inside the car. He jumped down and opened the car door and grabbed the phone from the center console, hoping it was Chevy. The caller ID said JUDY ROPER. His heart sank. He tossed his phone onto the seat and shut the car door. He planted the sole of his shoe on the bumper and hauled himself up onto the hood again. He looked at the fog and the mist. He took in the smells and energy that were all around him, hoping that somewhere in the rolling clouds was the answer to the question of what to do next.

### 

John was at home in the garage tinkering with his old plow truck. There was no better time to fidget with something than when his thoughts and feelings were jumbled.

The garage door opened. He glanced over to see Ruthie coming over with a loving smile and a glass of grape Kool-Aid in her hand, then turned his attention back to the truck.

"I thought you might want something to drink," she said.

He offered no response.

"Honey," she finally said, to get his attention.

He looked up from the engine, exchanged the wrench in his hand for a socket wrench, and continued what he was doing.

"Hey," she said. "I was nice enough to bring you something to drink. I don't know where you want me to set this."

"All you want to do is nag and bitch!" he snapped.

Her eyes narrowed as the sweet smile melted from her face. "What's wrong with you? It's Kool-Aid! I was thoughtful enough to bring you a glass, and you're being rude to me by making me stand here and ignoring me. All you have to do is acknowledge me, maybe say thank you, and tell me where you would like for me to set it down." She sounded fed up with his mean and thoughtless treatment.

"You expect me to drop what I'm doing just because you walked out here?" he barked.

She recoiled from his reaction. "No, I don't expect you to stop what you're doing when you are in the middle of something, but when you pause, I do expect you to acknowledge me. I expect good treatment. Being rude is not good treatment."

"Then quit fucking nagging me!" he yelled as he walked over to the garage button. He pressed it, and the garage door began sliding upward.

John looked across the field to the sea of reporters, vans, tents, lawn chairs, and cameras that were waiting.

"Too bad this isn't summer when the corn is tall," she commented, stepping beside him and looking out.

He didn't say anything. He turned and started back to his truck.

She glanced out, then paused at something that captured her attention. "John, come look at this."

He stopped and turned. He did a double-take and moved back to the open garage door for a closer look.

Turning into their long drive was a flatbed tow truck with its amber lights on, carrying a tarp-covered vehicle.

"Did you buy something?" Ruthie asked.

"No!" he shot back quickly. "But it looks like you did."

Ruthie gave him an irritated look. "What's that comment for? No, I didn't buy anything. You know better." She turned and walked back inside the house, slamming the door behind her.

The tow truck pulled up and an older man got out.

"I have a delivery for a John or Ruth Westen," he said.

"What is it?" John asked.

The man looked at him. "Well, you see, son, I am a tow truck driver. This here is a flatbed tow truck, and lo and behold, I am bringing you a vehicle."

### 

Ruthie put the unwanted glass of Kool-Aid in the sink. She grabbed a beer out o the fridge for John. She paused, then grabbed one for herself, too. She returned to the garage She walked back to John in time to see a frustrated expression on his face. It forced an instant smile on hers.

Sarcasm danced in the driver's eyes. "Well, son, since my delivery address is here, I would assume that it belongs to someone here by the name of John or Ruthie Westen."

She said nothing, wanting desperately to laugh. The driver put his hand on his hip. "Where did you want to stick it? Is right here in the drive good for ya?"

She put her head down, closed her eyes rolled her lips under—trying to contain herself.

"I want to see what the hell you are trying to drop off."

The man walked over and began undoing the ratchet straps that held the tarp on, then walked to the back of the flatbed and pulled the tarp off in one big motion.

There before them was Chevy's car, Skunk.

The smirk instantly fell from Ruthie's face. She covered her mouth with her hand and turned around, took in a deep breath, then squeezed her eyes shut, trying to keep her composure. She turned back around in time to see John's jaw clenched tight. Seeing Chevy's car was haunting. Her car was like a coffin being placed in the driveway—Chevy's coffin. It was a sickening reminder she was missing, somewhere out of their reach. The photos of the dead girl who resembled Chevy flashed through her mind.

The man retrieved a clipboard from his truck and started walking toward them.

Ruthie stepped in front of John as she handed him a beer.

"I need a signature," the driver said.

She scribbled her name on the paperwork, then watched as the man unhooked the car and slid it from the back of the tow truck. Without a word, he got back in the cab and drove off.

208

She turned to John and started for a hug.

"Get the fuck off me!" John barked as he pushed her away.

She looked at him, holding her arms out. "I would like a hug," she said.

"That's all you ever want. Give me a hug, spend time with me," he whined, making fun of her feelings and speaking to her like she was a child to be belittled.

Slowly she began to lower her arms. "You know you should be glad that I still love you, in spite of the fact that you are acting like an ass," she hissed.

John laughed at her. "Everybody is replaceable." He shook his head.

"What's that supposed to mean?"

"Just like I said: you think I am such an ass. Oh, well, then find someone else," he taunted.

She went into the house to the bathroom. She turned on the water in the sink, splashed some on her face, and started to cry. She wasn't sure what hurt more: the gut-wrenching reminder that Chevy was missing sitting in the driveway, or the way John was treating her. She knew that with each day the likelihood of Chevy coming home alive, or even being found at all, decreased. It tore at her soul. She began to cry harder. She felt like she was going to implode. Her heart was thumping in her ears, reminding her that she was helpless in finding Chevy. Huge tears ran down her cheeks. She grabbed the box of tissues and slid down the wall until she was sitting on the floor. She was hurt, sad, rejected, and mourning a daughter she wasn't sure would ever come home. She sat there sobbing into the palms of her hands—alone.

# Chapter 18

Late Saturday afternoon, Neal pulled on the rope beside the door at Little Sweeden, then waited.

The butler opened the door.

"I'm Neal Sterling. I have a reservation." He smiled.

"Welcome, Mr. Sterling. I am Bruce, your butler. We've been expecting you," he said.

Neal stepped in with a small suitcase at his side and another suitcase over his shoulder. "My driver wants to know where to park."

"Right. If you will excuse me, I will let your driver know where to park, then I will show you to your room."

Neal waited in the entry. He looked up to see Chevy and Veronica come around the corner and start down the stairs. There she was, no longer just a name or a face in a photo. She was much prettier in person than she was in the pictures. Her brown wavy hair flowed around her face and down her shoulders.

She spotted him, and her light-colored eyes locked on his. She paused for a moment as he gazed up at her.

Neal smiled, partly at her beauty and partly at the unique nature of the story. All the stories he had done were about places and situations. They had never been about a particular person. If he wrote about people, it was about what happened to them. This time it was a story about one particular girl with a catchy name: Chevy.

He was still smiling as they reached the bottom of the steps. "What a pleasure, to see two beautiful ladies descending the steps."

Chevy gave him a strange look. "Thank you for the compliment. Would you like us to go back up and descend again?" Her voice had a hint of Southern drawl.

"Perhaps later, after I clean up. I just finished a long flight. I'm Neal Sterling, by the way." He held out his hand. "And you lovely ladies would be?"

Chevy met his hand with hers. "I'm Chevy, and this is my good friend Veronica." She smiled.

Veronica's face was guarded. She shook his hand without a word.

Neal turned his focus back to Chevy when the butler came back in.

"Have you already made introductions?"

Neal glanced at the butler. "Yes, as a matter of fact we have," Neal smiled.

"You speak American English. Are you from the States?" Chevy asked.

"As a matter of fact, I am," he said, giving her his attention.

The butler cleared his throat. "Anytime you are ready, Mr. Sterling. The ladies will be here for several days. You will have a chance to speak with them again."

Chevy nodded. "If you would like some company once you get cleaned up, I'm on the second floor." She hesitated and looked at the butler. "I'm sure the butler would have no problem showing you which room is mine."

"Why, of course," he agreed, with a nod. "Allow me to show Mr. Sterling to his accommodations on the third floor, then I will be right down to serve your dinner."

"Sure." Chevy smiled and started down the wide hall with Veronica.

"So, tell me about that Chevy," Neal leaned to the butler.

He smirked. "Well, Miss Chevy...has a very distinctive name."

"Yes, that she does," Neal agreed, as they trailed up the steps.

"She's here for several days, so you have a chance." His eyes twinkled. "Come downstairs when you're ready. Mr. Sweeden would like a moment of your time to go over details."

### 

Neal sat in a chair next to Jack Sweeden, showered and freshly cologned. "These are the four women who are available," Jack told him as he spread out four 8×10 headshots on the table.

Neal glanced at the pictures. "I saw a girl in the hallway.

211

Actually, she and her friend where coming down the stairs when I came in. I spoke to them briefly. She spoke English. I want her."

"What girl are you speaking of?" Jack asked.

"She said her name was Chevy."

Jack sat back in his chair, suddenly serious. "Why that girl?"

Neal leaned back in his chair, realizing that he had struck a nerve. "Have you seen her? She's a pretty little number." He paused. "And the best part is she already speaks English," he said, with a gleam in his eye.

Jack gave him a half smile. "She's a looker, isn't she? I'm sorry, but she's not part of our auction."

"You mean to tell me that particular girl just happens to be here, at your bed and breakfast, on vacation?" Neal asked, with a certain amount of excitement.

"I would assume she's on vacation, she and her friend. I trust you understand that I don't ask a lot of questions about my guests."

"Jack." Neal stood up and held out his hand for him to shake. "That's the best news I have heard all day. I came all this way to find a wife, and lo and behold, there just happens to be a cute English-speaking girl on vacation who isn't going to cost me anything." Neal let go of Jack's hand. "When is the auction?"

"Thursday. The men who have come for the auction need several days to become acquainted with the women."

"All right." Neal smiled with delight and started to turn away. "Oh, do you have any recommendations for places to eat?"

"There's a place around the corner. It's very good," Jack suggested.

"Excellent. Don't count me out of the auction. I'm going to keep my options open, but I'm going to try my hand with this girl. She's cute, and she's personable," Neal said, then turned and walked out.

### 

Jack watched the door close behind him. He returned to his

chair, put his chin in his hand, and sat there thinking, trying to decide what to make of the man and his purpose there.

With all the upheaval around Chevy, Jack had to be careful about this man. Was this Neal Sterling really there for the wife auction, or was he there to retrieve the girl? Jack picked up his cell phone and dialed.

"This is Sandro."

"Sandro, Jack."

"Did they make it to you?" Sandro quickly asked, concerned.

"Yes. They arrived last night, tired and wanting to relax. I wanted to tell you several things. The first is rather disturbing, so I need to make sure you have time to talk."

"I have time."

"Well, after we spoke about Veronica and the girl in transit, I called Chris and asked if this girl was one of his." Jack paused. "I have to tell you that I didn't realize when I made the call what was going on. My apologies for that. We were both to blame. Regardless of how you and I inadvertently failed to fully communicate, we need to make sure we are disclosing all information to each other from here forward."

"You called Chris?" Sandro repeated, sounding disturbed.

"I had no idea. None of us have ever had a problem like this girl has created. Did you know that she is the girlfriend of Chris's son?"

"Not at first I didn't," Sandro answered. "I got two upsetting calls from Chris in less than twenty-four hours. There were people yelling in the background both times. Chris wanted me to send this girl home, so I put her in transit and got her and my wife off the yacht as fast as I could. First, I don't want to get into legal issues because of Chris's screw-up. Second, Chris wanted me to send Chevy home, so I wasn't sure what action Chris might take to make sure she does go home. I want both Chevy and my wife out of harm's way. My plan is to get this girl back to the States."

"Aren't you worried about this girl identifying you?" Jack asked.

"It certainly is a concern, absolutely. But I don't see that

213

about her. We have been good to her. My wife and Chevy have become friends. Could Chevy identify us? Sure, and with people looking for her my best options are what? Killing her? Not this one," Sandro said adamantly.

"I understand," Jack said sympathetically. "Here's the disturbing part, and then I have some good news, our window of opportunity, if you will. When I talked to Chris I thought Chevy was his. I thought maybe you were following Chris's request since you said she was in transit. So I called Chris to make sure he knew about my upcoming auction, and what he told me set off alarms. He told me that Chevy has been nothing but a problem, and I should auction her off to get his money out of her, and then make her go home. Make it look like an accident, natural causes, overdose, he didn't care. I wasn't happy to hear that. I told Chris I have a reputation to uphold."

"Right," Sandro agreed.

"All I told Chris was that I would see what I could do, then we hung up. When I got off the phone I did an Internet search, and a bunch of sites came up.

"He told me to send her home, too. Then there was yelling in the background, and Chris hung up. When we got off the phone I looked up the name. Instantly, a dozen different sites came up. I learned very quickly what I had on my yacht."

"Well," Jack said, "I'm still concerned about the pressure Chris is under and what lengths he might go to to make this girl go away. I'm not sure if Chris is thinking clearly. Here's the good news. I have this guy from the States here for the auction. He apparently ran into Chevy and Veronica when he came in. When I met with him to go over the women we have, this guy wanted to talk about Chevy. I told him Chevy wasn't part of the auction; she and her friend were staying here on vacation. The man was pleased that he had come all this way and Chevy she not only spoke English but also was from the States, and she wasn't going to cost him anything. I told him that he has several days before she leaves. Now, this man did tell me not to exclude him from the auction. He wanted to keep his options open. Here is what I'm thinking. This man from the States does concern me, because I'm not really sure who he is. I'm not concerned about the American government looking for dirt on us. Otherwise, I think this guy would be more interested in the auction. I do think that this guy is a very nice way out of this—for both of us. Chevy's not part of the auction, so if Chevy takes a liking to him, she's off our hands. You should have Veronica encourage Chevy to spend time with this guy," Jack suggested.

"I see where you are going with this. Do you feel this man is there to ensure Chevy goes home?" Sandro asked.

"No, I don't think so. He doesn't strike me as the hit man type. I'm more inclined to say he was just taken with her. She's a pretty girl. My next guess is that he was sent looking for her to take her home. In that case, I say fine, let him. Either way, it takes her off our hands."

"I'll call Veronica and tell her she should encourage Chevy to pursue him and go back to the States with this guy. Whatever you do, make sure my wife's safe and out of harm's way," Sandro requested.

"Of course," Jack assured him. "I'll do my best to keep watch over her."

### 

Neal located Chevy and Veronica eating dinner in one of the rooms on the main level. A roaring fire in the fireplace created flickering light that danced around the room.

"Ladies," Neal said as he walked in. "I found you. May I join you?"

Chevy smiled. "Of course you can. Pull up a chair. We're just about to have dessert."

Veronica sat there, looking unsure.

"You're from the States?" he asked Chevy.

"Yeah. Rudle Mills, Kentucky."

"So you're a Southern girl?"

"Yes, I am. What about you?"

Neal had his spiel ready on who he was and where he came from, but oddly, he saw something in her he liked. He looked at her and felt like he had known her for years. He paused. "Do you mind if I have a drink of your water?" he asked, feeling thrown off balance.

215

She glanced at her water. "Sure." She handed him her glass. Veronica looked at him, seeming wary.

Neal took a sip and set the glass down as the butler came in with dessert plates. From across the room, Neal could tell it was chocolaty and wonderful.

Veronica's phone rang. She looked down at the screen. "It's my husband. I'm going to step outside and take this. Neal, you go ahead and have my dessert."

"I—"

"No, I insist. I am going to be a while," she said sweetly. She headed for the door, leaving Neal and Chevy alone at the table.

Chevy's eyes followed Veronica out the door with uncertainty.

The candlelight danced between them with a soft, warm glow. The aroma of fresh flowers and warm chocolate filled the room.

The butler set a plate of dessert in front of Chevy, then another in front of Neal. He drizzled a clear liquid over each plate, then lit it. A brilliant blue flame shot upward.

Chevy smiled at the dazzling spectacle in front of her.

The butler opened a bottle of wine, pouring it for him to taste.

Neal took a sip. "Perfect! It's not Merlot."

"You don't like Merlot?" Chevy asked.

The butler cleared his throat. "I felt that the two of you need something with spark and flair, something sweeter. This particular wine is more like a Champagne and goes well with the chocolate. If the two of you don't mind, I will leave you now and come back to check on you in a while."

Neal looked at Chevy. "Are you okay with that?"

"Of course," she replied. She turned to the butler. "Thank you for the fabulous dessert. It looks wonderful."

Then Neal saw it—a quick flash, then it was gone. Just before Chevy looked back at her plate, she and the butler had made eye contact, and in that split second his eyes had flicked toward Neal, as though the butler was telling her something.

"I'm glad it's to your liking." He turned to Neal. "I trust

Miss Chevy will be safe in your company, Mr. Sterling."

"I'll guard her with my life," Neal replied, lifting his wine glass and catching her eye.

### 

The third time the butler checked on them, he cracked the door and found them sitting on the sofa next to the fireplace, laughing, talking, and sharing stories. He had seen the chemistry between them when Neal arrived. Now, after having a chance to observe them, there was no mistaking it: Neal and Chevy came together like two lost halves that made a whole.

### 

"Your eyes are looking heavy," she said. The flames from the fireplace cast shadows on his cheek.

Neal smiled. "I had a long flight and a long day, but I'm enjoying your company. I'm trying to stay awake."

"That's sweet. I happen to enjoy my time with you as well. There'll be tomorrow. Come." She stood up, holding out her hand for him. "Let's take you night-night."

"Night-night? Did you really just say that?" He looked up at her.

"Yes," she said sweetly. "Thank you for having dessert with me and keeping me company. It was nice. I really enjoyed myself." She smiled, looking into his eyes.

"I was thinking, since we're in the same place, that maybe I could see you again tomorrow?"

"I would be disappointed if you didn't," she said, trying not to sound eager. "That'd be nice."

"How about a hug from my newfound friend?"

"Of course," she said as she wrapped her arms around him and closed her eyes.

# Chapter 19

The next morning, Chevy was lounging in her room in her pajama pants and a tank top, her hair in a ponytail and a brown mud mask drying on her face. She had just picked up her bowl of rice pudding when there was a knock at the door. She set the bowl down, walked to the door, and opened it.

Neal stood in front of her with a bouquet of red roses.

Her eyes grew wide. "I figured you were going to be Veronica," she told him.

"These are for you." He smiled, a twinkle in his eyes as he handed her the flowers.

She put them under her nose, closed her eyes, and inhaled. "Mmm. How did you know roses are my favorite?"

Two women were coming down the hall behind Neal in high heels and cheap, revealing outfits. They stared at him. As they got closer, Chevy saw that they had leathery skin, deep wrinkles, and brittle straw-like hair. "Why, hello," the one in the gold lamé said, undressing him with their eyes. The other winked and pouted at him.

Neal turned at the interruption. "Ladies," he said in a flat tone, then immediately turned back and gave his attention to Chevy.

Chevy grabbed his hand and pulled him in her room, shutting the door behind him. She looked startled. "I would have invited you in more formally," she said softly. "Those women were scary and you looked uncomfortable."

"Thank you. They *were* scary and I *was* uncomfortable. That's a beautiful clock," he said, stepping to the fireplace.

She huffed, giving it a hateful glare. "You should hear it tick. It's is the loudest clock I have ever heard. I stopped the pendulum so I could sleep." She picked up a vase from the mantel, took it to the bathroom, filled it with water, and carefully arranged the roses.

"I was thinking we could get an early dinner at a place around the corner, then come back and watch a movie," he

218

suggested. "We can watch the movie in my room. I promise I will be a perfect gentlemen."

"Okay. That sounds nice."

Neal gestured to the bathroom. "Go get ready. I was thinking we could do some sightseeing and shopping until dinner. Do you mind if I wait out here? I would like to avoid those women," he told her, with a shiver at the thought of them.

She laughed. "What's wrong?" She got close to him. "You don't want a little foreign action? They might have some fun foreign diseases." She winked.

Neal made a repulsed face. "That's not funny." He crinkled his lip and shook his head playfully.

"You do realize its eleven in the morning. Dinner is a long way off. Are you planning to come back and change before dinner?"

"Yeah. Just wear something comfortable."

She stepped into the bathroom. There was something about him, something she liked. She leaned over the sink, splashing water on her face until the mask was gone. She straightened her ponytail, pulled on a pair of jeans and a blouse, and slipped on her boots. She was applying some lip gloss when she heard him call out from the main room: "There's a really interesting carved candlestick on the mantel. It's huge. Did you see this?"

Chevy called back from the bathroom: "Yeah, I saw that. It must weigh a ton." She took one last look in the mirror and opened the door. "I'm ready!"

His face lit up when he looked at her. She noted the twinkle in his eyes—it was like looking at her future. She picked up her jacket and moved toward the door. "I need to let Veronica know where I'm going." She glanced down at the table and paused. She looked at him. "You ate the rest of my rice pudding."

"It was really good."

"What if I had germs or something?"

"I like your germs."

She looked at the empty bowl. "It *was* really good. Maybe the butler will bring us more," she said. She smiled and led him out the door.

Around the corner, she knocked on Veronica's door.

Veronica pulled it open.

"We're going to leave and go sightseeing, then we're coming back to change for dinner—"

"It's a place right around the corner," Neal said, standing behind her. He paused, and looked at Chevy. "I'm sorry. I didn't mean to cut you off." He turned to Veronica. "Jack recommended it. We're going to eat, then I'll bring my new friend back. We're planning on a movie in my room tonight, so if you need to find her, she will be upstairs with me."

Veronica smiled. "Have a great time," she said, looking down and closing the door.

Neal grabbed hold of Chevy's arm and looped it around his. "Stay close to me." He spoke softly. "I don't like those ladies, and I rather not give them any indication that I could possibly be interested in them."

"You got it—no indication," she repeated, cuddling closer to him.

"So am I protecting you, or are you protecting me?" She nudged him playfully.

"We protect each other." He laughed.

"You don't want them to think you're interested? Why not?" She teased. "You could have lots of babies that look just like them," she whispered into his ear, then giggled, looking at his profile.

The two women were by the front door, looking out, waiting.

Chevy leaned to his ear and whispered softly. "Look— you're in luck. The one on the left is eyeing you." She beamed up at him, close to his face. She kissed the side of his cheek and said loudly enough so they could hear, "I love you, babe."

The woman's face fell when she saw them. She pushed her lips to the side with disappointment and looked down.

"Miss Chevy, Mr. Sterling." The butler stopped them. "Shall I expect the two of you for lunch?"

Chevy looked at Neal.

"No. We're going to go sightseeing and shopping. My

220

driver will be with us, so he won't be here, either. We'll be back to get ready for dinner. Would you make a reservation for us at the place around the corner that Jack mentioned? Seven p.m.?"

The butler nodded. "Very good, sir. Have a most magnificent time."

Chevy smiled at the women as she and Neal walked by. "Have a lovely day," she told them sweetly. Neal nodded at them.

Outside Sweeden's, they walked down the paved street, talking and admiring the architecture. An hour later, they stopped in front of a restaurant whose aromas were irresistible. "Wow!" Chevy said, peering in. "This looks great. Let's eat." Excitement danced in her eyes.

"Already? Didn't you just eat?"

"It was a snack. I had two bites, and *somebody* ate the rest of it." She looked at him.

"It was really good.

"You said that. It's my favorite, and you ate it. That's all I've had today."

"Then let's eat."

She examined her reflection in the glass. "I feel underdressed."

Neal reached for the door and opened it. "Even in jeans with your hair pulled back, you're prettier than the other women here. Trust me." He held out his arm and guided her in, touching her back as she passed.

### 

It wasn't very long until they had plates in front of them. "You never answered my question," Chevy said.

"What question was that?" Neal took a sip of his water.

"Where are you from?"

Neal paused and stared at his food, thinking back.

She sipped her wine, paying close attention. "Did I strike a nerve? You look haunted."

"A bit," he started. "I come from upstate New York, where my parents and siblings live." His voice tightened. "I also come from Texas, where my uncle lives."

"So what is it about your past that upsets you?"

"We all have issues with family that are difficult to handle, don't we?" He smiled.

Chevy laughed and rolled her eyes. "You should meet my father. He can have a big heart and be quite thoughtful and understanding, but then he can also be a giant jerk. I can't even describe him. You'd have to meet him and see him at his full jerkiness to truly understand." She shook her head.

"Really," Neal said, remembering her father at the restaurant. Her father was very much like his own—a man who was never pleased.

"I'm sure you'll get to meet him one of these days."

"You're sure?" They looked into each other's eyes.

"I know so." She smiled.

### 

Chris sat at his desk. The bottle of prescription painkillers sat next to his bottle of brandy. His foot was up, then he brought it down to the floor. It wasn't in any one place for long. It hurt no matter how he positioned it. Moving it around felt the best. He was irritated and fidgeting. He hadn't heard from Jack, and it was bugging him.

Restless, he picked up the phone and dialed. The phone rang again and again and again, until it went to voice mail. He hung up, even more irritated.

### 

Back at Little Sweeden, Chevy lay next to Neal, watching the flat screen.

Suddenly, the door handle twisted and clicked as the door came open.

They looked over as the two women from the hall entered.

"Hey, hey, hey!" Neal said. "What are you doing?" He jumped off the bed. "What if I was in the throes of passion with my girlfriend here?" he asked, walking toward them.

"That's your girlfriend?" one woman asked, peering around him.

"Yes." Neal held out his arms, herding them out of his room.

"I thought you were one of the men here for the auction. I'll

222

be your wife." She paused and smiled, sidling closer to him.

"What auction? I'm not sure where you got your information, but why would I want you to be my wife when I don't know you and have the woman of my dreams right here? But now that you mention the word *wife*, I think that's a great idea. Hey, honey!" he turned and called out to Chevy, who was propped up on her elbow watching with amusement.

"Yeah, babe?"

"I want to marry you! What do you say we get married?"

"Oh, sweetie, really?!" Chevy sat up in bed with excitement. "Do I get a nicer proposal later?" She smiled.

"Yes, you do!"

Chevy bounded off the bed.

Neal opened his arms, catching her as she leaped into them and wrapped her legs around his waist.

"I love you so much!" she told him, putting her hand on the side of his cheek and gazing into his eyes, feeling his skin under her fingertips. His lips were warm and perfect, moving against hers.

He looked into her eyes. "I love you, too."

She looked at the women and made a shooing motion. "Out! You need to go. Go!"

He turned back to the door with her around his waist. "Out!" he ordered. The women slunk off. He shut the door behind them and locked it.

She tightened her grip around his waist as he held her tighter in his arms.

They looked at each other with only the blue hue from the television.

He kissed her lips, holding her body close to him as he walked to the bed and set her down. "Stay here with me tonight?"

She reached up and touched his face. "I'll stay," she said, trailing her finger down the front of his shirt.

He flipped the television off and turned off the bedside lamp, leaving them with only the streetlights glowing through the curtains. He intertwined his fingers with hers, stretched her arms above her head, and leaned down to meet her lips, then continued kissing down the side of her neck. After a while, she snuggled into his arms and they drifted off to sleep.

# Chapter 20

Chevy woke up next to Neal and softly ran her hand down the side of his arm, feeling his skin under the tips of her fingers and liking the way it felt to wake up next to him. She kissed his shoulder and pushed the covers back.

"You're up?" he groaned, turning so he could see her.

"I'll be back," she mumbled.

He reached for his phone and looked at the time. When she came back to bed, he curled next to her.

"Hey, babe." He stroked his fingers through her hair. "I have something I want to show you," he said softly, waiting for her to wake up.

She looked across her pillow at him. "Hmm...?" She asked, her eyes sleepy but intrigued.

"Come." He tossed his covers back. "We have to go outside."

"Outside?" she groaned. "I don't want to get up."

"Trust me. You'll love it."

"Right now? All the way outside to where?"

He slid on his shoes and grabbed a long-sleeved shirt from his bag.

She rolled onto her elbow and rubbed her eyes. "Outside sounds chilly."

"No, it's not bad." He smiled. "What do you like to drink in the morning?"

"I like coffee or tea with hazelnut creamer—a lot of creamer."

He tossed her a pair of thick socks with a hunting emblem on the side. "You'll need these so your feet don't get cold." He picked up the phone and pressed one.

"Good morning to you also! We need two coffees, one with hazelnut creamer."

She leaned forward to get his attention. "One fourth creamer," she said softly.

His eyes shifted to her. "One fourth creamer—if you got it.

Bring it to the tower if you don't mind…"

"The tower?" she repeated, mumbling.

"Great. Thank you." He hung up and gathered the comforter while she pulled up her second sock. She followed him out the door and up the stairs. At the end of the hall on the fifth floor was an old wood door. On a table beside the door was a black lantern with a single candle flickering in the center. He pushed the creaking door open. Behind the door was a wrought iron spiral staircase.

"Where are we going?" She stuck her head inside the doorway and looked up the stairwell. The steps were old and rusty, and the air was musty. A window allowed the start of the morning sun to shine in from somewhere above.

"We're going up here." He looked up the stairwell then back at her. "Trust me, you'll love it."

At the top of the creaky stairs was a small half-size wood door. He opened it and squatted to move through. Chevy followed him. On the rooftop the cool, salty air hit against her face, forcing her hair back.

Neal spread the comforter and sat on one of the ledges between the notched brickwork. "Come on," he encouraged her. He opened his arms, waiting for her to climb in.

She walked over cautiously. "I'm afraid of heights." She stood on her tiptoes a safe distance from the edge and peered down, then reluctantly sat down. She reached over and wiggled the wrought iron railing. The iron didn't budge. She scooted back against him until she was warm in his arms. He wrapped the blanket around her, covering them.

The tower was taller than the structures around them, allowing them to see for miles. The sun was coming up. The ocean was in the distance, with the faint sound of waves splashing onto the shore. The streets were quiet and the cobblestone looked like a painter's canvas beneath them.

She loved the feel of his arms around her, safe and warm. He made her feel whole, as though she had only been half a person before now. She lovingly squeezed her arms against his, rubbing his arm with her hand.

He kissed the side of her face.

226

"Neal."

"Yeah."

"I have a question. What do you do exactly?"

"I'm CEO of a large corporation." He paused. "I write a lot of reports."

"I see. The socks that I have on, do you hunt?"

He smirked. "I do." He paused. "Do you?"

"I love to hunt—I grew up in the country."

Neal squeezed her tight again, rubbing the top of her arm with his hand. The colors in the sky were changing and the clouds reflected magnificent colors. The small door opened, and the butler came through the opening with a tray and stood up.

"Good morning!" He nodded politely. "Chevy, I was told plenty of hazelnut creamer. I hope it is to your liking." He handed her an oversized mug. "Sir," he said, handing Neal a mug with steam rising from the top.

"Thank you." Neal smelled the steam.

The butler gestured to a delicate-looking bowl heaped high with clouds of whipped cream. "Miss Chevy, would you like some whipped cream?"

Chevy's eyes lit up as a big smile stretched across her face. "Yes, please. How did you know?" She looked eagerly at her cup as he spooned some whipped cream on top of her coffee.

He smiled. "My daughter loved hazelnut creamer as well. A little whipped cream was always a treat." He continued to smile, remembering. "You remind me of her in many ways, Miss Chevy. Sir, would you like some whipped cream as well?"

Neal held up his hand. "No, I'm good. Thank you."

The butler turned and went back through the small door.

They watched the spectacular colors dance around the moving clouds as the sun rose, while they snuggled in the big fluffy comforter and sipped their coffee.

"This is a moment I want to burn into my mind forever," she said, taking another sip, enjoying the crisp breeze against her face. "The salty air—beautiful sky—spectacular streets and buildings—this is beyond perfect."

Neal had come there with a purpose: to get the girl and catch the story. He was sure the story didn't matter any more. The only thing that had been captured was his heart.

### 

Chevy stood in front of Veronica's door with her second cup of coffee in hand and knocked. Veronica pulled her door open.

"Good morning!" Chevy smiled, raising herself up and down on the balls of her feet.

Veronica rubbed her hand against her pale face.

Chevy's smiled faded. "You don't look so good."

Veronica shook her head. "I just woke up, and no, I'm not feeling good. Are you okay?"

"I came to show you the tower. Neal took me up there to watch the sunrise. It's so pretty. Do you want me to get you something?" She raised her hand to the side of Veronica's face, feeling for a fever. "I can have the butler bring you some toast," she offered.

"No, I'm okay. I called for some hot tea and lemon. I am going to lay down. You go and have fun today. You should have the butler show you the artifact room. I know you will love it, it's pretty amazing," she said, sounding sleepy. "I do appreciate you offering to get me toast." She smiled and slowly shut the door.

### 

The butler slid the pocket doors open. The artifact room was full of old paintings that hung on the walls in thick frames and pedestals that held vases and others items that looked to span hundreds, even thousands of years, from all over the world.

"I thought the two of you could have lunch by the fireplace." He stood, waiting on their response.

A smile pulled onto Chevy's face and her eyes lit up. "I think that sounds great." She looked at Neal. "What do you think?"

"Sounds great to me."

"Then I shall start a fire and leave the two of you to wander around the artifacts." He looked around. "There's a lot to see

228

and take in." He went to the fireplace and pressed a button at the side. With a small click the gas erupted into flames that flickered around the logs.

"I'll leave you for now and be back after a while with your lunch." He walked out of the room and closed the pocket doors behind him.

Chevy turned to Neal and smiled. "Look at this place, and we have it all to ourselves." Her eyes beamed as she looked around, not sure where to start first. "Look at these paintings." She walked up to one. "Can you imagine dressing like that?"

Neal looked at a small description next to the painting. "1402, Constance of Messerfly," he said aloud, looking closely at the painting. "She was very pretty."

Chevy stepped next to him. "She was. I wonder who she was?" She paused. "The look on her face, the glint in her eyes—it's like she has a story she wants to tell."

Neal stepped to a gold vase with red glass and large jewels embedded into the curved sides. "Wow, look at this. These look like real jewels." He picked up the vase, examining it closely.

"I'm going to guess yes." She turned to grass skirts that hung on mannequins, carefully took one off, and put it around her hips.

Neal set the vase down and turned to her. "What are you doing?"

She swung her hips from side to side, waving her hands in the air in front of her. "Here. Try it with me." She carefully pulled the other skirt from the other mannequin and put it around his waist. "Hula with me." She smiled, moving her hips again.

He stood moving his hips with her. "I don't think this is such a great look for me." He laughed, stepped to her, and put his arms around her. "I think we look better in these skirts with you dancing close to me." He took hold of her hand and swayed to no music.

She looked at him. "Everywhere you look in here it's like an adventure, a story from some place in time, wanting to be told."

He looked around. "Yeah…" His eyes twinkled and he walked to a wood tribal mask with long feathers that stuck out around the sides, held it to his face, and jumped around, making sounds.

Chevy laughed, pulled the grass skirt from her waist, and put it back on the mannequin. She stepped closer to him. "If you are a tribal man, will you come eat me?" She gave him a seductive look, then walked back to the painting of Constance of Messerfly. The woman's back was half turned. Her hand was on a doorframe and she was looking over her shoulder. Chevy turned, mimicking Lady Constance in the image.

"Can we go on an adventure? I can be Constance of Messerfly and you can fall hopelessly in love with me and rescue me." She turned around and carefully took the skirt off his waist, draping it across the vase.

He wrapped his arms around her and picked her up.

She wrapped her legs around his waist and looked into his eyes.

He returned her gaze. "Chevy, I will follow you to the ends of the earth to any adventure, rescuing you from whatever you need rescuing from. I am hopelessly in love with you."

She half laughed. "You can't be in love with me. You don't know me."

He pulled a fur from its display and draped it over her shoulders. "My heart knows what my mind doesn't yet understand." He set her down on the top of a tall trunk and kissed her.

She closed her eyes. Something about the way his lips moved with hers, the way they felt, and the way his body felt next to hers gave her a since of life, wholeness, and contentment she couldn't begin to articulate.

He lifted her off the trunk. "Stand on my feet." He grabbed hold of her hands.

"Stand on your feet?"

"Yes."

She put one foot on top of his, then the other.

He moved then around the room, dancing from one section of the room to the other. "All of it, Chevy. I want to do all of it with you. Do you like staying up late and sleeping in, or going to bed early and getting up?"

"Both. It depends on what I'm doing the next day. I don't like to be tired," she answered, as they whirled around the room.

She lifted an old black floppy-brimmed hat from a mannequin head and put it on his head as they continued to dance around the room. "That's a good look for you." She smiled.

They whirled to a par of old flight goggles. He pulled them from the display and put them on her face.

"Do I look beautiful now?" she asked.

"You look like a bug."

She laughed, seeing the goggle straps flopping in her peripheral vision. "You put them on me. Careful, I bite."

They whirled around the room. Her foot slid off his. "Wait." She looked down and put her foot back on his.

"Why are your feet so cold?"

"I don't know," she shrugged.

They danced to the sofa in front of the fireplace and sat down. He pulled his socks from his feet. "Here, put them on."

She looked at the hunting emblem, which reminded her of home, and pulled them on.

He leaned back on the sofa that sat in front of the fireplace and pulled her alongside him.

### 

Later that evening in Chevy's room, Neal dialed one. "This is Neal. I am going to take Chevy to dinner tonight. However, she would like a new dress. Would you please direct me to a clothing shop that would have appropriate evening clothes...Really?" he said, sounding surprised. "That would be very much appreciated...I'll let her know." He hung up the phone.

"What are you going to let me know?" She sipped her cocktail.

"The butler said they have a dress room. He's coming to take you there. While you do that, I'll go to my room, take a shower, and get ready." He gently pulled the cocktail from her hand and kissed her forehead.

Chevy closed her eyes, wrapped her arms around him, and pulled him closer. "I like this," she said softly.

"I like this too," he whispered.

Suddenly, she tackled him to the ground. His phone fell out of his pocket and landed by the fireplace. Straddling him, she stretched his arms above his head. "One-two-three!" she said quickly. "I win!" She made a muscle with one arm, then the other.

"No, no, no. If you want to play, you need to play fair." He smiled, and with a twinkle in his eye grabbed hold of her and sent her to the floor.

"Whoa!" she yelled out, playfully wrapping her legs around his waist as he held her arms above her head.

"Ha! Now what?"

"You're right where I want you—"

A knock came at the door.

He smiled ruefully. "Your dress awaits."

"We'll finish this later." She released her legs.

He pulled her from the floor. "I'll go take a shower. You, my dear, find a dress, and I will meet you back here. I have a place picked out for dinner." He pulled the door open.

"Miss Chevy, are you ready?" the butler asked graciously.

"I am." She smiled.

He turned to Neal as Chevy stepped through the doorway. "I'll have her back as soon as we find a suitable dress."

"Sounds perfect."

"Very good, sir." He smiled and gave him a small nod.

### ###

Agent Ward walked into the conference room. "I got news! I just got word that Chris Roper just got on a flight, by himself, for Barcelona."

"Why?" Cook asked, squinting his eyes to understand. "What good does that do?"

The man in the dress blues spoke up. "So he can remove Chevy himself."

Ward looked at the man. "We know he's not getting on the plane with firearms or weapons."

232

"Maybe not, but how many contacts does he have, when he arrives, who do?"

The surveillance man shook his head. "Who says that he's going to kill this girl? Roper would have somebody else do that for him. He wouldn't do it himself." He moved a pen back and forth in his hand.

The man in the black suit looked at the man in the dress blues. "Call Neal and get them out of there and back on the plane for the States, now. Have your men in position and ready to take out anyone who looks like they are going to hurt or attempt to kill either of them. I want your men in place yesterday!" He pressed his finger to the top of the table.

### 

Back in his room, Neal stepped into the shower. On the floor in Chevy's room by the fireplace, his phone screen lit up, ringing.

### 

The butler opened the door to the dress room and flipped on the light, revealing rack after rack of dresses of all colors. Chevy stepped in and looked around, noting the stale smell of the room. "I believe the dresses in this area will fit you." He pointed to a corner of the room and glanced at her figure. "You are a six?"

"Usually, depending on the dress." She started sorting through the rack.

"If I were you, I'd go with the basic black. You don't want to draw attention."

Chevy paused, looking at the dresses. "These belonged to women that never made it home, don't they?" Her face suddenly turned pale.

"Yes, Miss Chevy. They did."

Instantly, she remembered the girl in Lost Row chained to the floor, her pleas as she stretched out her hand for help. "How can I wear any of these?" She looked ill.

He put his arm around her. "You're a very lucky girl, Miss Chevy. Unlike the others, you get to go back to the States." He looked at her and tilted his head. "I know just the dress for you." He walked to the corner and reached for a dress at the very end of the rack. He pulled out a black bag that zipped up the front and handed her the bag. "Here. Tell me if you like this one."

She unzipped it, pulled out a black evening dress, and held it up. "This is beautiful," she said, holding it against herself and looking in the full length mirror.

"Try it on," he encouraged her.

Chevy set the dress down on a chair and began stripping off her tank top and pajamas pants.

"Miss Chevy." He turned away.

A moment later, Chevy said, "All right. What do you think?"

He opened his eyes. "Wow." He smiled. "You look radiant. The dress fits you very well." He sat in the chair.

She stood in front of the mirror, looking at herself. "It's disturbing to know that the person who owned it never went home."

"It was my daughter's," he said with a distant look in his eyes.

She turned from the mirror and looked at him. "You mean, she…"

He nodded. "Most girls aren't lucky like you. They don't get to go home." Tears welled in his eyes.

"I'm so sorry," she said, stepping to him and touching her hand to his. "You said earlier that she used to like whipped cream. I wondered. Would you like to tell me about it?" She sat on the arm of the chair.

He shook his head. "She was taken. I went after her. Before I could get to her, they killed her. That's it." He shrugged. "When I tell you you're lucky, I know. Trust me. You're a very lucky girl." He looked at her. "That dress fits you very well. I want you to keep it."

She shook her head and took in a breath. "I—"

He held up his hand. "I insist," he said firmly. "The dress is timeless. If you pull it out of your closet in another thirty years, it will still be in style. Now, whether or not you will able to get into it, well…" He tilted his head and gave her a mischievous smile.

234

Playfully, she swatted at his arm. "Hey! It will fit just fine."
She stood and looked at her reflection in the mirror again.
"May I ask you a question?"

"Of course."

"There's something I have been struggling with. I have a
boyfriend at home, but since I met Neal…"

"You're blown away by him, aren't you?"

She hung her head. "Yeah." She paused. "I am." She sat
back down on the arm of the chair. "I would have staked my
life on how much I love Brandon. Then came Neal. I want his
arms around me. I love him close to me. Was I wrong about
Brandon, or is this ordeal messing with my emotions?"

"Well, the situation could cause you to misinterpret what
you're feeling. But I see the way Neal looks at you. I bet, he's
wrestling with similar thoughts. I think the two of you are
designed for each other. You have chemistry. I saw it when he
arrived. Keep in mind, he came here to bring home a girl, not
find love. I think love is what he found. In all my fifty-four
years—"

"You're fifty-four?!" She looked at him. "I thought you
were younger."

He smiled. "Well, thank you, but no, I'm not." He stood up
and started straightening dresses on the racks. "As I was
saying, in my years, I have learned a lot of things. One of them
is that we're able to love and be in love. We can go from day to
day, week to week, year to year with a person and truly believe
we know what love, sex, and happiness are. Then one day, you
can meet someone else, and suddenly something changes. The
flowers you have looked at and smelled for years, they have
color you never saw before, they have aroma you didn't think
possible, the world feels like it comes alive. It causes you to
take a step back. You thought you knew what love was, you
thought you knew what happiness was, you thought you knew
what sex was. The truth is, you didn't know, and now you have
met someone who allows you to experience all the things you
thought you knew with a new level of awareness. The world
does come alive. If you find that kind of love, keep it. Hang on
to it and treat it like gold, because it is gold." He took in a

breath and reached for a pair of black shoes that sat under one of the clothing racks. "My advice is go to dinner. Have a good time. Wait until you get back home and have time to readjust. Trust me, sweetheart, if it's love, deep love, it won't go away." He handed her the shoes. "Try these on."

### 

The butler waited patiently in one of the chairs by the fireplace as Chevy finished putting on her makeup. When the bathroom doorknob twisted, he looked up to see Chevy in his daughter's dress. The dress showed off her curves, and her hair flowed over her shoulders and around her face.

He stood. "Wow! You look stunning."

"Thank you." She smiled warmly.

"Chevy?" Neal called out as he opened the door. He spotted her, glowing and vibrant. "You look…my Lord," he struggled, shutting the door behind him, standing there looking at her.

"Your cologne smells nice," she said softly, looking at him with dazzling eyes.

The butler noticed the energy around them magnify into something he could almost see. "I believe, sir, that your driver is downstairs waiting."

Neal's eyes shifted from Chevy's to his watch. "We have a reservation." He grabbed hold of her hand, pulling her close to his side.

### 

The driver pulled in front of a nondescript building with a neon sign that she couldn't read. Lights surrounded the plain front door, and a poster featuring oddly dressed dancers, painted or dressed in bodysuits with wild colors hung next to the door. Some looked angelic with feathery wings, while others looked like human rocks and other bizarre things.

Inside the door was a stairway with black lights that illuminated insets in the wall that contained oddly dressed people acting out a variety of things.

On the second level was a doorway that emptied into a huge room. The room was dimly lit with blue and pink lighting and filled with large glass tables. All of the tables had several people in the center acting or dancing. At one table, a person was singing. In one section of the room, people were dressed in shiny costumes and hung from long dangling pieces of fabric, performing in the air. "Wow!" Chevy looked around, taking it all in. "Bizarre—yet cool."

The hostess stood at a pedestal. "Two this evening?"

"Yes. Our reservation is under Sterling."

"This way." The hostess motioned for them to follow her.

Chevy leaned to his ear. "How did you find this place?"

"The butler suggested it. He said it is a place we'd never forget."

"This is your table tonight." The hostess pulled out a chair for Chevy. "Ben and Mya will be your entertainment." She smiled. Mya had on a black bodysuit that covered everything except her face, which was painted with different colors and shapes, making it appear that her face was absent—a black hole of nothing but shapes. Ben's brown body paint made him look like a tree.

The waiter walked up and handed Neal the wine list. "May I start the two of you with some wine?"

Chevy nodded. "No Merlot," she told him. "Sweet wines."

The waiter shifted his eyes to Neal.

"No Merlot. Something sweeter that's crossed with Champagne if you have it?"

"Absolutely." The waiter nodded, turned, and walked away.

"Nothing like starting with a tension tamer." She smiled.

"You and I never needed a tension tamer," he said with certainty.

# Chapter 21

Chevy woke up and blinked a few times, putting her hand on her pounding head and waiting for the room to stop spinning. She propped herself up on her elbow. The morning light seemed especially bright. She realized she was naked beside Neal, who was sound asleep and snoring. *What did I do?* she thought. Images of Brandon flashed through her mind.

She took a deep breath and looked around at their clothes, which were strewn about the room. She rubbed the temple of her throbbing head and looked at Neal, doing a double-take, then started to laugh. "Mud mask," she said out loud. "I really need to leave the wine alone," she mumbled to herself as she climbed out of bed, paused, then curiously lifted the covers. "Nice." She smiled, lowering them.

Her head pounded even more relentlessly when she stood up. She paused and looked down at her feet. She had on his black socks. She squinted, trying to recall why that would be. She pushed the socks off. "No more wine," she told herself, then picked up the phone and dialed one.

"Good morning, Miss Chevy. I trust that you slept well," the butler said, way too chipper for the state of her head.

"If half passed out constitutes sleeping well, then yeah, I slept great," she said softly, sounding groggy.

"Well, Miss Chevy, it's good to hear you haven't lost your sense of humor."

"Speaking of lost, I want to apologize for last night. I don't know what possessed me to get drunk. I don't remember exactly what happened, and my head's pounding."

"I do believe it was the wine that possessed you." The butler chuckled. "I must say, you don't need to apologize. What's the last thing you remember?"

"Getting ready to leave the restaurant."

"Oh my. Allow me to fill you in."

"Mr. Sterling's driver brought the two of you back— blitzed. He helped Mr. Sterling in, and I helped you. The two of you insisted on sitting by the fireplace in the artifacts room. The two of you wanted more wine. I must admit, as tipsy as you both were, I decided to dilute it with some ginger ale. The two of you were sitting by the fireplace on the sofa, snuggled up to each other, talking and drinking for quite a while.

"I had the most fun watching the two of you try to climb the stairs. The two of you spent the better part of twenty minutes crawling up the stairs. It seemed the gravity at the base of the stairs was especially powerful last night. The two of you kept sliding down the first few steps. The both of you hung on the spindles—he pulled you up and you pushed him. Each of you was determined to help the other. I decided then the two of you could use come supervision. I'll say, the energy between you is magnetic. By the time you guys made it to your room, it had been decided a bubble bath was in order. I got the bath ready and found the two of you struggling to undress. To make it even funnier, you were trying to come to each other's aid, undressing each other. I must say, Miss Chevy, it was a scream." He sounded like he was trying not to laugh.

"A scream," Chevy repeated, holding her head. "I'm so sorry."

"Oh, my dear child, don't be sorry. That was the best night laughing I have had in years." He cleared his throat. "What may I get you for breakfast?" he asked, trying to remain professional.

"I'm embarrassed," she groaned.

"Don't be. I shall always remember it fondly. If I die today, I will pass a happy man. You have put much delight into my life, Miss Chevy. What would you like for breakfast?" he asked again.

"Crepes with strawberries and cream cheese, some scrambled eggs, and a truckload of Alka-Seltzer." She rubbed her temple.

"And for Mr. Sterling?"

"I don't know what he likes for breakfast, so I say either bring whatever you think he would like, or wait until he wakes up."

"I'll have breakfast up to you in about an hour. The kitchen is a little backed up. But I can bring you some headache relief right away."

"All right. I'll be here resting my throbbing head."

"Very good," he said, and hung up.

She took in a deep breath and laid back down.

On the floor by the fireplace was Neal's phone, occasionally lighting up with missed calls.

A short while later, there was a knock at the door. Chevy got up, causing her head to thump harder, and pulled the door open. There stood the butler with a tray containing four glasses of water and five different pill bottles.

Her eyes lit up. "You are a saint!"

"I try, Miss Chevy." He nodded thoughtfully and set the tray down on the small table. "I brought you two glasses of salt water. One has more salt than the other. The other two are for Mr. Sterling when he wakes up." He handed her a glass.

She made a face.

"I know," he said. "Trust me, I've had many hangovers. A saline IV and some vitamins works best; however, this is an excellent second." He picked up a brown bottle, twisted off the cap, and shook several into her hand.. "These are B vitamins. You will feel better soon."

She popped the vitamins into her mouth and drank the salt water in large, fast gulps. She made a face of disgust as she set the glass down.

"That wasn't too salty, was it?" the butler asked.

"No, it wasn't bad. There was just a lot of it."

"Now, wait fifteen minutes, then drink the other glass. Do you have a preference in pain relievers?" He gestured to the other three bottles on the tray.

She looked at the bottles and selected one.

"I will leave this for Mr. Sterling," he said, leaving the two glasses of salt water, the vitamins, and pain relievers.

Neal turned as he slept and stopped snoring.

The butler quieted his voice. "I'll be back with your food in a little bit." He winked at her, and turned for the door.

"Thank you," she said after him in a whisper.

"You're quite welcome." He pulled the door shut behind him.

### 

Chevy got back into bed and snuggled against Neal.

"Good morning, babe," he said, not fully awake, wrapping his arm around her.

"Good morning," she whispered. She leaned up on her elbow, kissed him, and lay back down. Her head was resting comfortably on her pillow and she was looking across to the nightstand at the roses when she noticed her phone and purse sitting beside the vase. Instantly, she sat up, reached over Neal, and grabbed her phone. Under her phone was a cream-colored piece of paper folded in half. She picked it up and opened it.

*Chevy—*

*You have given me many realizations, all positive and overdue. For that, I am indebted to you.*

*In your purse you will find a debit card. On it is $35,000. It's yours. Use it for whatever you need. It's a token of my appreciation not only for my enlightenment, but also for keeping my much-loved wife safe.*

*It was a pleasure getting to know you. I am sure we will see you again someday under appropriate circumstances. Take care, Chevy. Now go home!*

*Sandro*

She bounded out of bed for the door.

"Hey, babe, where are you going?" Neal called out, half awake. "Is everything okay?"

"I think they left!" she said, turning the door handle and bolting out of the door.

"Veronica!" Chevy knocked on the door feverishly.

241

"Veronica!" She tried the door handle, which turned effortlessly. She pushed the door open, peered around the edge, and saw only an empty room, the bed made, and no Veronica. She looked around and took in a deep breath. She held her hand to her chest and let her breath out slowly, trying to regroup.

Neal stepped beside her in boxer briefs and put his hand on the top of her shoulders. "What's wrong?"

### 

Back in Chevy's room, on the floor by the fireplace his phone was ringing.

### 

Chevy glanced down at the floor, thinking. Her eyes shifted around; her nostrils flared. "They left. I didn't get to say good-bye." She ran her hand through the top of her hair.

He wrapped his arms around her. "I'm sure there was a reason your friend left."

"I suppose."

"Come on, babe, let's go back to bed. I could use another hour." He held his hand against his head and reached out his other hand to her.

"There's no way I can sleep. I can lay down beside you. I need to think." She tilted her head and grinned. "You may want to wash the mud mask off."

He paused, feeling his face. "That's why my face feels tight."

"That's probably why, yeah."

He went straight to the bathroom. "Ugh!" he said, standing in front of the mirror, then stuck his head out of the doorway. "I don't remember doing this."

She crawled back into bed, trying to avoid the smears of dried mud mask. "I don't remember it, either. I saw it when I woke up." She fluffed her pillow to get comfortable. The water was running in the bathroom.

With a clean face, Neal stood at his side of the bed, looking at his pillow and covers. The pillowcase, sheets, and blankets were smeared with the mud mask. He shook his head with his fingers at his temple. "I say we go to my room. I will finish sleeping. Hopefully my head will stop pounding and you can think." He started getting dressed.

She tossed the covers back and scooted out of bed. "I'll call the butler and tell him to bring our food to your room."

"You ordered food?" His eyebrows raised.

"Of course. He brought us hangover relief, too." She pointed. "Those glasses of salt water are yours, and there are vitamins and three different kinds of pain relievers."

He turned to the table. "Oh! Just what I need." He downed the first glass, opened a bottle of the pain relievers, popped several in his mouth, and downed the second glass as she made the call to him.

"I woke up with your socks on," she said with a frazzled look.

"I always knew there would be someone who would fill them."

She smirked at him and grabbed her purse. "I didn't know what you wanted to eat, so I told the butler to either guess, or wait until you got up." They stepped into the hall and pulled her door shut.

"You're fabulous!" They headed toward the stairs to his room.

###

In Chevy's room, on the floor by the fireplace, Neal's phone began ringing again.

###

Neal shut the door to his room. "I woke up naked." He paused. "Do you remember exactly what we did last night?"

She smiled as she crawled into the fluffy covers. "I don't remember anything after we got home. The butler said we were drunk when we got back." She giggled.

"You know what? I think we might have done something." He leaned in and kissed her.

"You think so? Like what?"

"Yes. You must have scooted close to me, wrapped your arms around me, and kissed me." He looked into her eyes. "Like this…" he said, then pressed his lips to hers, then softly squeezed her butt and pulled her leg over his.

243

"Yes…like that," she groaned, tilting her head back. She ran her hands down his arms and up his back. "You've got on way too many clothes." She pulled his shirt over his head and pushed his pants and briefs down.

"You know what? You're right." He pushed the back of his briefs down while she pushed the sides down with her feet.

"I like the way you wrap your legs around me." He kicked his briefs off his feet. "You've unwrapped the package."

"Did I do that?" She smiled.

He pushed the bottom of her tank top up and kissed her breasts.

She pulled off her tank top and tossed it to the floor. She looked into his eyes as he kneeled down and pulled her pajamas from her legs, kissing her ankles and working up to her thighs, over her hipbones, and to her stomach. She put a fingertip beneath his chin and guided his lips to hers, wrapping her legs around him.

She felt him hard against her abdomen as he kissed her with force and passion. He kissed down her neck, and she ran her hands down his back, feeling his skin against her fingertips.

She wanted him. The feel of his skin was intoxicating and stirred a deep desire in her.

He reached down and pulled her leg over his lower back.

She kissed his face, his neck. The need to feel him inside her grew into a deep ache. He kissed the hollow of her neck and moved himself at the opening of her canal. She reached down, grabbed his butt, and pulled him to her.

He slid into her.

She gasped and took in a deep breath as his length stretched into her. They moved together, finding an easy rhythm. "Yes…Oh God…Don't stop…" she moaned.

He squeezed her butt in the palm of his hand, moving deep inside her.

She ran her hand down his back.

"You feel so good," he said gruffly.

She tightened her legs around him, moving her hips with him.

He ran his hands up her arms and intertwined his fingers

with hers.

"Oh my God…" she whispered, feeling herself tighten around him and starting to pulse in orgasm.

He moved faster, then lost himself inside her.

### 

There was a knock at the door. Chevy got out of bed, grabbed her clothes, and headed to the bathroom. Neal pulled on his boxers and answered the door.

"Breakfast, sir," the butler said, wheeling a cart into the room.

He looked at Chevy as she emerged from the bathroom, then at Neal. A smile drew across his face and a knowing sparkle came into his eyes. Saying nothing, he stopped the cart next to the table as Chevy took a seat.

He uncovered a plate and sat it in front of her. "My dear, crepes with strawberries and cream cheese, and scrambled eggs. I hope it's to your liking."

"Oh, perfect," Chevy said, with excitement, looking at her plate.

He looked to Neal. "Sir, I took a guess." He uncovered the second plate to reveal eggs over easy, French toast, and potatoes.

"Nice," Neal said looking at his food. "Thank you."

"I must tell you, I have never seen two people more perfect for each other than the two of you." He smiled, turned, and started away.

### 

Neal's driver was lying in his room watching television when his phone rang. "Hello."

"Get them out of there and back to the plane." The driver sat up and reached for the remote, turning the volume down on the television. "We have been trying to call Neal since last night and haven't gotten an answer. Chris Roper is on his way there. We have reason to believe assassins may have been called to remove Chevy."

The driver sat up straighter. "I will get them now. Have the plane waiting."

"The plane is being prepped as we speak. Call back on this

245

number when they're on the plane."

"Of course."

The man on the other end of the line hung up.

He pulled his gun from his shoulder holster and checked it. He grabbed his jacket, hat, and bag, then headed for Chevy's room.

He knocked with the back of his knuckles several times, then opened the door. Empty. The driver darted for the stairs to the third floor, Neal's room. The butler was coming out of his room, wheeling a cart of dirty breakfast dishes. "Are Chevy and Neal in there?" He pointed.

"They went for a walk. I assumed you were with them."

"No." He headed back down the hall.

### 

Walking arm-in-arm down the cobblestone street, she leaned into Neal's neck. "You smell good."

"Then the cologne is doing its job." He rubbed her hand.

"Look at the flower cart!" Chevy glanced at his profile. "So picturesque." She beamed.

The cart sat in front of an old brick building.

She slowed, fidgeting with her shoe.

He walked ahead of her to the cart and picked up a couple of arrangements. "Which ones do you like?" he asked, looking at them then back at her.

"Hang on, I got…" Her words trailed off as she bent down, struggling with her shoe. An odd, airy whizzing sound, like an arrow zigging through the air, rang out.

She heard a thud in front of her and looked up. The person in front of her had collapsed to the street.

"Chevy!" Neal yelled, dropping the flowers and looking up at the buildings around them. "We need to go." He ran for her.

"That—" She looked at the person in front of her, unsure what had happened, then saw the blood spreading onto the cobblestones. She started to stand, taking several awkward steps back.

"Keep your head down!" He pulled her beside him and covered her head with his arm. They walked quickly.

A crowd of people began to form around the person on the

246

street. Loud, panicked words rang out in another language from behind them.

"This side of the street," he said, as their fast walk became a slow jog.

He turned to see a cab coming down the street, put his arm up, and stepped in front of it.

The cab stopped.

Chevy pulled the door open.

"Hurry! In!" Neal yelled as she dove into the backseat. He hurried in behind her and pulled the door shut. "Around the corner to Little Sweeden," he said loudly. "Hurry!" He looked ahead of them to the crowd.

"It looks like there is something going on in front of us," The cab driver said leisurely.

"Go, just go! Back up!" Neal yelled, looking out the back window.

"Well, I—" A shot hit his window, shattering the glass. The cab driver looked at it, stunned, then threw the cab into reverse and hit the gas. Cars honked and people shouted and veered to avoid them. He turned hard, spinning them around, and threw the cab in drive. They raced down the street, turning and twisting until they were in front of Little Sweeden.

"Out! Get out!" the cab driver yelled, bobbing his head up and down for protection.

Neal pushed the car door open and pulled Chevy behind him. They ran under the stone-covered entry and up the stairs, two at a time.

The cab squealed away.

They bounded through the door, slamming it open and slamming it closed behind them.

"I need my driver and my bag," Neal told her, bolting up the stairs with her beside him.

Without knocking, he turned the doorknob of his driver's room. It was locked. He pounded on the door.

His driver instantly pulled it open.

"We just got shot at! They almost got Chevy!" he said, breathing heavy. "We need to get out of here!"

"Get your things. I went to your rooms. Neither of you were

247

there. Where's your phone?" the driver asked.

Neal paused, feeling his pockets and realizing he didn't have it. "I'm not sure."

"Forget it." The driver stepped through the doorway and pulled his door shut. "Never mind it. I'll get the car and have it out front."

"We need to get our things." Neal turned toward his room. "Chevy and I will meet you in front!"

"No. I will pull the car up and meet you at her room. Lock the door behind you and don't leave there until I come to get you," the driver called after them, moving quickly down the hall with his things in hand.

"All right." Neal felt his pockets again.

"Where did you leave it," Chevy asked.

"I don't know." He pushed his door open and threw his things into his bag. He grabbed her hand. "We're good. Now, your room." They hurried out the door, down the hall, down the steps, and around the corner to her room.

They pushed her door open. "Just grab the essentials. We can replace everything else later."

She let go of his hand, then suddenly he stopped her. "Chevy." He looked at her. "I love you." He held his hand against the side of her face, rubbing her cheek with his thumb.

"I love you, too." She paused, gazing into his eyes. "I love you." She grabbed her bag and collected her things as quickly as she could.

On the floor next to the fireplace a small light caught Neal's eye. He saw his phone, reached down, and grabbed it. The screen lit up—seventeen missed calls.

###

On the main level, the butler and Jack were talking when the doorbell rang. They paused their conversation. The butler strolled down the hall and opened the door to a man with a large bouquet of flowers in front of him. "I have a delivery for Chevy," the man said.

At that moment Chevy turned the corner at the top of the stairs.

Jack poked his head out of the room down the hall.

248

"Ah, yes. Miss Chevy," he acknowledged politely.

From behind the flowers the man pulled a gun with a silencer. Two airy shots whizzed through the air into the butler's chest.

The butler seemed to pause, then collapsed to the floor.

Wide-eyed, Jack stepped back into the room and shut and locked the door.

From the top of the steps, Chevy took in a sudden breath.

The man with the gun looked up and dropped the bouquet. The vase crashed to the ground and broke into pieces. Flowers scattered everywhere.

### 

Neal was paused in the doorway of Chevy's room, trying to listen to his messages. His phone rang again as he was listening. He tapped the screen with the tip of his finger. "Hello," he answered hurriedly.

"Neal, get Chevy and get out of there!" the voice on the other end of the phone said. Neal looked over as Chevy ran toward him from the stairwell. She pushed him through the doorway, slamming the door behind them, and locked it.

"He shot the butler!"

The doorknob twisted behind her feverishly. They moved toward the fireplace.

"Who?"

"Some man!"

Neal's nostrils flared and his eyes widened. A loud thump hit the door, then another. The door flexed inward, then bounced back. Suddenly, the door burst open.

Without hesitation, Chevy pushed Neal out of the way.

The man lifted his gun.

Neal reached for her as he fell backward.

### 

Chevy looked at the gun and blinked. Everything happened in slow motion. Every sound was amplified. She could see herself from all sides. She could see Neal falling to the floor beside her, as though she were watching from outside the room.

There was a strange sharp wisp of air and suddenly, as she

249

looked at the man, red liquid and fleshy-looking chunks flew through the air in front of the man's forehead. The man's knees buckled, and he fell to the floor in front of her.

She stood there, numb. Neal's driver stepped into the doorway, his gun in hand. She looked down to see blood running from the man's head in pulsating waves that made a thick puddle.

"Car! Now!" the driver yelled, moving out of the doorway and down the hall ahead of them.

Chevy stood there, the slow motion fading, her mind and thought processes coming back from the paralyzed void.

Neal moved back to his feet. "Are you all right?"

"Yes." She picked up her backpack and swung it over her shoulder, grabbed the bag with the black dress, and stepped toward the door.

"Wait a minute there, Chevy," a man came into the doorway and said slowly. He had a black eye and rocked carefully into the room on a hard walking boot.

"The man in the corner with the cigar," she said, confused.

"Chris Roper?" Neal said, stepping beside Chevy protectively.

"Roper?" she repeated, squinting her eyes.

"That's right, Chevy," Chris said slowly. "I'm Brandon's father." He looked at her.

"Brandon's father?" She looked at Neal. "How do you know Brandon's father?"

"I did a story," Neal explained, looking at Chris. "You donated money to the local school." He watched Chris cautiously.

The dark circle around Chris's eye made him look evil. "It was a nice article. I read it. Thanks." He snickered.

Chevy looked at Neal. "An article?"

"Neal here's a reporter." Chris's face became serious as his eyes shifted to Chevy. "But you, you little bitch," he snarled. "If it wasn't for you, I wouldn't have needed to donate money."

"Me? What do I have to do with your donation?"

"Oh!" Neal repeated, slowly. "I get it. That's why her

250

parents showed up at your house. I didn't make the connection. Her boyfriend and your son are the same Brandon." Neal gestured to Chris. "He's the one behind all this. This guy here, he's the one responsible for stealing you."

She struggled for words.

Neal watched Chris closely. "We need to get going," Neal said. "Glad you liked the article." He watched Chris walk around the body in his boot.

"I don't think so," Chris said. He pulled a small .22 from his pocket.

Chevy starred at the handgun. "Are you serious?" she snapped, enraged. Without warning she picked up the decorative candlestick from the mantel, swung it with force, and knocked the .22 out of Chris's hand. "You're the one who did this to me?!"

Chris dove for the gun.

She swung the candlestick above her head. "Touch it and I will kill you!" She yelled. She stepped closer, allowing her bag to slide off her arm so she could get a better grip.

Chris reached for the gun, stretching to keep his hand out of her reach.

Watching him move for the gun enraged her. Her face turned red and her eyes went wild. She swung the candlestick, hitting his knee just above the walking boot. "How dare you!"

His knee made a crunching sound. He clutched it with his free hand.

Neal dove for the gun, wrestling with Chris. The gun was above their heads, pointed at the base of the wall, going off, one shot after another. They rolled one way, then the other, making it impossible for her to get another solid hit on Chris. The gun went off until there was only empty metallic clicks.

Infuriated, she turned around and swung the candlestick, clubbing the dead assassin repeatedly. Blood splattered around the room with the force of her swings, crushing the dead man's skull until his face was a warped, deflated, inhuman-looking shell.

Neal and Chris paused, looking at her with terror.

Neal stood up and backed away, wide-eyed, leaving Chris

251

there writhing on the ground, trying to get up.

Chevy let out a wild, blood-curling scream. "What the fuck is wrong with you?!" she screamed at Chris, hitting him in the thigh, creating an unnatural bend. There was a fire in her eyes as she watched Chris roll around on the floor, twisting in agony, holding his leg and whimpering. "Why would you try to kill me? You don't know me! Why would you do something like this to me?" She stomped on the bridge of his nose with her heel. A deep crunch filled the air as his nose skewed to the side.

She readied to stomp again.

Neal grabbed her. "Whoa, whoa!" He held her back. "You're going to kill him."

"I grew up on a farm and wrestled more than one head of cattle!" she yelled, looking at Chris with blood splattered wildly on her face.

"Do you really think a little .22 is going to hurt me?" she screamed at Chris.

"Come on, babe," Neal grabbed her hand, picked up her backpack and bag, and pulled her out the door behind him. They hurried down the steps. She looked at the butler as they ran past. Blood trailed from his chest. His eyes were open and staring into nothingness. She didn't have time to pause and say good-bye, which felt rude. He had been so kind.

Diving into the car, she pulled the door shut. The tires squealed against the pavement. The forward momentum pressed them against the seat. They left Little Sweeden shrinking in the distance behind them.

As she sat there, her fierce and mighty defenses began to melt away. Now that they were out of Little Sweeden and Chris was no longer within her grasp, she had nothing but the reality and emotion of the situation. She held her stomach, started to cry, then crumpled into a ball on the seat beside Neal.

He leaned over and pushed the hair from her face. "Hey, hey, hey. Talk to me."

The driver's arm came over the seat handed Neal several tissues. He wiped some of the blood from the side of her face. "Shh. It's all right, babe." He wrapped his arms around her and

252

pulled her close.

###

Chevy finally pulled herself from Neal's side. "Where are we going?" she asked, looking out the window.

"Home," he said, as he glanced out the back window.

The driver saw Neal glancing from his rearview mirror. "Don't worry. So far no one is following us."

She began shaking her head. "I can't go home. I don't have a passport. I need to find the American embassy." Worry sat heavily in her eyes.

"I have your passport." He smiled.

"How? I don't have a passport. I've never had one."

"I was given a passport for you."

"How do you have a passport for me?" Her eyebrows crinkled together, remembering what the butler told her about a man from the States coming for her as they danced around the room with no music.

He went into his bag, shuffled around, then pulled out a few things, thumbing through them. He held up a passport. "This one's yours." He winked at her and smiled.

Her eyes shifted to the little navy blue book. She pulled it from his fingers and opened it. There was her picture. Shifting her eyes, she gazed out the window without a word.

"Are you all right?" Neal asked.

She shook her head, speaking softly. "No."

"What's wrong?"

She pulled her eyes from the window and looked down at her lap. "I'm upset about the butler. I liked him. He was nice. He told me the first night I was there that someone was coming from the States to take me back, that I shouldn't drink the wine unless he gave it to me, and that I should think of him as my guardian angel." Her eyes began to well. "When he took me to the dress room, he handed me the dress I wore last night and told me it was his daughter's. She had been taken. By the time he got to her, they had killed her."

Neal looked at her. "He saved us both. If he hadn't opened the door, that guy probably would have killed us both." Neal lifted her chin so their eyes met. "He protected both of us," he

253

said gently.

"Do you realize how close I came to being killed?" She looked at him, the realization finally sinking in.

"You came closer than I did, and that was too close for me."

"Why didn't you tell me you were a reporter? Why did you make up a story about being a CEO?"

He put his hand to the side of her face while looking intently at her. "Do you know how many times I wanted to tell you? I came over here for a story I could write. Do you know what happened? Instead of me capturing a story, you captured my heart. The moment I saw you, I was instantly drawn to you in a way I can't explain. After you were shot at, I stopped and told you I love you. I told you because I didn't know what was going to happen. I wanted to make sure you knew. I know we've known each other only a few days, but my heart loves you. That could've been the last time I had the chance to tell you."

Chevy's eyes dropped to her hands, which were fidgeting in her lap. "I've been trying to figure this out since I saw you. I shouldn't feel so taken with you. Then there's Brandon. I would have staked my life on…" Her words trailed off. "You make me feel things I didn't think possible. I've been trying to figure out what to do with it." She paused and looked at him. "Now Brandon's father was behind this and tried to kill me himself."

"He didn't realize who he had. Once he figured out you're John Westen's daughter, he needed to correct it. It wasn't anything personal about you. He was just trying to protect himself and clean up his mess."

"If I were talking to someone, I would be able to see what his father did logically and without emotion, but it's me that he wanted dead. It's hard to not take it personally."

"You know what I want?" Neal said.

She looked at him, waiting.

"I want you. My heart wants you. It needs you. The truth is, my father's a CEO and he does have his own corporation, so to me it's not a stretch. I met your parents. Your father reminded me of my own father, a man who can never be pleased. They

254

always have a negative comment for everyone and about everything. My father's worse than yours. He wanted me to be part of the business, but I can't stand not being able to measure up to his ideals. I realized after I met your dad that I'm like my father in the aspect that I run all over the world writing about situations that are wrong to take the focus off my shortcomings. Because of my father, I spent a lot of time with my uncle on his ranch in Texas. My uncle taught me all those outdoor skills. I have a brother, who works with my father. He's an ass, too. I did have a girlfriend who was a news reporter, but she was more concerned about climbing the corporate ladder than having a relationship, so I left. I tried to be content at a small-town newspaper, but I didn't fit. My boss was a jerk. The best thing he did was give me the Chris Roper story. I met your mom, and she wanted to find her daughter. I saw a story I needed to write. I quit my job at the newspaper, left my girlfriend, and flew over here. Then I met you. You captured my heart, all of it. Am I wrong about us?"

She looked down and shook her head. Then looked back up at him. "Every time I look at you, I swear I see myself and my future in your eyes. But I need time to think. I need time to figure this out and wrap my mind around everything that's happened." She looked down at the seat.

# Chapter 22

The driver pulled beside the plane. The stairs were in place and the door was open, waiting for them.

The driver collected their bags as Neal helped Chevy scoot out of the backseat.

Chevy followed him up the stairs onto the plane. The driver followed behind her. The two men already on board stood as they stepped in, the same two men who had accompanied Neal on the flight over.

"Agent Smith, Agent Heater." Neal winked at them. "This is Chevy."

The man in the khaki jacket held out his hand with a pleasant smile and nodded to Chevy.

Chevy shook his hand and nodded to his partner. "Hi." She smiled, but her eyes seemed to be disconnected from that smile. She sat down next to Neal on a sofa across from them.

The driver stowed their bags, shook Neal's hand, and left the plane. The door to the plane closed. In moments they were taxiing toward the runway.

### 

"Chevy," The man in the khaki jacket began. "I have to tell you, it's nice to have the girl behind all the fuss in front of us, and alive," he said. His voice was powerful and authoritative.

Chevy looked at him, then at Neal. "So that guy was Brandon's father?" she asked, still trying to process everything that had happened.

Neal nodded. "Yeah, that was him—Chris Roper. I was assigned to do a story on his donation to a local school. I got the sense there was a larger story there. When I started to investigate, the government pulled me in and asked me to undertake a mission to rescue you."

His partner chimed in. "Do you mind if we record the conversation?"

She shook her head. "I don't care."

The man in the khaki jacket asked, "Did you know who

Chris Roper was?"

"No. He was just a guy. I didn't even know his name. He came into the club one night. He sat in a dim corner and watched me intently. He held up large bills and placed them on the table so I would come to him. He was smoking a cigar. I'd never met or seen a picture of Brandon's parents." She looked at Neal. "Did you know Brandon was my boyfriend?"

"No." Neal shook his head. "Not until Little Sweeden. I knew you had a boyfriend named Brandon. Your parents were at Chris's house—"

"Why were my parents at their house?"

The man in the khaki jacket interrupted. "Let me give you some insight. From what we have been able to gather, Brandon, your boyfriend—"

A flight attendant brought a tray with water for everyone. "Brandon," the man in the khaki jacket continued once she had left, "didn't know anything about what his father did for a living. He knew his father was a businessman and had a variety of companies, some of which dealt with overseas partners. But beyond that, he didn't know anything. His father was always careful to hide it. We feel that Brandon knew something wasn't right, and he was smart enough to leave it alone. His father, Chris Roper, has been under surveillance for a while. Now that brings us to your question about how your parents ended up at Brandon's house. He went home and overheard his father on the phone talking about you. This caused him to realize his father had a hand in your disappearance. He got into a verbal confrontation with his father that turned into a physical confrontation over bringing you back. Brandon wanted you brought back immediately, and his father wanted you killed, silenced, removed." The man paused. "Select whichever word you want."

"Why would his father want to take me to begin with?"

"Well, that's why Chris has been under surveillance. He's part of a large human trafficking group our government is trying to stop. He's taken hundreds of women and sold them in his sex trafficking operation."

The butler's words when they were standing in the dress

room rang in Chevy's ears. *You're a very lucky girl, Chevy.*
"How many woman has Chris taken?"

"In all the years he's been doing this, probably thousands. Do you know how many missing women and children we've had in our country in the last thirty years?"

"I have no idea. I'm afraid to ask." She paused. "How many?"

"Thousands. There were thousands," he emphasized. "Most of the missing women are age seven to twenty-five. You see them on the backs of milk cartons."

"That doesn't make any sense." She blinked. "These people have parents, friends, and family who would go looking for them."

The man shook his head and laughed. "You would be surprised. He was very careful to pick girls, teenagers, and young women who came from low-class and uneducated backgrounds. He took a lot of runaways or women strung out on drugs. If some of these girls came from good families, then they had been such problems their families didn't want anything to do with them any longer." He paused. "You, on the other hand…"

"Oh…" Chevy closed her eyes, then opened them, staring at the floor, recalling. "I told him at the club that my family life wasn't so great. My father was in prison, and I was raised by my grandmother, who passed away." She looked up. "If you tell them a good sob story, they tip better."

"So that was part of it," he said.

Chevy took a sip of her water.

"Most people don't give their child a nickname like Chevy. Your name's as unique as your situation. Between your name, the fact that he found you in a strip club, and what you told him about your family, he had the impression you were the perfect prospect. You're a pretty girl, so I'm sure he thought he could get a lot of money for you. We also went through your sugar daddy profile. Chris has an account on every site out there. He was on your profile twice. The last time was the day before you disappeared."

"How did my parents end up at his house?"

258

"Oh yes…back to that part. After Brandon and his father got into the argument about you, Brandon stormed out. News reporters photographed him at your parents' house the next morning. So, the best we can figure, he talked with your parents and alerted them. We assume he gave your parents the address to his parents' home." The man in the khaki jacket shrugged his shoulders. "A short time after Brandon was photographed at your parents' house, your mom left, then your father. Your mom showed up at Chris's house while Neal here was in the middle of an interview."

"Oh," Neal said, as he came to some sort of realization. "I was sitting there with Chris, who had a bruised eye. I was curious about it, but didn't ask. When your mom came in, one of the things she asked about was his eye. He said he had a mishap with a ladder and a wall. I didn't know what had happened to his eye until now. Brandon clearly said something to your mom. That's why she made the comment to him," Neal said. "Anyway, I needed to write an article about Chris's donation to the school. I'm sure he intended to make himself look good just in case the situation with you got out of hand, like it has. Then in walks your mom. At first Chris was being nice, because he had a reporter in front of him. Then your mom became very pushy—nice but demandingly pushy. Chris made the mistake of telling her he was in the middle of an interview for an article. Your mom realized I was a reporter. We spoke and I gave her my card. Oddly, I had seen a news report about a missing girl from Kentucky. The story caught my eye, and I felt drawn. Then, a day later, there I was talking to your mom. Your mom called me a couple hours after I left Chris's house and wanted help finding you. I didn't know until today how your parents ended up at Chris Roper's. I had no idea about Brandon. I will tell you, your mom is quite the woman. I see where you get it. She seems sweet, and she is, but she can be feisty."

His partner spoke up. "Your mom shot Chris in the foot."

The connection suddenly clicked. "Oh! That was the reason for the boot he had on!" Chevy smiled proudly. "My mom did that."

The man in the khaki jacket smiled. "The government has been working to take down this trafficking group. Once you were taken, the publicity created one hell of a problem. When your mom involved Neal, it was clear your parents were ready to make a big stink. That's when we stepped in. The government didn't want this to grow into an international incident, so we had to move quickly. We showed up at Neal's door. Neal was packing to come find you, and we streamlined it. The government needs it to appear that Neal left the country and rescued you by himself. It has to be perceived the government had no involvement. That's the only way to keep doing our undercover work and bring these guys down."

"It'll look to the world that the reporter brought you home," his partner said, and he smiled.

Chevy leaned forward and covered her face with her hands.

"We'll leave you and Chevy for a while," The man in the khaki jacket said to Neal as he and his partner stood to leave. "I think she's had enough to take in for the time being."

### 

The surveillance man sat at the conference table with the rest of the team, waiting for an update. Suddenly his phone rang. "Hello...Thank you...Let me knew when you are a couple of hours out" He pressed End on his phone. "I have great news," he told the team. "Neal and Chevy are on the plane en route for the States."

"Excellent!" the man in the black suit said, cracking a smile. "Make sure the press knows Chevy's on her way. I want this covered and Neal Collins looking like the hero. Call her parents, her co-workers, Brandon, and his mother. I want all of them, everyone—even the detectives in Boston and Rudle Mills."

"No one will be allowed close to the plane," one of the men in the room said.

"Have the plane routed to a small airport and have exceptions made," the man in the black suit instructed.

260

# Chapter 23

Chevy looked out the window as they landed and saw dozens of television trucks, cameras, and reporters standing in a clump by a hangar, waiting. "My Lord!" she said. "There's a sea of reporters out there! I just wanted to go home, but now…" She looked at Neal reluctantly. "They can take their time opening the door."

The two agents came up from the back section of the plane. The man in the khaki jacket cleared his throat. "We won't accompany you off the plane. Its only going to be the two of you. Don't mention us to any of the reporters. Say nothing about passports, credit cards, or anything about the government. It's better that way. It will help the other girls get home." He looked at Chevy. "Remember, Chevy, Neal's the hero."

She nodded. "I wasn't prepared for a mob of people." She was nervous.

"Well, you might want to wipe the rest of the blood splatters from your face," his partner suggested.

Chevy felt her skin and a look of horror crossed her face. She glanced at Neal, then headed for the bathroom. "Oh, dear Lord!" She stuck her head out the bathroom door. "Why in the world didn't any of you tell me?"

The man in the khaki jacket answered. "You were distraught when you got on the plane. It wasn't the time to mention it, then you went to the bathroom how many times? I sorta figured you had looked in the mirror. When you're put through that kind of traumatic situation, what else are you supposed to look like?

"Well one of you could've said something," she mumbled, wiping her face down with a damp washcloth then poked her head out again. "Better?" she asked.

Neal looked at her. "I personally thought the blood splatters created intrigue." He winked at her.

The man in the khaki jacket gave Neal an unimpressed gaze.

"Your car is in the parking lot by the letter D. Someone will walk up to you, shake your hand, and hand you your car keys. As for the things from your apartment, they are in a storage unit. I'll call you in the next couple of days to find out where you want us to take them. You still have my number?"

Neal nodded. "Are you ready, babe?" He held out his hand.

She looked out the window. "There's another group of people off to the side," she said, glancing at Neal then back out the window.

Neal looked out, then did a double-take. There, in the distance, was Megan. A smirk formed on his face. "I guess everyone needs closure." He shook his head, then looked at Chevy. "You ready to do this and get it over with?"

"As ready as I'm ever going to be," she said, looking reluctant. "I'm following you. There are certain times in a person's life when you don't want to be the leader, you want to be the follower. This is one of those times."

Neal stepped out of the plane and onto the metal steps with Chevy a step behind him.

She looked at a sectioned-off group of people she knew. Some were holding banners that said WELCOME HOME!

### 

As they approached the line of reporters, the reporters leaned over the ropes, yelling questions over one another. Their microphones displayed the logos of their stations and blurred together in a line of colors.

"Neal! Neal!" he heard Megan call out.

He turned to see her pushing to the front of the crowd.

He waited.

"Weren't you going to at least tell me good-bye?" she asked, standing next to the rope.

Neal looked off into the distance, formulating his thoughts with his hands in his pants pockets, then looked at her. "Why? You would've been too busy to take the call."

"Dinner tonight?" Her eyes twinkled.

Neal laughed. He had seen that twinkle before. Here he was, the reporter fresh from the fire that she had found so alluring and sexy. But in a few days that allure would fade, just as it

262

had before. "I'm sure you have a story to cover other than this one." Neal winked at her. "Right, Megan?"

Megan's smile fell, and the twinkle left her eyes.

A man walked up. "Neal." He held out his hand.

Neal nonchalantly pulled his hand from his pocket and held it out. The man grabbed his elbow and gave him a firm locking handshake. "Good to meet you. Glad you brought her home. Good work," the man said, unclasping his hand and leaving Neal's car keys in the palm of his hand before he turned and walked away.

Neal stuck his hand back in the pocket of his pants and stepped behind Chevy as a man with short, stick-straight reddish hair and a rough complexion stepped out from the crowd. The man held out his hand. "Hello, Chevy. I'm Detective Hemming, Boston PD. I'm the one who took your missing person report."

Chevy gave him a blank look, then smiled. "Thank you. It's nice to meet you." Through the crowd she caught a glimpse of Brandon, then she shifted her eyes back to the detective.

Neal held out his hand. "Thank you," he said. "Your help and fast action were a key factor."

Chevy kept an eye on Brandon, who was intermittently peering through the crowd at her. "Yes, thank you. If it wasn't for you—"

"It's good to met you. Most missing girls don't come home," Hemming told her, as Jen walked up beside him. "Chevy!" she yelled with excitement, throwing her arms around her. "You're home! I'm so sorry. If I had any idea…" She shook her head.

"Its okay. Neither of us knew."

Jen hugged her again. "I'm so glad you're back and all right. You have no idea how worried I was. This detective here gave me the third degree." She smiled, with her hand on his shoulder.

"It was just part of the job," he said. "Chevy, it was good meeting you. I won't take any more of your time." He turned away.

Chevy smiled at Jen. "Well, you don't need to worry

anymore." She paused. "Guess what? I have some tuition money for you," she said with eyes that dazzled.

"Tuition money?" Jen repeated, crinkling her eyebrows together.

"Yep, sure do."

"Where's Becky?" she asked, looking around. She caught a glimpse of Brandon in the crowd again, making his way toward her.

"Oh, she's in jail." Jen shrugged.

Chevy's eyes widened. "You're kidding!"

"Becky was with her latest boyfriend at a bar somewhere and a fight broke out. I guess police were called, and they were picked up for cocaine possession." Jen rolled her eyes. "I don't really know the whole story. It's not my problem. Becky and her endless bad choices aren't my issue."

"I'll call you. I'll explain the tuition money later," Chevy told her, as she was pulled away to the next person in the huddle to greet her. It seemed like she might drown in the sea of questions, cameras, reporters, and well-wishers. Slowly, the huddled crowd dwindled. In the distance, waiting patiently, by her dad's truck stood her parents. Off to the side stood Brandon, waiting, with an unsure smile on his face.

Chevy looked at him with an emotionless expression that almost turned to a scowl.

She turned her back to him and looked at Neal. "I can't do this." She began to fight back tears.

"Hey, hey, hey...What's wrong?"

"That's Brandon. I'm not sure how I'm supposed to feel. I'm not sure what I think. And isn't there something between you and me, or were those just words during a high-intensity situation that created some kind of strange faulty emotion?"

"Chevy, look at me." His eyes looked intently into hers. "I meant everything I said. Get in my car. Come with me. I can't promise you perfect, but I can promise I'll give you my heart and every part of me. I'll always love you. I'll listen to what you want and try to make you happy."

Chevy looked at him, her eyes red.

"You want rose petals in your bubble bath? Done. If

finances are tight I'll go buy some artificial roses and cut the petals off so we can reuse them—that way, you can always have them in your bath."

Chevy smiled and laughed through her now welling eyes.

"I also know your parents are waiting and you need to figure out Brandon. Maybe Brandon's where you need to be—but I'm hoping not."

She stood listening, thinking.

"We need to walk over and talk to your parents. They've been waiting patiently. I don't want them to spontaneously combust."

Chevy laughed while fighting back emotion.

"It's just not a good scene." Neal smiled.

Chevy took in a deep breath.

"Chevy!" Brandon called out. "Chevy!"

She turned to him with no excitement, her head tilted down.

"Chevy." He searched her face as she walked up. He held his arms open for her.

She put her hands up to ward him off. "Do you have any idea the hell I have been through?! Your father did this to me—your father." She stared at him. "Are you aware he came to Barcelona, where I ended up? Did you know he tried to have me killed? When that failed, he tried to kill me himself. Did you know that?" She stood there looking at him.

Brandon stood speechless. "I had no idea. I've been wandering in the Ozark Mountains since I left your parents." He pressed his lips together and looked away, upset.

"Remember I told you about the man at the club who kept holding up hundred-dollar bills for me, the one who sat in the corner?"

"Yeah." He blinked.

"That was my introduction to your father!"

"My God." Brandon shook his head. "Babe, I'm so sorry." He took hold of her hands.

"What would you like me to say? Considering all that has happened, I think that means we're done." She pulled her hands from his and stepped back.

"Chevy!" Brandon stepped after her. "My God, wait! My

265

father did this to me, too. The FBI detained me for questioning. My father couldn't even show up. When I found out he was behind this, I went straight to your parents and told them."

Chevy paused for a moment and held her hand to her stomach.

"Chevy, please, I love you. I didn't do this," he said. "I didn't do this."

### 

Neal stood in the background with the Westens, watching.

"Well, she can't very well stay with him," John said, watching. "He seemed nice. The problem is his father." John stuck his hands in the front pocket of his jeans.

### 

With tears welling in her eyes, Chevy looked at Brandon. "I love you, too, but where do we go from here? Do we continue with our relationship, and where does that go? My future in-laws had me drugged so they could sell me in the sex trade. That's a little awkward. What if we have kids? Do we allow your mom around them. Is it safe? What about your father? He tried to kill me, and I beat the crap out of him. He won't stay in jail forever. What do we tell our children about their grandfather? Even if you're not in the family business, who's going to hire Chris Roper's son? Would we ever be able to have a normal life? Ever?" Chevy paused. "I love you," she said, as tears began to stream down her cheeks. "But I would rather not start out life struggling to get out of an impossible hole."

Brandon looked at her, his eyes welling with tears. "Chevy, no, don't do this." He reached out and grabbed her hand. "I got you a ring, even before any of this happened."

She squeezed her eyes shut and struggled to keep her chin from quivering. The tears won. She shook her head and walked away.

Brandon stood there alone. His mother watched from the background.

"Chevy, please don't do this!" He called after her.

She didn't turn around.

Her parents finally rushed to her and hugged her between

them. Ruthie pushed the hair from Chevy's face and kissed her cheek. "I know, sweetheart. It will be all right," Ruthie said, trying to comfort her.

### 

Deep down, seeing just how much his little girl appeared to love Brandon, broke John's heart. He looked at his wife and for the first time in his life wondered, *What if it were Ruthie walking away from me? It would kill me. After all these years, I can bitch and moan, I can be a jerk and lash out at her. But in the end she has always been there at my side, helping me, supporting me, making sure I was all right. Every night she kisses me and snuggles next to me with that same heartfelt look in her eyes she had the first time we said I love you.* Suddenly John had an epiphany. He had everything to be thankful for, and he hadn't appreciated it nearly enough. He looked at Brandon and knew that if it were his Ruthie walking away, he would be devastated. John looked at the ground as he opened the truck door for all of them.

### 

On the drive home Brandon and his mother were silent for a long time before she reached her hand to his and squeezed it. "Are you all right?"

Brandon shot her a nasty look. "Not particularly."

"You know your father and I only want the best for you—"

"Then let me ask your opinion. My father was involved in my girlfriend's disappearance, and it ends up that he's a sex trafficker. I was detained for questioning, which has thrown me into suspicion, even though I had nothing to do with any of it. I'm going to be looked at suspiciously for years to come. It's going to limit my job prospects. I have lost the girl I was going to marry. So tell me, Mom, your opinion of how this has turned out?" He looked at her.

"I don't know what to say."

"That's right, Mom—there's nothing. How you thought any of this was a good idea to begin with—it's beyond me. How were you able to sleep at night knowing Dad took someone's daughter?" He shifted in his seat.

###

The men sat around a big-screen television in the conference room, watching the news as Chevy and Neal made their way off the plane. The man in the black suit watched, pleased that the news stations were making Neal Collins look like the hero. He twisted in his chair toward the others. "Wait until Brandon returns home. Then I want the two of you"—he looked at Ward and Cook—"To go to the Roper home and give Chris Roper's wife an update on her husband. Let her know he was hurt and is in custody and on his way back to the States. I want Chris Roper made an example for everyone to see," he stated.

Ward leaned forward. "What about the rest of the associates? As soon as they see what is happening to Chris, they are going to scatter like roaches."

The man in the black suit shifted his eyes to the man in the dress blues. "As soon as I give the go-ahead, I want all the associates taken out, all expect Sandro Nath and his wife. Don't touch them. Put men in place to follow the other associates until I give the order."

"What?" Cook blurted out hastily.

The man in the black suit shifted his eyes back to Cook. "Sandro Nath and his wife, as of this morning, have allowed the other associates to buy them out. Aside from a handful of things that take more time to get rid of, they are no longer involved. It's clear they want out, and they are getting out as fast as they can."

"They have been involved for an awfully long time!" Cook said loudly, irritated.

"They aren't any longer," the man in the black suit stated. "Nath didn't want Chevy dead and neither did his wife, or we would've never seen that girl again. They kept her safe. Nath and his wife did the right thing. Leave them be."

"That's like exterminating all the roaches but one!"

"I said, leave them." He gave Cook a firm look. "Nath and his wife kept that girl safe and kept me from having to clean up one hell of a goddamn mess!" He shifted his eyes to the man in the dress blues and raised his eyebrows. "I hope I made myself clear and you understood that Nath and his wife will be left alone."

268

The man in the dress blues gave him a nod. "Understood."

# Chapter 24

Chevy was sitting at the counter at home in Kentucky when the garage door opened. She looked over to see Crysta and the boys coming through the door, backpacks over their shoulders and bags in hand.

"Chevy!" Nicholas and Alex blurted out in unison.

A faint smile pulled across her face.

They dropped their bags, hurried to her, and threw their arms around her. They squeezed her tightly between them, then picked her up and wiggled her back and forth. "We missed you!" Alex said, as they both kissed either side of her face.

Chevy was blank.

They sat her down with troubled looks. "Are you all right?" Nicholas asked.

"I'm okay," she replied softly, moving back to the chair.

Nicholas gave her a long look. "All right." He picked up his backpack and motioned with the tilt of his head for Alex to follow him upstairs. "We'll be upstairs if you want to hang out with us," he offered.

Chevy nodded at him, then looked down.

Ruthie, John, and Crysta shot each other looks of concern and said nothing.

Chevy suddenly got up. "I've had a long day. I'm going to get some sleep," she announced, hurrying away up the steps ahead of her brothers, who were still standing in the kitchen.

Nicholas put the palms of his hand in the air. "Hey, where are you going?"

Crysta put her hand on Nicholas's arm to get his attention. "She's been through a lot. She needs time. Go easy on her, and be delicate. We have no idea what she's has been through."

### 

A few days later, Ruthie passed Chevy's bedroom with a basket of laundry, glanced in, then stopped in the doorway.

Chevy stood in front of her father's old easel, a canvas in front of her, painting.

Ruthie walked up behind her, looking intently at the canvas. "What are you doing?"

Chevy stared at the canvas, eyeing the way the colors blended while she moved the brush through the slippery paint. "Painting," she finally said, focused on the canvas.

"The colors are dark and your lines are intriguing. It looks…interesting," Ruthie said slowly, both terrified and amazed.

Chevy glanced at her mom and continued with the brush.

"Your father was always such a great artist. Your brothers have a good ability. You never had much interest. Were you stowing it away to surprise me?" Ruthie forced a smile, wanting to encourage her. She kissed the side of her face, turned, and left the room, alarmed by Chevy's antisocial behavior and dark painting.

### 

A day later Chevy came downstairs to the kitchen and saw a vase full of beautiful deep red roses on the counter. The aroma hung in the air. The petals looked soft and velvety. She looked away.

Ruthie watched as she put scoops of cookie dough on a baking sheet. "Would you like some cookies? I have some on a plate. They're warm."

"No, no cookies." She went to the refrigerator and pulled out a plastic cup of red grapefruit and started back to her room.

"Don't you want to know who they are from?" Ruthie asked. "They're for you."

Chevy paused, not turning around, but listening.

"They're from Neal," Ruthie said gently. "The card said, 'Since we had to leave your roses, I bought you new ones. I miss you.' You should call him. His number is on the card."

Chevy said nothing, and went back to her room.

### 

A couple days later, John and Ruthie stood as an older dark-haired woman wearing jeans and a blouse came down the stairs. They met her at the landing.

"Well?" Ruthie asked.

"Is there a place we can sit?"

271

"The kitchen," Ruthie replied, leading the way. "Can I get you something to drink?"

"No, thank you," the woman said, taking a spot at the table when John held out a chair for her, then took a seat himself.

Ruthie sat down. "So, please…What is going on with her. I want to help, but I'm afraid prompting her to talk could just make it worse."

"Just as we discussed on the phone, this is a very difficult situation. There are, of course, multiple levels to Chevy's pain right now. She's showing some signs of post-traumatic stress disorder—PTSD. It's a mental condition that can occur after someone experiences or sees a terrifying event. Being drugged and taken is a terrifying, helpless, venerable feeling. Event though she wasn't raped, tortured, or tied up, she watched this happen to the people around her. One girl said she wanted to go home, and they killed her. Chevy heard the shots. Your daughter was in a situation where she was never sure from moment to moment about her safety. Her captors were also her rescuers, to a degree, which creates confusion, doubt, and mistrust of the people closest to her. To top it all off, her boyfriend's father was behind it all, which creates an even deeper level of fear in trusting the people she loves."

The woman looked at John. "Of course, she was completely reliant on you, as her father. Then you took away her funding for school and everything that encompassed, which ultimately led her to do things she felt she had no choice about that got her to a situation where being stolen could happen. I know, Mr. Westen, that's not what you want to hear. As a parent myself, I know that's never what you intended."

John hung his head, looking at the table top in front of him. The woman's words trailed off as John sat there, realizing what he had put into motion.

### 

John walked into his bedroom and found Ruthie and Chevy deep in conversation. They suddenly stopped talking when they noticed him, and sat there quietly. "Sorry. I was looking for something." He slowly backed out of the room and pulled the door partway shut. From the hall he could hear them talking again.

He looked at the door, puzzled, then the light began to dawn. He went to the great room, grabbed a box of tissues, and went back to the bedroom. Once again, they stopped talking as he opened the door. "I thought you might need another box of tissues," he offered sheepishly. He set the box on the bed next to a pile of used tissue. "You know, Chevy, if you want to talk, I'm always here." He gave her a small smile.

Chevy shook her head. "That's all right. You wouldn't understand. Thanks, though."

Ruthie gave him a knowing I-told-you-so expression, but then followed it with a warm smile, acknowledging his efforts.

Not sure what to say in the awkward silence, he headed for the door. He realized the damage he had done. Ruthie had been correct: not accepting that Chevy was an adult had pushed her away. He had always thought he had to be right. It had always felt like a game to him with Ruthie. Now he realized that it was never a game. In his stubbornness and unwillingness to cooperate, he had excluded himself from Chevy's life—even Ruthie's. The reality had teeth that bit at his soul, making him feel small and sick inside.

### 

Brandon paused as he passed the French doors to his father's office. He twisted the knob and flipped on the light. The house felt different without his father. It felt lighter, freer. He could hear his mom crying herself to sleep at night. Part of him wanted to go comfort her, while the other part held no sympathy. He looked up at the ceiling toward the sound of her cries. "If you play with fire, eventually you get burned," he said, and walked out of the room, flipping off the light behind him.

In his bedroom he sat on the side of his bed and opened the drawer of the night stand. He pulled out a small black velvet box and opened it. The diamond ring dazzled. He watched how it sparkled. Tears welled in his eyes. He felt lost without her, but it was time to put the ring away and move on with his life.

He put the ring in the far back corner of the drawer and shut it.

"Chevy!" Ruthie yelled upstairs, the third vase of roses in her hands.

Chevy came out of her room and looked down from the top of the stairs.

Ruthie smiled up at her. "There's a card."

Chevy looked down from the top step. "Oh," she grunted, unamused.

"Well, don't you want to know who sent you flowers?" She held out the vase. "They smell wonderful."

"You should put them in the kitchen so you can enjoy them," Chevy said as she turned, walked back into her room, and shut the door behind her.

"Don't you want to know who they are from?" Ruthie shouted so Chevy could hear her.

"No!" Chevy yelled from behind the door.

Ruthie hung her head and sighed.

"So who are the flowers from?" John asked from the sofa, turning down the television slightly.

Ruthie walked the coffee table and set the vase down. She plucked the card from the bouquet and read it out loud.

> *I think about you every day and dream about you every night. There should be nothing we can't overcome.*
>
> *I love you,*
>
> *Brandon*

John looked at her. "I think it's about time I had a heart-to-heart with her." He rose from the sofa.

"No!" Ruthie shot out quickly. "What are you going to say to her?"

"Relax," John said. He stepped to her. "You know, I haven't told you lately how much I love you." He looked at her, the sincerity in his eyes twinkling like stars in the sky. "I watched how Brandon reacted when Chevy walked away. I thought about how I would feel if it were you. I would have been devastated. I realized that I take you for granted. I'm sorry about that. I don't tell you enough how much I love you. I'm sorry for the way I have treated you lately. I don't know how you put up with me, but I'm glad you did."

A glow came to her face as a smile pulled across her face. "Xanax. If you were like that very often, I would have left years ago." She looked at him. "But you spent years being a wonderful husband and father. You were horrible during all of this. I knew it was the situation and temporary."

He cupped the back of her head with his hand and pulled her to his chest, hugging her. "I'm so sorry, sweetheart."

She looked up at him, her eyes searching his face.

His words seemed to come hard as his eyes reddened. "You have spent years taking care of all of us, making the food we love, ensuring a spotless house and clean clothes, and you're always there for anything I need. I watch you nurse the kids back to health when they're sick. You run any errand I send you on, and you always do it with love. You put the kids and me before yourself. How many times have I told you that I love you, or that I appreciate all that you do? I haven't done it nearly enough. I've expected that you'll just be here, that I'll have clothes ready to wear, food to eat, and all the other things you do. I'm sorry for that." He looked at her with sincerity welling in his eyes.

She stood there, not sure what to say.

"I realize now that you were right. Chevy is an adult, and I need to listen to her. I need to listen to you, too. I thought that in order to be the man I had to be right. Now I understand. We need to be right together. Sometimes you'll have the answers, and sometimes I will." His eyes shifted away from her, then back. His words tore at his pride. "I guess I'm not making much sense."

Ruthie looked at him. "You're making more sense than you have in a long time. Do you have any idea how much it means to hear you say that?" She stepped closer to him, put her arms around his waist, and hugged him tightly. "I love you," she said. He picked her off her feet and squeezed her.

An item on the news playing softly in the background

caught John's attention. He turned to the television, grabbed the remote, and turned up the volume.

"Chris Roper died today of an apparent heart attack. He had been detained in Spain and returned to the U.S., and was currently awaiting a bail hearing on charges of human trafficking related to the October disappearance of Charlotte Westen…"

John flipped off the television. "Wow. He's dead."

Ruthie looked at him, stunned. "If Chevy wants Brandon, his father being dead certainly does remove a hurdle."

### 

Chevy was sitting in her room on her bed. Her face wet with tears, and her eyes were puffy. She had a mound of used tissue next to her. Suddenly, there in her doorway stood her father, his blue eyes were peering over the top of three vases full of deep red roses in his arms. "Chevy."

"Yeah?" She looked at him with a sad expression.

"Can I come in?"

She looked at him, unsure. "This is a first. You never ask. You always just do as you please." She looked at his blue eyes against the deep red of the roses, then put her head back down. "Of course you can come in," she told him softly, pushing the mound of gooey tissue to the side.

He set the roses on the nightstand and put the small cards down next to them. He sat beside her on the bed and held out his arms for her. "Chevy, come here," he coaxed her patiently.

"Normally you're abrasive and direct. Trying to talk to you about much of anything is impossible." She looked at him doubtfully, but snuggled up next to him. Even grown, she was small in his long, tall frame.

He wrapped his arms around her. "You know…" he began.

"What?" She looked at him reluctantly.

He nodded at the roses. "Don't you want to know who they're from?"

"No," Chevy looked away. Her chin quivered.

"What if the flowers are from Brandon?"

Chevy's shook her head.

"What if they are from that good-looking reporter, Neal? He

276

was nice." He watched her response.

"Yeah. He was nice," she agreed.

"I had breakfast with Neal the other day."

Chevy stared at him.

"I thought that would get your attention. Tell me about it. What are you feeling?" He tapped his finger to her shoulder.

She put her head down, closed her eyes, and shook her head. "It sounds crazy," she said, fighting to hold back tears.

"You know, if you get teary-eyed over how you're feeling, that's something you should talk about." He reached for a tissue. "I've had forty-three years of screwing things up. I don't know everything, but I know a few things. So talk to me. Maybe your dumb old dad can save you a couple of screw-ups."

She looked at him, apprehensive. She shook her head. "You'll just tell me I'm full of it."

"I promise I won't." He stuck his pinky in the air like they used to do when she was seven and there was no greater promise in the world than a pinky swear.

Chevy smiled seeing his pinky waiting for her to wrap her pinky around it. She glanced at him a few times, unsure.

"You know why I don't have brown eyes?" he asked.

"Because you didn't receive that genetic trait," she answered.

"All right, quit with the education," he teased. "I don't have brown eyes because brown eyed people, well, people say they are full of shit. I have blue eyes. You know what that means."

"That you have the blue-eyed genetic trait?" Chevy said, a smile starting to form on her face, knowing that wasn't the answer he wanted.

"Stop that." He nudged her. "I have blue eyes because I'm so full of bullshit my head is in the clouds."

Chevy smiled, then began to laugh for the first time since she had been home.

"So what does that say about me and my hazel eyes?"

John shook his head. "I have no idea, but you laughed." He paused. "Talk to me," he encouraged.

"I would have sworn I loved Brandon, and I do. Then Neal

277

came along…"

"Blew you away, did he?"

She nodded. "Yeah, he did."

"So why are you so upset? It sounds like you have it figured out."

"Can you really be in love with someone if another person can come along and steal your heart? The first time I saw Neal, I knew it was something…" She paused to think about the right words, remembering the butler's description. "It was like the world had suddenly come alive. Colors—it was as though the world didn't have color, sound, or smell before I met him." She looked at him.

John smirked.

Chevy was instantly angry. "See! I told you, you would laugh at me!" She pulled herself out of his grip.

"No, no—I'm not laughing at you," he told her lovingly as he took her hand. "Did you know I dated a girl in high school before your mom? Man, she was pretty. I would have followed her to the ends of the earth. Then I met your mother. I took one look at your mom, and guess what I saw." John smiled. "A rainbow of colors."

Chevy's anger melted away, and a spark came into her eyes. "Really?" She sounded doubtful. "You knew it was something rare?"

John nodded. "Sure did. I felt bad. I really did love that first girl, but I loved your mother more."

Her eyes instantly brightened, and her face lit up. "I feel so guilty. I don't want to hurt Brandon."

"You know what you do?"

"What?"

"You and I can take a road trip and see Brandon, test the water, see how it feels. Then we'll go see Neal."

Slowly, she started nodding, liking the idea. "All right, that sounds good." She smiled.

He handed her the cards from the flowers. "But first you have to read the cards. Don't make any decisions yet. Go see them, see how it feels."

She pulled the first card from his fingers then stared at it reluctantly.

"Read the card," he told her again. "Go ahead. It won't bite."

Chevy pulled the card from the small envelope.

*Roses are red,*

*Violets are blue,*

*I have socks that are empty without you!!*

*Neal*

"That's sweet," she said with sadness.

"Remember, it's about how it feels, not just sweet words. Read the rest of them. Then, go take a shower. You smell." He patted her leg and left her to think.

### 

Chevy and John pulled in front of Brandon's house on an overcast day. Chevy looked out the window. "This is it?" She look apprehensive.

"This is it."

"It's huge." She reached for the door handle and pulled the door open. "I thought ours was mammoth." She made a face as she got out and walked toward the door.

Standing in front of the door, she turned and looked back at her father, who turned the truck off and made a shooing motion with his hand in the air above the steering wheel.

She turned back to the door and pressed the doorbell. One side of the door cracked open, to a short, round-faced Hispanic woman. "Yes?"

"Hi," Chevy smiled. "I'm Chevy Westen. I'm here to see Brandon."

The woman nodded and opened the door further. In the hall just inside the door stood Brandon, waiting, his hands in his pockets.

The woman walked off.

Chevy stood there in front of him.

He opened his arm.

She wrapped her arms around him, silent and without enthusiasm.

"I was thinking we could go get dinner," he said.

Chevy fidgeted with her hands. "That would be great. I'm hungry. It was a long drive." She looked down at the floor, not knowing what to say.

"You haven't met my mother yet." He seemed to find some bubbliness. "She's been pretty upset. She's not quite herself." He grabbed hold of her hand and walked her through the house to a family room. The family room was huge, with woodwork that spanned from floor to ceiling and beams that crossed the ceiling in a square pattern. Big windows lined the outside wall, allowing a beautiful view of the outdoors—what was left of the autumn leaves and now mostly bare trees that were waiting for snow. Judy sat on a leather sofa, quietly looking out as they came into the room. Brandon cleared his throat to get her attention. A mound of used tissues sat beside her. She wore no makeup and her eyes were swollen, puffy, and red. An aura of deep-seated heartache and dismay hung around her.

"Mom, this is Chevy. Chevy, this is my mom, Judy Roper."

Graciously, Judy stood from the sofa. More tears welled in her eyes. "Chevy," she said, taking hold of her fingers. "It's so nice to meet you."

Chevy smiled, noting the confusion of thoughts running just behind Judy's eyes. "Its wonderful meeting you as well."

"You'll have to excuse me. It's been a very difficult time lately," she said, deeply distraught and distant.

"Of course," Chevy said, not sure what to say. She looked at the windows. "The view is beautiful."

Judy sat back down, pulled a tissue from the box, and wiped her eyes. "Yes, I suppose it is," she said sweetly.

"We're going to go get dinner. Would you like me to bring you back something?" He waited.

"No." She wiped her eyes. "I'm not sure I can eat."

He nodded. "Okay. We'll be back in a while." He took Chevy's hand and led her out of the room.

### 

Chevy sat across from him at the table. "So, what have you

been doing?"

He looked away, toward the tables near the window. "Listening to my mom cry, mostly."

"Oh." There was a long pause. "Are you finishing this semester?"

He looked at her. "I need to get a lot of things taken care of and situated."

"I understand."

"I have a lot of paperwork to go through—business stuff. I've only begun to figure out all the different companies my father either owned or had a partial ownership in, and sort out which were legitimate and which weren't. He didn't leave me any lists in case of his death, so I'm on my own to figure it all out."

Chevy nodded, giving him a half smile.

"He did leave some sizable life insurance policies, so I'm set." He paused. "I'm thinking about changing my name."

"Name change. Wow." She lifted her eyebrows. "I know it's socially polite to at least give condolences, since he's gone—"

"Well, you beat the hell out of him, and can't say I wouldn't have done the same thing. It's strange. He was my father, so part of me wants to be angry with you, while the other part is upset you got to him first. I'd like to bring him back so I can beat the hell out of him myself. I'm still wrestling with what he did for a living. How do I process that my father took and tried to kill the one person…" His voice trailed off and he looked away. "Anyway."

Chevy looked down at the table and swallowed hard.

### 

It was a bright sunny day. Chevy sat in the passenger seat as they drove down a long dirt road. "Wow!" Chevy said. "This is a lot of land."

"Yeah, it is," John commented.

Off in the distance was a large white farmhouse. "Is this it?" she asked, looking out the window eagerly.

"No," he told her. "Apparently there's a lodge-style home if we keep going."

"Oh!" she said, sounding disappointed. "Lodge

281

home…hmm…isn't that interesting. Just like ours."

The road made several more twists and turns before they saw the house off in the distance. He pulled into a large circular drive. The front door of the house opened before Chevy had a chance to get out of the truck. Out stepped Neal in a pair of jeans, brown boots, and a fitted white T-shirt. His blondish-brown curls looked sexy. She grabbed the door handle and leaped out of the truck. A smile covered her face, and her eyes were fixed on him.

He opened his arms, waiting.

She ran and leaped into his arms like she had in Barcelona, wrapping her legs around his waist. He wrapped his arms around her tightly. The feel of his body in her arms was perfect. The smell of his skin in the warm sun was intoxicating.

He put a hand on the side of her face, pulling her lips to his, which were soft, warm, and waiting.

"God, I missed you," she said as she tightened her legs around him and ran her fingers in his hair.

"I missed you more." He looked at her. "Are you here to stay?"

"Yes." She looked into his eyes. "I'm here to stay. I heard you had socks that needed filled."

He gazed into her eyes. "What took you so long?"